SUSPICION

"You can't be serious," Barry said.

"Why not?" asked Dylan. "I have to get some answers, and the more I try, the fewer I get. Who better to ask than the guy in charge?"

Barry shook his head. "Look, I admit there are some odd things about Nicole's case—chief among them being the inordinate amount of attention given it by Reverend Fletcher—"

"Some odd things," Dylan said scornfully. "What about Nicole looking drugged at the hearing? The settlement offer to McConnell? Argent's refusal to provide medical records? The disappearance of that other woman? If this was a movie plot, any one of those things would have been enough to start the hero investigating."

"But you don't know—"

Dylan folded his arms across his chest. "I'm going. Will you help me or not?"

Books by Daniel Steven

Final Remedy
Clinical Trials

Published by HarperPaperbacks

CLINICAL TRIALS

Daniel Steven

HarperPaperbacks
A Division of HarperCollinsPublishers

HarperPaperbacks
A Division of HarperCollins*Publishers*
10 East 53rd Street, New York, N.Y. 10022-5299

This is a work of fiction. The characters, incidents, and
dialogues are products of the author's imagination and are not to
be construed as real. Any resemblance to actual events or
persons, living or dead, is entirely coincidental.

ISBN 0-06-101198-3

HarperCollins®, 📕®, and HarperPaperbacks™
are trademarks of HarperCollins*Publishers* Inc.

Cover photo © 1997 by Superstock

First printing: March 1998

Printed in the United States of America

Visit HarperPaperbacks on the World Wide Web at
http://www.harpercollins.com

❖ 10 9 8 7 6 5 4 3 2 1

ACKNOWLEDGMENTS

Thanks to my wife, Joyce Brody, M.D., for reviewing the first draft and her assistance with the medical issues. She deserves the credit for what is accurate; any factual errors are mine. Thanks also to my agent, Evan Marshall, for his enthusiastic support and advice on plot issues.

PROLOGUE

Jason Conner walked along the most photographed fence in the world, putting his hand inside his surplus Army jacket to feel the envelope. Twice before he had tried to mail it, once actually putting his hand into the letter box.

Tall and gaunt, his cropped blond hair sticking straight out from his head, Conner looked like a forlorn stork. He stopped to cough into his handkerchief, then sucked in the frigid air, fighting a wave of nausea.

A few moments later, he felt better and replaced the handkerchief in his hip pocket, considering his options. Mailing the letter was definitely out. Phone calls, too—he would never convince a White House operator that he was a friend of the new President. It was strange, he thought, that any human being could be so isolated. Yesterday, before his inauguration, Thomas Banfield had been a free man. Today he was a prisoner of his position, in a constantly moving cocoon of handlers, aides, advisers, and agents.

Around Conner was the usual crowd of tourists, snapping pictures, gawking at the mansion.

Pennsylvania Avenue was closed to vehicles, and the street was a minimall for pedestrians and bikers, even in January. The crowd was good-natured and the President was too new to have any protesters. The only reminders of past troubles were the uniformed Executive Service cops patrolling the sidewalk.

An idea formed in Conner's mind. If he wasn't so weak and light-headed, he might have rejected the idea instantly—but in his present frame of mind, it seemed logical, almost a fait accompli. Adrift in his illness, in a stream-of-consciousness world, Conner's logical connections were facile, the hard edges of reality blurring easily into magical thinking.

He looked hard at the fence—three hundred yards of black wrought iron. In deference to one of the symbols of American democracy, there was no barbed wire or other impediment to climbing. He assumed there was some sort of sophisticated monitoring system—video cameras, motion detectors, sensors—but that was okay; his action was not meant to be covert.

Conner waited until the nearest cop looked in the other direction. Then, with the grace of a former athlete, he took two giant steps and leaped onto the fence. His adrenaline compensated for muscle weakness, and he was up and over the top in seconds, landing softly on the ground. He cringed, expecting the sound of alarms and sirens, but there was nothing, not even a shout from the guards. No one seemed to notice.

Directly in front of him was the massive fountain, shut down for the winter. Conner walked forward, steadily and slowly, deliberately not running. He wondered how far he could get before being challenged.

Ahead of him was a wide expanse of lawn leading to the north gate, and now he noticed a flurry of activity. Men in suits came down the steps; cars rushed up the driveway. He continued walking.

About fifty yards from the driveway, two uniformed cops and a man in a dark suit came around the end of the hedges directly in front of him. "You!" one of them shouted. "Freeze right there! Get down on the ground!"

Conner kept walking. They could see he was no threat. He was startled, however, to see the men kneel and pull guns out of holsters. It was weird—like being in a movie he'd seen a thousand times. He was close enough to see their faces, and realized they looked scared. Of *him*! He placed his empty hands in clear sight, palms facing outward. "It's all right," he said. "I just want to deliver something. For the President. This is the only way—"

He felt weak and light-headed again. He knew he might faint, that he only had a few seconds. With his right hand, Conner reached into his jacket for the envelope. Everything happened slowly: he felt the paper between his fingers and began pulling it out of the pocket. Then there was a tremendous blow, like the kick of a horse, in the center of his chest. He pitched backward, at the same time hearing the boom of the pistol.

Conner fell hard onto the frozen grass. There was no pain. He stared up at the cloudless sky, marveling at the *blueness*. The blood to his brain ebbed and he felt himself drifting away. He realized, with great regret, that he would never know how it ended.

■   ■   ■

Craig Hagen, Special Counsel to the President, walked away from his very first meeting in the Oval Office, his mind full of schemes. He clutched a heavy black briefing book under his arm as he nodded to the Marine sentry and headed down the hallway toward an appointment in the East Room.

The White House was still in chaos—everyone only partly moved in—and the new President was in a foul mood. Tom Banfield was always slightly testy in the morning, anyway, and when everything was going wrong, he could be intolerable. Hagen smiled, remembering how Banfield had pointed his finger at him like a gun, demanding answers to his questions about the delay in vetting his nominee for Secretary of State. Perversely, Hagen took Banfield's anger as a compliment: it meant that Hagen, not Turk Finnegan, continued to be the person on whom the President relied.

Roger "Turk" Finnegan was the new Chief of Staff—traditionally the second-most powerful person in Washington. But he was, and always would be, an interloper in the Banfield administration, chosen only because Banfield needed a Washington insider to guide him through the Congressional shoals.

Short, balding, and intense, Hagen had known Banfield since their college days at the University of Minnesota. He had been the county attorney in the administration of County Executive Banfield, and had managed both of Banfield's campaigns for governor. Hagen, T. J. Markham, and a few others popularly known as the "Minnesota Mafia" had suffered through the bad times as well as the good. That meant something to Tom Banfield.

As Hagen scurried down the hallway, passing the wide windows facing Pennsylvania Avenue, something on the periphery of his vision caught his attention. Through the windows he saw a man walking toward the White House, dressed in black pants and a military jacket too thin for the cold. At the same instant he heard the *boom!* of a large-caliber pistol and saw the man crumple to the ground.

"Jesus Christ!" muttered Hagen. Almost instantly, alarms sounded and a Secret Service agent rushed by, nearly knocking him into the window. Hagen spun around and jogged down the hallway, following the agent out the main entrance and onto the front steps.

T. J. Markham, former FBI agent and Minnesota state trooper, now the brand-new director of the President's Secret Service detail, was already on the driveway behind the hedge. He spoke into his wireless intercom. "Yeah, yeah, I know," he said. "It's just one guy . . . that we know about. I still want Point Guard in the safe room."

Point Guard—the President—would be even grumpier now, thought Hagen. His first day in office, and he was locked up in an underground bunker. But T.J. was right—this could be a diversion from a real attack.

Markham saw Hagen and put up his hand. "Stay there, Craig. We'll handle this."

"The hell you will," Hagen said. "You handle the cop stuff. I've gotta represent Point Guard."

Markham locked eyes with him for a moment, then conceded. "All right, just don't get in my way." He turned and walked quickly onto the lawn, Hagen following.

Two cops and a plainclothes agent were around the body. The plainclothes agent was kneeling next to the man, giving CPR. He looked up as Markham approached and shook his head. "He's gone."

"The paramedics are coming," Markham said. "Keep going."

The man shook his head again. "Forget it. He took it right in the heart." He pointed at the entrance wound in the man's chest.

"Shit!" Markham said. "Who fired?"

One of the uniformed Executive Service cops, a burly young man with a crewcut, spoke up. "Chris Potter, sir," he said, gulping air. "I . . . I thought he was going for a weapon. He reached into his pocket—"

"You idiot," Markham said tiredly, and sighed. "Give me your gun." The man complied, looking ready to cry. Markham made sure the safety was on, then shoved it into his waistband.

Hagen looked down at the intruder. He was very thin, in his late thirties, with pale, delicate features. His blue eyes were open but he had a relaxed, almost peaceful expression.

Markham put on a pair of surgical gloves and patted down the outside of the man's jacket. He slowly pushed aside the blood-soaked front, exposing what once might have been a white T-shirt. The jacket had an inside pocket, and sticking out of it was something red. Markham pulled on the object, revealing a standard business envelope with the upper third bloodstained. It was addressed to "The President, White House, Washington, D.C." There was a first-class stamp on it.

"This what he was reaching for?" Markham said meaningfully, glaring at Potter.

"I . . . guess so," Potter said.

"Yeah," Markham said. "A fucking letter." He tipped the body on its side and pulled the man's wallet out of his hip pocket, riffling through it quickly. He announced, "Jason Conner. Age thirty-eight. Lives in Minnesota."

Putting aside the wallet, Markham opened the bloody envelope, unfolded the letter, and skimmed it disdainfully. His eyes widened and he stood up straight, his jaw working.

"What is it?" Hagen said, but Markham waved him to silence until he finished reading. Then, with a strange expression, he handed the letter to Hagen.

Hagen read the letter, then looked at Markham. "Oh, my God," was all he could think to say.

The landlady was an old woman named Mrs. McGee, who was maddeningly slow at climbing the steps to the second-floor apartment.

"He seemed like such a nice young man," she whined nasally, laboriously removing a large key ring from the side pocket of her robe. "Always paid the rent right on time, never gave me any trouble."

They reached the top of the stairs, and the old lady fumbled with the lock. Markham had to restrain himself from throttling her; he consoled himself with the thought that she hadn't asked for a search warrant. Finally the door opened and Markham pushed past her into the apartment, trailed by three agents.

The apartment was tastefully decorated with Scandinavian-style furniture, all wood and light fabric. A high counter separated the living room from a small kitchen. Against the far wall was a home office consisting of a computer desk and bookcase.

In the short time since Conner had been shot, Markham had learned a great deal about the man.

Conner had worked for the county as a zoning inspector until he took a leave of absence for illness. He had never been married, never owned a home, and drove a ten-year-old Volvo. He was, apparently, a loner with few friends and no close family. It was just possible, thought Markham, that he hadn't told anyone what was in the letter.

Well, they would know soon enough.

Markham watched impassively as his men methodically searched the apartment, ripping open drawers, looking behind pictures and under furniture. The old woman stepped forward. "What are you doing?"

"We're searching," Markham said patiently.

"Oh, my."

"Did Mr. Conner tell you why he went to Washington?"

The old woman blinked. "Why, no, not really. He told me he had to go away for a while, and asked if I would take care of his goldfish." She sniffed. "I told him I don't like fish, and he got all huffy."

"Mrs. McGee," said Markham quietly, "please think about this very carefully. Did he leave anything with you, or ask you to mail anything or to contact anyone for him?"

"Nope," she said with assurance. "We weren't all that friendly."

Markham nodded as agents Timson and Brent approached. Brent said, "Found this in the bedroom behind the dresser." He handed Markham a thick leather-bound book.

"It's Conner's," Timson said, pointing to the name embossed in gold script on the cover. "His diary."

Markham quickly thumbed through it. The first

entry was almost ten years ago, and it looked like
Conner kept it pretty regularly for a while, averaging
at least a few entries every week. Then, after a couple of years, the entries tailed off for long periods,
followed by intervals of intense writing. He flipped
forward until he found the approximate date—and
there it was. He snapped the journal shut. "Good
work, Brent."

"You need an evidence bag?"

"No, thanks," Markham said grimly.

The red leather of the journal was dry and
cracked. It would burn easily.

CHAPTER ONE

Four Years Later

The fresh smell of new-mown grass and flowers blew through the hospital window into hell.

It's spring, thought Nicole Girard. Time to leave. She leaned over the bed, slid her hand under the mattress, and pulled out the stolen surgical scissors. The blades were curved, thin, and bright with sharpness. She glanced fearfully at the door, but it stayed closed. She didn't know how long the day nurse would be gone.

Nicole grasped the scissors with her left hand and clumsily cut away the white adhesive tape holding the intravenous line in her right arm. Then, breathing deeply, she grasped the hard plastic tube and pulled it out, slowly. It hurt—much more than she expected—but that was okay. There was also some bleeding, so she pushed down on the spot with facial tissue.

When the bleeding stopped, Nicole slid to the edge of the bed, put her feet on the floor, and stood. A wave of dizziness hit her, but after a moment the room steadied and she went to the window, pulling back the curtain. She raised the window sash and put one knee on the sill, slowly lifting herself onto the narrow outside ledge. The world spun briefly, vertigo from the height and the tranquilizers. She held tightly to the window frame.

Nicole expected she would be frozen with fear— she had never liked heights—but the vertigo was purely physical. She searched herself for panic and found none, not even anything that could fairly be called anxiety. That's what happens, she thought, when you run out of options, when there are no good alternatives to jumping out of a hospital window. She tried to picture what she must look like to the people below, and smiled.

The hospital was built in a U shape; her room was on the second floor of the inside of the short section. The courtyard below was bathed in clear morning sunlight, filled with people in folding chairs facing a temporary stage. The cool wind blew against Nicole, getting under the flimsy hospital gown, making it billow slightly.

So far, no one had noticed her; attention was focused on the stage, and the setting sun behind her. She felt steadier now, concentrating on the voice booming from the speakers below.

"And so it is with great pleasure that I present the Reverend Vernon Fletcher, director of the Evangelical Foundation of the Midwest, primary benefactor of University Hospital's AIDS Research Center, the Midwest Immunological Research Institute. Reverend Fletcher has personally—"

"Made a fortune from religion," a voice whispered.

Dylan Ice turned his head and frowned at Barry

Sasscer. Barry sometimes failed to realize when his humor was inappropriate. Dylan didn't think much of Fletcher, either, but Dylan believed this particular charitable endeavor was genuine. Certainly there were less controversial charitable purposes for an evangelical foundation than funding an AIDS research center. The *source* of the foundation's money was no secret: Fletcher's network of television and radio stations.

Dr. Mark Argent, director of the institute, finished his flowery introduction of Fletcher. Tall and Robert Redford-handsome, Argent wore a crisply pressed gray pinstripe suit. He stepped back as Reverend Fletcher came to the podium.

Fletcher, in his green linen sport jacket and khaki pants, looked dumpy next to Argent. That impression changed, however, when his warm baritone voice rolled over the crowd, and he began a speech dedicating the MIRI to the elimination of the "scourge of AIDS." Stroking his silvery mane of hair, Fletcher wove a spell of homilies and religious aphorisms mixed with self-deprecating humor.

"This institute will be on the leading edge of immunological research," Fletcher said, his voice reverberating through the speakers. "We cannot, and will not, stand by while so many of God's children are taken so early—and so unfairly. And we are committed to continued support of this institute, with both funds and resources, until a cure for AIDS is found."

There was a lot more in this vein; after a while, Dylan shifted his gaze to the dignitaries seated behind the podium, spotting Dr. Peter Rosati, head of the government's AIDS research program, and a frequent talking head on the network news shows.

Also among the business suits was a striking young woman with tousled red hair falling to her shoulders. She wore a black silk blouse and a short red skirt that was only marginally appropriate for the occasion. He nudged Barry with his elbow. "Who's the redhead?"

Barry leaned back in his chair and whispered, "That's Fletcher's daughter, Kristin."

"*That's* Fletcher's daughter!"

"Right. Doesn't look the part, does she?"

That was an understatement. Fletcher was probably the leading voice of the fundamentalist right, a proponent of chastity, morality, and traditional values. It wasn't surprising that Fletcher's daughter was a rebel—but it was odd that Fletcher tolerated the rebellion.

As Dylan turned his gaze back to the podium he noticed a movement on the building behind the platform. Glancing up, he saw a woman in a hospital gown standing on a second-floor window ledge. He had to shade his eyes from the sun to get a good look. Her face was obscured by long, black hair; the wind billowed the hospital gown almost up to her chest, revealing only a pair of white panties and no bra. He looked around. Didn't anyone else see her? She looked like she was going to jump—

And she did. It was about thirty feet to the grassy knoll below—certainly enough to break a leg or a neck. But the woman hit the ground softly, rolled, and staggered to her feet. Several other members of the audience now had seen her; people were pointing, but the speakers on the platform—facing the wrong way—were oblivious.

The woman briefly disappeared from view behind the speaker's platform, then reappeared as she climbed onto the two-foot-high platform from the rear. Dylan could see she was in her thirties, with pale, translucent skin and a fixed, unemotional facial expression.

She strode past the seated dignitaries in folding chairs, halting in front of Dr. Argent, who hastily stood up. Reverend Fletcher stopped speaking, suddenly uncertain, as his audience seemed distracted. The woman stood there a moment, swaying, as if trying to focus on Argent's face. Then she shouted clearly, "Vampire! Bloodsucker!" Argent said something quietly and urgently, then took her arm, guiding her to the edge of the platform.

She jerked her arm away, spitting in his face. As he reflexively stepped backward, she tried to rake his face with her fingernails. Argent fended her off with his arms as other men came forward to help, but the woman turned and ran to the end of the platform, coming—it seemed—directly at Dylan.

She reached the edge and jumped; this time, however, her landing wasn't on soft grass but on the hard red brick of the courtyard. She slipped to one knee and tumbled forward, striking her head loudly on the bricks. She rolled over, unconscious.

There was a moment of stunned silence, followed by a buzz as everyone began talking at once. Dr. Argent leaped over the edge of the platform and kneeled next to the woman; someone called for a stretcher. Dylan elbowed his way forward for a better look.

The woman lay facedown on the bricks, a trace of blood coming from her nose; her eyes were closed.

"C'mon," Barry said, pulling on Dylan's elbow. "Let's get out of here."

"Un-uh. I want to see what happens."

"They'll take her into the ER. She's a nut case."

"What about the dedication?"

"It'll be awhile before they start again. Let's get back to the office, we've done our duty."

Dylan shook his head. "Go ahead. I'll see you later."

Barry shrugged but stayed.

When the paramedics loaded the woman into an ambulance that was brought around from the ER, Dylan watched them place her on a backboard and carefully carry her around to the ER entrance. Then the dedication ceremony resumed.

Fletcher continued his speech without any reference to what had just happened. Kristin Fletcher, however, was no longer in her seat.

"Why the . . . the goddamn . . . hell . . . was she left alone?" Dr. Mark Argent was not used to failure, and in the face of utter incompetence he was almost incoherent. He leaned forward across the desktop, fists clenched.

The nursing supervisor shook her head and said, "It was just a few minutes. There was a Code Blue called in the next room—"

"She knew the rule! Never leave the patient alone! If the patient doesn't recover—"

"Mark." Linda Argent, standing beside Argent's desk, put her hand on his shoulder and nodded toward the doorway behind the nurse, where Peter Rosati stood uncomfortably shifting his weight, a look of embarrassment on his face. "I don't think Dr. Rosati needs to hear all this."

Argent took a deep breath and forced a smile. "Of course not." He nodded at the nursing supervisor and said, "We'll discuss this later." She breathed out in relief, turned, and nearly knocked over Rosati. "Excuse me," she muttered, pushing by him.

"Come in, come in," Argent said quickly. He leaped out from behind the desk and escorted Rosati to the conference table in the corner. "I'm sorry I left you stranded down on the platform, but I had to make sure the patient was all right—"

"Yes, I can see your concern."

Argent looked at him sharply, but there was no trace of irony in Rosati's face. Rosati was a plain, dependable-looking fellow with a receding hairline and a long nose; forthright, earnest—and surprisingly cunning. No one got to be the director of NIAID—the National Institute of Allergy and Infectious Diseases—without being a thoroughly political animal, capable of cutting enemies off at the knees. The federal AIDS research budget was well over three billion dollars a year, and Peter Rosati controlled most of it.

Argent cleared his throat and said carefully, "I just was trying to find out how this happened. I assure you it won't happen again."

Rosati shrugged. "What about the patient? It looked like she might have some head trauma."

Linda Argent spoke up. "I just spoke with the ER. She's conscious—it's probably just a concussion. Her neurological examination was normal."

Argent glared at her, annoyed. Although Linda was assistant director of the institute, with a master's degree in critical care nursing, she tended to take over in times of crisis. He usually valued that quality, but Linda didn't have the finesse to handle Rosati.

Actually, it infuriated Argent that he had to handle Rosati at all—but it was his own damn fault. If he hadn't stupidly sent Rosati the initial results of the clinical trial—or if he had at least suppressed the data on Nicole's blood—he wouldn't be in this position. Now Rosati wanted the patient for his own research.

Argent longed to tell him to go to hell, but he was too powerful. Aside from the federal money, a few well-placed words from Rosati could ruin Argent's reputation in the insular world of AIDS research.

"Good, very good," said Rosati. He pulled a mechanical pencil from his pocket and absently tapped it on the tabletop. "Her CD4 count still normal?"

"Yes, and so is her spinal fluid."

"Excellent. But this is the second incident of this type, isn't it? What do the psychiatrists think about this behavior? Bipolar? I hope not schizophrenia."

"Bipolar," Argent lied.

"On the phone you said you would have her legally committed to the hospital's care."

"We should have an emergency commitment by tomorrow."

"So when can she be transferred to NIH?"

Argent shook his head. "That's not possible. Under state law, our commitment is good only for ninety-six hours. After that, we've got to go to court for a twenty-one-day commitment, and then for a permanent—"

"I don't want excuses," Rosati said testily. "Just do what's necessary, the sooner the better."

Argent shrugged. "I have to deal with our chief of psychiatry—Volberg. He doesn't like the fact that we're keeping the patient here, rather than on the psych ward. He may not be willing to sign off on more than a twenty-one-day commitment."

Rosati stared at him icily.

"We'll do our best, Dr. Rosati," Argent said.

"I know you will." Rosati stood up. "I have great expectations for this research. And if it works out the way we hope, your contribution will be acknowledged." He stuck out his hand, and Argent shook it firmly, knowing it would be hellishly difficult to fool this man.

But it could be done.

CHAPTER TWO

Dylan Ice sat in an uncomfortably stylish chair in Paul Hudson's corner office, nervously drumming his fingers on the armrest, wondering why Hudson had asked to see him. A silver nautical clock on the bookcase ticked loudly, ominously. Hudson's desk—a slab of glass supported by two pillars of teak—was clear except for a few knickknacks and pen holders, but the floor behind the desk was piled high with bulging files. On the matching credenza were more file folders, butting up against pictures of Hudson's family.

Dylan stood up, walked to the floor-to-ceiling window, and looked out at the river. He was tall and slender, with long legs and broad shoulders. His brown complexion and wiry hair, combined with an aquiline nose, gave him a unique appearance that could only mean he was of mixed race. He wore a gray double-breasted designer suit with a pinpoint cotton white shirt and a dark green silk tie.

Dylan had graduated from law school three years earlier, and law firms from New York, Chicago, and L.A. had competed fiercely to recruit him. Although he was a top student at Washington

University Law School in St. Louis, the real reason for his marketability was that he qualified as African-American for the purposes of diversity formulas. And the fact that he didn't look *too* black was a bonus. He had received some incredible offers, but in the end had chosen Cameron, Barr, Haight, Waters & Kaster because he wanted to remain in St. Louis.

Cameron Barr, as everyone called it, wasn't a large law firm compared to those in New York or Washington, but it was one of the largest in the Midwest. Here in the firm's Gateway Tower office there were 126 lawyers, with another 40 in satellite offices in Kansas City, Chicago, and Washington.

The firm represented every major bank in the metropolitan area, plus many of the largest corporations. Dylan had two and a half years' experience in the litigation department—which left him about five more years to make partner.

On the river below him, the rapidly dropping afternoon temperature collided with the water's warmth, forming fog. A tugboat suddenly materialized through the mist, a ghost ship leading a long train of barges down the Mississippi. Watching the river reminded Dylan that it had been days since he had taken the time to go rowing.

He turned as he heard the door open behind him. Paul Hudson walked into the office and said, "Hello, Dylan. Sorry you had to wait." He sank with a sigh into his orthopedic leather chair, motioning Dylan to sit down. "That meeting was supposed to be quick."

Hudson was in his mid-forties, and looked older—hair gone, waist large and soft, double chins getting ready to reproduce. He wore an expensive vested suit that would have looked just right in an English club. Hudson's doughboy appearance, however, was in sharp contrast to his courtroom abilities. Juries liked and trusted him, and he was one of the city's top civil litigators.

As head of Cameron Barr's litigation department, Hudson demanded absolute commitment from his associates. Sixty-hour work weeks were the norm, seventy hours not unusual. Partners, of course, were not expected to work as hard (although some did). If you paid your dues as an associate and made partner, you had financial security for life.

It was all about billings. Having large annual billings wouldn't guarantee that an associate made partner, but without them there was no chance. And Dylan intended to make partner.

Hudson leaned back in his chair and put his hands behind his head. "Dylan. You were at the MIRI dedication ceremony, weren't you?"

"That's right." Hudson had required him to be there.

"What did you think of the incident? The woman who jumped out of the window?"

The image of her face immediately popped into Dylan's head. "She's obviously got some problems."

Hudson leaned forward and laughed. "That's for sure. How'd you like to represent her?"

"I . . . What?"

Hudson laughed again, a short bark. "You should see your face." He clasped his hands in front of him and stretched, cracking his knuckles. "Here's the deal. The woman's name is Nicole Girard, she's thirty-five years old, unmarried. She's got AIDS, and was part of some experimental clinical trial when her trolley left the tracks. The hospital originally got a ninety-six-hour detention order under the mental health law, then extended it for another twenty-one days. There's been no improvement, so her parents—Henry and Amanda Girard—want to get appointed as her guardians. Then they can have her committed to a psychiatric institution."

Dylan shifted uncomfortably in his chair. He didn't see why the firm would be involved in something like this.

Hudson smiled and continued, "Henry and Amanda Girard are original members of the St. Charles congregation."

"Oh." Dylan suddenly understood. The St. Charles Evangelical Church was the centerpiece of the Reverend Vernon Fletcher's empire of satellite churches, television networks, religious schools and colleges. Fletcher had started the church twenty years ago in a small clapboard building; now it was a marble-and-smoked-glass cathedral. The twenty or so families in that original congregation had become church elders—the apostles of the Reverend Fletcher.

And the conglomerate that was the Evangelical Foundation of the Midwest, Inc., also was Cameron Barr's largest client.

"Their daughter has AIDS? That must have been quite a shock."

Hudson rubbed his nose thoughtfully. "I should say so. Anyway, Fletcher has personally asked us to help the Girards. They'll need a petition for guardianship of the person and property, motion for hearing, that sort of thing." He swung around to the credenza, picked up a file folder, and shoved it across the desk at Dylan. "Monica opened the file this afternoon, but there's nothing in it except the client card."

Dylan took the folder. "Why me, Paul? And

shouldn't this be routed to T and E?" The firm's trusts and estates department normally handled guardianship matters.

"I want this to stay in our department," Hudson said meaningfully. "And I thought you would be a good choice to handle it, since you've got personal experience with guardianships."

Dylan opened the folder. The standard client card was pasted to the upper right edge; it included the client's name, address, and phone number; type of case; billing status; and computer bar code. The billing status was DNB—do not bill. This usually was reserved for pro bono cases or favors done for clients. He tapped the folder and said, "When do you want the pleadings?" He was in the middle of researching a complex trial brief in a securities case, for one of the more demanding partners; hopefully Hudson would take that into consideration.

"It's not a question of when *I* want them. You'll be counsel of record. I'll review them, of course."

Dylan looked up, startled. This kind of case was almost always handled by a partner, even if an associate did all the heavy lifting. After all, when you did a favor for a major client, you wanted the client to know *who* was being generous.

"Me?" he croaked.

Hudson said, "Yeah, I don't have time to go to guardianship hearings, and you've been second seat long enough. What's the matter? You don't look very happy. I thought you'd be thrilled to get out from under a partner."

"I am," he said quickly. "I mean . . . it's just that . . . they want her committed?"

Hudson frowned. "Yeah, that's right. She's flying on fumes. Why, you got a problem with that?"

Shut up and take the case, Dylan told himself. "No. No, not at all."

"Good." Hudson grunted. "It's all yours. Just keep me posted. E-mail reports once a week." He nodded in dismissal.

The cubicle of the secretary Dylan shared with another associate was empty, but there were messages in his half of the plastic message tray. He picked up the pink slips and went into his small office, allowing himself a discreet whoop of joy. He had been genuinely concerned when he was called to Hudson's office: such late-afternoon summonses were often the harbinger of doom. Instead, he had received manna from heaven: a simple case that would make the firm's biggest client happy.

His mood changed abruptly as he sorted through his messages. Most of them were typical—return calls from attorneys about depositions and minor hearings—but there was also one from Janis's high school principal. Actually, "Janis's principle," in Rhonda's large, ornate, typically misspelled handwriting.

Barry Sasscer poked his head through the door. "Was that a cry of pain, rage, happiness, or all of the above?"

Dylan was glad to see him. Barry was his only real friend in the firm—and his unofficial mentor.

Although in his late thirties, Barry wasn't a partner. Instead, he was one of a rare but increasing breed of creatures known as permanent associates. Permanent associates were usually brought in from outside the firm. Because of their unique legal specialty, they filled gaps in the firm's expertise. Some of them made quite handsome salaries, although they remained employees with no voice in managing the firm.

Occasionally a regular associate who failed to make partner would be offered such a position, but that was rare—too many hard feelings. Barry, whose expertise was in aviation law, had been hired away from a small boutique firm in Chicago, where he was twice passed over for partner. He had done well at Cameron Barr, increasing his billings annually, developing a nice practice representing local commuter aviation companies. He also had experience in defending shareholder derivative suits that meshed with Paul Hudson's specialty.

"Yes," Dylan said. "I just came from Hudson's office."

"Uh-oh," Barry said, taking a seat.

"Remember the woman jumper? Last week at the dedication ceremony?"

"Of course. But what—"

"Turns out she's the daughter of one of Fletcher's deacons, or assistants, or grand viziers or something. Anyway, Fletcher wants us to help her parents get appointed permanent guardians."

"And you—"

"Will be preparing the pleadings." He paused, then continued, "I'll also be counsel of record."

"Whoa," Barry said. "Aren't we the fair-haired boy." He grinned. "Actually, dark and curly-haired."

"Shut up," Dylan said, grinning back. Barry was the only one close enough to kid Dylan about his race. As one of the few "persons of color" among the firm's lawyers, Dylan was normally treated with exaggerated courtesy.

Barry picked up an orange Nerf basketball from

the floor and lobbed it toward the basket hooked over the door. The ball hit the rim and rebounded onto Dylan's desk, knocking over a cup of pens. "Sorry," Barry said. "What did you do to earn this honor? Have you slept with his wife? You got photos?"

Dylan grinned. "Not that I remember." He paused for a moment. "That's the thing. I really don't know."

It was almost seven thirty by the time Dylan pulled into the parking lot of his town-house development. He checked his mail and went inside, wondering whether Janis would have dinner ready.

Stepping into the foyer, he immediately sensed something wrong. The small kitchen was just the same as he had left it that morning; even the breakfast dishes were still in the sink. He called out, "Janis! Janis, are you home?"

He went down the hall and looked into her bedroom. The bed was unmade, clothes were strewn on the carpet, and the portable CD player was missing from her dresser. "Shit," Dylan said expressively. He should have called from the office instead of trying to show how much he trusted her.

Dylan went into his bedroom and carefully hung up his suit, changing into a pair of blue jeans and a T-shirt. He cleaned up the kitchen, boiled some water, opened a can of sauce, and splashed it into a pot. He had just poured the pasta into the boiling water when he heard the door open. He continued stirring the spaghetti until he felt her eyes on his back, then he turned.

She stood in the doorway of the kitchen, wearing a sheepish grin. "Guess I'm late, huh?"

"Where were you?"

She shrugged with the careless indifference of a sixteen-year-old. "At the mall."

He just stared at her. She stared back a moment before turning away. "Why won't you let me grow up?" she asked plaintively. "You treat me like a ten-year-old, when I'm not that much younger than you, really."

He slammed the metal spoon down hard on the stove, and she jumped at the sound. "Because you're not grown up!" He pulled a chair out from the small butcher-block table and sat down heavily.

It was futile, he knew. Although he was Janis's legal guardian, he was also her brother, and he didn't seem able to command the moral authority of a parent.

She lounged against the door, a defiant expression on her face. Janis's skin color was much darker than his, strongly resembling their mother. Like Dylan, she had their father's aquiline nose, but unlike Dylan, she had straight hair. Her body was fully mature, stuffed into a man's plaid flannel shirt and dirty jeans.

He took a deep breath and changed his approach. "Janis, I'm not trying to hassle you. You know that. I've been in your position—"

"Bullshit! You loved school. Getting As all the time!"

"You don't think I had problems?"

She rolled her eyes and said, "Dylan, all you did was study and row—row and study. You don't know anything about the real world. You never even had a girlfriend."

"No, I had to take care of you," he said hotly, and immediately regretted giving in to his anger.

Janis set her mouth and looked hurt. He continued, "I'm just trying to do what's right, Janis. You know you're supposed to come right home from school."

A fleeting expression passed over her face, quickly suppressed. He knew what it was. "Shit! You didn't go to school!" He remembered the phone message from the principal and stood up, angry again.

"I was there! Just not the whole day! I left after lunch, I didn't miss anything but PE and stupid math! So what—I don't learn anything anyway."

Dylan said carefully, "I won't permit this. I simply won't permit it. You're grounded."

"You can't lock me up! I'll run away!" She turned and stomped down the hallway to her bedroom, slamming the door melodramatically.

He started to go after her, then stopped. Instead, he returned to the stove and resumed stirring the pasta.

CHAPTER THREE

Henry and Amanda Girard lived in St. Charles, a small town across the Missouri River from the St. Louis Metroplex. At one time Missouri's state capital, St. Charles now was a quaint oasis in the shadow of St. Louis, a place where Mickey Rooney and Judy Garland would have made a movie.

It always gave Dylan a weird feeling of envy to see places like this, lifestyles so foreign to the way he had been raised. It was a *Leave It to Beaver* world mocked by his parents, yet one for which he had yearned. Now, as an adult, he knew it was no better an environment than his own childhood—just different. Still, it left him wistful.

Dylan parked his car in the concrete driveway of the red two-story Victorian that nestled in a cul-de-sac at the end of a tree-lined street. The front door opened as he walked up the steps, and a tall, reedy man in his sixties greeted him. "Henry Girard," the man said, shaking hands.

Dylan followed Girard into what could only be called a parlor. There was a sofa, some overstuffed chairs, and an ancient musket over the fireplace. On one wall was a large framed autographed picture of the Reverend Vernon Fletcher.

Amanda Girard sat in a wheelchair in front of the fireplace. Her hair was dull white and flopped loosely on her neck, and her face was slack. She motioned at the sofa, inviting him to sit.

"She don't like to talk," said Henry. "Since the stroke, it sounds funny."

"I understand."

Henry took a seat across from the sofa. "I appreciate your coming out here. I realize you lawyers don't do this much anymore, but Amanda don't like me to travel." Amanda looked embarrassed and smiled crookedly.

"That's quite all right," Dylan said quickly. "My pleasure, really. Gives me a chance to see St. Charles."

After he was seated and had refused coffee, Dylan started the interview, getting the background information he needed to prepare the petition for guardianship. Henry furnished all the information, with occasional nods from Amanda. Dylan asked, "When did you first learn that your daughter . . . was sick?"

"You don't have to beat around the bush, son," Henry said, lighting a pipe. "She's got AIDS, there's no gainsaying that. As to when we learned about it . . ." he leaned back to consider. "I guess it was 'bout a year ago, right, 'Manda?" She nodded. "Yep. She had to go into the hospital for some tests, and said it was time we knew. I can tell you, we was pretty shocked." He leaned forward and jabbed his pipe at Dylan. "She's our only child, you know."

"Yes."

"Yeah. Well, 'course I asked her how she got it. I mean, I thought you had to be a drug addict or hemophiliac or something. But she said, no, she thinks she got it from her husband. She was married, once, you know."

"No, I didn't," Dylan said, surprised.

"Yeah," said Henry. "She used to like men. Before she turned queer."

Amanda Girard made a strangled sound. Henry said to her, "Well, it's true. No use pretending different." He looked back at Dylan. "Amanda don't like me to say that. Anyway, Nicole got it, and now she's got to face what she done with her life. Mebbe that's why she tried to jump out a window."

Dylan asked a few more questions about Nicole's background, learning that she had attended the local high school, where she excelled at art. Afterward, she went to St. Louis University, earning a degree in psychology. After a few false starts, she settled into a career as an art therapist working for the public schools.

"It's a heavy burden to show that an individual is incapable of handling their own affairs," Dylan said. It came out sounding more pompous than he liked. "The courts don't like to do it without very strong reasons. Medical testimony, of course, will be critical."

"Dr. Argent will help you," said Henry.

"Yes, I'm talking to him this afternoon. But you're the one who will bear the emotional cost, Mr. Girard. You and your wife," Dylan said, nodding at her. "It may not be pleasant, having your daughter's condition brought out in open court."

Henry mulled this for a moment. "I understand. But it's really for the best, don't you think?" Henry looked at his wife, who looked away. He sighed. "Let's do it."

For the first time, Amanda Girard spoke. She could move only one side of her face, so the words were strange but still intelligible. "You will see Nicole too?"

Startled, Dylan said, "Uh, yes. Of course."

"Come with me. Please." She turned the wheelchair and rolled into the hallway. Dylan looked at Henry, who sighed and went after her. Dylan followed. At the foot of the stairs, Henry gently lifted his wife and carried her up the flight of stairs, trailed by Dylan.

On the landing at the top there was another wheelchair, and Henry gently placed his wife in it. There were some interesting paintings on the wall: landscapes and portraits done in an impressionistic style, full of color and texture.

"Nicole did those," said Amanda, watching him.

"They're beautiful," Dylan said sincerely.

They went into a small bedroom: Nicole's room. Mementos, trophies, and diplomas lined the walls and the surfaces of the white french provincial furniture. There were framed pictures of Nicole getting her high school diploma, in a cheerleader's uniform, and on her prom night with a tall blond kid in an ill-fitting white tux. Henry coughed and said, "Nicole calls this the Teenage Mausoleum. She can't stand to come in here, but—"

Amanda rolled over to the dresser and picked up a white leather photo album. "I want to show you my daughter," she said slowly, with much effort. "So when you see her tomorrow, you'll know that's not the real . . . Nicole."

"He's a busy lawyer," Henry said. "He don't have time to—"

"No, that's all right," Dylan said quickly. "I'd love to see the pictures, Mrs. Girard."

■   ■   ■

The University Hospital was a maze of linoleum corridors that smelled of antiseptic and decay. Dylan followed the yellow floor lines to the newly refurbished wing, where he walked through an archway with the words *Midwestern Immunological Research Institute* in foot-high letters. Just beyond the entranceway there was a bas-relief of the Reverend Fletcher and an enormous bronze plaque testifying to the multimillion dollar gift by the Evangelical Foundation of the Midwest.

Dylan checked in at the main desk and received a visitor's badge, then took an elevator to the second floor. There was a security desk outside the elevators, where a uniformed guard checked his badge, then directed him down the corridor.

He was not particularly fond of hospitals at any time, but he was particularly on edge walking down a hallway of AIDS patients. The smell of antiseptic was strong. Even though he knew it was ridiculous, he found himself taking short, shallow breaths, as if he could avoid breathing in the virus.

The director's office was at the end of the corridor, through two double glass doors, and smelled of new paint. Argent, wearing a crisply pressed white lab coat, was smooth and confident as he guided Dylan into a small conference room. After exchanging a few pleasantries about the weather and the progress of construction on the new wing, Argent said, "What can I tell you about Nicole Girard?"

"Everything." Dylan pulled a legal pad from his briefcase.

Argent nodded, stood up, and went to the window. After a moment he turned back to face Dylan.

"Nicole came to the hospital last month as an HIV-positive—without any AIDS symptoms—to participate in a new clinical trial. While she was here she developed some symptoms that indicated she had ADC—AIDS dementia complex."

"I've never heard of that," said Dylan.

"It's really a catchall diagnosis for multiple signs and symptoms, some AIDS-related and some not."

"What kind of symptoms?"

"Oh, lots of things. Poor concentration, short attention span, loss of memory, irritability, muscle weakness, impaired coordination and judgment, slowed thinking, personality changes, and, in more progressive cases, severe depression, psychosis, mania, sometimes paranoia."

Dylan digested this for a moment. "But you said something else could cause these problems?"

Argent stroked the side of his cheek. "Sure. Everything from ordinary depression to some opportunistic infections that affect the brain, like toxoplasmosis or lymphoma."

"So how do you sort out the—what is it called—the—"

"Differential diagnosis?" Argent smiled indulgently. "Oh, there are several tests we use. Brain scans are often useful, but didn't show much in this case. However, most patients with ADC have mild elevations of certain proteins and white blood cells, and Nicole's CSF—cerebrospinal fluid—had those elevations. Also, her CD4 cell counts were down, and her viral load was up."

Dylan dutifully wrote this all down, not really understanding, and not really caring, either. But he was curious about the clinical trial. "Wouldn't the drug you were testing have helped her? I mean, that's what the drug is for, isn't it? To prevent the patient from developing AIDS?"

"Who told you she was getting an antiviral drug?"

"I just assumed—"

"No, no. This is a national trial of PHT—passive hyperimmune therapy." At Dylan's blank look he continued, "PHT uses blood plasma from donors, like Nicole, who are HIV-positive but don't have any symptoms of AIDS yet—or none that we know about, anyway—and who are apparently controlling the virus well. We take their blood plasma, sterilize it to avoid transmitting any new mutation of the virus, then infuse it into patients with AIDS. The plasma contains antibodies to help the patients fight the virus."

"That's amazing!"

Argent nodded. "It's not a new idea, but the results have been inconsistent. Some studies were very successful, others not so much. And in some cases, there was a rebound effect after the treatment was stopped—an increased rate of opportunistic infections, wasting, and neurological deterioration. We're using a redesigned protocol to test PHT's efficacy once and for all."

"Sounds like a good idea," Dylan said.

"If the results validate it." Argent glanced at his watch. "It's time to meet the patient."

Dylan picked up his briefcase and followed Argent out of the conference room and into the corridor, just as a pair of workmen carrying cans of paint passed the doorway.

"Must be tough working through all this," Dylan observed as he followed Argent down the hall and into a stairwell.

"Yeah. But it's good to have the extra space." Argent took the steps quickly, and Dylan scrambled to keep up. Argent continued, "Before we got the donation from Reverend Fletcher's group, my research division was crammed into the internal medicine floor over in the East Wing. We really need two floors—one for patients, the other for our research facilities and administrative offices. With Fletcher's money, we were able to refurbish the two floors of this wing. Here we are." He stopped outside a closed door, knocked twice, and opened it.

Dylan followed into a dimly illuminated room, painted in light green. It was a "private" room—only one bed. The double-sash window had wooden bars nailed across it.

Argent nodded at the male nurse who rose from an upholstered chair facing the bed, blocking Dylan's view of the patient. "This is Mr. Ice," said Argent formally. "He's Ms. Girard's attorney." The man nodded at Dylan; he looked more like a professional wrestler than a nurse.

Dylan started to say that no, actually he represented Nicole's parents, but thought better of it. Instead he looked at Nicole Girard.

She sat upright in the bed, an IV line flowing into her left arm, foam-rubber restraints around her legs and arms. This was the second time he had seen her, and now he noticed that she had full lips, pale skin, and large brown eyes that stared dully at the wall opposite the bed.

Even in these circumstances, he could see she was an attractive woman. Then he remembered that a deadly virus was circulating in her veins, which made his skin crawl. "Can she talk?" Dylan asked tentatively.

"Sure," said Argent. "If she wants to." He walked forward and stroked her right hand gently. "Nicole."

She slowly turned her head to look at him. "Yes."

"How are you feeling?"

"How am I feeling?" she repeated.

"Yes," said Argent, pulling an ophthalmoscope out of his lab coat and peering through it into her eyes. "Any pain or discomfort?"

"Any pain or discomfort?" she said. She tried to jerk away from him, but with the restraints she couldn't do more than move her head.

"It's okay," said Argent soothingly, as the nurse hurried to the other side of the bed. Argent turned his head and said to Dylan, "This may not work out. As you see, she's not very cooperative today."

"I'd like to try." Dylan added, "And I'd like to be alone."

"Alone?" Argent seemed surprised—and not at all pleased—as he straightened up.

"That's right." Dylan quickly continued, "I have to make an independent evaluation of her condition for the court." He really had no particular right to a private meeting; on the other hand, he had already learned that when a lawyer—even a very young and inexperienced one—said something authoritatively using the word *court*, people listened. It was, he had come to learn, one of the few remaining perks of the profession.

Argent thought about it for a moment, then said abruptly, with an undertone of anger, "All right. Just remember, she's not lucid. She's liable to free-associate, say anything, anything at all."

"I understand." Dylan waited until they left,

then closed the door. He looked at Nicole; she now stared out the window, expressionless. He pulled a wooden chair to the other side of the bed, effectively blocking her gaze. He reminded himself again that he couldn't catch AIDS through casual contact. He said, "Ms. Girard, I'd like to talk to you. Can you understand what I'm saying?"

She stared at him for a moment, then said slowly, "Can you understand what I'm saying?"

Dylan groaned, ready to give up before he started, except for the tiny movement he saw at the corner of her mouth. After a moment, he said, "Yes."

She smiled, dimpling her left cheek. "That's good," she said. "You know, I didn't think my parents believed me, but they came through. They finally *listened*!" She chuckled. "Sorry for the weird way I acted in front of Argent, but I'm not gonna give in to him. So, what's next? When can you get me out of here?"

Dylan was taken aback by her sudden transformation. Well, Argent had said it wouldn't be easy. He cleared his throat and said carefully, "Ms. Girard—"

"Nicole." She looked directly at him as she spoke and appeared disconcertingly normal. He hadn't expected rationality. "Uh, actually, Dr. Argent didn't introduce me properly. I'm a lawyer retained by your parents, and I represent your parents, not you." He added quickly, "The court will appoint another lawyer to represent you in the hearing. I'm just here to evaluate your . . . condition."

She looked puzzled and tried to sit up, but was stopped by the restraints. "Shit," she said, and with her right hand grabbed for the bed control. She raised the whole head of the bed until her eyes were level with Dylan's. "What are your talking about? Why would my parents need a lawyer? I'm the one"—she nodded at the bed restraints—"all tied up!"

There goes rationality, Dylan thought. "Ms. Girard, your parents want the court to appoint them as your guardian."

She sucked in her breath. After a few seconds, she said, "Bullshit! I can't believe this! Those bastards, you know how often they've come to see me? Once! One time! I told them what's happening, I told them what that vampire Argent is doing, and I asked them to get a lawyer to help me! And this is what they do!"

The door opened and Dr. Argent stuck his head in. "You need help?"

"No. No, we're fine," said Dylan, annoyed at Argent's eavesdropping. "Please leave us alone."

Argent shrugged and shut the door. His appearance had an effect on Nicole, however; she took a deep breath and said calmly, "Sorry I yelled at you, but . . . look, if you were tied up like this twenty-four hours a day, you might be a little cranky, too."

"I would be."

She looked at him without speaking for an uncomfortable amount of time, then said, "You're pretty young, aren't you?"

"I don't think that—"

"I mean, you can't have been a lawyer very long. You must be about twenty-five or -six."

"Twenty-seven," he said, instantly regretting it.

"Oh," she said. "That's different."

They both smiled, and he found himself warming to her. Her face had lost its hard edge, becoming softer, more human. And for an instant, he had forgotten she had AIDS. He pushed that thought aside and said, "Could you tell me why you're under restraints?"

"I'll try. Can I have some water?" She nodded toward the side table. He saw a covered plastic cup with a straw. There was also a thin sketch pad and a box of colored pencils.

"Oh. Sure." He picked up the water cup.

"You'll have to hold it for me, my arms won't reach."

Dylan forcibly pushed aside his fears of infection and brought the cup to her pale lips. She took a few sips.

"Thanks."

As he replaced the cup on the table, she said, "I was here for a clinical trial, a study of passive immunotherapy. I was supposed to check into the hospital for a complete physical and evaluation, then donate plasma twice a month. But the day I was supposed to go home, I started getting dizzy and blacking out. Dr. Argent wanted me to stay another day while they figured it out, and I agreed. He started giving me all kinds of tests, then finally told me I was suffering from an early form of AIDS-related dementia." She paused and looked him in the eye. "That's a lie."

"Why do you say that?"

"Because I know the real reason." She blinked. "They've been drugging me. I *saw* the nurses put drugs in my IV lines. And I know how I felt. I'm telling you, I was drugged, that's why I kept passing out, that's why I acted so weird."

Dylan nodded as if he understood and said, "Do you have any idea why they might be doing this— drugging you?"

"Yes," she said gravely. "They're vampires. I think they drink my blood."

"I see," Dylan said carefully. "All right, then—"

She giggled, then exploded with laughter. "You should see your face."

Dylan reddened, then eventually laughed too. "So you didn't really mean it when you called Dr. Argent a vampire at the dedication ceremony?"

She shook her head. "Not literally, of course. But he *is* a vampire in the sense that he's taking my blood without my permission." She leaned forward and said, "I don't know what they're doing with it, but they're taking much more than they need for the PHT trial."

"I'm sure it's an appropriate amount, they wouldn't endanger you—"

"No! I read all about PHT before I agreed to participate in the trial. They take blood from all the volunteers, then pool it for infusion. They're taking two, three tubes, twice a day. It's made me anemic, for God's sake! What's all that blood for?"

"Maybe your time sense is off—maybe they're not taking it all on one day."

Her eyes narrowed. "I know what time it is."

Dylan tried a different tack. "Look, Ms. Girard—Nicole—you realize, don't you, that you've been acting rather strangely? I mean, you jumped out of this window." Dylan didn't know if it was therapeutically correct to confront her directly, but he had to find out the extent of her illusions.

"I was trying to escape."

"Escape? Escape from what? From treatment for AIDS?"

She started to reply, then sighed. "If my parents are appointed my guardian, what exactly does that mean?"

"It simply means they'll make decisions about your medical care until you're able to."

"I've already lost my right to make decisions."

"Yes, but it's being done under a temporary detention order given to the hospital under the mental health law. This would be more . . . permanent."

"So they could have me *permanently* committed, right? I'd have to stay here?"

"No, not here. A psychiatric hospital."

She laughed. "Right. There's a psychiatric ward in this hospital. And I still would need treatment for AIDS. So maybe I would just be *permanently* committed here. What do you think?"

"I don't know, I hadn't thought about that. I guess it's possible. That will be up to your parents, once they are appointed guardians."

She just looked away.

Dylan decided to get the conversation away from this subject, see if she was otherwise rational. He asked her about art therapy, something he had barely heard of before.

Her face lighted up as she described her profession. "You see," she said, "children—and adults too—usually reveal their feelings in their drawings. For example, if they draw themselves much smaller than other members of their family, they have low self-esteem. If someone is hurting them, they'll draw that individual large, or with big, powerful hands. There are all kinds of feelings that people will express in their drawings that they either can't or won't express otherwise."

That topic led to a discussion of how she got involved in art, and Dylan was surprised when he looked at his watch and saw almost an hour had passed. "I'm sorry, but I have to leave."

Her face became hard again. "So what's the verdict? Are you gonna help my parents get me committed to this . . . torture chamber?"

"I don't know. I—I'm sure your parents will do what's best for you."

She leaned back against the pillow and turned her face away. He stood and said lamely, "If there's more you'd like to tell me, I'll visit you again, if you like."

Her head swiveled back. "When?"

He found himself saying, "Uh, how about tomorrow?"

"I'd like that," she said. "I'll be here."

After he left Nicole's room, Dylan stopped in the hospital cafeteria for some coffee. The place was busy and he had to wait for a table, but he didn't feel like going right back to the office.

As he sat down, he wondered why he had volunteered to see Nicole again. It wasn't necessary—he had all the information he needed—but now it was an obligation. Dylan could imagine Hudson's reaction when he saw the entry on his time sheet. He felt sorry for Nicole, of course, but—

"Mind if I sit here?" said a female voice.

He looked up and saw a woman with red hair holding a tray—Reverend Fletcher's daughter, he realized. Before he could say anything, she added, "You look familiar."

"Uh—I was just about to say the same thing—I saw you at the dedication ceremony. I was in the audience."

She stuck out her hand as she sat down. "I'm Kristin Fletcher."

"Dylan Ice." Her grip was strong and her hand seemed to linger. She wore a white blouse and black jeans, and was as attractive up close as she was at long range. Her hair was truly red, falling straight to her shoulders, with bangs in front. She had green eyes—probably contact lenses, but very striking. She wore little makeup, and he could see small freckles on her nose and forehead. Until now, he never thought freckles were sexy.

"Why were you at the dedication?" she asked.

A little surprised by her directness, he said, "Uh, I'm a lawyer with the firm that represents you father's business interests. We were there to . . . uh, show support and respect for your father."

"Perhaps you should have a little less respect."

"I–uh–oh."

She laughed at his expression. "Sorry. I didn't mean to upset you."

He countered, "You don't sound like a minister's daughter."

"Have you known others?"

"Actually, no." He searched for something to say. "Do you work here?"

She grinned. "No. I have some business with Dr. Argent's office." She opened her purse and handed him a card: KRISTIN FLETCHER, INTERIOR DESIGN & SPACE PLANNING. There was a Clayton address and phone number.

"You're doing his office? It certainly needs it."

"I might," she said vaguely. "If he can afford me."

Dylan laughed. "I'm sure he can. I've seen the suits he wears."

"Very observant." She looked at him appraisingly. "You dress well yourself."

"Thanks," he said, and it slowly penetrated his brain that she might be attracted to him. He looked around the cafeteria; there were other seats available. *Ask her out, dummy.*

"Well," she said, finishing her coffee. "Nice talking to you."

"I'd like to learn more about interior decorating," he said clumsily.

"Oh? Is that so?"

"Yes. Maybe I could take you to dinner?"

She smiled. "What a nice idea."

CHAPTER FOUR

"All right, I think we're finished," Douglas Kaster said. As the senior managing partner of Cameron, Barr, Haight, Waters & Kaster—and the only "name" partner not dead or senile—Kaster sat at the head of the long oak table occupied by seven other members of the firm's management committee. It was his decision when to start and end the weekly meetings.

"One other item," Paul Hudson said laconically from the other end of the table. "I forgot to mention something during Case Reviews."

"Well, what is it?" Kaster impatiently looked at his watch.

"I took a DNB case this week," Hudson said as casually as possible. "From Reverend Fletcher."

"Fletcher?" repeated Tim Portland, head of the tax department. He and the others looked at Kaster for reaction.

Kaster stared at Hudson and said slowly, "Why don't you tell us about it, Paul."

"Not much to tell. Fletcher called for you last Monday, Doug, when you were out of town. When he learned you weren't here, he asked for another managing partner. I was available."

"My secretary knew where I could be reached."

"Really?" said Hudson. "I thought you were on vacation. Anyway, reception put Fletcher through to my office."

"I see," said Kaster coldly. "And what did Fletcher want?"

Hudson briefly described the Girard case.

James Gould, white-haired and years past retirement—but a Kaster loyalist—said, "It should have gone to Doug's department."

"It is a T and E case," Portland said.

"Just a simple guardianship," said Hudson. "Any first-year associate can handle it."

"So why are *you* handling it?" Kaster asked.

Hudson had to keep himself from laughing with delight. Kaster was furious. Fletcher had always been his client, passed on to him by Fletcher's original lawyer, Percy Barr. And controlling the firm's largest client meant, effectively, controlling the firm. *But all good things must come to an end, Douglas.*

"I'm not. I assigned it to an associate," Hudson said.

"Who?" said Portland.

"Dylan Ice."

"The Negro fellow?" Gould asked, to the dismay of the others. They had to restrain themselves from looking around to see who was listening.

"He calls himself biracial, actually," said Hudson dryly. "In any event, he has personal experience with guardianships, and he does good work."

Everyone turned to Kaster, waiting for his reaction. He just tapped his fingers on the table and said, "I'm frankly surprised, Paul. I intend to speak with Reverend Fletcher about this."

"Oh, I already have," said Hudson smoothly. "I

explained that you might be perturbed. He said it was just a small matter, he couldn't understand why you would care."

They locked glances, and Hudson knew it would have to end soon. One of them would have to go—and it wasn't going to be him.

"Meeting adjourned," said Kaster.

"Just like that?" Barry said, squinting his eyes from the smoke of the barbecue. He slipped a spatula under a sizzling burger and skillfully flipped it. "You got a date with Kristin Fletcher just by bumping into her in the cafeteria?" He shook his head. "Dylan, I sincerely apologize. I have definitely underestimated you."

"Believe me, I surprised myself," Dylan said from his perch on the wooden deck railing.

Barry stepped back from the barbecue kettle and rubbed a forearm across his sweat-beaded forehead. "Since I've been with the firm, I know of at least half a dozen lawyers who have asked Kristin out—and been shot down. Either she's very selective, or she doesn't date much. So when are you going out?"

"This Friday." Dylan swished the ice in his gin and tonic and took a drink. They were on the wide redwood deck of Barry's suburban home. Stretching before them was a manicured lawn with a wooden play set; a tall white stake fence separated Barry's property from the three-story Victorian behind it. On the deck of that house, Dylan could see another family, also barbecuing. The combined smoke from this neighborhood probably was killing trees all the way to the Amazon.

The sliding patio door opened, and Janis stepped out onto the deck.

"And you think you can handle her?" continued Barry.

"Handle who?" said Janis.

"Never mind," said Dylan.

Janis stuck out her tongue. "Elaine wants to know when the burgers will be ready," she said grumpily.

"Five minutes," said Barry cheerily. "Tell her to warm her buns."

Janis laughed. Dylan said, "And put your shirt on for dinner." She was dressed in jeans and a tiny halter top; Dylan hadn't known she was wearing the top until they arrived at Barry's house and she removed her blouse. Janis didn't acknowledge Dylan; she just turned and slammed the sliding door shut.

"Shit," said Dylan.

"Lighten up," said Barry. "She's a teenager."

"That's a chronological category, not an excuse."

"Sheesh. You're not really that much of a tight-ass, are you?"

Dylan took another drink. "It's not like that. Your kids are still young. You don't know what it's like."

Barry smiled genially. "But she's not your kid, Dylan. That's the whole point. You're her guardian, not her parent."

"From a legal viewpoint, there's no difference."

"From a legal viewpoint! Listen to yourself—"

The door opened again. This time Elaine stuck her head through. She was a pretty, plump woman in her early thirties, with frizzy brown hair. She smiled and said, "You guys want beer or wine?"

"Beer," they said quickly, together.

Before they went into the house, Barry said, "You know, there was one guy in the firm who dated Kristin Fletcher. An associate, like you."

"Yeah? Who?"

"You don't know him. That's the point."

"What point?"

"He's not around anymore."

It took a moment to sink in. "Oh. Wait a minute, you don't mean—"

"I think her old man didn't want to see his face in the halls when he came to confer with counsel."

"That really sounds absurd."

"Maybe it is. I just hope you don't test it."

"Look, it's just one date."

"Yeah." Barry leered. "That's what Samson said about Delilah."

As they pulled out of Barry's driveway, Janis tapped her fingers on the dashboard of Dylan's Buick, humming a little song he couldn't make out. When they turned onto Page Boulevard, she started telling him a long, involved story about a rock star and the way he was getting screwed by MTV. He glanced over at her, and in the light from a street lamp, saw that her face was flushed, eyes wide and bright. He hoped she wasn't getting sick—she couldn't afford to miss any more school.

Two days earlier, Dylan had had an alarming meeting with Janis's high school principal, who told him that the school was having trouble with gangs. Apparently, inner-city kids were using drugs—even heroin—to infiltrate the suburban high schools, and Janis had been seen hanging out with some known gang members. She also was missing classes. The implication was obvious, and the principal was warning all the parents of kids who might be involved.

Dylan had assured the principal that Janis would never use drugs—not with her history—but he had agreed to watch her more closely.

He suddenly realized that Janis was waiting for him to answer. He couldn't recall the question. She said, "Jesus, didn't you hear anything I said?"

"I'm sorry, I didn't."

Janis turned her head and stared out the window. He apologized again, but she was thoroughly offended.

When he turned into the parking lot of their townhouse development, his headlights illuminated a car parked in one of his two reserved spots. It was a late-model BMW, cherry red. Lounging against the driver side door was a tall black youth wearing a red knit skullcap, an oversize gray sweatshirt, and dark athletic pants. Another man, dressed similarly, was sitting on the front steps of their town house, leaning backward.

Janis suddenly slid down in her seat and said urgently, "Keep driving, Dylan. Don't stop."

"What are you talking about?" Dylan said as he turned into the adjacent parking spot. "Do you know these guys?"

"No! I mean—just go! Please!"

"If these are friends of yours—" Dylan said as he opened his door and got out. He realized that the two men had suddenly materialized next to his car— one outside each front door. The man in the red hat stood next to him. He was in his early twenties—and mean-looking.

"Get out the way," the man growled. "We wanna talk with the bitch." The second man was outside Janis's car door, which she had locked.

"Who are you?" said Dylan. "What do you want?"

The first man said impatiently, "Bizness, man. Now move." He put his hand on Dylan's shoulder and shoved him aside. Dylan instinctively reached out to shove him away but was met with a razor-sharp knife inches from his nose. "Back off, man."

Dylan fought a surge of panic and put up his hands. "Hey, take it easy. Can't we talk about this?" The man sniffed in disgust and ostentatiously returned the blade to its sheath on his waist, also revealing a pistol in a shoulder holster. "Get lost, man, or I'll cut you bad." Leaning into the car, he reached across the driver's seat and grabbed Janis's left arm as she jammed herself up against the passenger-side door. "Dylan!" she screamed.

Adrenaline surged through Dylan. He grabbed the back of the man's sweatshirt and pulled with all his strength, yanking him backward through the door opening. The back of the man's head hit the inside door frame with a thunk! and reluctantly followed the rest of his body. He was unconscious as Dylan dropped him onto the pavement.

Dylan looked up in time to see the second man coming around the front of the car. Dylan backed up quickly, expecting an attack, but the second man simply picked up his friend and half dragged him to their car, all the while looking anxiously past Dylan's shoulder. Dylan turned around and saw a police car, its red dome light on, slowly cruising down the parking lot. The BMW backed out of the parking spot before the police car arrived.

"She's lying," said the cop named Bradley, a short, stocky man in his thirties with a neck pumped up from weight training. As he seated himself in Dylan's study, he looked with interest at the rowing trophies displayed on the bookcase.

Bradley's partner was in the living room with Janis. Their fortuitous appearance on the scene was no accident; one of Dylan's neighbors had reported the suspicious appearance of the two black men.

Despite the obvious, Janis maintained that she didn't know the two men—not really. She had seen them hanging around the high school campus. Yes, they were probably gang members. She had no idea, she said, why they were after her.

"I know she's lying," Dylan said. "What the hell am I supposed to do about it?"

Bradley shrugged. "I don't know, but you better do something. My guess is she's dealing drugs, and those dudes were her source."

For the tenth time, Dylan cursed himself for not getting the tag number of the BMW. "That can't be right," he said. "Janis has a lot of problems, but she doesn't do drugs. I would know."

Bradley stared at him and laughed. "Excuse me, sir, but what planet are you from?"

Dylan felt himself redden. "You don't understand. It's not that I'm naïve, it's that—well, there's a certain family history. Janis would never—"

Bradley put up his hand. "Sure, sure. Whatever you say. All I'm saying is that those guys were in a gang—didn't you see their colors? And gangs deal drugs to make cash. You were lucky this time. No one got hurt except the bad guy." He paused, then continued, "Of course, that might be bad for you, later. You got a security system here? No? Well you might think about getting one." Bradley took a card out of his pocket and handed it to him. "A detective named Carl

Peterson runs our gang investigation unit. Here's his card. If your sister decides to tell the truth, call him."

After the cops left, Dylan sat down across from Janis. They played the heavy silence game for a while, Dylan looking at her, Janis staring at the wall. Eventually Dylan won. Janis said softly, "You don't understand."

"Maybe I would. Give it a try."

She gave an exaggerated sigh and folded her legs under her on the couch. "I have some friends," she began. "They're not the kind of friends you would approve of, but they're *real*, not like all the phonies at school. They accept me the way I am, they don't care that I'm half-white or half-black or half anything. You don't understand what it's like, it's different than when you were a kid."

"Janis, that was only ten years ago. Things haven't changed that much."

"Yes, they have, but you don't know it. You've become part of the Establishment, just like Howard said. You've sold out."

Dylan almost smiled at the way she parroted their father's ancient hippie lingo. Still, the words hurt. "I'm not gonna argue this with you."

"Good!" she said.

"That's not what I meant!" Then he added, "Those guys today were your friends?"

She made a face. "No way."

"But you know who they are."

"Yeah. They were . . . *enemies* of my friends. So they're my enemies, too."

Dylan thought about this for a moment, his heart sinking. "And what did they want from you?"

Silence. She changed positions, hugging her knees to her chin.

Dylan said gently, "Did you owe them money?"

"No!"

"Then what did they want?"

"I told you, they don't like me because of my friends, that's all."

"Groovy, does it involve drugs?"

After a moment, she said very softly, "No."

She had never lied to him, not when he called her Groovy—her childhood nickname. He sighed with relief and decided against pressing her any further. She was already mashed into the corner of the sofa, her hair in her face, looking more like a little girl than a neophyte adult. He reached out and patted her knee. "We'll talk more later. Go to bed now."

She reached out her arms to him. Dylan sat on the sofa and hugged her. He stroked her head. "It'll be all right, Groovy. We'll work it out."

She smiled at him gratefully.

CHAPTER FIVE

The next day Dylan was immersed in researching a complex discovery motion when Rhonda buzzed him. "There's a woman in the reception area wanting to see you. Says her name is McConnell—Charlene McConnell. I told reception you weren't expecting anyone." Dylan could hear the disapproval in Rhonda's voice—not only for the woman, but for Dylan, who, she assumed, had forgotten about the appointment.

The name sounded vaguely familiar, but Dylan couldn't place it. "Can you find out what she wants?"

"All right," she said grudgingly. As the secretary to two of the most junior associates in the firm, Rhonda didn't go out of her way to please. Dylan knew she thought her skills were suitable for a junior partner, at least.

A moment later his phone chirped again. "She says she's the roommate of Nicole Girard. Isn't that the nut case you're doing the guardianship for?"

"Yes," said Dylan. "And she's not a nut case."

"Whatever. This McConnell woman is pushy. Do you want me to get rid of her?"

"No, thanks. I'll see her. Tell reception I'm coming."

He took the stairs to the main reception area, a grandiose hall of wood paneling, deep pile carpet, and English club chairs surrounding a central reception pedestal. He almost walked right past McConnell before he realized that she must be the tall black woman. It hadn't occurred to him that Nicole Girard might have a black lover.

"Ms. McConnell?" he said tentatively. When she nodded, he continued, "Hello. I'm Dylan Ice."

"Nice to meet ya." She stood up, unfolding an angular frame in a red pullover and gray cotton pants. She was in her thirties, very dark, with high cheekbones and almond eyes.

"You're Nicole's roommate?"

"We live together, yes."

"I see," said Dylan. "Is there something . . . you wanted?"

"Well, of course, honey, you think I enjoy sitting in this funeral parlor?"

Dylan couldn't help grinning. "It is kind of formal in here. Why don't you come with me?" He took her down the hall to one of the small auxiliary conference rooms, designated for use by associates.

She looked at the grass cloth wallpaper and abstract art, murmured, "Nice," and sat down at the round faux wood table.

Dylan took a yellow legal pad from the side cabinet and sat down across from her. "Now, how can I help you?"

"Like I said, I live with Nicole. Or did, anyway. I've been out of town for a few days, and when I saw her this morning she said her parents are trying to get appointed as her guardians. She gave me your name—said you were the lawyer doing it."

"That's right. I represent Mr. and Mrs. Girard."

She snorted. "Right. The King and Queen of Soul."
"Pardon me?"

"Never mind. Look, Nicole says she's talked to you, and you seem okay. In fact, she likes you."

"Well, thanks."

"I mean, she said you didn't act like a typical lawyer, or at least a lawyer"—she waved her hand around the office—"that works in one of these places."

"Thanks again. I guess."

"You're welcome. I'm a social worker for the county, I deal with lawyers all the time, but not from firms like this." She paused and then said abruptly, "You think Nicole is crazy?"

"If you mean do I think she is psychotic or a danger to others, no. But I do think she's delusional, perhaps paranoid, and a danger to herself."

She grimaced. "Now you sound like a shrink. Who fed you that garbage?"

"I observed it," Dylan said patiently.

"You mean, the stuff about the blood? That's what you mean by 'delusional'?"

"Well, yes."

"And why, do you think, is she delusional *now* but wasn't before she went into the hospital? Because she wasn't, you know. Nicole was about as centered a person as there is."

Dylan found it strange to hear her talk about being "centered." It was such a California term. "Things happened in the hospital. She learned that she had progressed to AIDS—that's enough to drive anybody—"

"Bullshit!" McConnell slammed her hand on the table. "Nicole had been expecting that. She came to terms with it. Believe me, I *know*. We discussed it seriously at least once a month. No, something else happened to her in the hospital—something that screwed up her head."

Dylan tapped his pen on the yellow pad. "That may be true. But you should discuss it with Nicole's parents, not with me."

She laughed without humor. "I don't think you get it. To the Girards, I'm scum. I'm the person that turned their little girl into a lesbian. That's not true, of course, but they believe it."

"I'm sorry to hear that," Dylan said in what he hoped was a soothing manner. "But there's nothing *I* can do."

"You could get me her medical records so I can find out what really happened. You're the lawyer for the Girards, they won't refuse you. And if they did, you could subpoena them."

Dylan pushed his chair back and stood up. "Ms. McConnell, you say you're a social worker, so you must understand the principle of client confidentiality. Even if I were to obtain Nicole's records, I couldn't just give them to you without my client's permission."

"I expected you to say that." She reached into the purse slung over her shoulder and pulled out a piece of paper, sliding it across the table.

Dylan sat down again to read it. It was a piece of lined notepaper, handwritten: "I choose and appoint Charlene McConnell as my guardian if a judge decides that I am unable to make my own decisions." It was signed "Nicole Girard" and dated that day.

"I've done my homework," Charlene said. "According to Section 475.050 of the Code, Nicole has the right to make her own choice of guardian, and she wants me."

"That's not quite true," said Dylan, glad that he had recently looked at that section of the statute. He started to say more, then realized he shouldn't be arguing legal points with someone whose interests were adverse to his clients'.

She grabbed the paper back from him, folded it, and carefully returned it to her purse. "I don't want to fight over this, but I will if I have to. Will you help me or not?"

"The issue isn't about helping, it's what I can do, legally and practically . . ." His voice trailed off.

"I see. All right, at least I know where you stand." She rose and stuck her hand out. "If you change your mind, let me know." He took her hand and she shook it firmly, then turned and quickly exited. "I'll find my own way out."

Dylan was left standing in the empty room, thinking that maybe client contact wasn't so great after all.

Like her personality, Kristin Fletcher drove fast, her hair flying out from behind the Cardinals baseball cap, eyes hidden by designer sunglasses. Dylan sat in the passenger seat of the white Jeep Wrangler—the automobile of choice for Generation X—his right hand clutching the door armrest as Kristin maneuvered the Jeep through heavy traffic on Interstate 270.

Long ago, Dylan had decided that there were few things in life sexier than a blonde in a convertible. Kristin wasn't blonde, but the principle was the same.

Dylan had been more than a little startled when Kristin called at nine o'clock that morning and asked him to accompany her to church. Realizing how odd that sounded, she had quickly added that her father was giving one of his rare sermons and she was obligated to go. "I know it's a lot to ask, but I was hoping you would keep me company."

It wasn't a lot to ask, although Dylan was still trying to accelerate to Kristin's speed.

Their first date had been a unique experience: he had picked her up at her apartment in a Clayton high-rise, experiencing the usual first-date jitters. Kristin had opened the door, pulled him into the foyer by the arm, all in one motion, without saying a word. Reaching up, she grabbed his face with both hands and kissed him fiercely on the mouth, her tongue battering at his teeth. He was too surprised to respond. After a moment, she stepped back, grinning. "There," she said with satisfaction. "Now that's out of the way, and we can enjoy the evening."

Dylan had struggled to say something witty, managing only a squeak.

They went to dinner at a Chinese restaurant, saw a movie, and talked over coffee until three A.M. She was knowledgeable on a wide range of subjects, and seemed truly interested in Dylan's opinions. When he took her home, she kissed him on the cheek and demurely bid him good night. He hadn't been sure whether he should call her again or not.

Then she had settled the issue by inviting him to church this morning.

They passed a large truck, then zoomed up behind a small Japanese car poking along in the passing lane. Kristin flashed her lights, but the driver didn't notice, so Kristin leaned on her horn. The driver, a woman with Marge Simpson hair, visibly jumped, and her car almost swerved onto the shoulder. She recovered but remained in the fast lane.

"Damn," said Kristin over the sound of the wind. "What do I have to do, send her a letter?" There was a Mazda to their right, and Kristin nosed the Jeep into that lane, barely clearing its front bumper. As they came alongside, Kristin stuck out her left hand and gave the driver the finger. Dylan groaned, and Kristin turned to grin at him.

By the time they arrived in St. Charles, with its Victorian houses, well-tended lawns, and twenty-five mph speed limits, Kristin was driving reasonably. She even used her turn signals as she pulled into the enormous parking lot of the St. Charles First Evangelical Church.

The church was an incongruous structure squatting on the edge of town, dwarfing the homes. It had grown from a clapboard one-room building to this dreadfully immense cathedral, testament to the Reverend Fletcher's fund-raising prowess. Fletcher was no longer its pastor—preferring to concentrate his energies on his empire of real estate, radio and television stations—but this was his home base, his original source of power and money.

As they walked toward the entrance, passing scores of well-scrubbed midwestern families in their Sunday best, Dylan felt very conspicuous. It was an all-white crowd, and the men were dressed in suits. He wore a blue blazer with gray slacks, blue shirt, and red tie, and felt too casually dressed. Kristin had removed her baseball cap, and her black knit dress looked respectable.

Inside, the place was so big that from the main doorway to the altar there was enough room to play a game of regulation football; Dylan was somewhat surprised the altar wasn't shrouded in fog. They walked down the aisle, Kristin returning the greetings of several parishioners, and took seats in the very front pew.

For Dylan, who had only rarely been in a church, and then only for weddings and funerals, the Baptist service conducted by the regular pastor was fresh and interesting. He followed along in the hymn book and tried to look like he knew what he was doing. Kristin, however, made little attempt to hide her boredom.

When Fletcher finally was introduced—coming out from a side door at the back of the sanctuary—the entire congregation rose to its feet and applauded. Fletcher waved his hand graciously and ascended to the podium, then launched into a strongly worded sermon about violence and sex in the media, replete with sports metaphors and references to such diverse public figures as Madonna and Clint Eastwood. His delivery was compelling, but Dylan found it hard to believe that anyone could take the content seriously. Looking around, he saw that the congregation was listening raptly—even Kristin, who stared at her father with an adoring expression.

When it was finally over, Fletcher came down the steps directly to Kristin, who hugged him in congratulations. "Daddy, I want you to meet someone," she said, introducing Dylan.

"Ah, yes, Mr. Ice," Fletcher said, squeezing his hand firmly. "One of my lawyers."

"Nice to meet you, Reverend."

"You too, my friend. I'd like to talk to you after the service." He sat down between them as the regular minister took over the podium and finished up the service with a couple of hymns.

Fletcher accepted greetings from the parishioners, then Dylan and Kristin followed him to a door behind the altar. On the door was a small brass plaque with Fletcher's name.

Inside, a small office was carpeted in plush green. It had a wall of bookcases, a small, beautifully restored antique desk, a leather sofa, and matching easy chairs. As Fletcher led them in, he said to Dylan, "This is my little hideaway. I don't get here often, but the congregation decided to keep this office available for me." He motioned them to the couch as he went to the wall and folded down a minibar. "Can I offer you something, Dylan?"

"Soda would be fine."

"I'll have something stronger, Daddy," said Kristin.

He poured a bourbon for himself and Kristin, then sat down in the big upholstered chair. "How long have you been with Cameron Barr, Dylan?"

Kristin groaned, but didn't say anything.

"Almost three years."

"You like it there?"

"Well, uh, yes."

"You don't sound too sure."

"No, I am, I mean, I just have to pay my dues like everyone else."

"Meaning what?"

Dylan glanced at Kristin, a little surprised by Fletcher's insistence. She said, "Daddy's very nosy, in case you hadn't noticed."

Fletcher laughed, apparently not taking any offense. "She's right, Dylan, I am nosy. That's what got me where I am. I like to learn about people. So. Tell me what you mean."

"In law firms, associates have to do a lot of scut work before they're allowed to handle cases on their own. Sometimes associates will spend years in the law library, writing briefs and memoranda, before they meet their first client."

"And you don't think it's like that in other businesses?"

"Not in other professions, no. In medicine, for instance, it's just the opposite. Young doctors aren't prevented from treating patients."

Fletcher drained the last of his glass and went for a refill. With his back still turned to Dylan, he said, "But you've been given a case of your own, haven't you? The Girard case, I mean."

Dylan was only mildly surprised that Fletcher knew he had been assigned the case. Obviously, Fletcher's attention to detail was great—he had probably asked Hudson. "That's right," he said.

Fletcher nodded and resumed his seat. "So how come?"

"You mean, how come I got the case, to handle by myself?" Even as he said it, it suddenly occurred to him how odd it was that Hudson had made the assignment. For a moment, as he looked at Fletcher's permanent half smile, he thought Fletcher was behind it; but that was impossible. "I have some experience in guardianship matters. And it's really too small a case to bother a partner with."

"I see," said Fletcher. "And maybe it's because your boss has confidence in you."

Dylan shrugged.

"Daddy, is there a point to this?" said Kristin impatiently.

Dylan was wondering the same thing.

"No point," said Fletcher expansively. "Just curious. However, there is something I'd like to ask you."

"Uh-oh," said Kristin. "Watch out, Dylan."

Fletcher clucked his tongue. "Enough, young lady." He turned back to Dylan. "As you know, Nicole's parents are very good friends of mine. We go a long way back. It's *very* important to them, and therefore to me, that this guardianship goes smoothly. So I'd appreciate it very much if you would keep me informed."

"Keep you informed?" Dylan repeated, puzzled.

"That's right. Just let me know how things are going. Weekly reports would be fine. I understand that there may be some trouble with the young woman's roommate, that she's looking to hire a lawyer—"

"Excuse me, sir, but how do you know that?" Dylan said, sharply.

"That's not important. Let's just say I have my sources."

"I see," said Dylan. After a moment, he continued, "I assume, in that case, that Mr. and Mrs. Girard will give their authorization to release information about their case to you. Otherwise, of course, such information is privileged—"

"Yes, yes, of course." Fletcher waved his hand dismissively. "Whatever you need from the Girards, they'll give you." His tone hardened and he looked directly into Dylan's eyes. "Just make sure you tell me everything important, as soon as it happens. Is that clear?"

Dylan swallowed, starting to feel intimidated. "If the clients agree, of course."

"Good," said Fletcher. "That's settled, then. And one other thing—if you need any help with this case, anything at all, you let me know. Me, *directly*. Got that?"

"Well, sure," said Dylan, mystified, but seeing no harm in this.

"Excellent." Fletcher tossed back the remainder

of his drink, then rose ponderously. "I've got to get back to the city." He looked at Kristin.

Kristin said, "If you don't mind, Daddy, we'll stay a while."

Fletcher shrugged. "Okay. Just lock up when you leave." He shook hands with Dylan, kissed Kristin, and left.

Kristin closed the door behind him, then turned to face Dylan. "You handled him well."

"You think so?" said Dylan, still standing. She had a strange look on her face and moved seductively toward him, stopping inches from his body, but not touching.

"A lot of men have problems dealing with my father," Kristin said, stroking his arm. "They're either too kiss-ass or too hostile. You held your own."

"Thanks," he said.

Kristin was a smoker, and her clothes and hair had a stale tobacco smell that she covered with some very expensive perfume. *It must be expensive*, he thought, *because it sure is intoxicating*. He breathed deeply, and she moved her body softly into contact with his, hands reaching around his back to his buttocks. She squeezed gently while pressing her thighs into his front.

Very softly, she brushed her lips against his neck and under his chin. Dylan was immediately and majestically aroused.

"Wow," said Kristin, looking down at the front of his pants. She pushed him backward onto the couch. Then, in quick, precise motions, she skinned off her dress, slip, bra, and panties.

"Omigod," Dylan said. "Look, I'd love to, but we can't do this here."

"Why not?" she murmured, rubbing his thigh. "There's no one around, and I want to do it."

"But—"

She kissed him fiercely. When she lifted her lips from his, he said, "Did you lock the door?"

"No one but Daddy ever comes in here." She undid his necktie and pulled his shirt over his head. "Oh yes," she said, pulling back to admire his shoulders and chest, developed from years of rowing. "I knew it. I knew you were big and beautiful."

"I think we should lock the door," Dylan said, trying to get up, but she pushed him back hard.

"It's more exciting this way." She moved slowly down to his waist, pulling his pants and underwear down to his knees. Without first touching him, she put her head down and swallowed. Dylan uttered a long, low gasp, instantly ready to explode, but she sensed it and released him quickly, moving back up to kiss him.

He did his best to hold himself back until she got up and lay down on the thick pile carpet, beckoning.

I've got to lock the door, Dylan thought, but it was too far away. He joined her on the floor, and a last vestige of common sense made him say hoarsely, "Wait . . . I don't have a . . . I mean I need . . . a condom—"

She reached up and pulled him down, and his resistance was vaporized by the heat. Frantically, he pushed inside her, more excited then he thought possible, so taut with lust he almost screamed. When the explosion came—too quickly, yet not soon enough—it was almost painfully intense.

Afterward, while Kristin lay on the floor, eyes half-closed, Dylan rose, went to the door, and flipped the locking button. Sighing in relief, he returned to Kristin.

CHAPTER SIX

When Mark Argent was a boy, perhaps eleven or twelve, he would sit in the backseat of the family Chevrolet, lean forward, and tell his slightly bemused parents how famous he would be, how destiny had a special place reserved just for him. Quite naturally, they responded with indulgent chuckles.

He had learned since then that many children have such thoughts—especially somewhat spoiled children of professional parents. But his parents' lack of faith in his ultimate fame only acted as a spur, a challenge to make it so.

Some people might say he had already accomplished his goal. Argent was a graduate of Yale Medical School, a researcher of some note, and now the director of one of the top AIDS research institutes in the country. Among his peers, he was well-known, respected, admired, and—most satisfyingly—envied.

It was not enough. He wanted true fame, the kind of fame that brought instant name identification, TV news fame, fame that allowed contact with other famous people. Fame like that of Dr. Christiaan Barnard, who pioneered the heart transplant; like Dr. Jonas Salk, who beat polio.

He knew it was a shallow, ultimately unfulfilling goal, a goal probably more likely obtained by those not pursuing it. He also sometimes wondered what he would do after he achieved it.

But he had to have it.

Argent reflected on this and other things as he breathed the spring air on the hospital's sundeck, waiting for the distinguished Reverend Fletcher. His Holier than Thouness, as Argent's wife often called him.

The deck was a broad expanse of roof, planked with redwood, landscaped with shrubs and small trees in rough concrete tubs. At one end was a working fountain—a pair of interlocked Cupids—a small gazebo, numerous small tables, chairs, and chaise lounges. At the other end was one of the hospital's two helipads.

The whole thing was a gift from a grateful, very rich, former cancer patient. And although designed for recuperation, the sundeck primarily was used by hospital staff for cigarette breaks and sunbathing.

It was amazing how many health care workers smoked, thought Argent, as he walked by a cluster of smokers near the stairwell. He continued to the far side, near the fence that surrounded the deck, and took a seat at a white metal table. He glanced at his watch: Fletcher was late.

The noonday sun drenched him with light, and he turned his face toward it, enjoying the warmth. For some reason, the sun made him think of Nicole, practically chained to her bed, and he felt a twinge of guilt. He shoved it away.

But the thought of Nicole brought the PHT clinical trial to his thoughts, and he had to suppress a foolish grin.

It really was a remarkable set of circumstances that had put him in this position. If he had simply followed the course of least resistance, he would be immersed in testing one of the new protease inhibitors, drugs that blocked an HIV enzyme so the virus couldn't infect new cells.

Instead, he had unaccountably been drawn to some rather obscure studies involving passive hyperimmune therapy. Until recently, the serious rebound effects that occurred when patients stopped PHT—together with the difficulty and expense of the therapy itself—had relegated PHT to a footnote of AIDS research. But then a small drug company called ImmuCare submitted a new drug application to the FDA for approval, proposing studies of PHT combined with the company's proprietary immunoglobulin antibody concentrate. ImmuCare would pay the expenses, and his instincts told Argent something big was possible.

At about the same time, researchers at NIAID made a startling discovery. For years it was known that most animal cells reject the HIV virus—even if the cells were set up with transplanted human CD4 receptors. Clearly, humans, and not animals, had some "cofactor" that allowed HIV to infect human cells. The researchers, following this line of reasoning, had identified a previously unknown cell-surface receptor called fusin, a chemokine receptor. Their findings suggested that fusin and other chemokines were the "missing link" in HIV infection. That would explain why some people were less susceptible to HIV infection than others.

Putting this data together with hyperimmune therapy led him to some rather startling hypotheses, but he had no idea how important these ideas might be until after he had arranged for MIRI to sponsor a PHT clinical trial and he had received a surprise visit from Dr. Rosati, the director of NIAID.

And then he had discovered Nicole—

A solid slap to his back and he nearly bit his tongue. "Argent, my friend, good to see you!" Fletcher's voice boomed from above, his body blocking the sun.

Argent caught his breath; he hated when Fletcher did that. "Reverend, it's good to see you again. Here, have a seat."

"Beautiful day," said Fletcher, sitting next to him. "Glad you agreed to get out of that stuffy office."

Fletcher, Argent knew, hated being inside the hospital. Like many people, he found the thought of being near so many AIDS patients disconcerting. He was always trying to get Argent to meet him at his office, and Argent usually acquiesced, but today there hadn't been time. The sundeck was a good compromise. Anyway, it was time for Fletcher's status to change from benefactor to grateful supplicant. Argent looked around the deck, then lowered his voice and said, "I've completed the animal tests."

Fletcher's large eyebrows raised. "And?" he said anxiously.

"It works. No question, it works in rabbits. But rabbits aren't humans, and—"

"Dammit, is it safe or isn't it?"

My, aren't we testy, thought Argent, pleased. "Oh, I've never been worried about the safety. The worst that could happen is that it won't work, and we'll have to continue the way we are now."

"Yeah, so you say. But you're not the one who's going to use it, are you?"

"No, but I'd be willing to."

Fletcher said ominously, "I may hold you to that."

Argent shook his head and said, "Look, Reverend, this isn't a joke. If this works the way I expect—"

"Shut up!" Fletcher said fiercely. He leaned forward, invading Argent's space. "I've got a lot more at stake than you do, and you better not forget it. You haven't won the Nobel Prize yet, and without me, you never will."

Argent slid his chair backward, biting back an angry reply. The truth was he did need the fatuous old buzzard. He took a deep breath. "No one is going to get anything unless we keep Nicole."

"So? What's the problem?"

"The problem is that it's not easy holding someone against their will. If I don't keep her either locked up or sedated, or both, she'll walk out of here. This isn't a psychiatric ward with secure rooms and corridors. And if I transfer her to the psychiatric ward, I won't have sufficient access."

Fletcher frowned. "Is there some danger to her health?"

"Of course. She's already anemic because of all the blood I'm drawing. There's no help for that, of course, but she needs to eat or she'll get weaker and succumb to some infection."

"Can't you feed her intravenously?"

Argent delayed his answer while he waved at one of the hospital's ER surgeons, up for a smoke. Then he lowered his voice and said, "We're giving her fluids and nutrients, of course, but it's not the same as eating. We're taking a risk."

"Tell you what," said Fletcher. "The foundation

has its own security force. I'll assign some men here. You can use them as you like."

Argent laughed. "Rent-a-cops? We can't trust them with this."

Fletcher smiled thinly. "These aren't from an outside agency. They're my own people, all of them. True believers, you might say. You can trust them with anything."

Argent considered it. "They'll have to wear different uniforms."

Fletcher shrugged. "Fine."

"What about this court case?" said Argent. "When will we have her permanently committed?"

"The guardianship hearing will be soon, don't worry."

"That lawyer they put on the case—name of *Ice*, for Christ's sake—he's still wet behind the ears."

Fletcher's face creased in a warm chuckle. "You don't have to be Gerry Spence to handle a guardianship."

"No, but this isn't an ordinary case. There's too much at stake, and I don't like that kid's attitude."

"Forget it. I want to talk about the new treatment. When will it be ready?"

"A week or so."

"That's good, Mark, very good." His face creased in his trademark grin. "You've made me a happy man."

"My pleasure," said Argent.

CHAPTER SEVEN

Cameron Barr didn't have official coffee breaks for support staff—secretaries, messengers, and other nonlegal personnel—but they were taken informally at the various minikitchens and coffee stations scattered around the firm's three floors. In addition, many of the lawyers, especially the younger associates, carved out customary spots where office gossip could be exchanged.

Dylan, Barry, and Marsha Fields, one of the new securities associates, were in their accustomed corner near the copier room, drinking coffee and discussing the foibles of the partners.

"Kaster gave me two days to put together a hundred-page private placement memorandum for a new offering," said Fields, a plump woman with brittle brown hair. She had been number one in her class at Stanford Law, a fact Dylan knew because she had told him. "I explained that my parents were in town and we had tickets to the ballet," she continued. "He didn't even have the grace to say he was sorry."

Barry smiled indulgently. "You shouldn't have mentioned the ballet to Kaster. He thinks all dancers are fairies."

Fields sputtered, swallowing her coffee. "You're not serious!"

"Absolutely." Barry nodded. "'Screaming homos,' he calls them." He patted her arm. "Don't worry, Marsha, it wouldn't have made any difference if you said you were going to the Cardinals game. You're a first-year associate."

"Get used to it," said Dylan, from his lofty status of second-year. "It's like being in a fraternity or sorority, except that pledging is seven years."

Fields dumped her coffee into the sink. "I've been told that over a hundred times since I came here. It still doesn't make it right." She grimaced. "And truthfully, I thought it was exaggerated. I mean, you know, let's scare the newbies. It *couldn't* be as bad as everyone said."

"Except—" said Barry.

"Except it is," finished Fields. "I haven't had a weekend off in two months. I'm here until nine or ten every night, in at eight the next morning." She rubbed her hand over her face in a strange gesture, and Dylan noticed that her eye makeup was streaked. "And Kaster won't let me go to the fucking ballet."

Dylan and Barry exchanged glances. Barry said, "It gets better. Really. Have you talked to your mentor lately?"

Recently the firm had adopted the idea of mentors for the first- and second-year associates. These were some of the younger partners—ostensibly chosen for their empathy—who were supposed to help ease the transition into the firm's culture. Dylan's mentor had been a glib bond lawyer who took him out to lunch once a month and whose stock of advice consisted solely of billing tips and clichés about hard work. Luckily, Barry had taken him under his wing.

Fields said hopefully, "You think that might help? I haven't talked to him for a while. Would he talk to Kaster for me?"

"You mean about the ballet?" said Barry. Dylan could see he was puzzled that she still didn't get it. "That's not gonna change. But he might help you deal with—"

"I don't *want* to deal with it!" Fields said suddenly, wildly. Heads in the secretarial cubicles snapped in their direction.

"Take it easy," said Dylan quickly. "Why don't you—"

"Dylan!" interrupted Rhonda, coming down the hallway from his office. "Paul Hudson has been looking all over for you!"

"C'mon, Rhonda, I was just down the hall."

Rhonda tugged at her sweater and sniffed. "Well, I'm not a mind reader. Anyway, he wants you to come to his office right away."

"Okay, thanks." He looked at Fields, who appeared grateful for the distraction; she had composed herself. "Gotta go," she said suddenly, turning and striding quickly down the hall.

Hudson's door was closed, but Monica, Hudson's secretary, grudgingly nodded at him to go in. Inside, Hudson was at his desk, and there was a woman seated in front of him. She stood and faced Dylan: middle-aged—at least forty-five—with dark black hair streaked with gray, a smooth face, and blue eyes. Attractive for an older woman, thought Dylan.

"Pamela Holtz," she introduced herself before Hudson could say anything. "I represent Charlene McConnell."

Dylan did a pretty good job of not letting his jaw drop. He wasn't surprised that Charlene McConnell had followed through on her threat to get a lawyer; he *was* surprised, however, that the lawyer should be Pamela Holtz.

An able trial lawyer and a superbly prepared advocate, Pamela Holtz's name carried weight even in the chauvinistic conference rooms of the city's old-line law firms. One of the leading family lawyers in the state, she had handled the divorces of the sitting governor and both U.S. senators. She also was a gadfly to the state legislature, city government, and any employer she perceived to be sexist, making headlines by winning a sexual harassment suit against the CEO of an aerospace contractor. And, as head of a major feminist group, Holtz lobbied or brought lawsuits involving gay marriages, pregnancy rights, and battered women.

After Dylan and Holtz shook hands, Hudson explained that he and Holtz "went way back"—law school classmates, co-editors of the law review, that sort of thing. She had just attended a deposition downstairs in the big conference room and dropped in to say hello and "do a little business."

"I asked Paul if I could meet the attorney handling the Girard guardianship," she said in a strong contralto as Dylan took the seat next to her. "Maybe I can still talk you out of it."

Hudson said, "Now come on, Pamela, you know us better than that. Anyway, what's your interest in a run-of-the-mill guardianship?"

"My client has an interest, not me."

"Yes, yes, of course, but there are other lawyers—"

"Spare me that speech, Paul. I don't want to give

the 'how I pick my clients is my fucking business' lecture. Why don't we just discuss the facts?"

Hudson grinned and swiveled his chair to face Dylan. "She's cute when she's angry, don't you think?"

"Don't be an asshole, Paul," Holtz said cheerfully.

Dylan had to bite his lip hard to keep from grinning; no one dared talk to Hudson that way.

"Go on, Dylan, give her the facts," Hudson said curtly. "Tell Pamela about Nicole Girard."

"Well, I'm not sure what you already know."

Holtz waved her hand dismissively. "Tell me everything."

Dylan glanced at Hudson, who nodded and said, "Just don't reveal any client confidences."

"Of course not," Dylan said smoothly, knowing from experience it wasn't worth getting defensive in the face of one of Hudson's jabs. He described what happened in the hospital, the incident at the dedication ceremony, and his meetings with Dr. Argent and Nicole.

"So," said Hudson to Holtz, stretching his hands in front of him and cracking his knuckles, "what's your client's position on this?"

"Very simple," Holtz said crisply. "We agree that Nicole needs a guardian. We do not agree that the best candidates are Nicole's parents. Parents who, by the way, all but disowned her when they learned that she was living with a woman—my client. Parents who haven't seen their daughter for more than five minutes in the last five years—"

"Parents who are related by blood to the proposed ward," said Hudson. "In contrast to your client, who is not related by either blood or marriage.

Correct me if I'm wrong, Dylan, but isn't there a priority for appointment in the statute?"

"Yes," said Dylan. "Parents have priority over everyone but spouses."

"Exactly," said Holtz.

Dylan and Hudson looked at each other. "Exactly?" repeated Hudson.

"Exactly."

"Uh, sure," said Hudson. "Look, what's the problem, anyway, with her parents being guardian? I mean, what difference does it make to your client?"

"Let me ask you a question. Why do you think Ms. Girard is acting irrationally?"

"I don't know, I didn't talk to her doctor. Something to do with AIDS, isn't it?" He looked at Dylan.

"That's right," said Dylan. "AIDS dementia, it's called."

"Uh-huh," said Holtz. "You know she had no indications of such problems before she entered the hospital? No episodes of aberrant behavior at all? How do you account for that?"

Hudson said, "What's your point? That it's the *hospital's* fault she's seeing vampires under her bed?"

Holtz smiled. "Maybe. Anyway, my client wants to know exactly what happened in the hospital. If your clients also want to know this, then we don't have a problem. Otherwise, we will challenge the appointment."

Hudson drummed his fingers on the glass top of the desk. After a moment, he said, "Is this what this is all about? A potential malpractice suit against the hospital? C'mon, Pamela, you've never been an ambulance chaser—"

She stood up, cutting him off with a wave of her hand. "Don't go there, Paul. I won't listen. I thought I'd give you the courtesy of telling you our position. I was hoping this wouldn't be adversarial. It is, after all, just a guardianship. But if that's the way you want it—" She turned to Dylan and stuck out her hand. "Pleased to meet you, Dylan. I'm sure we'll be talking again."

As she left the room, Hudson muttered, "Bitch," then grinned at Dylan. "Looks like you got your work cut out for you, Dylan. You're gonna have some fun."

"You don't think she's bluffing? I mean, she really has no grounds to challenge—"

"Pamela doesn't bluff. She may be full of shit, but she *believes* her shit. So we'll have to—What is it?" Monica had opened the door.

"I'm sorry to bother you, Mr. Hudson, but there's an urgent phone call for Mr. Ice."

"An urgent phone call? From a client, I hope," he said ominously.

"From the police," said Monica, with satisfaction.

"Oh, yeah?" said Hudson, momentarily nonplussed. "You can take it there." He pointed at the phone on the conference table.

If Dylan had an idea what this was about, he would have taken the call privately. His first thought, however, was that it was a mistake.

"This is Dylan Ice," he said into the mouthpiece.

"Mr. Ice, this is Detective Carl Peterson, St. Louis County Police. I believe Corporal Bradley gave you my card the other day?" It took a moment to register, then Dylan remembered the cop who showed up the night Janis was attacked.

"Yes, of course. What's going on?"

"I'm afraid I have bad news. Your sister is in the hospital."

Dylan felt curiously calm. He said clearly, "What happened to her?"

"Drug overdose. Heroin."

Heroin. The word bounced around Dylan's skull like a tennis ball. "Where—how—"

"Why don't you come down to the hospital."

"But how *is* she?"

Dylan could almost hear him shrug over the phone. "Don't know, the docs are working on her."

"Where—what hospital?" Dylan said frantically.

"Barnes."

"I'm on my way."

Detective Peterson met Dylan in the waiting room of the ER, a big man in his thirties with light blond hair, dressed in a brown sports jacket and slacks. "Your sister's stable," he said quickly. "It looks like she's gonna be all right."

"Thank God," Dylan said. "What happened?"

Peterson frowned. "I'm with a special unit investigating street gangs. We got a tip about a drug deal going down in the high school parking lot, and we saw your sister make a heroin buy. She got a ride with some friends to Forest Park, and we followed to see what she was gonna do with the stuff. When we moved in to arrest her, we found three kids loading up and your sister already passed out under a tree. We arrested the others for possession, called an ambulance for your sister." He paused and looked squarely at Dylan. "We're gonna have to charge your sister with distribution. You better get her a criminal lawyer, they might charge her as an adult."

Dylan could find no words. He collapsed onto the nearest chair and put his head in his hands. Peterson continued, a little more kindly, "As soon as she's well enough, we'll take her to the station for processing. Since she's a juvenile, they'll probably release her to you. She doesn't have any priors, does she?"

Dylan shook his head, then struggled to his feet. "I want to see her."

Peterson led the way to a treatment room. Outside the door, writing on a clipboard, was an attractive but tired-looking female physician in her early thirties. "Dr. Karen Moore," said Peterson. "This is Dylan Ice, the patient's brother."

Moore's eyes widened as she looked at Dylan. "Her brother?"

"Yes, that's right, I'm her brother, and I know I don't look it. I'm also her legal guardian. Now tell me how she is."

She gave him a contrite smile and said, "Sorry. Your sister is very lucky. When the paramedics found her, she had no pulse. They gave her CPR and were able to support her respiration until we could counteract the heroin."

"Can I see her?"

Moore considered it. "All right. But she's very weak. Don't ask her any questions." Dylan nodded and pushed past her into the room.

Janis lay with her face to the wall, an IV snaking out of her wrist, a cardiac monitor beeping softly on the wall above the bed. Her eyes were closed, her breathing slow and regular. Dylan pulled a chair next to the bed and watched her.

Sleeping like this, Janis's face took on the contours of a child, and she resembled the little girl he had failed to protect.

It had been tough enough for him, growing up as the interracial love child of two totally irresponsible, frozen-in-the-sixties hippies. But at least his early years had been happy. He remembered many nights spent camping under the stars, and the easy atmosphere of communes and rock concerts. To a kid, living in a VW camper was a continuous adventure. Howard and Angela loved each other, loved their little boy, loved making love.

By the time Janis was born, however, things had changed. The 1970s were over, it was the Reagan Administration, and there was little sympathy for aging hippies. Even worse, Howard's trust fund had been exhausted; he actually had to work. Angela couldn't adjust, couldn't give up a life of drugs and pleasure—so she didn't.

Inevitably, the memory of that October day rose to the surface.

It had been raining for hours, and the metal roof of the trailer leaked in several places. Howard was at work, and Dylan calculated algebra problems at the tiny kitchen table. It wasn't easy doing homework while trying to keep track of a five-year-old and periodically changing the pots underneath the leaks.

Angela, as usual, was in the bedroom, getting stoned after a strenuous day of child care and soap operas.

For weeks Howard had promised Dylan that he would get Angela into a rehab program, but Howard's heart wasn't really into it. It was too much of a betrayal, not only of his wife but of his whole life. In the end, though, he would have to do

*it—or Dylan would. Dylan loved his mother, but in
six months he would be eighteen—* "Groovy!"
*snapped Dylan, noticing that Janis was getting ready
to give her Barbie doll an impromptu bath in one of
the leak collection pans.* "Leave that alone."

*She shrugged and reluctantly pulled the doll back.
At the same moment, a huge black beetle started
marching across the thinly carpeted floor. Janis said
excitedly,* "Look, Dylan, it's a bug monster!"

Dylan looked at it and chuckled. "Wow, you're
right, Groovy. I've never seen one that big. Why, it's
a . . . bugster!"

Janis squealed in delight. "Groovy!" *she said,
inevitably. Dylan watched her follow the beetle
across the room until it darted behind the sofa. She
tried to entice it out again, then lost interest and
returned to her dolls. Dylan resumed work on his
quadratic equations. He was concentrating deeply
when the bedroom door crashed open and Angela
emerged.*

*One glance told Dylan it was bad—very bad.
Probably acid. Her usually pretty face was a mask of
terrified eyes, open mouth, and stretched skin. She
started forward . . .*

"Dylan!" Janis whispered from the hospital bed.

"I'm here, Janis."

She licked her lips. "I screwed up, Dylan. And I
lied."

He felt an urge to reach out and slap her.
Instead, he knelt beside the bed, a terrible cramp in
his chest and throat. He grabbed her hand tightly
and said, "It's all right, Groovy, it's all right. It's
gonna be all right."

She managed a smile and closed her eyes again.

"Mr. Ice?" Dr. Moore opened the door and

approached the bed. "Would you mind stepping outside a minute while I check on your sister?"

As Dylan went to the waiting room, he suddenly
thought of Nicole Girard, tied to her bed. Probably,
he thought, the association with a hospital room.

Still, it was odd he should think of her.

CHAPTER EIGHT

Dylan spent the rest of the day and part of the night at the hospital. The next morning Janis was well enough to be taken to the police station for booking.

At the station, they were met by Jared Tabler, a lawyer specializing in juvenile criminal law, referred by Barry Sasscer. Although Cameron Barr had a small criminal law department, it handled only white-collar crime.

Tabler was firmly reassuring. "The cops were just shaking your tree," he said as they waited to see the juvenile court commissioner. "They won't charge Janis as an adult on a first offense. We should be able to get her probation and a drug diversion program."

At the hearing—the equivalent of a bond hearing for an adult—the issue was whether Janis should be confined to the juvenile detention center or released to Dylan's custody. Dylan thought it might be a problem that he was essentially a single parent, but the commissioner didn't seem to care. "The Juvenile Center is over capacity," Tabler whispered in his ear. "They're glad to dump her back on you."

By the time they got back home it was midafternoon, and they were both exhausted. Elaine Sasscer came to stay with Janis. After Janis was settled in, Dylan showered, shaved, then drank some coffee until he felt reasonably human. He drove to the firm, where he was immediately summoned to Paul Hudson's office.

Hudson looked up from a file and said, "About time."

"You knew I had a family emergency," Dylan said hotly.

"You should have called to say when you were coming back."

"I didn't think it was necessary." To Dylan's certain knowledge, Hudson never paid this much attention to a junior associate's absence. He suddenly noticed that it was the *Girard* file that was open on the desk. Hudson followed his gaze and picked up some papers from the file. "This came today." Hudson pushed a document toward Dylan.

Mystified, Dylan picked it up and glanced through it.

It was Pamela Holtz's opposition to the Girard's Petition for Guardianship—with a twenty-five-page Memorandum of Points and Authorities. Dylan gave a low whistle. "I guess she wasn't bluffing."

"I told you, Pamela doesn't bluff. Review it, then come back." As Dylan headed for the door, Hudson continued, grudgingly, "How's your sister?"

"She's all right," Dylan said stiffly.

"Good," said Hudson.

"Well, it's certainly creative," Dylan told Hudson later.

Hudson stood at the big window, staring out at

the river. "I'm not interested in a literary review. I want to know what you think of the legal arguments."

"The issues are pretty simple," Dylan said carefully. "They've got a document signed by Nicole purporting to appoint McConnell as guardian, but it's not a power of attorney, or properly witnessed, and it isn't dated before Nicole's incapacity. That leaves two routes to appointment: first, if Nicole, at the time of the hearing, is competent to make a reasonable choice, she can do so. Otherwise, it's up to the judge, based on the testimony at the hearing."

Hudson was silent for a moment. Then he said, "So it comes down, really, to whether Girard is well enough to testify at the hearing, doesn't it? Because if she is, she undoubtedly would pick her cunt-licking roommate."

Dylan was startled by the crudity of Hudson's words. "From what I saw of Nicole, I think there's a good chance that she will be allowed to make a choice of guardian. She may not be competent to take care of herself, but she appears cogent."

"Yes. But if that's the case, we'll lose, won't we? So let's be optimistic and assume the judge thinks she's *not* competent to choose her own guardian. Don't our clients, as parents, have priority of appointment, like under the probate statute?"

"Yes," said Dylan. "Uh, that's probably why Holtz calls McConnell a 'surrogate spouse' in the motion—"

"Bingo!" said Hudson, spinning around and pointing his finger at Dylan. "That's it! I knew there was something else going on here!"

"I don't understand."

Hudson walked to his desk and sat down with a

satisfied sigh. "It's the feminism agenda. Holtz has been trying for years to get the legislature to pass a 'domestic partners' bill allowing gay people to marry, or at least to have the same legal rights and obligations as heterosexuals. This is a perfect vehicle for her philosophy."

"But the Defense of Marriage Act—"

"Is a federal law, applying only to federal benefits. This is a state issue."

"I see." Dylan thought it over. "So if they lose the battle over Nicole's competency to choose her guardian, they fall back on the argument that McConnell is Nicole's spouse and should be given priority over the parents. It makes sense!"

"Certainly. Like I said, Holtz is tough. I want you to prepare a response to their motion and hit her with everything you can. State law, public policy, religion, family values, whatever."

"Right," Dylan said, jotting down some notes. "When is the hearing?"

"It hasn't been set yet, but I'm expecting a call from the clerk's office momentarily. The twenty-one-day order expires next Wednesday, so it will have to be before then."

"Shit. I'll be out of town. You'll have to handle it yourself."

"I will? You're not gonna assign someone else? A senior associate?"

Hudson smiled. "What's the matter, don't you want to go solo?" His smile vanished and he said, "It's important to me that you handle this alone, without the help of any other member of the firm." At Dylan's unspoken question, he continued, "Let's just say I advertised this as an easy case, one that didn't have to be handled by the T and E department. And it's a great opportunity for you, Dylan. A chance to shine. Don't fuck it up."

"I'll do my best."

Hudson rolled his eyes. "Just win."

Creve Coeur Lake was small but pretty. Although fronted on one side by an ugly highway and a row of power lines, it was surrounded by a band of thick woods and picnic areas. It was about twenty minutes from West St. Louis, and Dylan knew it well.

His rowing shell skimmed across the lake's warm surface, the oar blades dipping in and out of the water without a ripple. A tape player strapped to his chest fed Mozart to his earphones.

Already he could feel the tensions of the day dropping away. He had guiltily driven to the lake after making dinner for Janis, extracting a promise that she would do her homework and go to bed. Now, with the sun setting across the lake, he could feel the sweat popping out of his skin, his heart rate rising, the endorphins kicking in. He pushed up his stroke.

He rowed a MAAS Single Scull, bought used last year, and stored in the boathouse of the St. Louis Rowing Club at the lake's edge. The MAAS was a top-of-the-line racing single, made of carbon fiber with a carbon-fiber ball-bearing seat, titanium oar-lock pins, and carbon-fiber foot stretchers.

Dylan had rowed for the club during law school—winning a national junior's title—and still was a member, although he no longer competed. Then he had rowed almost every day; now he was lucky to get on the lake twice a week. His rowing had definitely suffered; although still classified as an elite rower—the highest category—by the United States Rowing Association, he knew he could no longer compete even at the intermediate level. Anyway, he was twenty-seven, and that meant rowing in the masters' division.

Of course, he also could teach. There were plenty of college programs that needed experienced crew coaches; it was a growing sport. But the pay was abysmal.

The idea of spending all his time around the water was truly intoxicating, and he shoved it aside. Law had to come first. Everything in his life—and Janis's—depended on that.

It was still incredible to him that Janis could have been involved with drugs. Even marijuana would have surprised him—but heroin! Considering her fucked-up background, though, it probably was inevitable. After all, she had been named after her mother's favorite singer, Janis Joplin, who had died of a heroin overdose.

At least things were going well with his career. Working directly with Hudson, for all of its pressure, meant that if he successfully handled the guardianship hearing—if he could beat the respected Pamela Holtz—it would put him on the road to partnership. This hearing could really be his start as a litigator.

Of course, winning for him meant a loss for Nicole. He couldn't help feeling guilty about that. In a perfect world, Charlene would be Nicole's guardian.

He shook his head. *I gotta cut that out*, he thought. *I represent Nicole's parents*.

He rowed harder and tried to think of something pleasant. Kristin came to mind. He smiled at the memory of her seducing him in her father's church. It had been an awful thing to do, right there in *church*, for God's sake, and he knew he should feel guilty—but he didn't.

Most of all he was glad she hadn't noticed his sexual inexperience—or at least, he didn't think she had. But then, how would he know? That was the problem.

In college and law school almost all the women were white, and weren't interested in interracial dating. Those who did usually were discouraged by his single parenthood. He always was taking care of Janis, or going somewhere to pick her up or drop her off—day care, school meetings, Brownies, Girl Scouts. And he never had much money to spend on baby-sitters, anyway.

In the end, Dylan had sublimated his sexual drive into rowing, studying, and—now that he was in the firm—working.

With that kind of history, Kristin was an amazing, unexpected gift. He had to remind himself not to get his hopes up, that the relationship was brand new, that she might not, probably did not, already feel so strongly about him. He sat up straight, catching a crab in his stroke, and glanced at his watch. Was it too late to call her? He turned the shell and headed back to the boathouse, rowing smoothly.

The guardianship hearing was scheduled for Wednesday, precisely the day when the hospital's twenty-one-day inpatient detention order expired.

On the day before the hearing, Dylan went to see Nicole again.

She was reading a book when he entered the room, her hands free, although the chest and leg restraints were still on. It had been almost a week since his last visit. The male nurse looked up and, recognizing Dylan, left the room.

"Hello, Mr. Ice," Nicole said.

"A little formal, aren't we?" said Dylan. "Mind if I chat for a while?"

She shrugged. "You're the third lawyer I've seen today. I don't have many answers left."

"The third?" said Dylan, sitting in the chair vacated by the nurse. "Who were the others?"

"Pamela Holtz, and the guy the court appointed to represent me. Jonathan Keller. He's not too swift."

Dylan nodded. Keller was a golfing buddy of the administrative judge, and according to one of the T&E associates in the firm, Keller's name often turned up in these hearings; he had almost made a career out of it. "Yes, I knew he was appointed."

"He hardly said a thing at my first hearing, for the twenty-one-day detention." She grimaced. "Not that I remember much of that."

Dylan said diplomatically, "Well, he has to do what you want."

She sniffed. "He suggested that I ask for a jury trial."

Keller would love that, thought Dylan. A jury trial would take much longer and earn him a bigger fee. But he had to tread carefully here; it would be unethical to give legal advice. On the other hand, she was entitled to know the facts. He said, "If you request a jury, it will delay the hearing. In the meantime, the hospital will apply for another temporary detention order, under either the guardianship statute or the mental health law."

She seemed to relax. "Yes, Pamela told me that. Mr. Keller, however, wasn't so honest."

"Oh," said Dylan, glad he had told her the truth.

They chatted amiably for a while, but she was more reserved than on his previous visits, and he was very conscious of his role as the attorney opposing her choice of guardian.

The problem, he admitted to himself, was that she seemed perfectly reasonable. The witnesses he was about to present in court believed she couldn't take care of herself; his own senses disputed that.

"Well, I'll see you tomorrow," he said lamely, getting up.

"Yeah," she said without emotion.

As Dylan turned to leave, Nicole said, "Oh, just a minute."

He glanced back and saw her holding a piece of paper torn from the sketch pad. "I almost forgot this. I drew it for you last week."

It was a beautifully rendered line drawing—a self-portrait of Nicole in bed, attended by a doctor who looked remarkably like Bela Lugosi. "This is great," Dylan said enthusiastically. "I love it."

"Look at the doctor."

He peered closer and saw a tiny imp, with angel wings, squatting on the doctor's shoulder. The imp had Dylan's face.

"I'm flattered," Dylan said, grinning. "But the size . . . I take it this means I'm not very powerful?"

"No, you're a magic imp," said Nicole. "If you choose to use your magic." Her face became emotionless again. "See you in court." She turned away.

"Good-bye, Nicole," said Dylan.

In the hall, he straightened his tie, turned, and nearly collided with Dr. Argent.

"Mr. Ice," said Argent breathlessly. "I just heard you were here. I was in the lab."

"That's all right," said Dylan, surprised. He had spent almost an hour in Argent's office just the previous day, preparing his testimony. "You didn't have to come. We covered everything yesterday. I just wanted to check on Ms. Girard's mental status before the hearing."

Argent pulled at his collar. "No, I must be present for all your visits. This institution has custody of the patient and must be represented. Is that clear?" His tone implied it better be.

"As long as I can see her alone, I don't care if you're outside the door."

Argent shook his head. "According to hospital counsel, only her court-appointed counsel has the right to see her alone. I've allowed it before, I know, but I won't anymore."

There was no point in arguing, Dylan thought, letting Argent escort him to the elevators. The hearing was tomorrow, and once a guardian was appointed, there would be no need to see Nicole.

He realized he was sorry about that.

CHAPTER NINE

The first trial of Dylan's legal career was really a hearing. There was no jury, and there would be no final judgment, only a guardianship order.

But it was close enough. He hardly slept the previous night, and almost threw up in the men's room minutes before entering the courtroom.

He couldn't be more prepared, having discussed every aspect of the case with Barry Sasscer, Paul Hudson, and a couple of senior trusts and estates associates who treated his foray into their subject matter with amused condescension.

The Girard case was first on the morning calendar, so everyone seated themselves at the counsel tables. Henry and Amanda Girard sat next to Dylan, while Jonathan Keller, Nicole's court-appointed attorney, sat apart from them at the end of the table. Also present was Gerald Rabb, the hospital's attorney.

At the other table sat Pamela Holtz, looking composed and confident, with Charlene McConnell.

Dylan unpacked his briefcase and looked around the courtroom. Like every other neophyte litigator, he feared most the possibility of embarrassing him-

self by messing up the basics. Laying evidentiary
foundations and handling objections was a skill that
came with experience, and he didn't have any. Good
litigators also needed a thorough knowledge of the
complex and arcane rules of evidence, combined with
an ability to think quickly. Dylan thought he had
these capabilities but so far had tested them only in
depositions and minor hearings.

As if on cue, the rear doors of the courtroom
opened and Dr. Richard Volberg, the hospital's chief
of psychiatry, entered. He was followed by Nicole,
sitting in a wheelchair, pushed by a uniformed hospital orderly.

Dr. Volberg went to the swinging door separat-
ing the audience area from the counsel tables and
paused, obviously wondering where to go with
Nicole. After a moment he opened the swinging
door and motioned the orderly to push the
wheelchair through; he placed her squarely between
the two counsel tables and stood behind the
wheelchair.

Dylan now had a clear look at Nicole. She
stared fixedly into space, her arms and feet strapped
down. Henry Girard went over to the chair, and
Dylan followed him.

Girard said, "Honey, how are you?" Nicole
didn't react; she hardly even blinked. Then, suddenly, she smiled lopsidedly and said, "Papa."

"Why is she sedated?" asked Pamela Holtz. She
and Charlene McConnell stared at Nicole from their
counsel table. The question was directed at Dr.
Volberg, who answered, "She's not. Dr. Argent tells
me she has these episodes occasionally, as a result of
her condition. It's unfortunate one came today—"

Volberg's explanation was cut off by the bailiff's

voice, ordering everyone to rise. Dylan guided the Girards back to the counsel table as Judge Rosemary Panaro came on the bench. She stared impassively at the parties as the court clerk called the case.

Short, thin, with an equine face reminding Dylan of the British royal family, Rosemary Panaro was considered tough but fair. She always was well prepared, and courteous to both parties and lawyers. Unfortunately for Dylan, she also was a feminist and a frequent lecturer on women's issues. Dylan couldn't have picked a less sympathetic judge for this case.

After the usual preliminaries, Panaro said, "Now, Mr. Ice, your client's petition was filed first, so I'm going to treat Ms. McConnell's petition as an opposition and cross-petition. You still have the burden of proving incapacity by clear and convincing evidence."

Dylan's stomach did a flip-flop. "Your Honor, I thought the Court would take judicial notice of Judge Thomas's finding of incapacity under the twenty-one-day detention order."

Panaro shook her head. "That finding was for a different purpose, under a different statute, and it expires next week. If you wish to prevail, you'll have to prove to the Court that the respondent is incapacitated, and if so, that she either chooses your client to be her guardian or that her incapacity is severe enough that she is unable to make and communicate such a choice. Then you still must convince this Court your client is best suited to be guardian." She looked at Holtz. "Ms. Holtz, the same applies to you on your cross-petition for guardianship. Does everyone understand?"

"Certainly, Your Honor," said Holtz.

"Yes, Your Honor," echoed Dylan, thinking furiously. This was a surprise, but it shouldn't be fatal. He planned to prove Nicole's incapacity in any event, and had the court-appointed psychiatrist available to testify, as well as Dr. Argent.

"Good," said Panaro. "Mr. Keller, I see that your client isn't paying attention. Do you want time to explain this to her?" Keller looked over at Nicole, who now stared at the floor without expression.

"No," said Keller. "I explained everything to her yesterday, Your Honor. She seemed to understand."

Panaro looked skeptical. "And what about a jury trial? Are you willing to waive it?"

Keller, a big, fleshy man with an obvious hairpiece, looked down at his legal pad. "She definitely told me that yesterday. But perhaps you should ask again."

Panaro didn't look happy with that answer. She looked at Nicole and said, "Ms. Girard? Do you hear me?"

Nicole stared at the floor. Henry Girard leaned over, put his hand on Nicole's shoulder, and whispered, "Nicole? Nicole, honey, what's wrong?" There was no reaction.

What the hell was this? thought Dylan. She had never acted this way before. She might be paranoid, but she wasn't oblivious. Was this her way of protesting the proceeding? Or was she suffering from a medication overdose?

Keller said, "Your Honor, she was cogent yesterday. I don't understand."

Holtz, frowning, listened to McConnell, who whispered furiously in her ear. Panaro glanced from Nicole to Keller and tapped her fingers on the bench. Finally she said, "I'm going to accept the jury waiver from respondent's counsel. Mr. Ice, call your first witness."

Dylan intended to begin with Henry Girard, but he changed his mind on the spot. "We call Dr. Mark Argent."

Argent was brought in from the hallway, glancing quizzically at Dylan. In his well-tailored dark suit and crisp white shirt, he was an impressive figure. After qualifying him as an expert witness, Dylan asked Argent to describe how he first came into contact with Nicole.

"Ms. Girard volunteered to participate in a new clinical trial for patients who are HIV-positive but have not yet developed AIDS."

"Can you tell the Court the details of this clinical trial?"

"Certainly. It's a randomized, double-blind study of passive hyperimmune therapy—PHT. PHT uses blood plasma from donors—that is, HIV-positive individuals such as Ms. Girard—who haven't yet developed AIDS. Basically, we're assuming that these people are controlling the virus naturally and that, at least temporarily, their bodies have a way of defeating it. We believe that if we infuse elements of their plasma into patients who have developed AIDS, we can significantly reduce the symptoms of AIDS and of opportunistic infections."

Panaro interjected, "Aren't there some new drugs that are quite successful against AIDS? I understand some people are talking about a cure."

Argent shook his head emphatically. "You mean the protease inhibitors? They are difficult to take, extremely expensive, and appear to work best for people whose HIV disease is not far advanced—people who probably still feel perfectly fine, despite being infected. And once you start taking them, you can't take them irregularly because of the danger of resistance mutations." He shook his head again, sorrowfully. "No, what we need is something that will knock out the virus for sure, completely and forever. We haven't found it yet."

Dylan asked, "And Ms. Girard—the respondent—she would have been a plasma donor, not a recipient, in your clinical trial?"

"Right. She had no signs of AIDS, and her CD4-plus cell count was normal."

"CD4-plus cell count?"

"Yes, often referred to as T-cells, for short. The CD4 count is the measure of the T-helper lymphocytes in the blood, which organize the body's immune response; without them, the body can't defend itself against disease. The HIV virus kills these cells. We also have other, more accurate indicators now—a viral load test—but the CD4-plus measure is still the easiest and most commonly used."

Dylan flipped a page on his legal pad. "And was Ms. Girard required to be hospitalized for her participation?"

"Not required, no. But we ask all participants, donors and recipients, to come into the hospital for a few days for a complete examination, a complete physical."

"I see. And what happened during the respondent's admission?"

"Dates?" interrupted Judge Panaro, irritation in her voice.

"Sorry, Your Honor," Dylan said quickly. "What was the date of her admission?"

"April eighteenth."

"Okay," said Dylan. "What happened after her admission?"

"Well, the first day she was there, I noticed something wrong. I do a complete H and P—history and physical—on all the participants in the clinical trial. Part of this physical examination is what we call a mental status exam. We do this because—"

"I'm familiar with it, Doctor," said Judge Panaro. "Please continue."

Argent seemed a little annoyed at the interruption, but he continued, "Well, the mental status exam was equivocal. By that I mean she seemed to have some problems with concentration and abstract thinking. She also had some short-term memory problems—she couldn't recall a string of numbers longer than five. Her affect was low—meaning she seemed depressed. On the whole, however, the test was within normal limits."

"And what happened next?"

"Well, by the end of the next day, her behavior really became aberrant. She was clearly depressed, but she also had some personality changes, some mood swings, almost manic."

Dylan heard a strange sound come from behind him, like a strangled cry. He turned and saw Nicole's face twisted in a grimace. He returned his attention to Argent. "Go on, Doctor."

"I was able to convince her to remain in the hospital a few more days while I ran some tests to confirm my provisional diagnosis."

"And that was?"

"AIDS dementia."

Charlene McConnell made a sound of disbelief, drawing a stern glare from the judge.

"Describe that condition, please," Dylan said.

Argent sat up a little. "AIDS dementia complex—ADC—is basically an HIV infection of the brain. It eventually affects twenty to thirty percent of all AIDS patients in one form or another, carrying a spectrum of psychiatric and neurological symptoms. These symptoms include poor concentration, forgetfulness, loss of short- or long-term memory, social withdrawal, slowed thinking, short attention span, irritability, apathy, paranoia, impaired judgment, and personality changes."

"And did the respondent exhibit any of these symptoms?"

"Very definitely. In addition to the problems with the mental status exam, she was often depressed, extremely irritable, and also delusional, resisting the drawing of blood because the nurses were 'vampires.' Then she tried to leave the hospital via the window."

"The window?" Panaro repeated, puzzled.

"Yes, Your Honor," Argent replied, and went on to explain how Nicole leaped from her window during the dedication ceremony.

Dylan asked, "Did you perform any objective tests to confirm your diagnosis?"

"Certainly. Examination of the cerebrospinal fluid, obtained by a spinal tap. She had mild elevations of certain marker proteins and of white blood cells, and her CT and MRI scans showed signs of brain tissue atrophy. Finally, we performed a SPECT scan—that's a special type of CT scan—using a radioactive dye to measure blood flow in the brain. This also was indicative of ADC."

As he had rehearsed with Argent, Dylan asked the obvious question: "But, Doctor, you testified that the respondent had no signs of AIDS—in fact, that is why she was chosen to be a donor. She had normal T-cell levels. So how is it possible she had ADC?"

Argent sighed. "Unfortunately, we still know very little about ADC. It may be that she had a silent brain infection for years. Some researchers believe the key factor may be the development of neurovirulent HIV strains due to genetic changes in the virus. There's also a theory that the gradual increase in total virus load eventually triggers the syndrome."

"I see," said Dylan. "And what treatment is available for ADC?"

"We treat both the disease and the symptoms. For the disease itself, the best treatment, of course, are the anti-HIV drugs, such as AZT, the newer protease inhibitors, and the newest nonnucleoside reverse transcriptase inhibitors. There also are therapies to boost a patient's immune system, such as interleukin–2 and PHT itself. For symptomatic relief, we use the full range of psychoactive drugs— antipsychotics, antidepressants, anticonvulsants, antimanics, psychostimulants, and the like. Haloperidol is often very effective."

"Which of these treatments did you give to the respondent?"

"Only the psychoactives. We didn't wish to start the antiviral therapy, with all of its attendant risk and possible side effects, until this hearing was concluded. It's not something we want to start and then have to stop."

"I see," said Dylan. "And is it possible for the respondent to have this condition, ADC, and still appear cogent?"

"Oh, absolutely," said Argent. "It's a day-to-day thing in her stage of the disease. As you know from visiting her, Mr. Ice, there are many days when she seems perfectly normal. However, there are also other days—like during the dedication ceremony, or today—when she can be anywhere from mildly disoriented to incoherent."

"Okay," said Dylan, nearing the end. Holtz hadn't objected even once; he wasn't sure if that was good or bad. He drew a breath and said, "Dr. Argent, in your professional opinion, is the respondent, Nicole Girard, mentally competent to make decisions about her health care?"

"Objection!" said Holtz, on her feet. "The witness is not a psychiatrist, he's an infectious disease specialist. He shouldn't be expressing opinions on the respondent's mental competency."

Panaro looked at Dylan, who said, "Uh, he's a physician, Your Honor. He doesn't have to be a psychiatrist to express an opinion on whether a patient is competent to understand proposed treatments. That's the basis of informed consent, and—"

Panaro put up her hand. "I understand your position, Counsel." She tapped her fingers on the bench and continued, "And I agree. Objection overruled. The witness will answer."

Argent said, "I don't believe Ms. Girard is competent to understand the consequences of her actions, medical or otherwise."

Dylan had a few more questions on his legal pad, but it seemed a good place to stop. "No further questions, Your Honor."

Panaro looked at Keller and Rabb. "No questions, Your Honor," they chorused.

"I have some," said Holtz, stepping to the podium. She stared at Argent over her reading glasses for a moment; he shifted uncomfortably in his chair. Finally she said, "Dr. Argent, isn't it true that ADC is found more commonly in AIDS patients with system-wide symptoms?"

"Well, that's true."

"And Ms. Girard doesn't have such symptoms, does she?"

"No."

"In fact, except for this *alleged* diagnosis of ADC, Ms. Girard has no signs of AIDS whatsoever, does she?"

Argent visibly bristled. "What do you mean *alleged*? That's my diagnosis, and it's verified by the signs and symptoms."

Holtz seemed unfazed. "Yes, that's what you say. Has anyone else examined the respondent?"

"Certainly. We have residents who round on her every day."

"Other than residents?"

"No."

"You wouldn't expect a resident—a doctor-in training—to challenge your diagnosis, would you?"

"If he or she thought my diagnosis was wrong, of course I would. Residents question the diagnoses of attending physicians all the time."

"Sure, sure," said Holtz, sarcastically. "Now, you testified that the respondent was depressed. That's a common symptom of ADC, right?"

"That's right."

"But depression can also be caused by psychological stress, can't it?"

"I'm not a psychiatrist, but yes, I believe that's true."

"I see," nodded Holtz. "And how many people are in your clinical trial?"

Argent blinked, surprised at this abrupt change

of subject. "Right now we have six donors and about twenty recipients in the protocol."

"And who is paying for it?"

Judge Panaro looked at Dylan expectantly while Argent answered, "It's sponsored by a drug company; the protocol was designed by Dr. Peter Rosati at the National Institutes of Health. There also is additional funding—"

As Argent continued his answer, it dawned on Dylan that Panaro expected him to object.

He jumped up and said, "Objection!" at the same time frantically trying to think of the grounds. He didn't think that "the judge wanted me to object" was appropriate. But Panaro didn't ask, she just snapped, "Sustained. Ms. Holtz, this is going beyond the scope of direct and I don't see its relevance at all."

Holtz tapped her pen on the podium. "This is a credibility issue, Your Honor. If you let me continue, I can demonstrate."

"Bias?" said Panaro, skeptically. "All right, but get to the point."

"Thank you, Your Honor," said Holtz. She turned back to Argent. "Dr. Argent, isn't it a fact that ImmuCare Corporation is providing over eighty percent of the funding for this clinical trial?"

"That sounds about right."

"And isn't it also true that this funding is in connection with an NDA—new drug application—for ImmuCare's Immunase?"

Argent seemed startled. "How did you—yes, that's true. But that is perfectly normal. Almost every new AIDS drug undergoes studies sponsored by the drug manufacturer."

"Of course," said Holtz smoothly. "But in this

case, ImmuCare is only paying for successful, completed studies that can be incorporated in its database. Isn't that right?"

Argent looked at her, his eyes growing round. "Yes."

Dylan had no idea where this was headed, and he didn't know how to stop it. Should he object? On what grounds?

"And isn't it true, Doctor Argent, that ImmuCare requires that at least six plasma donors participate in each study or the sponsoring institution will not receive reimbursement?"

"No, that's not entirely true. There is a certain basic reimbursement we receive, regardless of the statistical validity of the trial."

Holtz stepped in front of the podium and stared at him. "And isn't it a fact, Dr. Argent, that you have only the absolute minimum of plasma donors in this trial, and if the respondent should drop out, your institution—and your program—would lose a considerable amount of money?"

Argent tapped his fingers on the bar of the witness box in front of him. "If you're implying what I think you are, you're dead wrong—"

"And what am I implying?" Holtz asked sweetly.

Argent's face was getting red as he said, "You know exactly what."

"Counsel, I think we *all* get the point," Panaro said. "Ask another question."

Holtz nodded. "Certainly, Your Honor. Dr. Argent, did you give the respondent any unusual drugs this morning, before bringing her to court?"

"Unusual?" repeated Argent, clearly startled. "No, she just received her usual medication."

"I see. Did you bring your medical chart with you today?"

"Yes. It's right here." He patted the folder on his lap.

"May I see it, please?" Holtz strode forward and put out her hand.

Dylan finally saw the opportunity to show he wasn't a potted plant. He stood and said, "Objection, Your Honor. Those documents are under physician-patient privilege, and only the respondent or her attorney can waive that privilege."

Holtz looked surprised. "The respondent's physical condition is at issue in this hearing. Privilege doesn't apply, or opposing counsel wouldn't have been able to call Dr. Argent in the first place."

"Of course," said Panaro. "Overruled."

Dylan sat down, his face hot. Holtz took the folder from Argent. "Court's indulgence, please," she said as she took a few moments to page through the chart. Then she said, "What meds did the respondent receive this morning?"

"I'd have to refer to the chart."

"Certainly," said Holtz, handing it back.

Argent opened the folder and after a moment said, "Fluoxetine. Haloperidol. Lorazepam. Methylphenidate."

Holtz gave a low whistle. "And can you describe the purpose of each of those drugs?"

"Of course I can. Haloperidol—popularly known as Haldol—is an effective drug for Alzheimer's disease and often works to alleviate ADC symptoms. Methylphenidate, or Ritalin, is a stimulant that alleviates apathy and increases energy and concentration. Fluoxetine—Prozac—is an antidepressant."

"And these drugs have side effects, do they not?"

"Some do, yes. But we watch the dosage very carefully." Argent sat up straighter and continued, "Look, I know what you're getting at, Ms. Holtz, but you're quite wrong. The reason Nicole looks like that today"—he pointed at her—"is a result of ADC. She has these episodes, which are quite characteristic of the syndrome, and tomorrow she may be fine, may seem perfectly cogent and coherent. It all depends on how her immune system is handling the virus on that day, and on the degree of neurological damage suffered. But it's not the result of her medications, I assure you. If we see unfavorable side effects develop, we adjust the dosage immediately."

"Of course you do," Holtz said, looking down at her pad. "That's all the questions I have at this time, Your Honor, but I have a motion as a result of this testimony."

"A motion?" said Panaro, puzzled. "What kind of motion?"

"I'd like to make it after the witness is excused, subject to recall in my case."

Panaro nodded. "Doctor, please wait outside. Your testimony may be required again."

When Argent was gone, Panaro said, "Well, Ms. Holtz?"

Holtz stepped forward and said, "Your Honor, based on the condition of the respondent and the testimony just given by Dr. Argent, I move for an immediate independent medical examination of the respondent, including toxicological testing of both blood and urine."

"Your Honor!" Dylan sprang to his feet. "Objection!"

"Yes, Mr. Ice?"

Dylan took a deep breath. He wasn't sure of the legal basis for his objection, but he knew he had to oppose this. He said, "Your Honor, this is wholly unnecessary. The respondent has been poked and prodded hundreds of times, and apparently this causes her mental, if not physical pain. I heard the same testimony as Ms. Holtz, and Dr. Argent gave a scientific, medical reason for respondent's condition having nothing to do with medication. I also respectfully challenge the Court's authority to order an invasive procedure—I think there are constitutional issues here."

Unexpected help came from Jonathan Keller, rousing himself enough to rise and say, "I agree, Your Honor, and I also object. I haven't heard anything that would require a court-ordered invasion of her body."

Panaro nodded and said to Holtz, "Counsel, he does have a point. Why can't you just look at respondent's medication records?"

"Because, Judge, I'm not sure they show what really happened."

There it was. It was a good thing, Dylan thought, that Argent had left the courtroom, or he would be frothing with affronted dignity. And Panaro seemed to be buying the argument. After a moment she said, "All right. I'll take your motion under advisement. Mr. Ice, call your next witness."

Dylan, still thinking about Holtz's comment, forced himself to concentrate. "Mr. Henry Girard."

Henry's testimony, at least, went as rehearsed. In a few halting sentences, he testified that he loved his daughter, hated to impose himself as a guardian, but she just couldn't take care of herself right now. She was normally so bright, so sharp. It broke his heart to see her this way, and it was his duty as her father to take over. He and his wife were the best persons to be her guardian. Who could be better than her parents?

Dylan was surprised when Holtz stood to cross-examine Girard. He couldn't imagine what she could ask that would be helpful to her case.

"Mr. Girard, were you close to your daughter?" Holtz began.

"Close?" repeated Girard. "How do you mean?"

"I mean, did you talk with her often?"

"Oh, sure, we talked."

"Every day?"

"Oh, no, of course not."

"Once a week?"

"Well, I don't know . . . I never kept track." He fingered his collar nervously.

"Once a month?"

"I guess so—I don't know."

Holtz sighed theatrically. "Mr. Girard, isn't it a fact that for the past five years, you and your wife spoke with your daughter only on the holidays of Thanksgiving and Christmas, and occasional birthdays?"

Girard drew in his breath, about to reply angrily, but then seemed to reconsider. He looked at Dylan imploringly, but of course Dylan couldn't help. Finally, Girard said softly, "That might be true."

Holtz let the answer hang for a moment, then said, "And isn't it true that your conversations on those occasions were short and combative?"

"We talked," Girard said stubbornly. "She's my daughter and we talked."

Holtz looked at his face for a moment and nodded; her point was made. "And isn't it true, Mr. Girard, that you were violently opposed to your daughter's lifestyle?"

"What the hell do you mean by that?"

"Mr. Girard, please watch your language and answer the question," Panaro said.

"Sorry," mumbled Girard. "I don't understand what she wants."

Holtz said, "Mr. Girard, I don't mean to imply anything negative about you or your daughter. I'm simply trying to understand the facts. Now, isn't it true that you believe your daughter is a lesbian?"

Girard looked at his wife, then slumped back into the witness chair. "Yeah."

"And you don't approve of homosexuality, do you?"

"The Bible forbids it," he said firmly. "But I still love my daughter."

"Of course you do," said Holtz soothingly. "But if you could change her lifestyle, you would?"

"Objection," Dylan said, springing to his feet.

Holtz said, "Your Honor, his relationship with his daughter is an essential element of his fitness as a guardian."

Panaro pondered this for a moment, rubbing her chin. She said, "I'm not so sure, Counsel. I think you're very close to the edge of relevancy. You better get to the point fast."

Holtz turned back to Girard. "Please answer the question, Mr. Girard. You would change her if you could?"

"Well, of course. She's committing a mortal sin, and her soul is in jeopardy every day." Girard paused, then added, "But I can't."

"No, you can't," said Holtz. "But that doesn't mean you won't try, does it?"

Before he could answer, and as Dylan was rising to his feet again, Holtz put up her hand and said, "No, no, never mind. Withdraw the question." She looked down at her notes. "Now, Mr. Girard, if you should be appointed guardian by this Court, is it your intention to continue your daughter's present care and treatment at University Hospital?"

"Certainly," said Girard, relieved to be on safer ground. "She's getting the best of care."

"Oh?" said Holtz, looking toward Nicole, who sat in the wheelchair, head lolling to one side with a vacant expression. "You think she's being helped by this . . . treatment?"

Girard followed her gaze and his brow furrowed. "She's not always like this, you know. Today is just a bad day. And the doctors are doing the best they can."

"Really?" said Holtz. "Well, we'll see about that. No further questions, Your Honor."

Dylan's next witness was the court-appointed psychiatrist, Dr. Faye Norris. Her report was already a part of the court file, but Dylan took her through it, step by step. She explained how she had observed Nicole, her conversations with her, the neurological tests performed, all without any objection from Holtz. Finally Dylan asked her, "Dr. Norris, based on your observation and evaluation of the respondent, do you have an opinion regarding the mental competency of the respondent, Nicole Girard?"

"I do."

"And what is that opinion?"

"Ms. Girard is not presently competent to care for herself or to make competent medical decisions."

"And what is the basis of that opinion?"

"That's complex. Ms. Girard's basic problem is AIDS dementia syndrome. This is a syndrome where—"

"That's already been explained to the Court, Doctor," said Panaro. "Counsel, you don't have to repeat all that. Just get to the point."

Dylan bit his lip. He had prepped Norris extensively on this issue. He said, "Dr. Norris, just describe the objective signs that form the basis of your opinion."

"Certainly," said Norris. "As a result of her organic disease, Ms. Girard is, in lay terms, delusional. She has insufficient ability to distinguish between the real and the imagined, and, although she can at times seem perfectly cogent and reasonable, she is truly unable to make informed decisions on her own behalf."

"Examples?" said Dylan.

Norris nodded judiciously. "Well, of course, there is the incident at the dedication ceremony, where she endangered herself by jumping out of the window and then disrupted the ceremony. She also is quite adamant that the physicians at the institute are trying to take her blood. She calls them vampires. When it is suggested to her that taking blood specimens is a routine part of medical care, she continues to deny the legitimacy of her physicians."

Dylan looked at Panaro; he seemed to have made his point. "No further questions, Your Honor."

"Just a few questions, Dr. Norris," said Holtz, jumping up. She paced a moment, then said, "Dr. Norris, isn't it true that delusional patients usually have a range of delusions, not just one?"

"Well, Ms. Girard does have more than one."

"That's not responsive, Doctor. Please answer the question."

Norris shifted uncomfortably in her chair. "Well, yes, usually they do."

"And the only 'delusion' that Nicole Girard has is the idea that her attending physicians are taking too much blood?"

"No, as I testified, there was the time she jumped out of the window. That clearly is delusional behavior."

"But isn't that the *same* so-called delusion?"

"I don't understand."

"Isn't it true, Dr. Norris, that Nicole jumped out that window in order to escape from the confinement, confinement imposed by the so-called delusion about 'vampires sucking her blood'?"

Norris cocked her head and considered this. "I suppose that's possible."

"And isn't it also true," said Holtz, moving closer to the witness stand, "that Ms. Girard admits her comments about vampires are meant as a joke, an overstatement, that she doesn't really believe Dr. Argent is a vampire?"

"Well, yes, that is true. But she does believe that Dr. Argent is taking too much blood."

"Right," said Holtz. "And do you know from your own personal knowledge, Dr. Norris, that Dr. Argent *isn't* taking too much blood?"

Norris's mouth opened and closed silently. Finally she said, "Well, no, I don't, but of course I know that—"

"Thank you," said Holtz, cutting her off. "No further questions, Your Honor."

Panaro didn't respond. She continued to stare at

Norris for a few seconds. *That's not a good sign*, thought Dylan. Finally Panaro said, "Thank you, Counsel." Turning to Dylan, she asked, "Any more witnesses?"

"No, Your Honor. We rest our case."

Panaro looked at the clock. "It's almost one o'clock, and I have a previously scheduled criminal matter this afternoon. We'll adjourn this matter until tomorrow morning at nine thirty. At that time, I'll rule on your motion, Ms. Holtz. I'll take memoranda of law on the issues this afternoon, if you can get them in by six o'clock."

Holtz stood. "Your Honor, by that time it may be too late. Any excess drugs in respondent's system may have been metabolized by then."

"I know," said Panaro sympathetically, "but I can't help that. I can't shoot from the hip. As Mr. Ice pointed out, there are constitutional issues involved."

"But, Judge—"

"I'm sorry, Counsel. Take it or leave it."

Holtz sighed. "I understand."

Panaro stood up. "Court adjourned."

CHAPTER TEN

"**I** heard you had an interesting morning," said Barry as he came into Dylan's office, picked up the little basketball, and executed a clumsy dunk into the basket over the door.

Dylan looked up from his computer, peering over a pile of *South Western Reporters*, yellow Post-its sticking out of the pages. "Yeah," said Dylan. "I looked for you when I got back. I've got to get this memorandum finished by six, and I'd like your opinion."

"Of course you would." Barry grinned. "On what issue?"

Dylan quickly outlined Holtz's motion for a blood test of Nicole, and Judge Panaro's response. "I've looked at the guardianship statute, and I can't see any justification for it. There's a provision for an independent psychological assessment, but that's already been done by Dr. Norris. There's no authority for a court-ordered physical examination, so it seems to me this is a substituted consent issue."

"Hold on," said Barry. "Let's think this through. . . . All right, first, the court already has granted the hospital custody under chapter 632. But the Court always retains supervision. The issue before the Court now is who should be the permanent guardian, not *whether* the ward is disabled, right? Okay. Well, since the court has jurisdiction over Nicole, it would follow that it could order a simple blood test."

"I disagree. If the hospital wanted to do a blood test, it could—in fact, it does, every day, precisely because the court has granted it custody under chapter 632. But can the court substitute its consent for the ward's to a medical test that is *not* requested by the hospital? I don't think so."

Barry pointed at the case books. "Nothing on point?"

"Not in Missouri, no. Some California cases."

They both laughed. No attorney liked citing California precedent.

"What about Jon Keller? He's Girard's lawyer. What's his position?"

Dylan snorted. "He doesn't believe it's necessary to prepare a memorandum."

"Not at the county rate of $75 an hour, anyway."

"Right. And the hospital's attorney is neutral."

Barry scratched his cheek. "Well, actually, Dylan, I don't think you should spend too much time on this, either. If you prepare a major pleading, Panaro might start wondering whether Holtz has something. You know, where there's smoke . . . Act like you assume Panaro knows Holtz's motion is off the wall, hardly requiring a response. I would file a cursory memorandum, just hitting the high points, dismissing Holtz's motion as obviously ridiculous."

Dylan nodded gratefully. This was exactly the kind of practical advice he needed.

"Tell me," Barry continued, "why do you think Girard acted so strangely? Assuming you don't buy Holtz's theory?"

Dylan sighed and turned toward his credenza, where he had taped Nicole's drawing to the wall. He focused on the little imp, which seemed to be mocking him. "I don't know. It doesn't make sense, either way." He shrugged and turned back to Barry. "I do know I feel terribly inadequate going up against Holtz in my first contested case. I mean, this should really be handled by a partner, even if it is a small matter."

Barry laughed. "Hey, you're getting trial experience, be grateful. Anyway, you didn't really expect our fearless leader to get into the same courtroom with Pamela Holtz, did you?"

Dylan frowned. "Why not?"

Barry looked at him, surprised. "I thought you knew."

"Knew what?"

"About Holtz and Hudson."

"I know they were law school classmates." Dylan struck his forehead with his hand. "Of course! They must have had a relationship! Is that it?"

"More than that. Jesus, I guess I should have mentioned this before. Hudson was in love with her, and they were engaged to be married. But Holtz kept putting off the wedding. Then she left him."

"That's it? He's a jilted lover?"

Barry grinned. "Not quite. You see, Pamela left Hudson to move in with another lawyer."

"Another lawyer?"

"Another *woman* lawyer."

"What!"

"Yes, it seems that Pamela 'discovered' she was a

lesbian while she was living with Hudson. Or so she told him, anyway."

"That hurts."

"Yeah, and Hudson didn't take it well. Probably something to do with his manly ego. It's one thing to lose your fiancé to another man—but to a *woman?*"

Now, Dylan thought, things make sense. He had wondered about the snide comments Hudson made during the meeting with Holtz in his office. Dylan tapped his front teeth meditatively. "I feel like I'm caught in a cross fire. Holtz and Hudson. Sheesh."

"Don't worry about it. It's not your problem."

Dylan wasn't so sure. He said, "Do you think I should call Hudson in K.C., get his opinion of what to do about this motion? He *is* the supervising partner on this case."

"Nah. He knew about the hearing. If he wanted you to keep him posted, he would have let you know."

"I guess so," said Dylan. "Well, I better get this thing finished." He swiveled back to face the computer screen.

Barry got up. "Good luck."

"I've read your motion, Counsel," Judge Panaro said to Pamela Holtz from the bench the next morning, "and Mr. Ice's opposition. I'm disposed to grant it, based on the issues you have raised and the Court's personal observation of the respondent." She looked over at Nicole, who seemed exactly the same as yesterday.

Well, I lost, thought Dylan. He wasn't sure if he

was sorry or not. He'd had trouble sleeping last night, wondering whether Nicole *was* overmedicated, and, if so, why Argent would have done it.

Panaro continued, "Unfortunately, I have been unable to find any authority for such an order. Although you have put the respondent's physical condition at issue, the guardianship statute allows the Court only to appoint a guardian, not to personally supervise the respondent. Now if the duly appointed guardian chooses to subject the respondent to a blood test—well, of course, choosing a guardian is what is at issue here. So we come full circle." She sighed, then said, "The motion for serological testing is denied. Ms. Holtz, are you ready with your first witness?"

Holtz betrayed no sign of disappointment. "Yes, Your Honor."

"Good. I assume you can combine the testimony on your opposition with your own case in chief?"

"That's fine, Your Honor."

"Proceed."

"I call Charlene McConnell."

Charlene seated herself gracefully. She was dressed in business attire: brown suit jacket over a crisp white blouse and a matching brown skirt. She looked serene and self-possessed.

"What is your occupation?" Holtz asked McConnell.

"I'm a county social worker," said Charlene.

"And what is your educational background?"

"I have a bachelor's degree from St. Louis University and a master's of social work from Washington University."

"How long have you worked for the county?"

"Almost eight years."

Judge Panaro said, "Just a minute, please. Would counsel please approach the bench?"

Dylan and Holtz went forward, and Panaro said to them, "Counsel, I want you to know I'm acquainted with the witness. I thought she looked familiar, and now that I've heard her occupation, I realize we served on a child welfare committee together. Do either of you have a problem with that?"

Dylan said, "I don't think so, Your Honor. I mean, you didn't have a personal relationship, right?" As soon as he said that, he realized how horribly wrong it sounded in the context of this case. Panaro's face reddened, and Holtz said, "I can't believe you would—"

"No, no!" Dylan said immediately. "I didn't mean it that way, I just meant you didn't know her personally! I'm sorry, Your Honor."

They both stared at him for a moment, and then Panaro's face softened. "I believe you, Mr. Ice. No apology is necessary. And the answer is no, I have had no personal relationship with the witness."

"Then it's fine with me, Your Honor," Dylan said quickly, and retreated to the counsel table.

Holtz shuffled some papers and said, "Now, please tell the Court how you first became acquainted with the respondent."

Charlene shifted position on the uncomfortably hard witness chair. "About six years ago, I was assigned to the child protective services unit." She looked at Panaro. "The Court, I know, is familiar with that unit and what we do."

"Of course," said Panaro, impatiently. "Please proceed."

Charlene seemed unfazed. "Well, I was assigned

to supervise a case involving a little boy who was molested by his stepfather. We—I mean the county—removed him from his mother's custody and placed him temporarily in one of our foster homes. The little boy was in pretty bad shape, psychologically—not physically—and our consultants recommended multiple therapeutic modalities to help him deal with his feelings of rage and hurt. Art therapy has been very successful with children, and Nicole was recommended. Well, Nicole saw the child and right away had an impact. I mean, this kid was practically catatonic, and she got him talking again. Eventually, he did all right and we were able to place him permanently in a good home."

"I see," said Holtz. "And after that?"

"Well, we started seeing more of each other. We would get together at least one evening a week, go out to dinner, see a movie. Then on the weekends."

She continued in this vein for a while, building a tale of what sounded like a traditional courtship. Dylan found the story fascinating, so fascinating that he almost forgot he was supposed to process information and determine objections. He wondered just how far Holtz would take this—would she overtly bring out the homosexual relationship, or leave it only implied?

"So you became quite close?" asked Holtz.

"Yes," said Charlene, her voice emotionless. Her tone remained the same as she said, "More than close."

Dylan glanced at Panaro, who seemed unfazed. Well, he thought, that was a benefit Holtz reaped by not having a jury. A sudden panic gripped him: What if *Panaro* was gay? Why hadn't he considered that before?

Holtz approached Charlene and said softly, "And what is the nature of that relationship?"

Charlene said firmly, "We love each other and have an exclusive relationship. We were married in a religious ceremony by a Presbyterian minister. Although we know such marriages are not yet recognized by civil law, we believe it's just a matter of time before our marriage is recognized by both God and man."

"Like hell!" Henry Girard whispered forcefully.

Panaro looked sharply at him and said, "Mr. Ice, please control your client."

"Sorry, Your Honor," said Dylan, glaring at Henry Girard.

Holtz took some photographs from her briefcase, premarked with exhibit stickers; she showed them to Dylan. They were snapshots of Charlene and Nicole together, in their apartment, in the park, at the beach. Holtz showed them to Charlene for identification, then moved them into evidence. Dylan didn't object.

Next Holtz took some sheets of paper from the counsel table—also premarked—and handed one copy to Dylan. It was a photocopy of the notepaper Charlene had shown him in his office, the first time she met him: "I choose and appoint Charlene McConnell as my guardian if a judge decides that I am unable to make my own decisions."

Holtz gave the other copy to Charlene and said, "I show you what has been marked as Petitioner McConnell's Exhibit Number 12. Can you identify it?"

"Certainly," Charlene said. "This is a document I prepared for Nicole's signature about—"

"Objection!" Dylan almost shouted, springing to his feet.

"Just a minute, Counsel," Panaro said patiently.

"Ms. Holtz hasn't moved its admission yet. She's just asking the witness to identify it."

Another rookie mistake, thought Dylan. "Sorry, Your Honor," he said, sitting down.

Charlene continued, "I prepared it for Nicole's signature about two weeks ago."

"Please describe what you observed of Ms. Girard's mental state at that time."

"She acted perfectly normal," Charlene said, glancing at Nicole, still slumped in her wheelchair. "Not like that," she added.

"And why did you prepare this document?"

Charlene shrugged. "Well, it was before you represented me. I had visited Nicole at the hospital and talked to Dr. Volberg; he explained that when Nicole's twenty-one-day commitment ended, he wouldn't ask to renew it—that he believed a guardian should be appointed for her. Well, I didn't have a chance to look at the law, but I discussed it with Nicole, and she asked me to prepare something in writing, because she wanted me to be her guardian. In fact she said that—"

"Objection!" said Dylan.

Panaro looked at Charlene and said, "Ms. McConnell, you've testified before. You know about hearsay. Don't repeat what Nicole said."

"Sorry, Your Honor."

"And exhibit 12 is what she signed that day?" said Holtz.

"That's right."

"And she did so freely and voluntarily, without any duress or coercion?"

"Yes."

Holtz turned to Panaro. "We move the admission of exhibit 12."

"Mr. Ice?" said Panaro.

"I object to its admission, Your Honor," Dylan said quickly. "The document does not meet the requirements of section 475.050(3) of the code, on several grounds. First, it is not signed before the inception of disability, as required by that section, and secondly, it's not signed by two witnesses, as required."

"Ms. Holtz?" said Panaro.

"We acknowledge the defects, Your Honor, and agree that the Court is not *required* to consider this document in making its decision. The code does not, however, *prohibit* the Court from considering the document, as part of all the other evidence before it. It does show the respondent's intent, and that is something that the Court *should* consider."

"Your Honor!" said Dylan. "This is just a back door way of getting an inadmissable exhibit into evidence!"

Panaro smiled at him. "Take it easy, Counsel. I understand the issues. Ms. Holtz, that is quite a creative argument." She thought for moment, looking at Nicole. "Considering the respondent's apparent mental state today, I can't allow this into evidence. Denied."

Holtz shrugged and returned her attention to Charlene. "Please tell the Court why you feel you are best qualified to be Nicole's guardian."

Charlene took a deep breath. "I'm only asking for the same right as any husband or wife. I'm her spouse—it's that simple. I have lived with Nicole day in and day out, for almost six years. I've seen her ups and downs. When the constant threat of progressing to AIDS got to be too much, I'm the one who held her in the middle of the night, and lied and told her it was gonna be all right." Her eyes were moist and she made a perfunctory pass at them with her hands. "And she has comforted me when my problems seemed insurmountable. We've laughed together, played together, planned together. We were a *couple*. And we were happy." She paused. "Now that she's sick, it's killing me that I can't help her, that I can't be with her. And it's even more disheartening to see decisions being made for her by doctors, decisions she should be making herself. Nicole always was so competent, so *grounded*. She would want to choose her drug therapy, not have it forced on her. And now, the thought of decisions being made on her behalf by people who don't know her one-tenth as well as I—" she looked directly at Henry Girard, "well, it's breaking my heart." She straightened up. "I'm the person who is best qualified to be Nicole's guardian."

Holtz let that answer hang in the silence for a moment, then said, "No more questions."

Panaro looked at Keller and Rabb. "Any questions of this witness, gentlemen?"

"None, Your Honor," they chorused, and Panaro looked at Dylan.

Dylan stood slowly and advanced to the podium. He had debated for days how he would handle the cross-examination of Charlene. Tough or soft? Lengthy or brief? But now, after hearing her testimony, he saw his course clearly. He had to puncture this emotional balloon, quickly, efficiently, and without rancor. He said, "Ms. McConnell, isn't it a fact that you are not the legal spouse of Nicole Girard?"

She stared at him. "What do you mean?"

"You don't understand the question?"

She stared at him a moment, looking angry, then finally said through compressed lips, "Technically, that's correct."

Dylan couldn't accept that. "Technically? Either you are or you aren't."

"Objection," said Holtz. "Counsel is making a statement."

Panaro said to Dylan, "We need a question, Counsel."

Dylan nodded and said, "Are you or are you not the legally wedded spouse of Nicole Girard?"

"Objection," said Holtz again. "Asked and answered."

"Not this way, Your Honor," said Dylan.

Panaro looked annoyed. "Overruled. Answer the question, Ms. McConnell."

Charlene looked a bit bewildered, but she said, "Look, I know what you're getting at. And yes, of course we're not legally married, but I—"

"Thank you," said Dylan quickly, successfully cutting her off. "You've answered the question." And he sat down.

He had pages of other questions, but his instinct told him to leave it alone. It was a good cross, he thought, considering what he had to work with. The bottom line was that she was *not* Nicole's spouse, while his client was the proposed ward's parent.

Holtz called a few more witnesses, all friends or coworkers of Nicole, to testify about the wonderful relationship had by Nicole and Charlene. Not much to work with for Dylan, and his cross-examinations were perfunctory.

Finally, Holtz wrapped up the testimony, and Panaro took a brief recess. When she returned to the bench, Panaro said, "All right, I'll hear argument now. Let's begin with the respondent's attorney. Mr. Keller?"

Keller went to the podium. "I'll be brief, Your Honor. Until recently, my client completely opposed the concept of guardianship, and I was prepared to oppose it on her behalf. In light of her present condition, and the testimony of the physicians, however, I do not oppose. However, I suggest a ninety-day review. As for the choice of guardian, I can tell the court that my client's wish, when she could still express it, was in favor of Ms. McConnell. Unfortunately, I cannot verify that at this time." He returned to his seat.

"Thank you," said Panaro. "Mr. Rabb? The hospital's position?"

Rabb said, "As I stated at the start of this hearing, Your Honor, my client believes the appointment of a guardian is necessary, and that further inpatient treatment is necessary. We have no position on the choice of guardian."

This was as Dylan expected. He felt his heart beating faster as Panaro said, "All right. Mr. Ice, your petition was filed before Ms. Holtz's. Why don't you go first." She leaned back in her big judge's chair and waited expectantly.

Dylan took the podium and said, "I also will try to be brief, Your Honor. I believe the issues before the Court are clear. The threshold question, of course, is whether we have proven, by clear and convincing evidence, that the respondent is incapacitated. The statute defines an incapacitated person as one who lacks capacity to meet essential requirements for food, clothing, shelter, safety or other care such that serious physical injury, illness, or disease is likely to occur. Ms. Girard has a disease—AIDS dementia—that has clearly left her in such an incapacitated state. The uncontradicted testimony of her attending physician, as well as the independent court-appointed physician, support this, as well as the obvious condition of the respondent in this courtroom." He gestured to Nicole, who was staring fixedly at some point over the judge's shoulder.

Dylan continued, "As for the choice of guardian, I turn to the law." Dylan picked up his photocopy of the guardianship statute. "Under section 475.050, the Court must choose a guardian from among three classes: first, any reasonable choice communicated by the respondent at the hearing; second, any eligible person nominated by the respondent in a durable power of attorney or other written instrument executed within five years of the disability; and third, if there are no individuals in the first two categories, then the court shall appoint a guardian from the class of 'spouse, parents, adult children, adult brothers and sisters and other close adult relatives.'"

"As to the first class, the respondent has not been able to express any choice of guardian at this hearing. There also is no valid power of attorney or instrument in writing executed by the respondent *before* the disability. That leaves the Court with only the third choice, selection from the class of relatives."

"Your Honor, my client is the father of the respondent. The respondent has no other close relatives and, notwithstanding the eloquent testimony of Ms. McConnell, she is not married to the respondent. Accordingly, assuming that my client is qualified to be guardian under the provisions of section 475.050—and I submit he is—then the Court must appoint him as guardian of his daughter. Thank you." Dylan sat down, relieved to be finished and satisfied he had stated the case correctly.

"Thank you," said Panaro. "Ms. Holtz?"

"May it please the Court," said Holtz, standing. "I have serious questions as to whether the respondent is disabled as defined in the statute. I think it is clear that she is not acting normally, and that—"

Panaro said, "Counsel, please don't reargue the drug issue. I've made my ruling."

Holtz nodded agreeably. "I understand, Your Honor. But what I was leading up to was a suggestion that, in light of all the evidence, the Court should simply continue the temporary mental health commitment and reschedule this hearing for a later date. If the respondent is suffering from a drug overdose—"

"We would object to that," said Rabb, rising to his feet. "The old disposition is no longer appropriate."

Panaro waved him down. "Ms. Holtz, that's not going to happen. If what you say is true, you can always file a petition to reopen. Now please continue."

Holtz sighed and said, "Yes, Your Honor." She looked at her papers briefly, then said, "Mr. Ice has argued that Nicole has not made a valid election in favor of my client as guardian. We dispute that. First, I think it is clear from the totality of the evidence that, given a choice between the woman she considered to be her spouse and her estranged father, Nicole Girard would choose my client as her guardian."

Clever, thought Dylan. She couldn't cite the note Nicole had signed, because it wasn't admitted into evidence. But Holtz had managed to remind Panaro of it anyway.

Holtz continued, "Now, if the Court accepts Mr. Ice's argument that it must choose a guardian from the third class—that of 'spouse, parents, adult children,' then I suggest to the Court that it may, under the statute, validly choose my client." She drew a deep breath and pitched her voice somewhat deeper. "This case is about much more than just guardianship. It's also about principles of fundamental fairness and basic equality for all citizens. Nicole Girard and Charlene McConnell love each other. They live together, share expenses equally, and were married in a religious ceremony. The Court has heard testimony of this commitment and love. I suggest to the Court that, in the truest sense of the word, they *are* married. But because this state does not recognize same-sex marriages, they do not have that magic piece of paper, that secular seal of approval." She slapped her hand on the podium for emphasis. "This, in my view, is unconstitutional, and I will work until the law is changed."

Panaro said, "Counsel, I believe you. But the point is that it is not changed *now*. Are you suggesting I ignore the law?"

All right, thought Dylan. She's not buying this.

Holtz shook her head. "Not at all. I don't believe the Court has to ignore or violate the law in order to appoint my client as guardian. I submit that, based on the evidence before it, this Court can rule that Charlene McConnell is in the nature of a spouse, and, for the limited purposes of this guardianship hearing, should be treated as such."

Panaro looked thoughtful. Too thoughtful.

Holtz quickly said, "For the Court to do so is

not without precedent. I have included in my trial brief several similar cases where a court has granted certain spousal rights to a same-sex partner, including property rights."

"I've read those cases," said Panaro. "They're all from California and Hawaii. Don't you have any Missouri precedent?"

"Uh, no, Your Honor. This case would be the first."

Again, Panaro looked interested in the concept. She certainly was not dismissing it out of hand. Maybe, thought Dylan, she was dreaming of making a new law.

"Your Honor," said Holtz quickly, "it's clear from the evidence that Mr. and Mrs. Girard were not close to the respondent. It is undisputed that my client and the respondent had a relationship that, if it were between a man and a woman, would be called a marriage. If the Court were to rule against my client, it would be an injustice on many levels, not least of all to her. Nicole Girard deserves better. Thank you." She sat down.

"Thank you, Counsel," said Panaro. "All of you. I'll take this case under advisement, but I'll make my decision today. My clerk will notify all counsel by four P.M." She looked at the clerk. "Call the next case, please."

Dylan rose slowly from his seat. He had to wait to find out if he had won. But looking at Nicole, and at Charlene hovering over her, he wondered if he really wanted victory.

CHAPTER ELEVEN

"**C**ongratulations," said Hudson, coming out from behind his desk and grinning broadly. "You beat the best."

It was the day after Dylan got the call from the judge's law clerk giving him word of his victory— Judge Panaro had appointed Henry Girard as Nicole's guardian.

Dylan accepted a handshake and tried to look pleased and humble. The humility part was easy—he knew that he had won despite his efforts, not because of them. And yet Hudson, who should know better, was uncharacteristically effusive in his praise. In fact, he looked positively giddy.

"Sit down, sit down," Hudson said, pushing Dylan into the side chair. "I wish I could have been there to see it. The great Pamela Holtz losing to a second-year associate!" He sprawled in his chair. "Tell me everything."

Dylan related it as objectively as possible, deliberately including his neophyte mistakes. When he finished, Hudson picked up a crystal paperweight and tossed it from hand to hand. "You did a great job, Dylan. I know it wasn't easy going up against a heavy hitter like Holtz in your first case, but I think you showed some balls. Keep up the good work and you'll get some nicer cases to work on."

Dylan tried to keep his voice even. "You mean, better than subrogation cases?"

Hudson laughed. "You bet. Now get back to work and bill some hours."

The Burning Tree Country Club and golf course, nestled inside a loop of the Washington Beltway, rarely was visited by presidents. Despite its beauty and its proximity to the Capitol, Burning Tree had one great defect: no women members. The restriction had cost the club its tax deduction, but its membership was wealthy enough to make up the difference.

President Thomas Banfield didn't care; he loved the course. He was doing reasonably well in the polls, and he decided to reject the advice of his staff and play on this rare late spring day of low humidity. If he took flak from the media, so be it. Anyway, it was well known that he was a strong supporter of women's rights—his opponent had even criticized his views as "too feminist."

Banfield coughed as he lined up his putt for par on the seventh hole, shutting everything out of his head except for the little white ball, the green, and the hole. It was a fifteen footer, but tricky; the caddy warned him the green broke left. Just as he swung, he coughed again, ruining his swing, and the ball rolled wide left, stopping a good five feet away.

"Goddamn it." Banfield cursed this dry cough that had plagued him for days: a tickling in his throat, probably from making too many speeches.

"Tough luck, Tom." Craig Hagen moved to take his own shot.

Banfield walked over the green to the remainder of the foursome, Senator Dobbs and Peter Laughlin, a corporate CEO.

Dobbs said, "I understand Ted Osborne is trying to get you to agree to a debate right after the conventions."

Banfield laughed, trying not to let it end in a cough. "That's right. He sent a letter over this morning. What, did he already leak it on the Hill?"

"I'm afraid so, Mr. President," said Dobbs.

They were silent as Hagen took his putt, making it for par. Then Banfield said, "I expected as much. He's almost fifteen points behind—he can't afford to wait until late September to debate me."

Dobbs nodded. "He'll claim you're ducking him, but I think it's a good decision to wait."

"You bet your ass it is," said Banfield. They walked to their golf carts and hopped on, Craig sitting next to the President.

"You know, Tom," said Hagen as the Secret Service agent started the cart, "you can expect some new trick from Osborne at least once a week, now. We've got to make sure Opposition Research is ready."

"I agree." Banfield felt slightly dizzy as the cart swooped over a rise. "Check into it when we get back to the White House." Banfield had already decided that, in this election, he would return every low blow sent his way by Osborne. He would take no chances with the man he privately called the Snake.

Senator Theodore Osborne, winner of most of his party's presidential primaries, was the presumptive nominee of the opposition. He was also—without hyperbole—Banfield's lifelong enemy.

Inextricably linked in the public's mind, the two Minnesotans had fought brutal campaigns against each other for mayor and later governor and senator. Banfield had won the governorship—twice; Osborne the Senate seat—three times. Both had jockeyed for position to run for President, but Osborne had been blocked by an incumbent in his own party, the incumbent Banfield defeated four years ago.

Now Banfield was running for reelection on a record of solid achievement, with a strong economy and an administration free of scandal. He had taken office on a pledge to reorganize and revamp a military that was still structured to defeat a nonexistent Soviet threat, and had accomplished what the experts said couldn't be done: eliminate the billions of dollars wasted by interservice rivalry, the separate air forces of the Army, Navy, and Marines.

The key to his success had been getting rid of the old generals and admirals whose careers were invested in the status quo. It had not been easy, but when his Defense Reform Act squeaked through Congress, the next layer in the officer corps turned out to be remarkably competent and creative. With their help, and tremendous effort from Secretary of Defense Hackworth, he had built a streamlined, highly trained, highly paid, and effective conventional army, and a much smaller but highly advanced Navy and Air Force.

And the billions of dollars saved had solved many other domestic issues.

The one arena in which he failed was in the area of "big ticket" items. The multibillion dollar bombers and submarine programs that even the old military deemed unnecessary and wasteful just couldn't be killed. There was just too much pork in those programs, too many jobs at stake.

It was no coincidence that the Congressional leader of the opposition to his military reform program was Theodore Osborne. Osborne, whose belief system was purely functional, and whose personal hero was Richard Nixon.

He would be a disaster as President. He would talk about family values and conservative fiscal policies while handing the government over to every special interest that could pay the freight. And he would destroy everything Banfield had accomplished.

The golf cart came to a halt on the eighth tee, and everyone piled out. Again, Banfield felt a wave of dizziness, this time followed by a spasm of coughing.

"You all right, Tom?" asked Hagen, coming closer and looking him in the eye.

Banfield knew what he was thinking, and said quickly, "Just a dry throat from campaigning," said Banfield.

Hagen looked unconvinced. "Maybe we should go back to the clubhouse."

"Forget it," said Banfield, striding toward the tee.

"Sounds like you've got a chest cold, Mr. President," said Laughlin.

"Too much campaigning," repeated Banfield, as he placed a ball on the tee. "I'm gonna birdie this next hole. Care to place a little wager?"

CHAPTER TWELVE

Nicole drifted in and out of a troubled sleep, dreaming of court. She kept seeing the judge talk about her as if she weren't there, hearing Argent's lies, seeing people decide her fate while she couldn't force any words past her lips. It was a Kafkaesque experience, a nightmare that seemed to go on forever, and now it played again and again in her head until the faces became dark and evil and monstrous and she tried to scream but had no breath, and opened her eyes.

There were shadows in front of her, shapes: Mark and Linda Argent. This was real, she thought, not part of the dream. She struggled to focus on the digital clock next to her bed. The digits read 3:12 A.M. Why were they here?

Dr. Argent didn't say anything, just stood to one side, while his wife stood next to the portable IV stand. From her lab coat pocket, Linda Argent removed a small drug vial and a disposable syringe.

Nicole lifted her head and tried to speak, but her head felt as big as a bowling ball, her tongue too thick to move. The expression on Linda's face set off an alarm deep inside Nicole's brain. "No," she managed to say, struggling to get her arms to work.

Ignoring her, Linda drew the medication—a dark liquid—into the syringe, then slowly inserted the needle directly into the IV line.

"You're sure you got the right dosage?" said Argent.

"Of course," Linda snapped.

Argent nodded, and Linda slowly depressed the plunger on the syringe.

Nicole watched in horror as the dark liquid disappeared into the IV, her eyes following its course down the flexible tubing, into the butterfly valve taped to the top of her hand. She wanted to sit up, tear the tubing out of her body, scream, do *something*, but nothing happened. She felt her brain exploding with futile effort, and pinpoints of light appeared before her eyes—flashes of light, then darkness, then light.

"How long?" Linda said.

Argent shrugged. "Not long. As soon as it gets pumped up to her brain."

Nicole heard with amazing acuity all the sounds of the room—the air conditioner, Argent's breathing, water surging through the plumbing in the wall, even low voices coming from the nurses' station. Then there was a hum, growing louder and louder, until it filled her head, expanding and becoming not sound but color, swirling red and white and more red and then white again, and she felt herself rising, rising. She was free of the bed, free of the restraints, floating near the ceiling, looking down on her body. She saw Argent reach out and place his stethoscope on her chest, saw him listen intently and then straighten up in satisfaction.

Nicole watched without emotion as her body's respirations slowed. She turned to face the bright light coming through the ceiling.

■   ■   ■

The Learjet lifted from the runway of Lambert International Airport, pressing Dylan back into the wide seat. The plane climbed rapidly, and they were soon at cruising altitude.

Fletcher's plane was small but luxurious. In addition to twelve airline seats, there also was an upholstered sofa, a narrow table with a parquet wood top, a fully equipped galley, several phones, a fax machine, and a complete entertainment center.

Kristin rose from the seat next to Dylan, stretched languorously, and said, "How about a drink?"

"Sure," Dylan replied, trying to act nonchalant, as if he was used to flying in private jets.

The only other passengers were Fletcher and his wife, Rae, who was short, plump, and prematurely white-haired. She hadn't said a word to Dylan since he and Kristin came aboard.

Fletcher was already in earnest conversation on the phone; Dylan caught something about "discount rate" and "federal funds" before Kristin brought him his drink—a single malt scotch on the rocks. She clinked her Absolut and lime against his glass and said, "To a great weekend."

"I'm ready for that," said Dylan.

They were headed for Lake Tahoe, where Fletcher and his entire family traditionally spent the Memorial Day weekend at his house on the south shore. Despite their short relationship, Kristin had invited Dylan along. It seemed a bit strange, but Kristin clearly was a woman who didn't play by the rules. Dylan barely hesitated before accepting.

He had left Janis at Barry Sasscer's house,

precipitating a major argument. "I'm almost seventeen," she had insisted. "I can take care of myself."

"Perhaps you could, normally," Dylan replied. "But you're on bond, subject to supervision. Unless you're supervised, the Court has a right to revoke your bond and keep you in jail until your trial in August. Is that what you want?"

She had no answer to that, of course.

"You're doing it again," said Kristin.

"What?"

"Furrowing."

He gave her a blank look. She pointed at his forehead. "Furrowing your brow. If you keep that up, you're gonna get permanent wrinkles." She brushed her fingertips lightly across his forehead; Dylan noticed her mother glance up from her paperback novel and then quickly look down again. "C'mon, it's the weekend. Let's party."

"Yeah," said Dylan, taking a sip of his Scotch, trying to get in the spirit. "Let's party."

In all his travels as a child, crisscrossing the country, Dylan had never been to Lake Tahoe. And if he had, he certainly would not have stayed in a million-dollar house right on the lake. He imagined that his parents would have parked their VW Microbus in a campground outside of town, then hitched a ride to the waterfront.

It was Saturday afternoon, and Dylan sat in a massive hot tub set deep into the deck of Fletcher's lake house. Kristin sat across from him. He settled more comfortably on the bench, getting the small of his back directly over one of the underwater jets, and said, "So this is how the rich live." He waved his hand around in the general direction of the house and lake.

Kristin wiped a sheen of sweat from her face. "When I was a little girl, we were just a typical minister's family, living in a run-down parsonage. But Daddy's had a lot of money for some time now." She looked at him quizzically. "Were you really poor?"

Dylan sighed and slid a little deeper into the water. "When you're a kid, you don't have anything to compare it with. Most of the time, I was pretty happy." He fingered the hole in his earlobe reflectively.

"You better leave that alone," said Kristin. "It'll get infected."

"Oh." Dylan withdrew his hand. Friday night, while walking in Tahoe, Kristin had pulled him into a little shop and insisted he get his ears pierced. Although it was a de rigeur fashion statement for his generation, Dylan had never thought to do it. On the other hand, he couldn't think of any reason not to.

She seemed to read his thoughts. "Tomorrow we get you a tattoo."

"No way!"

"Just a little one."

"Forget it. Why would I put something on my body that I'd be ashamed to hang on my wall?"

"We'll see." She smirked and lightly brushed his leg with her toe. "So you said you were happy. But what about your parents? How did you end up taking care of your sister? You promised you'd tell me."

Dylan thought about it for a moment. It was true that she had asked him—often—about his family, and that he always avoided the subject.

Well, if he really was going to have a relationship with her—and he desperately wanted one—she would have to know the truth, no matter how it humiliated him. "My mother's dead, I told you that," he said finally.

"Yes, but how did she die?"

"A drug overdose." It wasn't quite the truth, but close enough.

"Oh, really? I'm sorry." She brushed him with her toe again. "And your father? Is he still alive?"

Dylan rubbed his ear. "When my mother died, he sort of . . . lost it. Well, he had never been too stable anyway. He stopped going to work, couldn't concentrate on anything or anyone."

"Sounds like he was doing drugs, too."

"Probably," said Dylan without emotion. "Anyway, after a while it got to the point he couldn't take care of himself, much less my sister. I was eighteen by then, and in college."

"What about your relatives? Couldn't they help out?"

Dylan shook his head. "Only one set of grandparents were still alive—my mother's—and they disowned us long ago. There also were a couple of aunts, but we lost track of them. Luckily, I had some money—my mother had a small life insurance policy, with Janis and me as beneficiaries—so I was able to afford an apartment off campus. Janis came to live with me."

"You mean you were taking care of Janis all through college and law school?"

"That's right."

She whistled. "No wonder you're so . . . mature."

He grinned. "Thanks. That's a nice way of saying I've got a rod up my ass."

She laughed. "Yeah, but it makes you taller.

Seriously, that must have been very tough. College is supposed to be the freest time of life, and you must have missed so much. Didn't you resent it?"

"Sometimes," he admitted. "But it wasn't all negative. It forced me to grow up, to be responsible. And Janis and I had a lot of fun."

"What about your father? What happened to him?"

"He got some money together—dealing marijuana, probably—and bought land in Arkansas." Dylan paused, then said, "I really don't want to talk about this."

For a moment it seemed that Kristin would pursue it, but then she said, "I'm hot. Let's jump in the lake."

"You're not serious."

"You bet I am."

"That water is freezing!" Dylan pointed at the lake through the railing of the deck. Even in high summer, the mountain-fed water would be cold; this early in the season, the water temperature was probably in the fifties. There were plenty of boats and even windsurfers on the lake, but no swimmers.

"C'mon, don't be a wimp." Kristin stood up and smoothed down her one-piece bathing suit. "It's an incredible rush. When we start to get numb, we'll come back to the house and jump into the sauna."

"I don't think so," Dylan said firmly.

"Don't make me get you!"

Dylan was beginning to believe the cliché about redheads: They *were* all hot tempered. Already in their short relationship he had learned it was better not to cross her. Sighing, he stood up and followed her across the deck and down the stairs to the narrow, pebbly beach.

Kristin suddenly let out a yell, ran full speed down to the water's edge, and dove headfirst into the lake. After a moment her head emerged and she let out a yell. "C'mon, Dylan. It'll put hair on your chest!"

Dylan gritted his teeth, took a deep breath, and ran into the water, shrieking like a banshee. The water felt like melted ice, and it took a huge effort to keep from turning around and running back to the warmth of the hot tub. Instead, he swam over to Kristin.

They splashed around playfully for a while. He started to go numb, and the cold wasn't so bad until his ears started ringing. But about that time Kristin decided she had had enough and ran back up the little beach to the deck.

He followed her as she grabbed a fluffy towel from the rack next to the hot tub. They walked to a small wooden structure against the wall of the house, opened the plank door, and entered. Inside, there were bench seats along each wall, both low and high, and a metal sink full of hot stones reflecting heat from the hidden electric elements. The temperature dial on the wall read two hundred degrees; Dylan could feel his pores opening to absorb the warmth.

"Wow," said Dylan, as he lay on the bench above Kristin. "What a rush!"

"I told you," Kristin said smugly. They lay there silently for a while, breathing in the warmth and feeling their bodies shift from heat conservation to heat dissipation. In a surprisingly short time, Dylan felt sweat popping out of his skin. He glanced down at Kristin; she also was perspiring.

Suddenly she got up, opened the door, and went out.

"Hey!" said Dylan, but she came back almost immediately, carrying three more towels that she carefully spread on the lower bench. Then, looking in his eyes, she slowly pulled down the straps of her swimsuit, skinned it down her body, and stepped out of it. She dropped the suit lightly on his chest, then lay down on the towels, one arm behind her head, smiling.

Dylan levitated out of his swim trunks and joined her. Both their bodies were covered with perspiration, and they slid slickly against each other. It was a unique and very stimulating feeling. She reached down and fondled him.

"Feels like you've recovered from your immersion," she said.

"Did you hear the 'boing'?"

She laughed, and he kissed her hair, her mouth, her neck, her breasts, sliding down her body until he reached the junction of her thighs. After a few minutes there, she gasped and pulled him forcefully up her body again, twisting her hips to get beneath him, pressing him into her.

The heat in the little room, combined with Kristin's passion and her fair skin, turned her body almost as red as her hair. He slid into her, feeling like he was stoking a furnace, and she raised her legs off the bench, wrapping around him.

Dylan was pumping furiously when he heard the door open and felt a rush of cool air on his buttocks. A male voice said, "Holy Christ!"

In that moment of sheer panic, Dylan had one clear thought: *You idiot, you know she never locks doors.*

Dylan felt excruciatingly vulnerable, his bare ass literally twisting in the wind. He couldn't even back out of Kristin; the pressure of her legs around his back had, incredibly, increased. He turned his head to see who was there just as the spring-loaded door closed.

Dinner that night was a family affair. The house was occupied by several other families, all related to Reverend Fletcher: his brother, Nate, and his large brood, and his wife's sister's family. Several of Kristin's cousins also had families of their own.

The younger children had eaten earlier, and the massive split-log table was just being cleared by the live-in cook and the housekeeper. About seven adults and a few of the older teens remained as coffee was served.

"So, Dylan," said Frank Horner, a balding man wearing a Polynesian print shirt, pouring sugar into his cup. "What's it like being a hotshot lawyer in a big firm?" Horner was Fletcher's brother-in-law, and he wasn't smiling.

Dylan noticed the others watching his reaction. "I wouldn't know, since I don't think of myself as a hotshot. And for sure, my boss doesn't."

That brought a few titters from Kristin's cousins. In general, Dylan's treatment by the family had broken down by age group: the twenty- and thirty-something cousins had been cordial and warm; the fortyish and fiftyish uncles and aunts treated him politely but coldly. Now, with a few beers under their belts, Dylan sensed that the older generation was turning hostile. In addition to Uncle Frank, there was Fletcher's brother, Nate, who glowered at Dylan from across the table.

Dylan wondered if their attitude resulted from

the gut-wrenching sauna incident. He assumed that Kristin had seen the man who opened the door, but she insisted that her view was blocked by his arm. She was sure it wasn't her father, and beyond that she didn't care.

After the door closed, Dylan had leaped up and put on his bathing suit, then rushed back to his room. Every time he saw one of Kristin's male relatives in the hallway, he wondered if he was the one who had surprised them.

By dinner, however, he had come around to Kristin's attitude—what did it matter? Everyone knew they were having sex; she hadn't tried to conceal it. It was, he reflected ruefully, a prime example of how she could talk him out of something that, usually, he would have brooded about for days.

"What kind of law do you practice?" continued Uncle Frank in a friendlier tone.

"I'm a litigator," Dylan said, and he gave them a brief summary of his work.

Uncle Nate said suddenly, "You know, you don't act black at all."

Shit. Dylan looked at him: a big man with fleshy jowls and thick eyebrows. He resembled Reverend Fletcher only slightly. Dylan said gruffly, "What the hell does that mean? How does 'black' act?"

"Now, son, don't get offended," Nate said. "I'm just curious. I mean, you're half black, but your speech, your mannerisms, and especially your attitudes are white. Why is that? Didn't your momma have any effect on you?"

Obviously he had been briefed on Dylan's family background. Kristin, seated next to Dylan, said, "Uncle Nate, you've got no right—" but Dylan put up his hand.

"Both my parents were college graduates. My mother was the daughter of two professors. She was smart enough to get accepted to a Berkeley doctoral program in mathematics, where she met my father. And neither parent acted black or white, they just acted like . . . people."

Again Kristin tried to say something, but Dylan continued, "Anyway, I prefer to think of myself as biracial, because that's what I am."

Fletcher drawled, "That's nice, son, but unfortunately, society doesn't accept that category—you're either one or the other."

Dylan nodded and sighed. "You're right, there's not even a category for biracial on any government forms. But there are a lot of us now, and eventually things will change. In the meantime, if I have to choose, I say I'm African-American."

"Wrong choice," Nate said. "Give yourself credit, boy."

"Shut up, Uncle Nate!" said Kristin as Dylan rose out of his chair. She grabbed his arm.

"I don't have to take that shit—"

"From anybody," finished Reverend Fletcher. "I quite agree. Nate, you owe Mr. Ice an apology."

"Bullshit," said Nate, locking eyes with Fletcher. But after a long moment, Nate dropped his gaze first. Very slowly, he turned to Dylan and said, "As always, my brother is right. Dylan, I didn't mean anything by it. I was just joshing, that's all. People will tell you I'm always putting my foot in my mouth. I'm sorry, okay?" He stuck out his hand.

Dylan looked at it but didn't respond. Could he really believe Dylan would accept that apology as sincere? Kristin whispered in his ear, "Do it," and something in her tone made him slowly bring his hand up. He couldn't stand to shake it; he just sort of grazed his fingers and then dropped his hand again.

"Good," said Fletcher. Then he looked at Nate and slanted his head meaningfully toward the door. Nate stretched his arms and said, "Well, I think I'll call it a night," and left the room, trailed by his wife.

Fletcher waited until he was gone, then said, "Dylan, I'm sincerely sorry. You're a guest here, and my brother's behavior is unforgivable. Please accept my personal apologies."

"I understand," Dylan said tightly. "It's not the first time, nor I suppose the last." Somehow Dylan felt that it was his brother's rudeness, not what he said, that Fletcher found objectionable. Dylan had a lifetime of experience in bigotry, and its odor was strong in the room. Even after Nate's exit.

"C'mon, Dylan," said Kristin, standing up. "We've gotta get going. We're off to the casinos tonight," she said to the room at large. She prodded his ribs painfully, and he got the message. He said good night politely, then followed her out of the room. When they were in the hallway leading to the bedrooms, she stopped.

"Just a minute," she said. "I forgot something. Wait here." She started back to the dining room.

Something made him follow her. She reentered the dining room, walked over to her father, and said the words, "Thanks, Daddy," then kissed him on the forehead.

CHAPTER THIRTEEN

Sunday morning they slept late, made love twice, and had a big breakfast of sausage, eggs, and waffles. After breakfast, Kristin showed him a map of the mountain and proposed a hike on the Echo Lake trail. Together they picked out a route, then Kristin went back to her bedroom to get dressed.

Dylan was reading the Sunday paper on the deck when Fletcher came outside and pulled up a chair. He hadn't been at breakfast.

"This morning I got some bad news from the church," Fletcher said.

"Oh?" Dylan put down the paper.

"Nicole Girard died Friday night."

Dylan sucked in his breath. "What? She's dead?"

"Yes. Henry Girard was told she died of AIDS-related complications."

"That's terrible. I can't believe it." Dylan was truly shocked. It seemed very strange that she should die so suddenly, and he was surprised by how upset he felt.

Fletcher continued, "Henry asked me to call Dr. Argent, and I just got off the phone with him. Nicole apparently suffered a prolonged period of 'apnea'—

respiratory arrest—while she was asleep. There was no pain."

In other words, she stopped breathing, thought Dylan. "But why? She was in good health, except for the ADC."

Fletcher clucked his tongue. "*Except* for the ADC? She had AIDS, Dylan. There's so much we don't know about AIDS. What we *do* know is that she had a lot of nerve damage and was taking lots of drugs."

"Argent thinks it was the medication? An overdose?" It certainly sounded likely.

"I'm sure she was receiving appropriate dosages for each type of medication. However, Dr. Argent thinks there might have been an unpredictable drug interaction."

"Will there be an autopsy?"

"Argent ordered one." Fletcher sighed and leaned back in his chair. "The funeral is tomorrow. I owe it to Henry to be there, so I'm flying home tonight, after dinner. I'll send the plane back for you and Kristin tomorrow."

"No," said Dylan.

"Pardon me?"

"I'm sorry, I just meant—I'd like to fly back with you, if that's all right. I want to attend the funeral."

"Of course, you're welcome to come." Fletcher grimaced and continued, "But I'm not gonna be the one to tell Kristin. She won't like having her weekend cut short."

"I know. I'll tell her." He wasn't looking forward to it. "Uh, do you have Henry Girard's phone number?"

"Certainly," said Fletcher, getting up. "Follow me."

■   ■   ■

The hiking trip didn't go well, although it started pleasantly enough. The mountain trail had some breathtaking views, and the air was so clear and sweet it could be bottled and sold in the cities. The Rockies spread around them, snowcaps and fir trees and the smell of pine.

Kristin wore a thick thermal T-shirt and shorts that showed her muscular thighs to advantage. Her hair was tied back in a ponytail, and she looked adorably competent. Dylan wore his old jeans, a red flannel shirt he had bought in Tahoe, and a backpack filled with crusty french bread, various cheeses, and four bottles of Corona Light beer.

They chatted amiably as they climbed the trail, seldom seeing other hikers, and Dylan reminded himself how lucky he was. He had never hoped to have a relationship with someone like Kristin, someone who instinctively knew that he really didn't want to be so serious, someone who could make him forget all his responsibilities, even for a while. Someone who loved sex as much—or more—than he did. *I can't let myself screw this up*, he thought.

They reached the halfway point of the hike, a small campground overlooking one of the ski trails, and placed the bottles in a small stream. When the beer was cold, they ate the lunch sitting cross-legged on the top of a large, smooth boulder. Dylan decided Kristin was relaxed enough.

"Your father is flying home tonight." he said abruptly.

"What?" She stopped chewing her bread and stared at him. "Daddy's leaving? Why?"

"He has to attend a funeral."

"A funeral? Whose?"

"Nicole Girard's. You remember, the woman who

jumped out of the window at the dedication ceremony. We talked about her at your father's church. She died yesterday. And . . . I'm going back with him. For the funeral."

Kristin looked away. Finally she said, "You're leaving a day early just to go to the funeral of some crazy woman?"

Dylan felt suddenly defensive. "Well, yes, that's right."

Her face flushed. She picked up a rock, stood up, and threw the rock viciously at a tree. "Why don't you tell me the real reason."

"That is the real reason," he said, puzzled. "I'm sorry to lose our last day, but it's my duty. Anyway, I already told Mr. Girard I was coming—"

"Bullshit. You just want to go."

"It's got nothing to do with you, Kristin."

"Then why don't you call Girard, apologize, and say you can't make it after all? Say you couldn't change your travel plans or something."

That sounded eminently reasonable. "I can't do that."

"Why not?"

The truth, he suddenly realized, was that Nicole had affected him in some way, had touched him deeply—and she also was the subject of his very first trial. "I have to," he said lamely.

Kristin's lips compressed to a thin line. She didn't reply, just turned around and started walking.

"Wait a minute—where are you going?"

The answer was obvious.

She took that well, Dylan thought. After a moment, he cleaned up the campsite, finished his beer, and followed her down the mountain.

CHAPTER FOURTEEN

The Memorial Day funeral service at the St. Charles First Evangelical Church was brief but moving. Reverend Fletcher gave the eulogy, speaking eloquently of Nicole's "life of excellence," her successes and failures, how a cruel disease had taken her far too early. Henry and Amanda Girard sat in the first pew, eyes glowing with the light of faith. Occasionally their eyes would drift to the closed casket.

Fletcher spoke without notes about minor and major details of Nicole's life. Either he was a remarkably quick study or he had known Nicole far better than Dylan suspected. After Fletcher's eulogy, several other family members rose to say a few words—an uncle, a couple of cousins, an aunt.

Opposite the Girards and Dylan sat Charlene McConnell and a few women and men in their thirties: Nicole's friends. There was a brief moment of tension as Charlene started toward the podium; Henry Girard walked forward as if to prevent her. Fletcher caught the interchange and stepped between them, taking Charlene by the elbow and guiding her to the side of the church. They talked quietly for a few moments, every eye upon them; Charlene first shook her head emphatically, then nodded. Fletcher escorted her to the podium, causing a furious outbreak of whispering among the audience—even a few raised voices. Dylan caught the words "shameful" and "outrage."

Charlene ignored it. "Nicole Girard was my friend," she said without preamble. Her eyes were moist, but she stared fiercely at the congregation. "And I loved her."

There were a few gasps from the congregation, but no one said anything in the face of Charlene's obviously deep emotion. "Nicole Girard," she continued, "had a tough life. Not because she had AIDS, but because she never got to do what she really wanted. I've heard people talk about her drawing and her sculpture, like it was a sideline, some sort of hobby, not her real job. Well, it wasn't a hobby. More than anything else, Nicole wanted to be an artist. Wanted to spend all day, every day, creatively. She never had the money—or the courage—to do it. Maybe she wasn't given enough encouragement, I don't know. I know I tried." She looked steadily at the Girards. "And most of all, Nicole was a warm, loving person. A *giving* person."

Charlene paused to rub her eyes with the heel of her hand. "Well, Nicole, it didn't work out. But as long as your friends and *family*—" she looked at her group of friends, "remember you, you'll—" She stopped. Tears finally sprouted, and without wiping them away she turned from the podium and walked to her seat.

There was a moment of silence before Fletcher cleared his throat and the church's regular minister stepped forward to give directions to the gravesite.

■   ■   ■

The Gates of Harmony Cemetery, owned and oper-
ated by the Evangelical Foundation of the Midwest,
was five acres of land on a bluff overlooking the
Missouri River. Old-growth maple and oak trees
shaded many of the plots, and soft river breezes blew
across the granite tombstones planted in neat rows,
waiting for the final harvest.

Henry and Amanda Girard had a reserved
gravesite, big enough for the whole family—a choice
plot with a river view. The morning sunlight fell on
the newly overturned soil at the grave, and everywhere there was the moist and redolent air of early
summer. About fifty mourners came from the church
and formed a circle around Fletcher as he said some
final words.

Dylan found himself compelled to see this
through to the end, even though memories of his
mother's funeral inevitably crowded into his head.
Then there had only been himself, his father, his sister, and a few of his father's friends. He closed his
eyes and could almost see the drizzly cold morning,
the bored funeral director, the feeble poem read by
his father while Dylan held Janis's hand.

Opening his eyes, he watched Nicole's coffin
lowered into the grave, accompanied by sounds of
muffled weeping from Amanda Girard.

Standing apart from the Girards was Charlene
McConnell, head held high, surrounded by her
group of friends, avoided by the other mourners. *By
all the white folk*, Dylan couldn't help thinking. As
the ceremony concluded, he walked toward her. She
saw him coming and met him halfway.

"Nice of you to come," she said neutrally.

"Least I could do," Dylan said, instantly regretting it.

"Yeah, that's for sure," she said, but there was a trace of a smile on her lips. "More than that doctor of hers did, anyway."

Dylan had noticed the surprising absence of Dr. Argent. "Perhaps he had an emergency."

Charlene looked at him, then said, "You know how she died?"

"Uh, well, not really. Dr. Argent said it was respiratory arrest. Complications of AIDS."

Charlene snorted derisively. "That's bullshit. Nobody who knows anything about AIDS would buy that. I've seen at least a dozen people die of AIDS—close friends—and believe me, I was paying attention. Not one was anywhere near as healthy, as strong as Nicole." She reached out and tapped his chest forcefully. "Whatever she died from, it wasn't AIDS."

Dylan noticed, on the periphery of his vision, that Fletcher was edging through the crowd toward him. "Well, they've done an autopsy. That should tell us."

"Are you really that naive?" she said, just as Fletcher came up and put his hand on Dylan's shoulder.

"Please excuse the interruption, but I really need to speak with Mr. Ice for a moment."

Charlene raised her eyebrows. "That's all right. This conversation wasn't going anywhere. Goodbye, Dylan. See you in court." She turned and walked away.

"That doesn't sound good," said Fletcher.

Dylan shook his head. "I don't know what she means."

"Well," mused Fletcher, "I guess we'll find out

soon enough. Dylan, walk me back to my limo." It was an order.

As they walked, Fletcher said, "I sent my plane back to Tahoe to pick up Kristin. She'll be home tonight."

"I'm not sure she'll still talk to me."

Fletcher laughed. "Don't worry about that—my daughter angers quickly, but soon cools. Believe me, I know." They had reached his limo, and the driver opened the door for Fletcher. "Just one more thing." He put his hand on Dylan's shoulder. "Henry Girard asked my advice about how to wrap up Nicole's legal affairs. The estate, I mean. I suggested that he let you continue to handle things, and he thought that was a good idea. Don't worry about a retainer—I'll take care of it. Okay?"

Dylan thought it was strange that Henry didn't ask himself. And he really didn't want to do it. It would be a constant reminder of Nicole's death and meant he would, inevitably, have to deal with Charlene. She would know where Nicole's bank accounts were, whatever assets she might have. There would have to be an inventory of her possessions. On the other hand, it meant doing a favor for Fletcher. "Of course."

"Good. It means a lot to me that Henry doesn't have to concern himself with this. He's got enough to worry about." He pointed at Girard, slowly pushing Amanda's wheelchair down the paved path toward the parking lot.

"Yes," Dylan said. "That's true."

Dylan drove to his apartment, intending to change clothes before picking up Janis at Barry's house. He found the door unlocked.

Dylan's first reaction was anger. Janis must have stopped by the apartment while he was away and neglected to lock the door when she left. Typical.

As he walked into the apartment, however, he had a queasy sense that something was not right. "Janis?" he called. Then again, louder, "Janis? Are you home?"

Someone is here, he thought with sudden certainty. He started backing slowly toward the door, then stopped, straining his senses. He heard nothing.

Dylan had seen this situation in countless movies. Some character entered an apartment or house despite the evidence of an intruder, then, instead of leaving and calling the police, continued on to his doom.

But what if he was wrong? What if there was no one here, and Janis had left the door open? After all, there was no sign of forced entry. And everything in the living room looked to be in order. It could be very embarrassing.

Yeah, but what if I'm right? He answered himself.

There were no unusual sounds, just the hum of the refrigerator. You're paranoid, he thought, and started forward, walking down the hallway to his bedroom, striding in confidently.

There was no one there, not even in the walk-in closet that he casually glanced into. Everything was in order, including his small collection of jewelry on the dressing table—his college class ring, a gold chain, a fake Rolex.

More relaxed now, he went down the hall to look into Janis's room. It was bound to be a mess, but he wanted to see it. Her unmade bed could be seen directly from the hall; the rest of the room looked like a tornado had touched down. He sighed and entered the room.

As he crossed the threshold, he felt a presence at the same instant as an arm came around the door and grabbed his right arm, pulling him forward and throwing him violently onto the floor. He landed painfully on his left arm and chest, knocking his breath away, his chin burrowing into the carpet. This was followed by a kick to his kidney that felt like a hot hammer, and everything went black for a few seconds, before waves of searing pain.

His eyes were shut tight, not enough breath to scream his agony, as he was jerked upward into a sitting position. A stinging slap to his face opened his eyes and brought his breath back.

Barely visible through tears of pain, Dylan saw a face like a black moon. A face he had seen before: the man in the red hat, the gang member who had tried to attack Janis. There was another face, too, coming into focus behind the man, grinning.

The man grabbed Dylan's shirtfront and pulled his face close to his own. His eyes were bloodshot, the dark face smooth and expressionless. "Where is she, man?" he asked, his breath foul.

"Who?" Dylan croaked, although he knew the answer. That earned him another slap, hard enough to see stars, but it also gave him time to think. When his vision cleared, he croaked, "I don't know. I thought she was here. I've been away for the weekend."

The man considered this long enough for Dylan to say, "Who are you? What do you want?"

"What I want, nigger, is your sister."

"Why?"

"She got something I want. The bitch stole it."

"What is it? Let me pay for it."

"Fuck," said the man, pulling his face back a bit, "you ain't got that much money."

"He be lying," said another voice—the second man from the parking lot, tall and rangy. He had a large sore over his right eye.

"Maybe," the first man said. "But she ain't been here for a while, we know that." He looked at Dylan. "Lissen, Oreo, you tell that bitch if she wanna live, she come see me and bring the bag, and it better be all there. You hear?"

"I don't know what this is about, I told you—"

Whap! Another slap to his face that nearly blinded him with pain. His mouth was suddenly full of blood, and it felt like a couple of teeth were loose. He managed to say, "Okay."

The man grunted, then pulled out his knife, an enormous blade that seemed to fill up the room. He brought it up to Dylan's nose and sneered, "You be dead meat, nigger, if I gotta come back." With that, he stood up and gave Dylan a parting kick to the ribs.

When he could breathe again, they were both gone, and he slowly got to his feet. He staggered to the bathroom, barely making it to the sink before he started vomiting blood.

Now what? Call the police?

No. First he had to talk to Janis. He lurched back into the bedroom, to the phone.

"I'm so sorry, Dylan," Janis said, tenderly rubbing dried blood from the corner of Dylan's mouth. "I never thought they'd come back."

They were in the hall bathroom. Dylan sat on

the edge of the bathtub, bare chested, while Janis and Elaine evaluated the damage. "Ow!" he said, as Elaine touched the bruises on his side.

"You probably have some cracked or broken ribs," she said. "You've got to go to the emergency room for X rays."

"It hurts when I breathe. Is that a sign of a broken rib?"

Elaine shook her head. "I don't know. Dylan, you have to call the police."

"No!" said Janis.

"Why not?" Elaine said.

"It wouldn't do any good!"

Dylan thought for a moment, then asked Elaine to excuse them for a moment. When she closed the bathroom door behind her, Dylan said, "All right, Groovy. What did he want?"

She folded her hands across her chest.

"Heroin, I guess. What did you do with it?"

Still no answer. "All right, then. I'll call the police. I'll let them ask you these questions." He stood slowly.

"Don't," she said fiercely. "Or I won't be here."

He sat again. "What do you mean?"

"If you call the police, I'll walk out that door and never come back." She stared at him, and he could tell she meant it. "I know where to go."

"That's your choice," he said gravely. "But it doesn't have to happen. If you just tell me the truth, I promise I won't call the police." *Unless*, he added silently, *you're in danger*.

Suddenly her tough facade broke. "I don't have it anymore," she blubbered. "Dylan, if I did, I'd give it back. I never wanted you to get hurt!" She came forward and leaned into him. It hurt, but he put his arms around her and gently patted her back.

"I couldn't stand it if you were hurt, Dylan," she whispered. "You're the only one . . ." she couldn't finish the sentence, and he knew what she was thinking. The memory came back, unbidden.

Angela walked into the tiny living room, stumbling over Janis's Barbie doll. She looked down at the doll as if it were some loathsome creature, then kicked it against the wall.

Dylan stepped forward and grabbed Angela's arm. She only got hostile like this when she was having a bad trip; the only cure for that was time. But he had to get her away from Janis. Janis couldn't understand how Mommy could be so mean.

"I told you to keep your crap off the floor," Angela said to Janis. "Didn't I? Didn't I tell you that?"

"I'm sorry, Mommy," said Janis, backing away.

"C'mon, Angela," said Dylan, pulling on her arm. "Let's get some milk."

She turned to face him, then cringed away, a look of awful fear on her face. But just as quickly, the fear changed to anger, to fury, and she screamed at him, "You're not my son! You're not my son! You're a goat!"

She started cackling, and he almost got her into the kitchen before she suddenly stopped and pulled her arm back. He saw her eyes narrow, and then bam! she slapped him so hard it made his teeth rattle. He reached out to grab her arms, but her strength was amazing. She slapped him again, just as hard, then caught him a glancing blow as he ducked.

"Mommy! Mommy! Please stop, Mommy!" Janis screamed.

And then Angela turned to face her . . .

Dylan shook his head. No.

He hugged Janis again. "It's okay, Groovy. Just tell me everything."

"It's pretty simple," Dylan told Barry later.

They were in Barry's house, Dylan sitting awkwardly on a kitchen chair, trying to hold his upper body straight, waiting for the codeine to take effect. He had gone to the emergency room—saying he had fallen down a flight of stairs—and X rays revealed two cracked ribs on his left side. They would heal by themselves, the ER doctor told him, but would be painful for a while, until the swelling and bruises receded.

Dylan continued, "The guy's name is LaShawn, LaShawn Johnson. He gave her a kilo of heroin to hold when the cops busted one of his gang members. She put it in her school locker, and when she looked for it again it was gone. He's been after her since that time. She got depressed and scared, and the more scared she got, the more drugs she used."

"God, what she must have been going through!"

"I know. But the police will want her to turn in her friends. She says she'll run away first, and I believe her. She's sixteen years old; the streets are full of runaways much younger."

"That's true, I guess. But what else can you do?"

If you can't fight, and you can't run, thought Dylan, there's only one thing left—hide. "There are several court-sponsored drug rehab programs. One of them is residential."

"And she'll agree?"

"She won't know until it's too late."

"I hope you're right." Barry paused, then said,

"It may be a blessing in disguise that you came home early and had this little adventure."

Dylan groaned. "You wouldn't say that if the shit were kicked out of *you*. I'm lucky they didn't slit my throat." He gingerly touched his injured ribs and continued, "Also, I may have screwed up things with Kristin."

Barry looked at him strangely. "That, too, may be a blessing."

"Why do you say that?"

"I told you before—Kristin isn't for you. You're bewitched now, but you'll see that I'm right."

"Bewitched?" Dylan chuckled.

"I know it sounds corny, but I'm telling you, she's no good."

"She's *very* good," Dylan said flippantly, thinking of that smooth, freckled skin. "You've just been married too long."

"It's like a drug, isn't it? The sex, I mean?"

He wasn't joking, Dylan realized. "Yeah, I guess so. In a way. But it's not a drug, it's just screwing."

"Where do you think the urge comes from? A hormone called testosterone. And you've got an overdose."

"And you don't?"

Barry grinned. "Maybe I do, maybe that's my problem, too. Or maybe it's inevitable that wives can't satisfy their husbands. God knows I'm miserable sometimes."

"You're miserable?"

"No, no, not like you mean. I'm happily married, as they say. You know I love Elaine." He stood and paced around the room, then wheeled to face Dylan. "When you tell me about Kristin, it isn't easy . . . Elaine would kill me if I told you this, but she comes to bed in an old flannel nightgown, even in summer, and socks! When we first got married, she used to jump into bed stark naked, and we'd spend the whole night making love, talking, laughing, snuggling." He smiled wistfully. "God, I miss that!"

"Maybe you're being unrealistic. I mean, doesn't that happen to all married couples after a while? I mean, she's had two kids."

"Of course it does," Barry said, looking embarrassed. "Of course it does. Sorry, bud. Guess I lost it. The point I'm trying to make—badly, I'm sure—is that you're infatuated with Kristin. I wonder if you realize what you're getting into. . . ."

"I'm a big boy, Barry."

"Yeah, yeah. Ah, the hell with it." Barry grinned. "I'm jealous. Let's get a beer." He headed for the kitchen.

Dylan limped behind him.

CHAPTER FIFTEEN

It was almost a relief to get back to the firm on Tuesday, to the ordinary problems of litigants and intraoffice politics. There was a pile of mail to prioritize, motions to oppose, phone calls to return, widows and orphans to evict. He had barely dug into the pile when he got a phone call from Hudson. Jesus, he thought, maybe I should just set up a desk in his office.

"How about lunch?" said Hudson.

"Sure!" said Dylan. Hudson only rarely took an associate to lunch.

"I've got to go out of the office for a while. Can you meet me at the Pavilion in an hour?"

Dylan agreed, and hung up the phone, amazed. Not only lunch, but lunch at the partners' private dining room.

The Pavilion was a French restaurant not far from the firm's office. The owner was a longtime client, and the firm rented out a large dining room for the private use of the partners. Three waiters were always available for lunch and dinner.

The room was full of potted plants, dark paneling, expensive prints on the walls. Refinement and gentility. Dylan sat at a table with Hudson, looking over the menu, thinking, I could get used to this.

After they ordered, Hudson leaned back in his chair. "Christ, you look awful."

Dylan fingered the large bruise on his cheek. "It's beginning to fade," he said feebly.

"Don't tell me—you walked into a door."

"That's right." He had no intention of telling Hudson he had been beaten up by a drug dealer. Such things did not happen to Cameron Barr associates. "It jumped right out at me."

Hudson chuckled and took a drink of his bourbon. Dylan looked around the room; it was filling up with the firm's partners, mostly white, middle-aged men in $1,500 suits. A few of the partners had guests—clients or opposing attorneys they wanted to impress—and Dylan caught a few looking curiously at him. Probably wondering if he was Hudson's new protégé.

"So tell me about your trip to Tahoe."

"It was a lot of fun," said Dylan, understanding that Hudson's sudden interest had nothing to do with concern for his recreational activities. "Reverend Fletcher has a beautiful place, right on the lake. Unfortunately, I had to leave early."

"For the funeral. Yes, I heard. Very sad. I understood you went to Tahoe in Fletcher's private plane?"

"That's right."

Hudson nodded, then asked him some routine questions about his case inventory. Through lunch, Hudson did most of the talking, mainly war stories about difficult cases that he had pulled from the brink of disaster.

Finally, as they were sipping coffee, Hudson returned to the subject of Fletcher. "Dylan, you know your relationship with Reverend Fletcher can be a real asset to the firm."

"Uh, how is that?"

"Well, it never hurts to spend time with an important client. And Fletcher is our single most important client, you must know that."

He did. "Well, sure, but I was there to be with his daughter, not him."

"Kristin," Hudson said with a leer.

"That's right," Dylan said rather defensively.

"That's fine. Young love and all that. But I also happen to know that Reverend Fletcher has taken a personal interest in you. You know, he specifically asked that you be allowed to handle the Girard hearing on your own."

"What?" Dylan nearly spilled his coffee.

"I know, that's not what I told you before. But the fact is, he knew you were chafing at how long it was taking you to get into the courtroom, and he wanted to help you out. Of course, I wouldn't have let you do it if I didn't think you were capable."

"I see," said Dylan, not sure of what to make of all this.

"Anyway," continued Hudson, "the point is, Fletcher has taken a *positive* interest in you. For the first time, I might add."

"For the first time?"

"Well, you know, you're not the only lawyer in the firm that has dated Kristin."

"So?"

Hudson sighed. "Don't be dense, Dylan. Reverend Fletcher didn't like the other guy, and when things got too . . . hot . . . he let us know about it."

"Wait a minute," said Dylan, remembering what Barry had told him. "You mean you fired the guy? Because Fletcher didn't like him?"

"No, no," Hudson waved his hand impatiently. "Nothing like that. We just transferred him to one of our other offices."

"I see."

"We're not proud of that. But the fact is, Fletcher could pull his business like that—" he snapped his fingers. "There are plenty of other firms."

"But Cameron Barr could survive, couldn't it? I mean, we can't be that dependent on him."

Hudson stared at him. "Probably. Although these days, who knows? It's not like the old days, there's no client loyalty. They jump from firm to firm just to get a better hourly rate. Other clients might follow. And it would mean a significant dent in our income. But that's not the point. I'm trying to say that you can help the firm and yourself by—shall we say—remaining in the picture."

Dylan was finally seeing the point. "Look, we've only been dating for a few weeks—"

"I'm not saying you have to marry the girl, for God's sake. I just hope that you're smart enough to stay with her until *she* gets tired of you."

"That's no problem," Dylan said. Then he blurted, "I think I'm falling in love with her."

Hudson laughed. "I can see that. But there's something else you can do, too."

"Yes?" said Dylan, mystified.

"You can talk me up."

"Excuse me?"

"Talk me up. Tell Fletcher what kind of guy I am, how I handle things, how I run the firm's most important department."

Dylan looked to see if he was smiling. Either Hudson was a consummate actor, or he was dead serious. "I'm not sure I understand," he said slowly.

"It's no mystery. Right now, Fletcher's primary contact with the firm is through"—he lowered his voice—"Kaster." He nearly spit the name. "Kaster represented Fletcher's church in the old days, and everything—negotiation of fees, case strategies, liaison with in-house counsel in Fletcher's companies—it all goes through him. Kaster controls Fletcher, and because he controls the firm's biggest client, he controls the firm. *Capish?*"

"Yes."

"Now if you were to imply to Fletcher that he should switch his loyalty to me—"

"That hardly seems likely, just on my advice."

"You'd be surprised. Maybe he's ready to do it anyway; maybe all he needs is a little nudge. In any event, it can't hurt to try, can it?"

"Uh, no."

"Good. Then you'll do it?"

There was a plaintive edge to Hudson's voice, a certain pleading quality. Hudson *needed* him to say yes. He seemed desperate. Dylan had a sudden dizzying feeling of power. "I'll try."

"Excellent. And don't worry, Dylan. If this works out the way I hope it will, you'll be *very* glad you helped. You might even"—he pointed around him—"get to eat here on a regular basis."

"I understand," said Dylan.

It was just a form letter from University Hospital, almost lost among the other daily mail in Dylan's in-box, and it puzzled him. The letter was from the Medical Records Department, rubber-stamped by some minor functionary, and the little rectangle captioned "Insufficient, Improper, or Stale Authorization" was checked. Next to the check mark was handwritten *"Per Mark Argent, MD."* That was all.

Dylan looked at it for a moment, then pulled open his active file drawer and extracted the Girard file. He flipped open the inside cover, found a phone number, and dialed. He left a message, then turned to other cases.

Late that afternoon, Dr. Argent returned his call. "What is it?" Argent asked, without any preliminary.

"Uh, sorry to bother you, Doctor, but I just got a letter today from your Medical Records Department. I requested Nicole Girard's medical chart, and I got a letter back saying insufficient authorization. It had your name next to it."

"Yes, so?"

Dylan cleared his throat. "Well, I don't understand. What was insufficient?"

"Dylan," said Argent in a condescending tone, "as you know, there are special considerations when dealing with records of AIDS patients. State and federal law imposes higher standards than with other records. Because of this, any patient records released from MIRI must be personally authorized by me or my delegate."

"Well, certainly, I understand that, but—"

"And in this case, I couldn't give my consent because the authorization was not signed by the duly appointed executor of the estate of the patient."

"What?" said Dylan incredulously. "But it was signed by the next of kin, by the patient's father, whom you know personally! That's always—"

"You're not listening, Dylan. The Missouri code clearly states that medical records of a decedent may only be released to the duly appointed personal representative."

"Look," said Dylan, losing his temper but not caring, "this is ridiculous. Why would you want to keep these records from the Girards?"

"I don't have any desire to do that," Argent said coldly. "I'm surprised that you, a lawyer, wouldn't understand my position. As soon as you get Mr. Girard appointed executor, I will be happy to release the records. Good-bye." And he hung up.

"Fuck you," said Dylan into the silence, surprising himself. He rarely used strong language. It wasn't just the denial of the records, it was Argent's whole attitude, his patent lack of respect, his unwillingness to even go through the form of polite refusal.

It seemed only fitting, then, that Rhonda should enter his office at that moment, carrying a manila envelope. "This just arrived by messenger. It's regarding the Girard case, and you've got the file." She placed it on his in-box and left.

He stared at it for a moment, then picked it up. Rhonda had opened the envelope across the end, not down the long side, as he preferred, and he pulled out the pleading. "Opposition to Petition for Probate," it read, "And Cross Petition for Appointment of Charlene McConnell as Personal Representative." It was signed by Pamela Holtz, attorney for the petitioner.

"Of course," Dylan murmured, not really surprised. And there was more—a whole separate set of pleadings underneath this one. Mystified, he pulled them out. They were stamped "courtesy copies" and bore the caption "Charlene McConnell v. University Hospital, a public corporation, the Midwest Immunological Research Institute, Inc., and Mark Argent,

MD." The title of the pleading was "Complaint for
Wrongful Death—Medical Negligence."

"What the hell?" Dylan said.

Hudson shook his head sorrowfully. "She's really
gone off the deep end this time," he said, thumbing
through the pleadings.

Dylan carefully placed his cup of coffee on the
side table next to his chair. He had had some time to
think between his receipt of the documents, his call
to Hudson, and his summons to Hudson's office.
"It's really just a logical extension of the arguments
Holtz made at the guardianship hearing. If you
accept her premise that a domestic partner should
have the same constitutional rights as a spouse, then
McConnell should be allowed to be executor."

"But what about the wrongful death suit? Where's
her standing to sue? She's not a statutory heir!"

"She is if you buy the domestic partner argument."

"You know that isn't gonna happen. Certainly
not by a trial judge, and not by our supreme court.
She's doing this for one reason."

Dylan gave the only answer he could think of,
although it didn't make sense either. "You think
she's trying to get a nuisance settlement?"

Hudson snorted. "Nah. Pamela isn't after
money, although maybe that's the reason her client is
doing it. No, for Pamela the reason is simple—pub-
licity. It's all part of this radical gay rights agenda.
She's got plenty of friends in the media, they'll play
this up for all it's worth."

"But it'll be over quickly. The hospital's lawyers
will file a motion to dismiss, and that's it."

"Yeah, but then she can appeal. She can give seminars on the case, she can lobby the legislature using this case as an example. Oh, it's perfect for her. Made to order."

Having met Holtz, Dylan didn't share Hudson's opinion of her motivations, but he kept quiet. After what Barry had told him about Hudson's relationship with Holtz, he wasn't about to get in the way of Hudson's enmity.

"Well, maybe she'll give up after she loses the estate motion. We've got a hearing on that next week."

"You're dreaming."

"Well, I'm still young," Dylan said, trying to lighten Hudson's mood. "Anyway, there's nothing we can do about the wrongful death case. That's the hospital's and Argent's problem."

Hudson tapped his chin thoughtfully. "Yes, that's true." He swiveled in his chair and faced his computer terminal, an obvious dismissal. "Thanks for letting me know about this. I'll want to see your response to her opposition."

"Of course," said Dylan.

"I'm sorry, Turk," said the President. "But I've got to make a change."

Turk Finnegan knew what was coming. He stood slowly and looked around the Oval Office, as if expecting something or someone would rescue him. He returned his gaze to the President, who had the grace to look embarrassed and uncomfortable. Turk ran his fingers through his thinning gray hair and said, "It doesn't have to be this way, Mr. President. You don't have to do this."

The President looked even more pained, if that were possible. He pushed back from his desk and said, "Yes, I do, and you know it. You've done a hell of a good job, and I'm grateful for it. But with the election coming up, you'd be more useful to me over at campaign headquarters—"

"Is that the story for public consumption?" Finnegan asked bitterly. "Do you really think the press will buy that? Everyone knows that Craig has been undercutting me, how you've let him take over scheduling, how he's—"

"Turk!" said the President sharply. "That's enough!"

Finnegan took a deep breath, forcing himself to hold his anger in check. Banfield had made his decision, and Finnegan knew he wasn't going to win an argument with him. Hagen had done his work well, playing the Washington power game like a virtuoso.

For almost four years, Finnegan had been the loyal soldier, ignoring the thousand cuts and slights received from the small group of Banfield loyalists known as the Minnesota Mafia. The President had hired Finnegan because of his background on Capitol Hill, his reputation for independence and fairness, and his ability to deliver the goods. Banfield's military reorganization program was successful, the economy sound, and the White House free of the staff blunders and outright scandals that had characterized previous administrations.

And yet it wasn't enough. A few months before the election, Banfield was dumping him; he had served his purpose. Of course he was expected to go quietly, like a good soldier.

Finnegan sucked in his stomach and stood as straight as his bad back allowed. "Mr. President," he said formally, "I don't want to work in the campaign. I think a complete separation is better."

"Now, Turk, c'mon. You're just angry, and I understand. But I really need you." Banfield stood also. "Look, take a couple of weeks, think it over—"

Finnegan stuck out his hand. "It's been a great ride, Tom. A great ride. I wish you all the luck in the world."

Banfield took his hand and shook it. The President looked relieved there was no further argument. This was the man for whom Finnegan had ruined his health, his marriage, and maybe his career. In the final analysis, just another politician.

"I'll be out of my office by tomorrow morning," said Finnegan as he left the room. In the outer office, he wasn't surprised to see Craig Hagen perched casually on a corner of the secretary's desk. He walked over and said, "Congratulations, Craig. You're the new Chief of Staff."

Hagen slid off the desk. "I'm sorry it had to happen this way, Turk. No hard feelings?"

"Of course not. We all want what's best for the President, don't we?"

"Yes, of course." Hagen looked puzzled.

Not what you were expecting from the Turk, is it, you fuckhead? thought Finnegan as he smiled genially. You thought the Turk would go down swinging.

Finnegan was still smiling as he went into his office and closed his door. He pulled a cardboard box down from his closet shelf and began throwing his personal articles into it. They probably were all breathing a sigh of relief, even the President, thinking that Turk wasn't such a hard-ass after all.

They were wrong, of course. If they thought they could dump the Turk this way, they were deluded. He would get even. Hagen was just a prick, interchangeable with a thousand other guys; but Banfield—Banfield owed him more.

He had a lot of packing to do.

Kristin's apartment was like Kristin: uninhibited. The furniture, though expensive, was a mix of modern and traditional. There was an antique french provincial desk and a sectional sofa; a polished wood armoire and Eames chairs. Her bed was an incongruous canopied four-poster with lace flouncing.

They lay in that bed, awash in the afterglow of sex, Kristin's silky hair spread out on the pillow like a splash of red paint. She put her hand under her head and said, "You really sent Janis away? I can't believe it."

This was the first time they had seen each other since Tahoe, the first time they had talked since he called to tell her he was not returning, and why. She had been sympathetic about Janis, but distant, and he feared he had screwed up the relationship for good.

But then she called him at the office after his lunch with Hudson, offering to cook dinner. She said nothing about their prior argument.

When he arrived at her apartment there had been no talk. They had attacked each other fiercely, pulling each other's clothes off in the foyer, barely making it to the living room before screwing like sailors on liberty. The pain in Dylan's ribs went completely unnoticed. They continued their amorous progress into Kristin's bedroom, making love again—Kristin on top, to prevent further damage to his ribs—before they felt momentarily sated.

"God, I missed you," Dylan said.

"I can see that!"

"No, not just for the sex," said Dylan quickly. "I mean, I missed talking to you."

"Me too," she said neutrally. "Give me all the details."

Dylan told her more about the attack at his apartment, and his solution. "I had to put her in a residential program," he said. "There's no other way to protect her from the gang, unless I hired a twenty-four-hour bodyguard."

"But what about school?"

"It's almost over for the year. Anyway, she's no student."

"And you have no family she could stay with?"

"None that either of us would tolerate. Hopefully, she'll get herself straight; meanwhile I'll figure out what to do next." He breathed out. "The hard part was convincing her to go. But that's where the damage they did me"—he motioned at his chest and face—"helped. She couldn't deny the danger we're both in."

Kristin stroked his arm. "That you are *still* in. What if that guy comes back?"

"I don't think so. He's out of his league, and I think he knows it. He's used to the streets, to dealing with other gang members. If something happens to me, he knows the cops will be all over him."

"Well, that'll be comforting for those of us at your funeral," said Kristin with a grin.

"Yeah. I know. Also, I've decided to get a gun."

After a few seconds she said, "I think that's a good idea."

That's what I like about her, Dylan thought. No false fluttering, no "do you really want to do that, guns are dangerous" yipping. "Only problem is," he continued, "I don't know how to shoot. Guess I'll have to take lessons."

"I'll teach you. *I* wasn't raised by hippies, you know. My family all know how to shoot. I'll help you choose a pistol. You probably would buy something with a short barrel that's impossible to aim and wouldn't knock down a mosquito."

"Well, I—"

"You need a long-barreled .38 or 9 millimeter," she continued.

"Okay, okay," Dylan said, grinning. "You can be my gun consultant."

"What did your boss say about what happened?"

"He doesn't know. It doesn't affect my job, and I prefer that he doesn't know about my personal life, especially Janis. Anyway, he's got other things on his mind." He had debated whether he should tell Kristin about Hudson's strange request that he try to influence her father. It could be interpreted the wrong way; on the other hand, he wanted to share it with someone, and he couldn't get any closer to Kristin than he was at the moment. He told her about his lunch with Hudson, then watched her reaction.

She laughed, a deep, rounded laugh from her bare belly. "That . . . is . . . great. I love it. *You* trying to influence my father."

"Well, you know it's not impossible. I mean, he does talk to me," he said stiffly.

She laughed again. "Dylan, Dylan." She leaned over and kissed his shoulder. "Don't take it personally. It's just that you don't know my father. A tidal wave couldn't influence my father. An earthquake. An—"

"I get the picture."

She looked at him. "You're hurt. Ah, the male ego. I'm sorry, Dylan. I shouldn't have said it just because it's the truth. I should be punished."

"It's all right."

"No, it's not. I've been bad and I deserve a spanking."

"A spanking?"

"Definitely," said Kristin, rolling over onto her chest. "Right now, please!"

"Ah," said Dylan. He slapped her ass, lightly at first, then harder, until her cheeks were as red as her hair and they both were fiercely aroused.

Life was good.

CHAPTER SIXTEEN

The White House swimming pool on the lawn dated to the Ford Administration. The previous pool, in the White House basement—used by FDR for hydrotherapy—had been filled in by Tricky Dick to make an expanded press room.

As a dedicated swimmer, President Thomas Banfield often thought about reopening the basement pool. He was a former college butterflyer who had almost qualified for the '72 Olympic team. It was well known that he did his laps daily, and no one—certainly not the press—thought it strange that he walked through the White House in a bathing suit every day.

Dr. Peter Rosati also had swum competitively in college, and at least once a week he was admitted through the east entrance, ostensibly to provide Banfield a swimming partner.

The small changing area next to the pool was one of the few places the Secret Service did not follow the President, giving Rosati the opportunity to remove his instruments from his gym bag and conduct an examination, even take a tube of blood for analysis. Although this was usually done privately, in the residence area, Banfield didn't want Rosati visiting him there too often.

On this day Rosati was just lifting his stethoscope from Banfield's chest when Hagen entered the small locker room. "Everything all right?"

"The same," said Rosati. "I want to start the antivirals."

"Not this again," said Banfield curtly, although he desperately wanted to say, *Yes, of course, don't waste another minute, give me the stuff now.* "Not until after the election."

"I thought we settled all this," Hagen said.

"We did," said Rosati, putting away his stethoscope. "But that was when I had confidence in the alternative."

The two men gaped at him, their faces suddenly serious. Hagen said, "What do you mean?"

Rosati sighed and sat down heavily on a wooden bench. "Our best plasma donor died."

"Shit!" said Hagen. "Girard? What happened?"

Rosati shrugged. "I'm not sure. Her attending physician says she had a sudden episode of respiratory distress—which means he doesn't really know. She was taking a lot of antipsychotics for her bipolar disorder; I assume that had something to do with it."

Banfield had a sinking feeling. "Peter, don't you have any other candidates? You said before that you had other leads. . . ."

Rosati walked to the doorway and looked out. Then he returned and said, "No sir, we don't. None of the other long-term nonprogressors have yielded the same results. The Girard woman was unique." He sighed. "It's my fault; I shouldn't have put so much faith in PHT. We should have started aggressive drug therapy long ago, right after your bout with PCP. Now we don't have a choice—your CD4 counts are dropping again. We've got to hit it hard with everything we've got, wipe it out if we can."

"Can you guarantee I won't suffer side effects?" Banfield asked.

"Of course not, sir. These drugs are toxic," said Rosati, a little too cheerfully. "But the side effects are tolerable, in view of the alternative."

"Tell me again."

"Fatigue, body aches, chills. The RT inhibitors, in particular, often cause severe diarrhea and nausea. In some cases, anemia and liver damage."

"Oh, that's all," muttered Hagen.

"I see," said Banfield. "And when would I take the pills?"

Rosati said crisply, "It's a pretty rigorous regimen. With your schedule, it will require a great deal of discipline."

"Go on," said Banfield.

"Anywhere from twenty-eight to fifty pills a day, depending on what drugs we put you on. Multiple doses at three- and four-hour intervals, some taken with food, others without. And the doses must be taken scrupulously on time so that the blood levels never drop enough to let the virus regrow in a resistant strain."

"Jesus," said Hagen, shaking his head.

"Let's say I do it," said Banfield, his voice dispassionate. "Then I'll be free of the virus?"

Rosati looked pained. "I can't guarantee that, Mr. President. In some people the drugs just don't work; in others, there's a dramatic improvement, then an even more dramatic relapse. There's no way to predict it."

Hagen said to Banfield, "You can't be taking

drugs that way in the middle of a campaign. Someone will notice. And if you have side effects—"

"It's not your life, Craig," said Rosati. "Anyway, if he has another episode of PCP, or something worse, your campaign will be ruined anyway."

Banfield nodded in agreement. His first bout with an AIDS opportunistic infection had been a rude awakening. He had barely made it off the course that day at Burning Tree before collapsing with pneumonia. *Pneumocystis carinii* pneumonia— PCP—was a protozoal infection to which healthy people rarely succumbed. His immune system had been unable to handle it, and he had suffered from fever, fatigue, and liver abnormalities before Rosati had knocked it out with a spectrum of drugs. They had treated him at Camp David, under the guise of a working vacation.

"Mr. President," said Hagen formally. "I strongly recommend that we wait. Maybe we can find another PHT candidate. That could give you enough protection to carry us through the election. Then you could go on vacation and start drug therapy under Dr. Rosati's supervision."

Banfield thought of living day after day, this Damoclean sword over him, his CD4 count becoming his life's barometer. He thought about the pressures of his office, the upcoming election, the humiliation if he was exposed.

He also thought of Turk Finnegan. Maybe it was a mistake, deciding not to let him in on the secret. But Craig didn't trust him and had convinced Banfield the best course was to dismiss him. He could use Turk's advice now.

Banfield said slowly, "We always knew this day might come, Craig. That's why we worked so hard to accomplish what we did in my first term. Maybe I should just withdraw from the race."

Hagen's face lost color, and he said, "Mr. President, you don't mean that. You might just as well hand the White House over to Osborne now. Because that's what will happen, and then everything we've accomplished these last four years will go up in cigar smoke. At least wait until you're reelected, then resign and let Sinclair take over."

Banfield stood up and looked out at the cool water of the pool, the beauty of the mansion behind it. *Why am I doing this?* he berated himself. *I should just bow out gracefully, while I can. I've got a fatal disease.* He rubbed his arm where the blood had been drawn. He was terrified. Banfield knew all about the horrible afflictions, the intermittent pneumonias, the fungal infections, the cancers. But he thought that as long as he was President, he would be all right. As President, he could get the premier medical attention in the world, from the world's preeminent AIDS researcher. First crack at any cure. Finally he turned and said, "Right now my CD4 count isn't too bad, and it's stable. We'll hold off on the drugs at least as long as it stays that way."

Hagen grunted in satisfaction.

"I think I'll swim now," said the leader of the free world, picking up his bathing suit.

Turk Finnegan paced nervously in the anteroom of the Senate cloakroom. The room's peculiar decorations and intricately woven carpet were familiar to him: He had spent many hours here, but always as an arm twister, never as a supplicant.

"Turk!" said a booming voice from the doorway to the Senate chamber, followed shortly by Senator Lyle Barcus, squat and homely, coming into the cloakroom, smiling broadly as he clapped Finnegan on the shoulder. "Good to see you again, Turk! It's been a long time!"

"Too long, Senator," said Turk, wincing inwardly. Barcus was a throwback to the old days of party politics, his vote easily influenced or bought outright with presidential promises of pork. As a senior member of the opposition party, Barcus had often proved useful to the President's agenda. Strangely, Barcus's obvious sellouts hadn't affected his relationship with his party's leadership, and he was a natural entrée for Finnegan to that leadership.

Barcus's sentences always ended in exclamation marks, all his words delivered at the same high decibel level. It was his trademark, appropriate for a former car dealer. Barcus grabbed Finnegan's hand, shook it vigorously, and said, "We all think you got screwed by the President! Gotta watch your back in the executive mansion, you know!"

"That's true, Senator, very true—"

"I know, I know!" said Barcus, in what passed for a stage whisper. "Come with me, I've arranged the meeting, but we can't meet here! Too many people might see you! You gotta come with me!"

Finnegan followed Barcus out of the Capitol through a side exit, where a maroon stretch limousine idled. The interior was as big as a studio apartment.

Fifteen minutes later they cruised to a stop in an alley behind a large town house in Georgetown. Barcus exited first, looking around nonchalantly.

After a moment he hissed, "The coast is clear! Come on, let's get into the house!"

They scurried up a brick walkway into the rear entrance, the door held open by a plump Hispanic woman in a black dress and white apron. Barcus led Finnegan down a hallway into a wood-paneled library, closing the door behind them.

Three men in leather swivel chairs sat around an antique mahogany table. Cigar smoke swirled above the Tiffany lamp hanging above the table. The man closest to Finnegan rose immediately to greet him.

"Hello, Turk," said Theodore Osborne, senior senator from the state of Minnesota. Osborne was tall, not particularly handsome but with rugged features conveying strength and stability. His thin dark hair was gray at the temples.

"Good to see you, sir," said Finnegan, shaking hands.

"You know Mitch, don't you?" said Osborne.

"Certainly." Finnegan nodded at Mitch McPeak, Osborne's campaign manager.

They all took seats around the table, and Finnegan nervously refused a drink. After several minutes of strained small talk, Osborne got directly to the point. "Lyle tells me you have some information that might be useful."

Finnegan felt all their eyes upon him, and was suddenly conscious of the enormity of what he was about to do. He had been a close adviser to the President of the United States, and now he was in the very midst of the President's political enemies, ready to play Judas. He had a sudden urge to get up, to tell them it was all a mistake, go home, get drunk.

But then he remembered the years of loyalty, the endless days and nights on the campaign trail, the damage to his marriage—and the humiliating ending. The anger and bitterness welled up again, and the urge to leave passed. Revenge is the best medicine, he thought. "Information, yes," he said hoarsely. "Information that it's my duty to convey."

Osborne and McPeak exchanged glances, so quickly that Finnegan almost missed it. They're afraid they're being set up, he thought suddenly. I would think so, too. Well, there was nothing he could do about that. They would believe him, because it was true.

Without further preliminaries, he plunged in. First, he reminded them about the incident with the fence jumper, just after the President's inauguration.

"I remember that, of course," said Barcus. "Although it seems like that sort of thing is becoming routine."

"What you didn't know, Senator," said Finnegan, "is that the fence jumper—his name was Conner—carried a letter for the President."

"A letter?"

"A letter," said Finnegan. "Hagen took it, said it was just some rambling about how the guy was gonna get the President. I didn't think about it again until I was leaving the White House, when I opened our document safe to retrieve some private papers. I noticed a large manila envelope stuck way in the back. I thought it was one of mine, and opened it before I noticed Hagen's name handwritten on the outside."

This declaration was met with knowing looks all around. Finnegan didn't bother to defend himself; he just told them what was in the letter.

McPeak finally broke the silence. "Mary, mother of Jesus," he said, astonished.

Finnegan scanned their shocked faces. *God, this was worth it. They thought I was going to give them information on some minor peccadillo, or betray a dirty trick planned by the campaign. Instead, I dropped the Bomb.*

"God, this is unbelievable!" Barcus said excitedly. "Once this becomes known—"

"He'll deny it," Finnegan said forcefully. "I know him. He'll call it a dirty trick, a slander, and he'll make *you* look bad."

"Yes," said Osborne. "But you've got the letter—" he looked at Finnegan, "don't you?"

"Afraid not," said Finnegan. "I couldn't take a chance of making a copy."

They stared at him. "No, really," he said. "I put back the envelope just where I found it—I didn't want Hagen to know I had read it. And it didn't occur to me until later to do . . . to do what I'm doing now. And by that time I had given up my security card and clearance."

"So all we have on this is your word," said McPeak. "No offense."

"Just my word."

"Wait a minute," said Barcus. "Why can't we just quietly spread it around? A whispering campaign!"

"No!" said Osborne, and everyone looked at him. "Like Turk says, we have to be very careful here, or it will backfire." He stared into space for a moment. Then he said, "No one here will breathe a word of this. To anybody. Not even wives." He glared at them fiercely. "Is that understood?"

Finnegan couldn't conceal a smile as they all agreed. Promises from politicians. On the other hand, maybe they would keep the secret. Osborne was—potentially—the next President of the United States.

"But . . . how will we use this?" said McPeak. "You *do* intend to use it, don't you, Ted?"

"Of course," Osborne assured him. "At the proper time." His mouth formed a smile, but there was no humor in it. "At the proper time," he repeated.

CHAPTER SEVENTEEN

For Dylan's second hearing in the Girard case, the judge was Robert Pressler, an ancient no-nonsense jurist who was famously suspicious of women lawyers.

Pressler came onto the bench promptly at nine A.M.—God help the lawyer who was late—and glared out at the courtroom from beneath heavy brows as the Court Clerk called the case: "Case number 53933, Probate Division, Henry Girard, Petitioner, Estate of Nicole Girard, deceased."

"All right," rumbled Pressler. "What do we have here?" He shuffled the papers in the file, studying them for a long moment. Then he said, "Miss Holtz, you're opposing the appointment of the deceased's father as executor? Can that be right?" Pressler was incredulous.

Dylan had to cough to cover a laugh.

Holtz stood up and said clearly, "*Ms.* Holtz, if you please, Your Honor, as I requested the last time I appeared before you. Yes, my client is opposing Mr. Girard's appointment, for the reasons set forth in our memorandum."

Pressler sighed deeply as he thumbed through the memorandum, obviously looking at it for the first time. "All right, then," he said finally. "Let's get on with it. Make your argument." He might as well have continued, "So I can deny your motion." Holtz glared, but began. She made essentially the same argument as in the guardianship hearing: McConnell and the deceased, she said, were domestic partners, equivalent of husband and wife. As such, McConnell should be given the same priority under the probate statute as spouse, and should be entitled to be personal representative. Charlene McConnell was being denied the equal protection of the law because of her sexual orientation. When Holtz concluded, she called Charlene as her first witness.

Judge Pressler interrupted. "No need for that, Miss Holtz."

"*Ms*. Holtz, Your Honor," said Holtz tiredly. "Why not?"

Pressler grinned. "Because I'm ready to rule. I'll accept, *arguendo*, that you can prove through testimony that a spousal relationship existed between your client and the decedent. In fact, I'm willing to bet Mr. Ice will so stipulate." He looked directly at Dylan, who understood his cue.

"Your Honor, we so stipulate," said Dylan, standing, trying not to smile.

"I thought so," said Pressler. "That gives you your record for appeal, Counsel. I hereby deny your opposition motion, and appoint—" he shuffled the papers, "Henry Girard as personal representative of the estate of Nicole Girard. I'll give you a memorandum order in a couple of days." He looked at the Court Clerk. "Call the next case."

And just like that, it was over. Dylan had won the case as soon as it was assigned to Pressler, as both Barry and Hudson had predicted.

In the hallway, Dylan said good-bye to Henry Girard, then started toward the lawyer's lounge. Holtz called out his name, and he walked over. She congratulated him graciously. "No surprise here."

"You're filing an appeal?"

She opened her briefcase and pulled out a piece of paper. "Already prepared. Here's your service copy."

He took it, smiling.

"Of course, this isn't our only arrow, Dylan."

"You mean the wrongful death case?"

"Yes."

"You'll have the same problem there. You won't even make it to a hearing."

"I know that, too. But I think it's the kind of case the supreme court will take."

She meant the Missouri Supreme Court, of course. Or did she? "Well," said Dylan, "since I won't be involved in that one, I wish you luck." He stuck out his hand.

She gripped it and held on. "Dylan, I still think something weird is going on in that hospital. And I think you know it, too."

He started to answer, but she put a finger to her lips. "Do your client a favor. Ask his permission to get Nicole's medical records and give them to me. If I'm right, it's something he would like to know."

"I can't do that."

"Can't you?" she said, and walked away.

The Westwood Country Club in St. Charles was just what Dylan expected: a large, rambling, two-story red-frame building sited next to an artificial lake amid acres of manicured greens.

Dylan stood nervously on the superbly maintained fairway of the third hole, wondering what to do next. His caddy pulled a seven iron from the bag and handed it to him with a look of amused condescension.

"Keep your head down, Dylan, and follow through," said Hudson, who had walked back from his ball, spotted about seventy-five yards up the fairway.

Dylan smiled weakly. "At least it didn't slice."

Hudson laughed. "That's the spirit." With the caddy's help, Hudson coached Dylan through a swing, and Dylan managed to hit a decent shot that landed at the base of the green, on the edge of a sand trap. Then they walked to the green, where Fletcher and John Tyler were preparing to putt. Tyler, a tall, gaunt man with a sallow complexion and close-cropped hair, was the executive director of the Evangelical Foundation.

The golf invitation had come unexpectedly that morning. Fletcher had invited Hudson, and Hudson, sounding a bit giddy, called Dylan to tell him that he was also invited. Dylan protested that he didn't really play golf—he had played only a couple of times in college, with a fraternity brother—and didn't own golf clubs.

"Don't worry about that," said Hudson. "We'll get a loaner set at the club, and I'll help you. The point is that we'll be spending the whole afternoon with Fletcher." The triumph in his voice was clear; in Hudson's mind, he was winning the battle for the heart and mind of the firm's biggest client. "Kaster will have puppies when he hears this." Hudson chortled.

"You're going to tell him?"

"Of course. Have to keep my partners informed, you know." He laughed again. And Dylan laughed too, knowing that Hudson's triumph was in part due to *him*.

But now he was self-consciously trying to avoid embarrassing himself in front of these three good golfers, all with low handicaps. By the time they finished the back nine, Dylan was drenched in nervous sweat, and immensely relieved to sit with the others in the clubhouse, drinking ice-cold Heinekens.

After the usual postmortem of the round, and the exchange of money between Fletcher and Tyler, who had side bets on each hole (Dylan had thought Baptists didn't gamble), Fletcher began to discuss business, asking Hudson a number of questions about pending cases of the Evangelical Foundation. Dylan was impressed and somewhat surprised to find that Hudson was conversant with all of the matters, even the ones outside his department, and could give Fletcher informed answers. Obviously, he had been doing his homework.

For his part, Dylan felt slightly guilty that he hadn't yet done anything in connection with the promise he had given to Hudson; now it looked like his efforts wouldn't be necessary. And that he might be getting credit for it anyway.

"There's something else I want to discuss." Fletcher's tone was low and serious, as he looked at Dylan.

"My golf game?" Dylan asked. "You think I should turn pro?"

Fletcher chuckled warmly. "Son, I think you need lessons just to achieve the status of *bad*. No, what I want to discuss is the Girard case."

"The Girard case," Dylan repeated. "But that's all over. Henry Girard was appointed personal representative. You know, executor."

"Yes, I know. But the McConnell woman has filed an appeal."

"That's got no chance," interjected Hudson. "We'll take care of that."

Fletcher gave him an amused look, and Tyler spoke up. "There's another case going on, too—the wrongful death lawsuit against the hospital."

"Well, yes," said Dylan, puzzled. "But we don't represent the hospital or Dr. Argent—that's handled by the hospital's malpractice carrier and their defense firm."

"I know that," Tyler said impatiently. "The point is, it also involves the Girard family, doesn't it? I mean, it's gonna be a headache for them. Mr. and Mrs. Girard will have to relive everything—their daughter's AIDS, the incident at the dedication ceremony, her death."

Dylan thought that Tyler was remarkably knowledgeable about the Girards.

Hudson also had a quizzical expression. "I guess that's true, John, but there's not much we can do about it."

"Well, actually, there is," said Fletcher, and Dylan realized that this had all been a lead-in to what Fletcher would now tell them. "My gut feeling is that this McConnell . . . woman . . . is after some quick cash. She's just trying to extract some sort of a settlement from the hospital in this alleged malpractice case, and from the Girards in this executor matter." Dylan's sixth sense told him that Fletcher had been about to use a word other than *woman* to describe McConnell but had censored himself.

Because of Dylan's presence—another African-American? Or perhaps it was a sexual epithet.

"I guess that's possible," said Hudson diplomatically, "but I can assure you gentlemen that money is *not* what her attorney is after. I know Pamela Holtz from way back, and she's purely interested in the sexual equality issues."

"And I have to disagree about Ms. McConnell's motives," Dylan said firmly. "I've met her, and while I can't say I understand her motives, greed isn't one of them."

This statement was met by looks of disbelief all around.

Fletcher finally said, "Well, why don't we test it? Let's offer a settlement to drop the appeal of the executorship *and* the wrongful death suit. A package deal for one price."

This took Dylan's breath away, and Hudson's too, by the look of him. Hudson recovered first, saying, "A settlement, sir? But . . . who would pay it?"

"We'll take care of the financial arrangements," said Tyler crisply. "Now, as to the amount—" he looked at Fletcher, who nodded his head, "see if she'll take two hundred thousand dollars. And there's another fifty thousand if you need it."

Dylan gasped. "Two hundred thousand? Are you kidding?"

"Not at all," Tyler said blandly.

"But why would you pay that much money when you have no responsibility, and anyway, there's only a tiny chance of a judgment that high?"

Fletcher's words were cold. "I told you before, Dylan. I owe a tremendous amount to Henry and Amanda Girard. More than you'll ever know. And I won't stand for them to suffer emotional trauma when I have the means to prevent it. Not that it's any of your business, but the funds will come out of a special discretionary fund established by the foundation for this very purpose—to help the members of the original congregation."

Dylan felt a kick to his right leg, under the table. Hudson obviously wanted him to shut up. He was pissing off the client.

"We'll convey the offer," said Hudson. "Dylan will do it himself." He stared meaningfully at Dylan, then continued, grinning, "I'm not the right person to discuss anything with Pamela Holtz."

Fletcher had not missed the interplay, and he watched his reaction. Tyler, too, was looking at him, and the waiter hovered nearby, waiting to take their sandwich order.

"Of course," said Dylan. "I'll do it right away."

Then he drank his beer.

"Thank you for coming to my place," said Pamela Holtz as she escorted Dylan up the stairs of her firm's Clayton town house and into her office. "I wanted to give you our answer in person, and I really couldn't face the hallowed halls of Cameron Barr again, so soon." She grinned. "Also, I thought you might like to get out from under the shadow of Paul Hudson."

"Thanks." Dylan found it impossible not to grin back. He sat down on a gorgeous sofa covered in some silky flower-patterned material.

Pamela Holtz's office reflected her personality— pastel hues and comfortable furniture that would be equally appropriate in a living room. Apparently she didn't feel the need for a large power desk to intimidate clients; her work area was a V-shaped gray-and-white desk built into a corner, complete with computer and printer. On either side of the work area were glass-and-chrome-bookcases; in the center of the large room was a round, light-wood conference table with plush gray swivel chairs.

It had been just a couple of days since Dylan called Holtz and conveyed Fletcher's settlement offer of $200,000. Her shocked response had been what Dylan expected, and she probably didn't believe her ears until she got the faxed confirmation. Then, yesterday, she had called to set up this meeting.

A male assistant brought in a silver tray with a coffee service. Holtz poured for both of them. She seemed in no rush to get to business, talking amiably about local politics and the baseball season. Finally she said, "I guess you're wondering why I asked you here."

"Well, I'm guessing you want to negotiate. If you were going to refuse the offer outright, you could have told me on the phone." At least that was Hudson's rather pleased analysis of the situation, and Dylan agreed.

Holtz smiled at him over her coffee cup, considering him coolly. Dylan was finally forced to say, "Well, is that right?"

She put down her cup. "Dylan, don't you find it surprising that I have given so much time and attention to a rather simple guardianship, and now to an admittedly quixotic wrongful death case?"

"Frankly, we have."

"Yes. You see, I knew both Charlene McConnell and Nicole Girard long before this case. As you may know, I am very active in feminist politics in this state."

"Of course."

"But you may not have known that Charlene also has been involved. She's on the board of directors of the local NOW chapter, as well as on the steering committees of several ad hoc women's political action groups. I've known her for years, worked with her many times. And, through her, I met Nicole. Nicole wasn't very political, but I spent a lot of time with her and came to know her very well, too."

Dylan made a sound of acknowledgment. Where was this going?

"Anyway," continued Holtz, "it was natural that Charlene should turn to me for representation when Nicole had her . . . episode . . . at the dedication ceremony. I had a point of reference to judge Nicole by. Do you understand what I mean?"

"Uh, no."

"Dylan, I know for a fact—through my experience and judgment—that Nicole's behavior in the hospital was totally out of character. And you'll never convince me that it was a result of the emotional trauma of learning she had AIDS. People don't change that much, that fast. Then, at the hearing, when it was clear how sedated she was, I realized what was going on."

"You mean—"

"I mean there's only one explanation that makes any sense." She stood up and went to the window, then turned back to Dylan. "She had been drugged from the beginning."

"You mean, deliberately?" Dylan didn't bother feigning surprise. This was what Nicole herself had told him, of course, and it looked like Holtz had bought her story.

"Yes."

"You don't think she might have had AIDS dementia?"

She shook her head. "My experts tell me that is highly unlikely. I think Dr. Argent and his gang screwed up. They committed some error—and I really have no idea what it might have been—screwed up her medical care somehow, and then had to cover it up to avoid the loss of their research grant, and, more importantly, to avoid a costly lawsuit."

"But you've got no proof of that, do you?"

"No. We contacted the coroner, and he requested an autopsy but remarkably allowed Argent to arrange for it instead of bringing the body to the state morgue and having it done by a state pathologist. I still don't know what strings Argent pulled to arrange that. Anyway, we don't know what the autopsy showed, other than that it wasn't enough for the coroner to take any action. And we can't get Nicole's medical records. Now that I've filed the wrongful death lawsuit, though, they'll have to provide them."

"Unless your case is dismissed, first."

"Oh, I think I can get a deposition or two before we get dismissed."

"I see. I don't have the medical records, either," he mused. "Not yet, anyway." With Henry Girard now the duly appointed executor, however, Argent would have to provide the records. He looked at her expectantly. "But all of this was a preamble to your response regarding our settlement proposal."

"Yes, but at least now you can understand the context when I tell you that Charlene rejects the settlement. Completely and utterly. We are not simply establishing a negotiating posture. My client is not interested in money—she's interested in a much more valuable, and scarcer, commodity."

"The truth," said Dylan, feeling rather melodramatic.

"Right. And I want you to consider all this, too, Dylan. If I'm not right, then why in God's name would we be offered so much money to shut up and go away?"

She didn't know, of course, the source of the money. She figured it was coming from the hospital, and she also must be wondering why the hospital was using Cameron Barr as the financial conduit, rather than its own law firm. There were several reasons that might be done, none of them ethical, some even illegal. But she was keeping these suspicions to herself.

"I can't comment on that."

"No. Of course you can't. I've said my piece, and again I appreciate your coming here. I hope you'll consider what I said, and if you can, within the limits of client confidentiality, I hope you'll try to help me get to the truth in this case." She stood and put out her hand.

Dylan shook her hand, feeling her warmth, and found himself saying, "I'll do whatever I can."

It was, he thought later, probably the nicest rejection of a settlement proposal he would ever experience.

CHAPTER EIGHTEEN

The Nutcracker was dark, dirty, and reeked of stale cigarette smoke. Although it was a weekday evening, the bar was crowded, and most of the little round tables were occupied with couples, some kissing. The dirty linoleum dance floor was half-filled; the dancers moved to sixties rhythm and blues that came—too loudly—from the large overhead speakers.

Pamela Holtz sat among the women at the bar, sipping a soda. She glanced at her watch, then returned her gaze to the dance floor. At a nearby table, a large blond woman dressed in a jeans jacket, black pants, and thigh-high boots sat alone, occasionally drinking from a big mug of beer. She tried to catch Pamela's eye.

I've been stood up, Pamela thought. *Serves me right.* She found it hard to believe that she had agreed to come here. She'd been practicing law for twenty-five years and had never done anything like this. She probably should have turned around and left as soon as she saw the neighborhood. She decided to give it five more minutes, then leave.

Almost precisely five minutes later, a young,

attractive brunette in a blue print dress and high heels pushed her way through the crowd toward the bar, drawing appreciative glances from the women around her. She glanced down the line of people at the bar until she recognized Pamela, then came over.

"Ms. Holtz?" she asked, her voice soft.

"That's me," said Pamela. "You're . . . Astrid?"

"Yeah," said Astrid, smiling, showing brilliant white, even teeth. "Please come with me." She started toward the exit.

"Wait a minute. Follow you? Where?"

Astrid turned and said impatiently, "You don't want to talk here, do you?" She gestured at the bar.

Pamela shook her head. "No, but first I'd like to know who sent you. On the phone I was told you would have some information—"

"Shh!" hissed Astrid. "All in good time. C'mon, now." She walked firmly toward the door.

Reluctantly, Pamela followed her out the door and into the parking lot.

The street was lined with small bars—some straight, some gay—strip joints, and sleazy adult book and video stores. Astrid put her hand under Pamela's arm and pulled her toward the street. "My friend—the one with the information—will pick us up over there."

Pamela suppressed the urge to pull her arm away. She'd come this far, she might as well play along until she found out whether Astrid and Company really knew anything about Nicole's death. They had just reached the end of the parking lot when half a dozen motorcyclists came down the street, moving slowly. They were in full regalia— leather jackets with insignia, chains, and German World War II helmets.

Pamela recognized them—the White Lords, they called themselves. They were infamous for their gay-bashing activities. The police had just arrested a dozen of them for crashing an art gallery in St. Louis and beating up some of the patrons.

Now their Harleys idled noisily as they cruised down the street, calling out to the occasional hooker. When they were adjacent to Pamela and Astrid, the leader put up his hand and stopped. At this time of night there was very little traffic, and what there was made a wide detour around them.

The leader was a fat, slovenly man in his forties, with a scruffy three-days' growth of beard. His piggy eyes stared out from under a black military cap. The other riders were equally ugly, although several had women riding on the seats behind them.

The leader looked them over, spat ostentatiously, and said, "Fucking dykes."

Almost involuntarily, Pamela tried to pull her arm out of Astrid's suddenly firm grip, but Astrid wouldn't release her.

"C'mon, let's go back into the bar," Pamela said fiercely.

"I'm not afraid of these assholes," Astrid said.

"Well, you should be," Pamela whispered.

Suddenly the leader gunned his engine and rode into the parking lot. The others followed. Pamela felt a stab of fear. The sense of menace, of impending violence, was overwhelming. They were surrounded by the motorcycles, the deep-throated idling of their engines and the exhaust fumes confusing Pamela's senses.

"What do you guys want?" Astrid shouted, no fear in her voice.

The fat man slouched back in his seat and

grinned, then twirled his throttle and gunned his bike directly at Pamela. She scrambled out of the way, just as one of the other bikers turned into her path. Pamela was forced away from him, then to the side when another bike loomed in front of her. Soon the parking lot was a circling, roaring derby of motorcycles, each taking a run at Pamela and Astrid, forcing them to dodge and weave to avoid being run over. Pamela had the sour taste of fear in her mouth as she realized she and Astrid were being herded away from the street, toward the far end of the parking lot.

There was nothing she could do until, finally, her breath coming in deep gasps, she was forced over the edge of the parking area onto a dark, bottle-strewn vacant lot. The fat man put his forefinger up to his neck and made a slashing gesture across his neck. One by one, the other bikers cut their engines until the sudden silence was deafening.

Astrid stood next to Pamela, hands on her knees, panting. Pamela thought about screaming for help, but the parking lot was deserted, and it might incite the bikers. Maybe there was still a chance they could talk their way out of this. Anyway, Astrid probably was the one in danger—she was young and attractive, while Pamela was a gray-haired middle-aged woman. Pamela nudged Astrid and whispered, "I'll talk to them. As soon as you can, make a dash for the building." Astrid nodded.

The fat man heaved himself off his motorcycle and walked forward, stopping directly in front of Pamela. Pamela instinctively took a step backward but bumped into the hard leather chest of another biker. The man behind her grabbed a handful of her breasts and squeezed viciously; Pamela jumped forward with a shriek and bumped into the fat man, who shoved her back to the first man like a pinball.

Now the invisible man behind her put his arms around her chest and held on. She could feel his beery breath on the back of her neck. "Let me go!" she yelled, all semblance of control gone.

The fat man slugged her in the belly, knocking the breath out of her. When she finished gasping, she looked up and saw the man's face inches away, the pupils of his eyes like pinheads. More than anything else, that scared her; she realized he was stoned, and might do anything.

"I really hate dykes," the man said again.

I've got to stay calm, stay in control, thought Pamela. She turned her head to find Astrid, and saw that she was gone. Pamela felt a wave of relief. Incredibly, they had let her get away. She probably was inside the Nutcracker now, getting help.

"I'm not a dyke," Pamela said in as reasonable a tone as she could manage. "I'm a lawyer, and I'm here to investigate a case. My partners will be coming into the parking lot shortly."

The fat man laughed. His face really had a remarkable resemblance to a pig's. The skin beneath his scruffy beard shone pink; his nose was short and snoutlike. He looked around at the other bikers, and one of them yelled out, his speech slurred, "Take the bitch down, Jimmy!"

Jimmy grinned evilly, swayed, and reached out. Pamela tried to flinch away, but it was no use. The fat man grabbed the front of her blouse and yanked, ripping it off her chest and exposing her bra. Pamela began screaming, and the man behind her slapped his hand over her mouth. She tried to bite the hand, but he was too strong.

Jimmy put his hand under the front of her bra and pulled it down, exposing Pamela's breasts. "Shit. They ain't even a mouthful."

C'mon, Astrid, where are you? thought Pamela. She must have had time to get help by now. Where were the police?

Jimmy looked around again, then said, "Let's go over there," and the man holding Pamela dragged her deeper into the vacant lot. The other bikers followed, pushing their motorcycles toward several abandoned cars with their wheels up on cinderblocks.

"That one, Frankie," Jimmy said to the man holding Pamela, and she was shoved roughly against the rusty fender of one of the cars. Someone pushed a greasy handkerchief between her teeth, as a gag, and her slacks were pulled down, leaving her clad only in panties. In an instant these were torn off, too.

Now Jimmy stood before her, barely illuminated by the reflected light from the Nutcracker's parking lot. Slowly, he unzipped his pants and moved toward her, his tongue moving quickly over his lips, his stubby penis thickening.

Pamela remembered the advice she had heard so often about rape: If you can't prevent it, let it happen, your life is more important.

But Pamela had been a fighter all her life, and she was too frightened to control her reactions. Her right leg flew out in a vicious kick, her stiff toes catching Jimmy right in the balls. She had the brief satisfaction of seeing him collapse, grunting in agony, before the two-by-four crashed into the side of her head and the world disappeared in a flash of light and pain.

Fifty yards away, in the parking lot, the woman who called herself Astrid, unable to see what was happening in the darkness, shrugged and turned away. She got into her car, turned on the radio, and, humming softly, drove away.

CHAPTER NINETEEN

Dylan was having a generally good day. He spent the morning taking a deposition in a breach of contract case against a mortgage lender—he represented the mortgage company—and got important concessions from the plaintiff. Afterward, Hudson invited him to the Cardinals game on Saturday.

At lunch, when Barry heard about that, he said, "Christ, you're a regular teacher's pet. Those Cardinals seats are usually reserved for partners and clients." There was a tinge of envy in his voice.

"Yeah, but I'm not kidding myself. It's all because of my relationship with Kristin. Like you said, if she dumps me, I'll be thrown back into the pack with the rest of you wage slaves."

Barry took a bite of his sandwich. "I know what I said, but I'm not so sure anymore. You just may be one of those boy wonders that comes along sometimes. You know, the kind that makes partner in three years."

Dylan nearly choked on his tuna fish. It was such an unlikely—and tantalizing—prospect that he didn't want to jinx it.

Changing the subject, he told Barry about the good reports Janis was getting from the Second Start program. After an initial period of rebellion, she seemed to be adjusting well. More importantly, she was drug-free. Barry agreed that it looked like she had turned the corner.

In the afternoon, after a couple of hours spent in the law library researching an interesting discovery motion, Dylan went back to his office. There was a phone message from Henry Girard.

"Hi, Dylan," said Girard, answering the phone when Dylan returned the call. "Look, I'm sorry to bother you—"

"No problem. That's what I'm here for."

"Uh, yeah. Well, look, you know those papers I signed the other day?"

"The medical records authorizations?" Dylan had given them to Henry right after their victory at the hearing for personal representative. He had already received the officially sealed letters of administration, and he intended to take the letters and the medical authorizations to MIRI and ram them down Dr. Argent's throat. Argent's refusal of the records still rankled.

"Yes," said Girard. "I changed my mind. I don't want to get Nicole's medical records."

"What? Why not?"

"I just want to put all that behind us. It won't help bring back Nicole."

"Of course not," Dylan said, thinking that Henry's phrases sounded rehearsed. "But I thought you wanted to find out what really happened."

"It doesn't matter. It won't bring her back," he repeated.

Dylan tried to argue him out of it, but Girard was politely adamant, and finally said, "Look, I'm the client, right?"

"Well of course, but—"

"Then you have to do what I want. I want you to throw away those papers, right now." And he hung up.

"Damn," said Dylan, putting down the receiver. He had really been looking forward to getting those records—not only to tweak Argent, but also because Pamela Holtz had raised legitimate questions that had piqued his curiosity.

He wondered what—or who—had changed Girard's mind.

Dylan was packing up his briefcase when Barry came into his office and collapsed into the side chair. "Have you heard?"

"Heard what?"

"About Pamela Holtz?"

Dylan shrugged. "What now? Has she sued the pope?"

Barry's face was uncharacteristically serious. "She's dead, Dylan."

"What?"

"Murdered. I just heard it on the news. Her body was found this morning outside a place called the Nutcracker. It's a sleazy lez bar, out in the county." He grimaced. "She was pretty badly beaten up. Probably raped."

"Jesus! I just saw her yesterday!"

"I know."

"Do they have any idea who did it?"

Barry hesitated. "The cops suspect it was another gay bashing by the White Lords."

Dylan considered it. It was hard to imagine the refined, genteel Pamela Holtz going to such a place.

Well, sex made you do crazy things. He had a sudden thought. "Does Hudson know about this yet?"

"I don't know. Why?"

"I would guess it would hit him pretty hard."

"Maybe. Maybe not."

"Jesus," Dylan repeated. "I can't believe this." It suddenly occurred to him that this was the second death in the Girard case—first Nicole, then Charlene's lawyer. The two deaths had no relationship, of course, except that he had known and liked each person and their deaths were unexpected.

"Well, I thought you'd want to know."

"Yeah," said Dylan, thoughtfully. "Thanks."

After Barry left, Dylan swiveled to look at Nicole's drawing. He knew it was his imagination, but Nicole's eyes now seemed accusatory, and the little imp was barely visible.

The green-shuttered duplex house was on a pleasant, tree-lined street in Webster Groves. Most of the neighborhood homes were refurbished Victorians that could have been transported to the early 1900s without causing any comment.

There was a car parked in the cement driveway with a county government parking sticker on the rear bumper. Dylan parked his Buick on the street and went up the brick walkway to the front door. He pushed the doorbell; when no one answered, he pressed again, harder and longer.

Finally, a voice came out of the speaker grille above the button. "Who's there?"

"Dylan Ice."

There was a very long pause, then, "What do you want?"

"I'd like to talk to you. May I come in?"

"You're alone?"

An odd question. "Yes."

"Wait a minute."

It was more like five before the door opened and Charlene McConnell motioned him into the foyer of the house she shared—had shared—with Nicole.

"Okay, you're here," said Charlene, leading him into the foyer. "What do you want?"

Dylan looked around. To his left was the living room—overstuffed chairs mixed with more modern pieces—two people's furniture. To his right was the dining room table, stacked with several cardboard boxes of books, some taped for shipping. Directly in front of him was the staircase to the second floor; on the landing at the top he could just see the edges of two suitcases.

Dylan said, "I wanted you to know how very sorry I was to hear about Pamela's death. I know she was your friend, as well as your lawyer."

Her eyes locked on him, as cold as her expression. "That's very nice. But you could have called. Or sent a card."

"No, I wanted to say it in person. I wanted to talk about Pamela. I was afraid that if I called, you would say no."

"You were right," Charlene said curtly. Then her expression softened. "I guess you're not as big an asshole as I thought. You want to sit down?" She motioned him toward the living room.

Dylan sat on the sofa. There was an awkward silence, then he said, "You going on a trip?"

"No," she said too quickly. "What makes you think that?"

He pointed at the staircase. "I saw the suitcases."

"Oh, those. Those are Nicole's. I'm getting her stuff ready to send to her parents."

"Oh," said Dylan, thinking she was a poor liar.

A car backfired outside, and Charlene hurried to the bay window, kneeled on the dark oak window seat, and flipped down the Venetian blind slats to look outside. When she turned to face him again, he could see her anxiety.

"I think you better go."

On a sudden impulse, he said, "Did Pamela go to the Nutcracker often?"

Again, that look of panic on her face, quickly suppressed. "I'm surprised you have to ask. Don't you know?"

"No, I don't," Dylan said with exasperation. "I wouldn't ask if I knew."

His reaction was genuine, and she seemed to realize that. She sat down. "Maybe you don't," she said, surprised. Then, suddenly, "Do you know how Pamela died?"

"Only generally. She was outside a gay bar, and—"

"Do you really think that Pamela Holtz would go to a place like the Nutcracker?"

"I wondered about that. Especially after I saw it on the news last night. On the other hand, I know about some very prominent attorneys who have been caught in equally sordid places."

"Believe me," said Charlene fervently, "that was Pamela's first visit."

"Yet she did go that night," pressed Dylan.

Charlene considered him for a moment. Then she said, "She was lured there."

"Lured?"

"Yeah. She got a phone call about eleven P.M. A woman who identified herself as Astrid said she worked at University Hospital. She claimed to have information about Nicole's death, information that would help my case. She wanted Pamela to meet her at the Nutcracker."

"I see. How do you know this?"

"Pamela called me before she left. I told her not to go, that it sounded fishy, but you know Pamela."

"Interesting," said Dylan, not sure what to think. "There wasn't anything on the news last night, or in the paper this morning, about Pamela having a companion or a friend. So the White Lords must have gotten to Pamela before the meeting with this Astrid woman. Or maybe right after." He realized Charlene was studying his face.

"Either you're the best actor I've ever seen, or you really don't know anything about this. I guess they kept you in the dark."

"Look," said Dylan, feeling himself get angry, "I told you, I don't know what you're talking about. And I don't know what you think I know, but I do know you think I know something I don't."

After a beat, they both burst out laughing.

"Okay," said Charlene. "I believe you. Really." She stood again and walked to the window, checked outside, then returned. "You know, I never wanted to sue Argent in the first place. It was Pamela who suggested it, as a way of getting a test case on same-sex partner benefits to the Missouri Supreme Court." She stared gloomily into space, then said, "It was a set-up. This 'Astrid' woman got Pamela to the Nutcracker for the purpose of having the White Lords attack her."

"C'mon! Why do you think that?"

"With all that's happened, you have trouble believing it?"

"Well, yes. I mean—"

She looked disgusted. "I've said more than I should. I'm sorry, but I've got some work to do right now. Maybe we can talk some other time." She stuck out her hand, he shook it, and before he knew it he was outside, walking to his car.

He sat behind the wheel for a while, digesting what he had heard, then backed out of the driveway and drove away. At the end of the street, he turned around and drove part of the way back, pulled to the curb and parked. He was about seventy-five yards from Charlene's house.

A few minutes later, Charlene came down the steps carrying the suitcases he had seen earlier. She threw them into the back of her Toyota wagon, slammed the liftgate, and backed out of the driveway.

Dylan ducked his head as she drove past, then looked out again just in time to see another car, a tan Chrysler Concorde that faced him, pull away from the curb about one hundred yards beyond Charlene's house. It accelerated quickly, and the two men in the front seat had their eyes on Charlene's car as they drove by Dylan.

The driver was distinctive, even in Dylan's brief glance: a large bald head, bushy eyebrows, and a mustache. The top of his head seemed to brush the roof of the car.

Dylan memorized the tag number.

Back at the office, Dylan called Detective Peterson.

"Mr. Ice," Peterson said when he came to the phone. "How's your sister doing?"

"Not bad. She's in Second Start."

"That's a good program. If she makes it through, I think she'll be okay."

"Yeah, I think so, too. What about LaShawn Johnson and his buddy? Have you made an arrest?"

"Who's that—oh, the gang members that attacked your sister. No, they've disappeared. We're keeping an eye on the high school, though."

For a moment Dylan considered telling him about the attack in his apartment, then changed his mind. "Thanks. But actually, that's not what I called about. Are you familiar with the Holtz case? You know, the lawyer who was killed outside the gay bar?"

"Sure, I know about it. Why?"

"Well, can you find out the name of the investigating officer for me? I've got some information I'd like to pass on."

"I don't know his name, offhand. I'd have to find out. What kind of information?" He sounded dubious.

Dylan briefly told him about his meeting with McConnell, and the two men who were following her. "I've got the tag number. I could contact Motor Vehicles myself and find out the owner's name, but I'd like to know more. Whether he's got a criminal record, that sort of thing."

"To tell you the truth, it doesn't impress me. But tell you what, give me the tag number, I'll look into it, find out who's investigating it over in Homicide."

Dylan gave it to him. "Will you call me when you learn something?"

"*If* we find anything, yeah, I will. Have a nice day."

Dylan shrugged as he hung up. Well, it was worth a try, he thought. He picked up his basketball and threw it at the hoop, then opened his file drawer and took out the Girard file.

The medical authorizations were still there, clipped to the pleadings section. They seemed to reproach him.

On their face, they were perfectly valid.

Dylan thought about what Charlene had told him. He thought of Nicole, and of Pamela Holtz. He reminded himself of Argent's resistance to providing the medical records, and of Henry Girard's sudden change of heart.

Do it, he told himself. Argent is hiding something, and this is the only way to find out.

He could take the authorizations to the hospital along with the letters of administration, and Argent would have to turn the records over. No one could object.

And with that thought, Dylan realized he had reached a turning point in his short career. Henry Girard had specifically forbidden Dylan from using the authorizations. He was therefore required to either file them, return them to the client, or destroy them. Certainly not use them.

Yet he was consciously and deliberately contemplating their use, contemplating a breach of legal ethics. Until now, he had nothing but contempt for those lawyers who viewed the canons as rules to be circumvented, yet—

His father probably would say Dylan was on the cusp. It was one of the old hippie's favorite expressions, and Dylan never really understood where it came from. Something to do with astrology.

But, rubbing his jaw reflectively, he realized that even if he used the authorizations, there was no guarantee he would get the records. They probably weren't even physically present in the Medical Records Department, but in Argent's office. Argent would stall. And what if Henry Girard found out?

If that happened, he could end up without the records, facing an angry client and a disciplinary hearing. And fired. No, there had to be some other way.

It took him a while, but he finally thought of it.

Brown carpet, brown wallpaper, brown chairs, everything brown and muted—a typical psychiatrist's office. No one else was in the little waiting room, and there was no receptionist. Dylan was about to knock on the inner door when it opened, and Dr. Norris—the Court's independent consultant psychiatrist—greeted him warmly. "Please come in, Mr. Ice."

There were two couches, two chairs, a desk and a bookcase. Norris sat in the chair next to the couch; he took the other chair. "Thanks for seeing me so quickly. I hope you can help me."

"If I can," she said neutrally. "How?"

"I'd like to get copies of Nicole Girard's medical records. I know you got them from the hospital as part of your psychiatric evaluation." He reached into his briefcase and handed her photocopies of Henry Girard's letters of administration and a medical records authorization signed by Henry, as personal representative.

She looked them over. "I don't see why not." She went to a nearby file cabinet and removed a file. She sorted through the papers, then handed him a thick brown manila envelope. "Here you go. I don't have a copier; you'll have to bring them back."

"Of course," said Dylan, trying hard to restrain his enthusiasm as he opened the envelope and checked its contents. He didn't know if everything was there, of course, but it sure looked like it—history and physical, admission sheet, progress notes, lab slips. "Did you get a copy of the autopsy report?" he asked.

"No," she said, surprised. "My work was finished when I testified. Can't you get it?"

"Sure, sure. I just thought I would save myself some time if you already had it." He stood, promised to return the records the next day, thanked her sincerely, and left her office with the manila folder and a stifling sense of guilt.

"You can't be serious," said Barry.

"Why not?" said Dylan, dipping another corn chip into the salsa.

"I can't even begin to think of all the reasons."

Dylan shrugged and settled back on the vinyl seat of the booth. They were in a large Mexican restaurant, part of a national chain. They had stopped in the bar for a beer after work, a luxury Dylan could indulge now that Janis wasn't living at home. Although he missed her, this new freedom was nice.

Dylan took a sip of beer. "I have to get some answers, and the more I try, the fewer I get. Who better to ask than the guy in charge?"

Barry shook his head sorrowfully. "Look, I admit there are some odd things about Nicole's case—chief among them being the inordinate amount of attention given it by Reverend Fletcher—"

"Some 'odd things,'" Dylan said scornfully. "What about Nicole looking drugged at the hearing? The settlement offer to McConnell? Argent's refusal to provide the medical records? The death of Pamela Holtz? McConnell leaving town? What about the fact that McConnell was being followed?"

"But none of that stuff is necessarily connected. The settlement offer was crazy, I'll grant you, but that didn't come from Argent. And Pamela's death? You really think Argent would kill her just to avoid a malpractice case?"

"All right, I know it sounds ridiculous, but how else do you explain everything? I mean, if Argent is covering up his malpractice, he would want Henry Girard, not Charlene McConnell, appointed Nicole's guardian. And he would sedate Nicole so she couldn't express her own opinion. He probably arranged for the settlement payoff."

Barry sighed. "You haven't told the police your theory."

"Of course not. I understand the concept of evidence. And what about Charlene? What's your explanation for what she told me?"

"Just because she's paranoid doesn't mean you have to be."

"It wasn't paranoia that was driving that Chrysler."

"They might be process servers, for God's sake."

Dylan folded his arms across his chest. "I'm going. Will you help or not?"

Barry picked up his beer, took a long drag, and smiled. "Of course. Wouldn't miss it for the world. What do you want me to do?"

"I've got a deposition tomorrow and it's too late to cancel. The Appelman case. File's on my desk. It's discovery of assets in a subrogation case. Can you cover for me?"

"I think so. What are you gonna tell our fearless leader?"

"Nothing. If he asks, I'm sick."

"That's true."

Dylan ignored the jab. "I've got the first flight out of Lambert. I should only be away a day or two, however long it takes me to see Dr. Rosati."

"You mean you don't even have an appointment?"

Dylan winced. "Not yet. I tried, but he's busy until the next century. Don't worry, I'll get in to see him, it just may take a while." He tapped his fingers on the Formica top. "God, if I only had the autopsy report, too. That would help."

"So? Get it."

"I tried. I personally went to the Medical Records Department and presented my medical authorizations, but it had been removed by the attending physician—Argent—'for review.'"

Barry stared at him. "Sometimes I forget how new you are to this. Look, didn't Pamela Holtz file a complaint with the medical examiner, alleging it was a suspicious death?"

"Yeah," said Dylan. "So what—" and then it hit him. "There must be a copy at the medical examiner's office!"

"Bingo."

"Uh, Barry—"

"I know, I know. I'll get a copy tomorrow. You'll have it when you get back."

"Thanks, Barry." He looked at his watch. "I better get going."

"Where?"

"Ah—don't give me shit. I've got a date with Kristin."

Barry just rolled his eyes. "Call me from Washington. I want to know how long I'll have to cover for you."

"You got it."

Kristin looked especially good, Dylan thought. She was dressed in a pair of tight black jeans and some sort of peasant blouse he had never seen before. Her hair fell loosely to her shoulders and he longed to touch it.

They had a late dinner at an Italian restaurant, talking about nothing in particular, just drinking lots of red wine, eating linguine with clam sauce, and laughing. Then they rushed to make an Arnold Schwarzenegger movie.

Afterward, in the car, Dylan said, "I gotta get up early tomorrow, I'm afraid. I've got to catch an early flight."

"Oh. Business or pleasure?" She put a hand on his thigh. "Business, I hope."

"Uh, yeah. I'm going to Washington to meet with the head of the AIDS research program."

The grip on his thigh tightened. It was a pleasant sensation; he had to remind himself to concentrate on his driving. "Dr. Rosati? Why is that?"

"Actually, it's regarding the Girard case." He said it tentatively, knowing how she had reacted when he went to Nicole's funeral.

After a moment she said mildly, "Really? Why?"

"Well, there are some things I don't understand about her death."

"What, exactly?"

"Oh, some of the AIDS issues, that's all." He was a little surprised at her insistence, and didn't feel he could tell her any more than that, not with her father so tight with Dr. Argent. It wasn't that he didn't trust her, he reasoned, but their relationship was still very new.

"You don't want to talk about it?"

"Uh, no, not really."

"How long will you be gone?"

He shrugged. "It may take a few days."

"Well, since you don't know when you'll be back, I better spend the night."

"Oh, sure." He hadn't really wanted to do that tonight, but with her sitting there, the smell of her perfume, and her hand on his thigh, he wasn't going to protest. He had been driving toward Clayton; he pulled over to make a U-turn.

CHAPTER TWENTY

Peter Rosati filled his days with meetings, clinical research, paperwork, and more meetings. Too many meetings. As director of the National Institute of Allergy and Infectious Diseases, he was a man with too many responsibilities and too many demands.

Rosati saved the database file he was working in and pushed away from his computer, swinging his feet up and onto the edge of his desk—the same desk he had used on his first day of work at NIH. It was a point of some pride to him that his office, although much larger than that of an ordinary research associate, was no grander. He had the same government-issue metal desk and filing cabinets as any GS–13.

He put his hands over his head and rolled his head on his neck, stretching until the tendons cracked. It was almost five o'clock, and he had arrived at the office at six-thirty A.M. Outside his window, the western sun still was high in the June sky, its rays slanting through the clouds and hitting the side of the tall Clinical Center that dominated the Bethesda campus of the National Institutes of Health.

His career had started here, in one of the older

low-rise brick buildings, twenty-five years earlier. After his internship and residency in internal medicine at the University of Pennsylvania, Rosati had come to NIAID as a clinical associate, where he soon made a reputation for developing effective treatments for formerly fatal immunological diseases. When the Division of AIDS was created as part of NIAID, he first became its deputy clinical director, then its director, and did landmark research into the pathogenesis of the AIDS virus. Five years ago, he was appointed director of the entire NIAID, while also remaining clinical director of its AIDS division.

During this period he published hundreds of articles, wrote authoritative books, and won international acclaim as perhaps the leading AIDS researcher in the world.

That was then, he thought. This is now. "Now" was the piles of folders, memoranda, and computer printouts piled high on his desk; the stacks of unread journals and article reprints overwhelming the shelves of his bookcase. "Now" was the undeniable truth that he spent more time administering than researching.

He longed to resign his position and return full-time to the womb of the research laboratory, just another clinical associate, just another lab coat with a name tag.

It was fantasy, he knew. Especially now that he was both privileged and burdened by the secret known only to four other people. The knowledge of that secret was an almost paralyzing responsibility, and he felt profoundly uneasy about the rightness of keeping it.

There was, after all, the issue of the public's right

to know. The disease, if untreated, could certainly affect the President's judgment. Yet to reveal the secret would be a hideous breach of faith, as well as a breach of medical ethics. Which duty was higher?

There was also the issue of treatment itself, which he had examined from every angle. He concluded that there was only one viable solution.

The thought was interrupted by the buzzing of the intercom. Reluctantly, Rosati picked up the phone. It was his secretary, leaving for the day and reminding him that he was due at the White House at six thirty.

"I'll leave in fifteen minutes. Thanks, Beth," said Rosati. "And go home."

"One other thing, Doctor," Beth said. Her voice lowered, and he could tell she was cupping her hand over the mouthpiece. "That lawyer is still here. You said you'd see him this afternoon."

Rosati groaned. He'd forgotten all about the St. Louis lawyer who wanted to discuss the clinical trial for PHT. Normally, Beth wouldn't have given him an appointment for weeks, but he had showed up at the office and insisted on waiting until Rosati was free. Rosati looked at his watch. "I can give him ten minutes."

The lawyer with the strange name turned out to be quite young, and looked biracial. Rosati ushered him into his office. "Unfortunately, Mr. Ice, I'm due at a meeting downtown. Perhaps you would like to come back some other time?"

"No. I'll talk fast."

He did talk fast, but Rosati soon made him slow down when he realized that Ice's interest in the PHT trial involved Nicole Girard.

It was strange hearing about her from Ice's viewpoint, and as he talked, Rosati realized that Dr. Argent apparently had told Ice—and everyone other than Rosati—that the patient had AIDS dementia rather than bipolar disorder.

The diagnosis of ADC was absurd in a woman whose antibodies were good enough to be used in PHT therapy.

"You said you have the patient's medical chart?" Rosati asked.

"Right here." Ice opened his briefcase and removed a large manila envelope, which he pushed across the top of Rosati's desk.

Rosati opened the packet and pulled out the stack of papers. He was anxious to review them, but he didn't want Ice to know that. "Okay. I'll take a look. Call me in a couple of weeks—"

"Can't you at least skim them *now*?"

God, he's a pushy bastard, Rosati thought. He leafed through the chart. "You don't understand. The only way I can help you is by making a thorough evaluation of the records, and I can't—wait a minute." One of the lab slips had caught his eye. "When did you say the patient died?"

"I didn't. It was May twenty-sixth."

Rosati tapped the chart thoughtfully. "And the cause of death?"

Ice grimaced. "Good question. Dr. Argent called it 'idiopathic respiratory distress secondary to head trauma and immunosuppression.'" He grinned winningly. "I hope I said that right."

"Yes. But immunosuppressed? It doesn't make sense. What did the autopsy show?"

"I haven't been able to get the autopsy report."

Rosati frowned as he skimmed the chart. "This really is quite strange."

"What is? The way she died?"

"Yes. I don't see how she could have been immunosuppressed on her date of death when, according to this chart, just one week before her death she had normal CD4-plus counts. Although it's possible for T-cells to decline very fast, I've never seen it go *that* fast."

"So she was healthy, despite having AIDS?"

Rosati shook his head again. "She didn't *have* AIDS. She was HIV-positive for almost fifteen years. There are a surprisingly large number of people in that category—long-term nonprogressors, we call them. We know there's a specific genetic resistance; others, like Girard, have blood plasma that reveals an unusually high level of neutralizing antibodies."

"So what are you saying?" Ice said excitedly.

What I'm saying, thought Rosati, *is that Dr. Argent is lying. And I've got a big mouth. I shouldn't have mentioned this until I found out what really happened*. He said, "Look, Mr. Ice, don't overreact. I'm sure there's a reasonable explanation. Give me a few days to really look at this chart."

"Will you call Dr. Argent and tell him I've seen you?"

"Are you asking me not to?"

"Not necessarily. But I would like to know if you do. And, if your final conclusion is the same as your preliminary—that this is a very strange sequence of events—I expect you to initiate an investigation."

Rosati nodded. "I'll let you know."

Ice regarded him silently, as if judging this statement. "All right. In the meantime, I'll get the autopsy report and fax it to you."

"Good. I'll be looking for it." Rosati glanced at his watch. "Now I really have to go."

He escorted Ice out of the suite. When the elevator doors closed behind him, Rosati returned to his office. As he got ready to leave for the White House, he tossed Nicole Girard's chart into his briefcase.

Dylan took the elevator to the parking garage and retrieved his rental car, feeling remarkably satisfied with himself. Rosati's reaction to Nicole's medical chart had been exactly what he hoped, and was the first concrete evidence that his suspicions about Argent were well founded.

Unfortunately, the long wait in Rosati's outer office had ruined his travel plans. He would never make his 5:40 P.M. flight from Dulles. Of course, he could go to the airport and try to get on a later flight.

Instead, Dylan drove through the NIH campus to Wisconsin Avenue, then into nearby Bethesda. He took a room at the Ramada Inn, from which he placed a call to the Second Start program in St. Louis. He had to wait almost ten minutes before Janis came to the phone, somewhat breathless.

"Hi, Groovy. How's it going?"

"I was playing basketball. I'm okay." And she really sounded that way. "They're finally easing up on me. I even get to go to the bathroom myself." She giggled.

"I guess that's good. Are you still mad at me?"

There was a long silence before she said, "Yeah. But that's all right. Everyone in group feels the same way about being here."

"At least you're safe. They can't get at you there."

She sighed. "Yeah. When are you gonna come see me?"

"I'm in D.C. right now. On a business trip."

"D.C.?"

"Yeah."

They each knew what the other was thinking. Dylan said, "I think I'm gonna do it. Tomorrow morning." He tried to keep his tone light. "I could have gone home tonight, but I decided it was time."

"Good!" said Janis. "Good. I'm really glad, Dylan."

"Yeah." Dylan asked her a few more questions about the rehab program, and they chatted until the counselor told her she had to go. "Love ya, Dylan," she said, before she hung up.

Into the dead phone, Dylan said, "Love ya, too, Groovy," and grinned. It was a tremendous change from their last conversation.

He savored the feeling for a moment before calling Barry to tell him about his meeting with Rosati.

"Don't jump to conclusions," Barry said. "Rosati may change his mind after he reviews the full chart."

"No way. You should have seen his face."

"Well. If so, what are you gonna do about it?"

"Tell Henry Girard, of course. Once he knows about this, he'll want to sue. Have you got the autopsy report?"

"I'll get it tomorrow. Didn't have time today."

"If it shows what I expect, I'm going to the prosecutor's office with it."

"Whoa again. One step at a time, please."

"Sure, sure."

"When are you coming home?"

"Tomorrow."

"You couldn't get another flight tonight?"

"I didn't try. I've got some . . . personal business to take care of tomorrow."

"Personal business?"

"Yeah, personal business." Dylan wasn't going to answer the obvious question. "Can you hold the fort for me one more day?"

"Sure. Hudson thinks you've got the flu."

"I'll work on my cough. Thanks, Barry."

The meeting was in Craig Hagen's office. That way, Rosati's visit to the White House would be logged in as a visit to Hagen, not to the President. And it wasn't unusual for President Banfield to leave his office for a tête-à-tête with his closest adviser.

The President arrived after Rosati; he shut the door firmly behind him and locked it, then greeted Rosati warmly. He took a seat on the leather couch. "Let's get started," he said. "I've only got fifteen minutes."

Hagen nodded and looked at Rosati. "Peter, anything new before we make this decision?"

Rosati frowned. "Well, nothing that should change the decision, but something noteworthy in any event." He briefly summarized Dylan's visit to his office.

Banfield said, "I don't get the significance. Whatever the woman died from, she can't help us now."

Rosati said, "I'm not so sure. I know the clinical director there, this Dr. Argent, and I don't trust him. He's the worst kind of glory hound. He also is an absolutely brilliant man. It's just possible he's hiding something, some information that could be useful, not in the short term, but in the long term—"

"We're only interested in the short term," Banfield interjected harshly. "But"—and he looked directly at Hagen—"maybe it wouldn't hurt to look into this. Tell Markham to find out whether Dr. Argent is concealing something from us. Also, that lawyer who came to see Rosati—check him out too. He might know something about Argent that he didn't tell Rosati."

"Right away," said Hagen.

"Good," said Banfield, leaning back on the leather sofa. "Now let's get to the real issues, Peter. What's my latest CD4 count, and do we try some PHT antibody treatment using one of your NIH donors?"

"Your count is two hundred seventy, Mr. President," said Rosati.

"That settles it, then," said Hagen. "Let's start PHT."

Rosati folded his arms, and the two other men looked at him.

"Dr. Rosati?" said Banfield.

"I haven't changed my position, sir. PHT from the donors I have is nowhere near as effective as antiviral therapy. In addition, there is a rebound effect once the treatment is ended."

Banfield sighed. "We're not going over this again. I've decided to stay in this race, and I can't take the risk of getting side effects now."

"I respectfully disagree," Rosati said stubbornly. "As your physician, it's my duty to recommend against PHT."

"All right, you've made your point and covered your ass," Hagen said impatiently. "Your duty is fulfilled."

Banfield looked at his watch and got to his feet.

"It's my decision. We'll go with your PHT, at least until something changes. Peter, tell Craig when you're ready. He'll arrange everything."

"Yes, Mr. President," Rosati and Hagen said in unison.

CHAPTER TWENTY-ONE

Dylan slept late the next morning, then ordered a big breakfast from room service. He showered, shaved, and dressed, feeling detached from his emotions.

From the checkout clerk, he got directions to the nearest florist, where he bought a spray of yellow carnations, then drove back toward the Beltway. He went east on the inner loop. After a fifteen-minute ride that seemed much longer, he exited at Route 1 and followed the directions on the tattered piece of paper he took from his wallet.

Dylan entered the Laurel Rest Cemetery through two wide wrought-iron gates and parked in an almost empty lot. The administrative building was nearby; the entrance road extended from the parking lot and circled the large lot that comprised the bulk of the cemetery.

Dylan stood next to his car holding the flowers and frowning. The place looked different, and he had a only vague recollection of the grave.

Inside the administrative building, he identified himself and asked for a plot map. A few minutes later he stood near the crest of a small hill, looking back over a sea of headstones and grave markers.

The sun shone incongruously bright, and he felt small beads of sweat prickling his forehead. There wasn't anyone else around, not even the omnipresent grave diggers.

He looked at the little map; he was close. He walked forward, counting plots, until he found it.

This was very hard. His throat was constricted and he was on the verge of crying, feeling like a little boy again. He forced himself to look at the headstone.

It was big, almost five feet high. A large beveled cross was carved into the top two thirds, and below was the epitaph:

ANGELA ABBOTT ICE
b. 6–12–48
d. 8–23–86
"On the wings of angels"

Dylan groaned. Angela would have hated this. Absolutely detested it. It was the final revenge of her father, Lucas Abbott.

His hand shook as he gently placed the flowers at the base of the stone. They fell over, but he left them.

This is my mother's grave, Dylan thought. I'm standing over her coffin. Inside the coffin are her desiccated bones. . . . He shook his head violently. *No.* He took a step backward, as though he had been pushed, and thought of his mother, tried to visualize her face, her smell, her smile.

He couldn't. The mind picture wasn't there. Only the horror of that last day. Dylan sat down heavily on the sweet-smelling grass. He took deep breaths and closed his eyes, and didn't even try to avoid the memories.

He could hear Janis's cries of "Stop, Mommy, please stop!" as Angela slapped his face, harder and harder. He would always remember the awful sting of those slaps.

And then Angela wheeled to face Janis, whose tears streamed down pudgy brown cheeks, Cabbage Patch doll clutched to her chest.

"Shut up!" Angela screamed. "Shut up, you brat! I'm sick of you! I'm sick of you!"

Janis gaped in mid-cry, sucking air.

"She doesn't mean it, Groovy," Dylan said quickly, but Janis started wailing again.

And before Dylan could react, Angela strode forward, almost spitting with rage, grabbed Janis by the hair, and jerked her upward and off her feet.

"Shut up!" Angela screamed at her daughter, and with superhuman strength, picked up Janis by the arms and swung her around in a great arc. As Dylan reached out to grab her, Angela let go, and Janis flew into the cinder-block-and-board bookcase with an awful crash. The whole thing collapsed on top of her: books, magazines, knickknacks, heavy boards.

There was a moment of awful silence punctuated by the sound of Angela's stentorian breathing.

Dylan rushed to Janis, pulling debris off her body. Gently, he picked her up and cradled her in his arms. There was blood coming from her ears and nose, and she made no sounds.

Angela took two halting steps toward them, whispered, "Groovy," and reached out to touch Janis's forehead. Dylan fiercely batted her hand away, and Angela drew back with a gasp; then she turned and staggered uncertainly toward the bedroom.

Thank God, thought Dylan, as he checked Janis

for broken bones. If Angela was true to form, she would crash on the bed and they wouldn't see her until tomorrow.

Janis was covered with cuts, bruises, and scratches. She probably had a concussion, but at least now she was making sounds, little whimpers, as she clung to him. He would have to take her to the ER, and there would be a lot of questions. Well, he thought grimly, that's tough. He would tell them exactly what had happened.

A noise made him look up, and he saw Angela coming out of the bedroom again, hugging her arms to her chest. "I'm cold," she said. "I'm cold."

Dylan ignored her. She would have to crash without his help. He took Janis to the kitchen sink and tried to clean her up with some lukewarm water. When he finished, he went to the phone and called for a taxicab. Angela had disappeared again: She probably was back in the bedroom.

The rain had diminished to a mere misting when Dylan, with Janis on his shoulder, stepped out of the trailer to look for the taxi. Janis now was recovered enough to complain of pain and ask where they were going.

"To the hospital, Groovy. We have to let the doctors check you."

"Don't want to." Before he could answer, she said, "Look, there's Mommy!"

Dylan turned to see Angela, about twenty yards away, standing next to the trailer park's barbecue pit. She was thoroughly soaked; her sweatshirt and sweatpants hung like lead weights on her body, her hair plastered to her head. She waved at them, and he noticed she was holding Howard's Zippo lighter, the one he used to light hash pipes and bongs.

"*I'm still cold, Dylan,*" she said, flicking the Zippo on and off.

Odd that she could have gotten so wet, thought Dylan. It was hardly raining.

At the same instant, he noticed the can of barbecue lighter fluid on the ground next to her.

"*No!*" *Dylan screamed, dropping Janis. He ran to Angela, but seemed to move in slow motion, his legs churning. He almost reached her before she flicked on the Zippo one last time, casually touching the flame to her sweatshirt.*

There was a whoosh! *of air, and Angela turned into a torch.*

Dylan burned his hands throwing her to the ground, screaming at her to roll, roll on the wet ground. He tore off his shirt and tried to beat out the flames, but it was futile.

By the time a neighbor came out with a fire extinguisher, Angela was a charred corpse.

Now, at her grave, Dylan covered his face with both hands, rubbing his eyes. In his dreams (and he dreamed about it often) he was always one step short of grabbing the lighter, always one instant from pulling her finger away from the little steel wheel.

He had sworn he would never forgive her for what she did to the family—to Janis—sworn with all the fervor of a morally certain seventeen-year-old. And he had sworn he would never visit her grave.

But now he wanted to forgive Angela, to forgive everything. He wanted to remember the Angela from the carefree days of the VW Microbus, of sleeping under the stars.

His throat was dry, and there was a persistent pain behind his eyes.

He kneeled on the soft earth. "Mom," Dylan said to the headstone, "I'm sorry. I'm sorry I didn't help you. I'm sorry I hated you. I'm sorry."

He didn't cry.

The man in the Oakland Athletics baseball cap lowered the binoculars from his eyes. "Skoler. I think he's praying or something."

Skoler stepped out from behind a tree at the edge of the parking lot, the sun reflecting off his shaved head. His upper chest and shoulders were enormous, the result of hundreds of hours of lifting free weights, and he wore a tight black T-shirt underneath a white linen sport jacket. "He better pray," Skoler said gruffly, "if he keeps sticking his fucking nose where it don't belong."

Preston shrugged. "He's a lawyer. You gotta expect that. Just remember, we're not supposed to take him out. Just educate him."

"Yeah. But I owe him for that phone call to the cops."

Preston said, "Lighten up. We don't get paid if the job ain't done right."

Skoler scowled. This job had been fucked up from the beginning. They were supposed to keep Ice from seeing Rosati, at NIH. That shouldn't have been a problem—except that Skoler had missed his plane because of an unexpected visit from the cops wanting to know why he had been following Charlene McConnell. By the time they got a later flight to D.C., Ice had already been to NIH. Now their orders were to impress Ice with the wisdom of keeping his nose out of other people's business.

"Let's do it now," Skoler said. "Ain't no one around."

"In a cemetery? No way, not me."

Skoler laughed. "What are you afraid of—ghosts?"

"Not in a cemetery," Preston repeated stubbornly. "We got time, we don't have to do it now."

"You're a pussy." Skoler sat down with his back against the tree and opened a pack of chewing gum.

As he drove away from the cemetery, Dylan knew he couldn't go to the airport—not yet. What he wanted to do now was row. Row until his mind stopped, until his heart could pump no harder and until the endorphins pushed all the memories out of his brain.

He wasn't exactly sure how to cut through the city, so he went the long way around, taking the Beltway to Glen Echo, then down Clara Barton Parkway and Canal Road to Georgetown.

The Thompson Boat Center was at Rock Creek Parkway and Virginia Avenue, and he had many happy memories of the place. When he was in college at George Washington University, the varsity crew had rowed out of the boat center, as did Georgetown University's crew and the Capital Rowing Club.

He parked the rental car on the street and dug a T-shirt, shorts and light running shoes out of their customary place in his overnight garment bag.

He went inside the center and changed in the locker room. Then he showed his USRA certification card, rented a Maas Aero, and bought a cheap water bottle that he filled from the water fountain.

After a few minutes of stretching exercises,

Dylan was on the Potomac, skimming southeast toward the Memorial Bridge. It was a very hot day with high humidity, and there weren't many other rowers—just a few tourists in canoes, some water-skiers, and the omnipresent tour boats. The Aero wasn't very well maintained, and his port oar lock made a grinding noise on each recovery stroke, but he didn't care. It felt great to be back on the water.

He eased up as he passed the Lincoln Memorial and saw the Washington Monument. Washington might have its problems, but it was a uniquely beautiful city, even on a muggy, hazy summer day. He took a long drink of water and turned the shell around, heading back up river. He increased his pace and soon felt his heart pumping and his respiration rising, the shoreline flying by. He swooped past Roosevelt Island and the Roosevelt Bridge, then under Key Bridge, as the shore changed from parkland to cliffs.

He thought of his mother again, and this time Dylan could clearly visualize her face as it was . . . before. He remembered her smile, the way the corners of her eyes crinkled when she laughed, and the sweet smell of marijuana on her sweater.

The visit to her gravesite, he realized, had liberated him, had started a geologic shift in his emotions. It wasn't his fault she was a junkie; even if he had prevented her death that day, the end result would have been the same.

Dylan laughed, a great, big, deep laugh from his belly that felt absolutely wonderful. The end of the laugh, however, was drowned by the sound of a motorboat overtaking him on the left. As he concentrated on his stroke, his peripheral vision caught the sight of the twenty-foot pace boat with a big Evinrude outboard, moving upriver about fifty yards away. It was one of the Capital Rowing Club's pace boats, but he didn't see any of the club's shells around.

There were two men in the boat, and he instantly had the feeling he knew them; they were familiar, but he couldn't place the context. Maybe they were from his undergraduate rowing days.

The pace boat passed behind him and Dylan kept rowing, gradually picking up his pace. Eventually he reached his old turnaround point. Because rowers rowed sitting backward to their forward progress, it was dangerous to scull alone in waters with any hazards, and the Potomac beyond this point was quite rocky. He stopped rowing, gasping with the effort of his last sprint, his shirt soaked in sweat. Dylan stripped it off and threw it in the bottom of the boat, then took another swig of water.

Resting on his oars, he allowed the shell to drift slowly toward the western bank of the river, his back to the shore.

Now he could see no other boats, and Washington was out of sight around a bend of the river. He took a deep breath, getting ready to start back, when there was a sudden roar of an engine starting close behind him. Dylan twisted on his seat and saw the pace boat that had passed earlier, emerging from the deep shadows close to shore. The boat burst into the sunshine about twenty-five yards from him, the big outboard revving at full throttle.

In that instant Dylan saw the man kneeling in the stern—and suddenly recognized him. It was the driver of the car following Charlene McConnell.

That instant of recognition was followed by the realization that the boat was pointed directly at the side of his shell.

"Look out!" Dylan shouted, knowing they couldn't hear him over the motor's roar. He desperately unshipped his oars and tried to scull out of the way. Even so, he kept expecting the boat to change course. Then the bald man in the stern ducked below the gunwale, covering his head.

"Shit!" Dylan yelled as he dropped the oars and tumbled over the side of the shell, an instant before the collision.

As the water closed over his head, Dylan heard the thump of the impact, incredibly loud—even through the water—followed by an awful grinding noise. When he surfaced, gasping, he struck his head a glancing blow on a shattered piece of the shell.

His head reeled with the suddenness of the incident and the blow to his head; he treaded water in a daze as the pace boat, its aluminum bow dented, turned in a tight circle and headed back toward him. Dylan started swimming toward shore, knowing he would never make it in time.

The boat roared up on his left and then the engine was thrown into reverse. He heard a voice yelling, "Ice! Ice, you bastard, stop swimming!"

He turned to face the boat and looked up at the lumpy face of the big bald man, peering at him over the gunwale. The boat rocked violently in its own wake.

"Who the hell are you?" Dylan managed to say.

"Shut up," said the man. "You're a nosy bastard, Ice, and nosy bastards have short lives. You understand what I'm saying?"

"No," Dylan spluttered, slipping underwater for a moment. He came back up and tried to grab the boat for support. The bald man slapped his hand away.

"It's easy," the man said. "Just keep your fucking big nose out of the Girard case. You got that?"

Dylan felt a surge of anger, despite his vulnerable position. "No, I don't, and fuck you."

Almost instantly, the bald man leaned over the side and swung a fist at Dylan's head. Because of his position, it was an awkward motion, and Dylan was able to move so that the fist only glanced off the side of his head, but he slipped underwater again. As he surfaced, he heard a voice from the bow of the boat, "Skoler, you're not supposed to kill him!"

"The hell I won't," Skoler said.

Dylan started swimming as he heard the outboard rev up again. The boat made a tight circle, then came right at him. Dylan was still a good fifty yards from the shore, and he didn't know whether to break left or right, so he dove underwater.

He was unpleasantly surprised to find the bottom only a few feet below. Bouncing back toward the surface, Dylan frantically blew the air out of his lungs, then sank down again, knowing he had to get as low as possible in order to avoid the propeller. He flattened himself on the slimy bottom as the boat passed overhead, grabbing a hunk of weeds with his right hand and instinctively bringing his left hand up over his head as the motor noise was loudest. He felt something bump against his hand, pulling at it, and he jerked it back while burrowing deeper into the mud.

Then the boat was past.

As Dylan rose to the surface—he could stand now—there was a horrible grinding noise followed by a soft bump! He shook the water from his eyes. Directly ahead of him, the pace boat was hard aground. The big outboard had flipped up and nearly torn the rear transom out of the boat.

Skoler apparently had been tossed out of the boat by the impact; he was in the water a good ten yards ahead of the boat, already wading toward shore. The other man, younger and blond, was just getting up from the floorboards, bleeding from the scalp and holding his left arm like it was broken. He jumped into the water and followed Skoler.

Dylan felt an immense sense of relief, at the same time becoming aware of pain coming from his left hand. He held up the hand and saw it was covered with a mixture of blood and water. He must have cut it.

Then he looked closer. About half of the little and ring fingers were missing, cut diagonally across the first joint of each finger. Blood oozed out of the stumps.

Dylan fainted into the water.

CHAPTER TWENTY-TWO

"**M**r. President! Mr. President!" The White House press corps was like a kindergarten class clamoring for attention, hands windmilling in the air. Banfield leaned forward on the podium and pointed at a balding, overweight man in a blue seersucker suit. "Bob."

Robert Mendes was no friend of the administration, but Banfield already had taken questions from the usual suspects and he couldn't avoid unpleasantness forever. Mendes, a reporter for the *Wall Street Journal*, usually asked foreign policy questions that had no concrete answers, making Banfield appear either evasive or unknowledgeable.

Mendes stood. "Mr. President, your opponent recently released his complete medical history and the full results of his latest medical examination, but, up to this time, you have released only medical summaries, not your actual records. Do you have a reason, sir, for failing to provide full medical disclosure?"

Does he know? Banfield thought, his gut clenching. Or was this just a fishing expedition? He took a deep breath, keeping his face neutral, then forced a genial smile. He said, "My personal physician, Dr. Schreiber, has released a detailed report on my health. We're not required to do that, as you know, and in fact that's more than most of my predecessors have done. And I'll bet my cholesterol is lower than yours, Bob."

This brought laughter from the press corps—Mendes was famous for his doughnut intake. Hands shot up in the air again. As Banfield scanned for the next questioner, Mendes said loudly, "A follow-up question, Mr. President! If you're in such great health, why won't you reveal the results of your most recent blood tests?"

The bastard must know, thought Banfield. He turned to face Mendes again. Before he could say anything, Mendes continued, "Senator Osborne has released all of his laboratory test results, *including* those for sexually transmitted diseases."

It was one of those rare moments when the entire press corps shut up. Mendes, they were sure, wouldn't be asking such specific questions without a lead.

Stay calm, Banfield told himself fiercely. He glanced to the side of the stage, where Hagen stood with his other aides and handlers. Hagen, alone among his staff, knew the significance of this question, and he looked frightened and angry. Their eyes met briefly. *I've got to stonewall until we can figure out what to do. When in doubt, attack.*

He kept smiling and said genially, "Well, Bob, since you bring it up, I think it's fair for me to comment on that issue. I really don't know why Senator Osborne felt it necessary to *suddenly* release so much of his personal health history." His tone was both ironic and scornful. "But, as you know, I've been happily married for over twenty-five years. It's a matter of record that my opponent has, unfortunately, suffered through two divorces. If Senator Osborne thinks it is necessary to disclose every scrap of personal information, including testing for sexually transmitted diseases, that's his privilege. I guess he wants to prove he's still . . . active. Personally, I think Americans are more interested in the real issues."

Banfield could see from the nodding heads and body language that this had defused the situation. He immediately turned to face the other side of the room, searching for another reporter to call on.

Mendes didn't give up; the bastard was like a terrier. He shouted, "Well, if you don't have anything to hide, why don't you—" but the rest of the question was drowned by the new chorus of "Mr. President, Mr. President!"

"Thank you, Mr. President," one of the reporters said, and Banfield quickly strode off the stage and out of the C-SPAN picture.

Mitch McPeak picked up the remote control and pushed the power button. He turned to his boss, grinning. "Mendes did a hell of a job, didn't he, Senator?"

McPeak, Senators Osborne and Barcus, and Turk Finnegan—the gang of four, as Finnegan thought of them—were in a plush office in the party campaign headquarters, a ten-story office building on K Street.

Osborne leaned back in his swivel chair, an unlit cigar clenched between his teeth. He nodded. "Yeah, he did. But God, Banfield is slick. He must have been sweating bullets, but you'd never know it." He nodded at Finnegan. "What did you think?"

Turk Finnegan scratched the side of his face pensively. It still felt very strange being here, the headquarters of the party he had fought against his entire adult life. "He reacted the way I expected. But I guarantee there will be a hell of a meeting in the Oval Office in a few minutes."

Osborne made a tent of his fingers. The fluorescent lighting highlighted his prominent eyebrows, giving him a hooded, forbidding look. "Banfield will be on guard now, of course. And looking for the leak." He nodded at Finnegan again.

"So what's our next move?" said Barcus.

"What do you suggest, Mitch?" Osborne asked his campaign manager.

McPeak stroked his crewcut. "Turn up the pressure, Ted. Until he 'fesses up."

"Banfield can't do that!" said Barcus, his jowls jiggling.

"Why not?" said Osborne.

Barcus sputtered indignantly, "Several reasons! First, voters don't want to elect a man with a terminal disease! Second, there's the honesty issue—he lied when he said he was in good health. Third, there's the issue of how he got sick. If that becomes known, the first two issues don't matter—he's a dead man walking!"

"Exactly right," said Osborne. "He'll have to withdraw from the race. It's the only way he can finish his term in dignity. The question is . . . when."

"I get it!" said Barcus. "You want him getting nervous, but you don't want to lower the boom until after the convention!"

Osborne nodded. "If he withdraws before the

convention, the party will nominate someone else. I'm satisfied I could beat any of the contenders, but why take a chance? If it happens after the convention, they'll have to either hold a special convention or let the Vice President run in Banfield's place. Either way—"

That brought smiles to the faces of everyone. The Vice President, Arthur Sinclair, was a lightweight former Senator, chosen purely for ticket-balancing reasons. In addition, the President had made him point man on several unpopular issues.

McPeak said, "This is all fine, except for one thing. How *do* we lower the boom? We don't have any evidence. Rumor alone is not gonna bring the bastard down."

"That's true," Osborne said. "We don't have any documentary evidence. But Banfield doesn't know that. And can he take the chance?"

"They'll figure out that I'm the leak," said Finnegan. "And they'll have to assume that I made a copy of the letter."

"Yes," said Osborne. He looked at McPeak. "What about the other end of this? Have we learned anything about Conner?"

McPeak shook his head. "I've had two operatives checking him out, talking to his family and acquaintances, but so far, nothing. For a faggot, he sure kept his mouth shut."

They all laughed, except for Finnegan.

"So the bottom line is, we have no proof!" said Barcus. "That still bothers me!"

"You're all forgetting one thing," said Osborne. "Regardless of anything we do, the man does have AIDS, and Turk says he's had some symptoms already."

They all looked at each other for a long moment, absorbing the implications of that statement.

"How the hell did they find out?" Banfield said, pacing furiously around the Oval Office.

Hagen, looking out the window across the South Lawn, turned to face the President. "There are only five people who knew, besides Marianne—you, me, T.J., Dr. Rosati, and Dr. Schreiber. It wasn't me or you, and it sure as hell wasn't T.J. I assume we can count out Marianne. That leaves only the doctors."

Banfield frowned. "No. I don't believe that either one—"

"It doesn't have to be deliberate. A slip of the tongue, a carelessly placed lab report—"

"No! It doesn't smell that way to me."

Hagen nodded. Banfield's instincts in these matters were usually right. "There is one other possibility," Hagen mused. "But you're not going to like it."

"There's nothing here to like. Go on."

"Turk."

Banfield winced. He sat down heavily in one of the big wing chairs, his gray hair in disarray. He suddenly looked very old. "I thought you might say that. But Turk never knew."

"So we believed. But a couple of things make me suspicious. One, he has a motive—he hates us now. Second, he's been seen lurking around your worthy opponent."

"What!" Banfield's head snapped up. "I didn't know that."

"I'm afraid so. And he might have picked up on this before he left."

"If that's true, I'm done for."

Hagen ignored that. "We need to work out some contingency plans."

"Get me a drink, will you?" said Banfield. "Bourbon."

Hagen went to the wet bar in the corner and mixed a double Jack Daniel's over ice. He placed it in the President's hand. Banfield rarely drank during the day; now he took a deep gulp.

"We'll discuss this later," Banfield said. "Can you leave me alone for a while?"

"Of course. What should I tell Nachman? He's outside with your briefing books and appointment schedule for the rest of the day."

Nachman was his appointments secretary.

"Just give me five minutes, dammit!"

Hagen grinned. At least Banfield had some fire left. They could beat this thing, he knew, as long as Banfield didn't lose his nerve. "You got it, sir," he said, and left.

Banfield stretched his legs out toward the empty fireplace and took another sip of bourbon. He felt terribly, terribly tired, and old beyond his years. How had he gotten himself into this? What strange devil had possessed him to throw away his career—maybe his life—in one moment years ago? He closed his eyes and remembered that strange interlude during his campaign for governor, ten years and an era ago.

It was the first—and only—time he had had sex with a man. No one would believe that now, of course, sometimes even he had trouble believing it, but it was true.

All his life, Banfield had been a heterosexual macho man, a star athlete, a successful lawyer, and

finally the people's choice. And always he had felt
the urge, the need. Always suppressed, always
shoved down to the deepest level of consciousness.

He remembered.

It was almost one A.M. *when he finished his
paperwork, pulled on his sport jacket, and walked
down the hall to the "hothouse," the big room
where the volunteers worked the phones and stuffed
envelopes. He looked around for his campaign manager, but the only one in the room was Jason
Conner, a campaign volunteer in his twenties.
Conner wore a black polo shirt, black corduroy
pants, and western boots.*

*Naturally Banfield had to say hello and com-
ment on Conner's work ethic. They talked for a
while, then something made Banfield suggest they
get a drink. They walked down the street to a bar,
talking about the campaign and the results of the latest poll. Inside the bar, they sat at a small round
wood table in a dark alcove. Conner ordered beer;
Banfield drank two bourbons. He pretended that he
didn't notice how Conner looked at him. It was
harder to deny how it excited him.*

*Conner seemed to know what he was feeling,
and it seemed natural when he briefly touched
Banfield's hand: once as if by accident, the second
time by design. The third time, Banfield left it there.*

*It also seemed normal when they paid the bill
and walked back to the campaign headquarters.
Without further words, they entered the dark building and walked through the now-dark building to
his office. And then, suddenly, they were together,
crashing onto the couch, touching and fondling.*

*The sex was very strong, almost violent, and, for
the first time, Banfield was passive, the recipient, not*

the aggressor. To his amazement, it seemed natural that way.

When it was over, when Conner had dressed and left without a word, Banfield felt both relief and disgust. He had enjoyed it, truly enjoyed it, there was no denying that. At the same time he was revolted by the terrible danger in which he had placed himself. His political career was on the rise; if he won reelection as governor, he would be in position to challenge for the national party leadership. If Conner talked, if this were known . . .

He swore that he would never take such a risk again.

And he hadn't. By God, he hadn't. How many times had he wanted to? How many times had he resisted the urge?

Banfield struggled upward in the chair, rose, and went to his desk, thinking of Mendes's questions at his press conference. *Before all this, I was willing to bow out, to just finish my term in dignity. But now they're raising the stakes, and I find I don't want to go out so easily.* He hit the button on his intercom and ordered Hagen to return.

When Hagen entered, Banfield said, "We're gonna beat this thing, Craig, I swear it. First, we have to find out where the leak is, and how much they know. I want you to put a twenty-four-hour tail on Turk. I want to know everything about him—where he's living, who he sees, who he calls and who calls him. I want to know the color of his shit. You got that?"

Hagen grinned at him. "I got it."

"And get a progress report from Markham on that Dr. Argent in St. Louis. My instincts tell me he's hiding something, and I want to know what it is, and whether it can help me."

"Anything else?"

"Not right now. Tell Nachman to come in." Banfield sat down in his presidential chair, behind the desk cut from the timbers of the HMS *Renown*, and stared at the large portrait of Abraham Lincoln on the wall.

CHAPTER TWENTY-THREE

Dylan walked through the airport gate, his garment bag slung over his right shoulder.

"Dylan!" squealed Janis, running forward. He put down the bag and she stopped about a foot away, looking at him with wide eyes. Then she reached out and gingerly hugged him.

"Here, let me take that," said Barry, coming up behind Janis. He hoisted Dylan's bag. "How you feeling?"

Dylan shrugged. "The pain medication works pretty well, it just makes me a little woozy. Sort of like a dull ache."

Janis looked at his left hand, a bit fearfully. There wasn't much to see. The stumps of the two fingers were sewn up and hidden under a wide ace bandage that encircled his whole left hand, leaving only thumb and index finger free. "It must have been terrible," she said softly.

Other passengers swirled around them. "C'mon, let's get going," said Dylan, and they started walking down the concourse toward the terminal. He looked at Janis. "Did you have any trouble getting out of Second Start?"

Janis shook her head. "Barry took care of it for me. But I have to be back tonight."

"You will be," Dylan said. He was pleased to see how energetic she seemed. She wore a Chicago Bulls sweatshirt cut off at the arms, black jeans, and her Nike sneakers. She practically bounced down the concourse, eyes sparkling with life.

They went out to Barry's car in the short-term parking lot. A light, drizzling rain fell, and the air was heavy with humidity and ozone. Barry said, "Your car isn't here at the airport?"

"Un-uh. I didn't know how long I would be away, so I took a taxi on the way out."

As they drove out of the airport in Barry's late-model BMW, Barry said, "So. Tell us all about it."

Dylan sighed. "There's not much more besides what I told you on the phone."

"Have they caught the guys yet?" said Janis.

"No. And you wouldn't believe what I had to go through just to file a report. I was in the ER and asked them to get a cop. When the cop finally appears, he says it's not a D.C. police case, because of where it happened on the river. They call for the Maryland Natural Resources police. By the time the Maryland cop shows up, I'm up on the ward. He takes my statement, I tell him about Skoler and that I had turned his license tag over to Detective Peterson, here in St. Louis."

Barry nodded. "Detective Peterson left a message for you this morning. That's probably what it's about."

"Good! Can I use your car phone?"

"Sure."

Dylan took out his wallet; he had left it in his rental car at Thompson's, or everything in it would be soaked—and found Peterson's business card. He was lucky; Peterson was in the office.

"Mr. Ice!" Peterson said. "You're a busy man. How's your hand?"

"I lost a couple of fingers, but I'll live," Dylan said, amazed that he could say it with such bravado. "You talked with the Maryland police?"

"Yeah. Let me bring you up to date. I ran the make on the car, like you asked, just before you left on Tuesday. It's owned by a guy named William Skoler. We know him—he's got quite a rap sheet locally—mostly assault and battery. He's a small-time hood, a hired thug, acts as an enforcer for bookies and some drug dealers. I sent a uniform to his apartment to ask him about McConnell, but of course he denied everything. We can't do any more without some evidence."

"I'll swear out a complaint."

"Un-uh. Nothing's happened to you in Missouri. We've got no jurisdiction, and no judge is gonna approve a warrant based on an out-of-state assault, unless we get notification that Maryland has issued an arrest warrant. Even then—"

"Yes, I see," said Dylan impatiently. "Isn't there anything you can do now?"

"We'll keep an eye on him when he gets back to Missouri, don't worry. And as soon as the Maryland cops finish their investigation and file charges . . ."

Dylan felt like he should be doing something else, but didn't know what. It was an annoying sensation. He sighed. "Okay. I understand. Look, thanks for getting that information for me. I appreciate it."

"Sure. Now you try to stay out of trouble."

"I'll try." Dylan hung up and related the conversation to Barry and Janis.

"Good. Sounds like the cops are doing their job," said Barry.

Dylan settled back in his seat, adjusting his arm. Despite what he had told Janis, his hand was throbbing pretty badly. The ER doctors told him the pain would be worse the second day, and they were right.

The rain got heavier, and he looked at the familiar scenes of St. Louis flashing by the window, feeling a sense of displacement. Trauma did that to you, he knew. He closed his eyes, remembering that first sight of his hand, the bones of two fingers shining wetly through the blood. He had felt dizzy and sick, felt himself falling, then the shock of the water entering his mouth. Choking and spluttering, he had stood up and stumbled like a drunk toward shore.

When he emerged from the water, he saw Skoler and the other man scrambling up a steep slope, disappearing into the underbrush. He had stood there uncertainly for a while before taking off his shirt and wrapping it around his bloody hand. The blood loss made him feel faint, and he sat down heavily on the shore.

He had no idea how much time passed before a motorboat stopped and the occupants asked if he was all right. The boat took him to the nearest dock, where he was transported by ambulance to the Georgetown University Hospital Emergency Room. Although his injury was, by ER standards, comparatively minor, the doctors were willing to admit him to the hospital overnight, for "observation." He accepted gratefully.

Dylan was pulled from his memory as Barry stopped the car. They were in a guest space in front of Dylan's town-house complex.

They all went up to the apartment. Dylan sat on

the living room couch and looked around wonderingly. He had been gone only three days; it felt like a year.

"You probably should just rest today," said Barry. "I'm sure you lost a lot of blood."

"Absolutely," said Janis. "I'll make you some soup. Chicken soup." She went into the kitchen. Barry and Dylan looked at each other and smiled.

Dylan said, "Hudson? What did you tell him?"

"The truth. What the hell could I do? He's bound to notice you're missing a couple of fingers."

Dylan started and Barry said, immediately, "Sorry. That was insensitive."

"It's all right. I've got to get used to it. What did he say?"

"Not much. He acted concerned, for what it's worth. But you better give him a call."

Dylan shook his head. "Not yet. I've got some other business first."

"Other business?" Barry frowned. "What other business? You mean, with the police? I thought you just took care of that."

"Other business."

Janis came into the room with a tray of cookies and some coffee. "The soup will be ready in a minute," she said, returning to the kitchen. Dylan could tell she enjoyed acting parental.

Barry took off his suit jacket, loosened his tie, and poured himself a cup of coffee. "Let's get it all out in the open. What other business?"

"Did you get the Girard autopsy report?"

"Yeah, I got it yesterday."

Dylan felt a surge of excitement. "What did it say?"

Barry shrugged. "I'm no doctor, but it seems to

confirm exactly what Dr. Argent told you. Respiratory distress."

"Where is the report?"

"At the office."

"I need to see it."

"Fine. But I'm not leaving here until you answer my question. What other business?"

"Pour me some coffee."

"Jesus!" Barry said grumpily, but complied, as Janis came in and quietly sat down.

Dylan took a sip of coffee. "In the hospital, I had a lot of time to think. Here's what I've come up with. Assume for a moment that Argent did something terribly wrong in the clinical trial. Something that killed Nicole Girard, and maybe affected others we don't even know about. Anyway, it's something that could make him vulnerable to a malpractice suit, even lose his medical license, so he's got to cover up. That shouldn't be a problem, except that Charlene McConnell and Pamela Holtz won't leave him alone. They keep pushing, pushing, and he knows that eventually what he did will be revealed. So, first he tries to shut them up by offering a big settlement—"

"That settlement offer came from Fletcher," objected Barry.

"Yeah, I know, that doesn't make sense. But Fletcher is the major donor to MIRI. It would be quite an embarrassment to Fletcher if the director of MIRI turns out to be incompetent or worse. I'm not saying that Fletcher has anything to do with it, but he would probably be willing to help Argent out of a jam. And maybe there is some truth to the cover story about saving the Girards from further trauma."

"Okay," said Barry neutrally. "Go on."

"Of course, Holtz and McConnell don't take the settlement, so now Argent gets really desperate. He hires someone to either scare or kill Holtz. McConnell told me that Holtz had been drawn to that bar by a phone call from someone purportedly offering information about the Girard case."

Barry put up hand. "Hold on. There's a piece of information you don't have. While you were in Washington, the police made an arrest in Holtz's case."

"Yes!" said Dylan excitedly. "Who was it?"

"It's exactly whom everyone suspected—the White Lords. A couple of the members got drunk and bragged about it. The news reports are skimpy, but it looks like someone paid them to go after Holtz."

"I knew it! Argent!"

"So you think Argent also hired this guy Skoler to go after McConnell, and then you?"

"Don't you?"

"No. If Argent hired Skoler to scare you off, why not do it here, in St. Louis? What's the point of sending Skoler and his buddy to Washington? Come to think of it, how did he even know you were going to Washington?" Barry's face suddenly got grave. "I thought I was the only one who knew that. And I certainly didn't tell anybody."

"I believe you. And I don't know the answer. Maybe they were following me. Maybe it's got something to do with my seeing Dr. Rosati. I don't know."

But Barry was in his cross-examination mode. "You didn't answer my question, Dylan. Who else knew you were going to Washington?"

Dylan sighed. "Kristin."

"Aha!"

"Yeah, I know," Dylan said gloomily. "She may have mentioned it to her father. Fletcher may have tipped off Argent without knowing what Argent would do with the information. Anyway, I didn't swear Kristin to secrecy, you know."

"Who's Kristin?" Janis asked sweetly.

They both looked at her, startled; they'd almost forgotten she was there. "A friend," said Dylan. "I'll explain some other time." He turned back to Barry. "The point is, Argent is behind all this."

"Yes," said Barry, "that's what bothers me. It's *too* obvious. Argent isn't dumb. All it takes is for one of the White Lords or Skoler to identify Argent as the man that paid them, and it's over for him."

"They'll never connect Argent, he's too smart. Probably used three different middlemen."

Janis said quietly, "So what are you gonna do?"

Dylan looked at her. "That's a good question. I guess I'll wait to see if the police can link Argent to Holtz's death, or to Skoler."

"And if they can't?" said Barry.

Dylan started to say that there wouldn't be much else he could do, but something held him back. The words seemed to stick in his throat. He felt different, changed in some way. Maybe part of his personality had washed ashore in the strong current of the Potomac River, along with his fingertips. He knew now that he should have asked Detective Peterson for Skoler's address. Slowly, he held up his left hand. "Skoler isn't going to get away with this. And if Argent is behind it all . . ."

Barry and Janis stared at him. His words were spoken softly but with an unusual fierceness, disconcertingly out of character.

"Very dramatic," Barry said finally. "But I don't think it's a good idea to get consumed by this, Dylan. So far all you've lost are some fingers."

Dylan smiled at him. "You underestimate me."

"You need to get away," Kristin said the next evening, as they ate dinner in a small downtown Chinese restaurant. She reached over a plate of Szechuan chicken and gently patted his hand above the bandage. "My father has a place in the Caribbean—Barbados—we can go there for a few days."

"No, thanks. Not now."

"Too much work at the office? Can't they spare you?"

Dylan shook his head. "I've got a couple of trials coming up. Anyway, I'm in no position to ask for time off. Paul Hudson was none too pleased about my Washington trip."

"I would think not," she said, taking a big gulp of beer. "You're not in real trouble, are you?"

Dylan looked around the restaurant, eyes unfocused. "Well, yes and no. Hudson and I had a strange meeting today. He started off very solicitous about my hand, said we could get some dictation equipment—now that I can't type—and that the firm would make whatever accommodation was necessary for my . . . 'handicap,' he called it. He offered to give me some time off again, which I refused. Then he laid into me for taking time off without permission and for an unauthorized investigation into the Girard case."

"What did he think about the attack on you?"

"I don't think he quite believes it. It's too far-fetched, from his point of view. And he told me he doesn't care whether Nicole died of AIDS or not—it's none of our business unless the client wants to pursue it."

"I see."

"Then his tone changed, he almost started apologizing for reprimanding me. It was really weird."

"Not if you think about it," Kristin said thoughtfully. "I bet he suddenly remembered your relationship with me and my father. He needs you, Dylan. Or at least he thinks he does."

"Shit," said Dylan, knowing she was right, and hating it. "I don't want our relationship to be some kind of shield. If I'm wrong, I'm wrong, and I should suffer the consequences. Likewise, I want to be able to take credit for what I do on my own."

"Poor baby," said Kristin, laughing. "So is Hudson taking you off the Girard case? The estate case, I mean?"

"He didn't say that. Not yet, anyway. He just said that he would never have approved my trip to see Dr. Rosati. I'd bet the firm wouldn't even be handling the estate case if it weren't for the Fletcher factor."

"'The Fletcher factor!'" said Kristin. "I love it!" She finished her second beer; she really could drink an amazing amount of beer.

He also took a sip of his Heineken and said as casually as possible, "By the way, you didn't mention that I was going to Washington to anybody, did you? Your father, perhaps?"

She looked at him through half-closed eyelids. "I don't think so. Why?"

"Well, I'm trying to figure out how this guy Skoler knew I was in Washington."

"What would that have to do with my telling Daddy?" Before he could answer, she continued, "Oh, I get it. You think I told Daddy, and he told Argent."

"The thought had crossed my mind."

She chuckled. "And you were nervous about asking me. It's all right, I'm not offended. The truth is, I really don't remember telling him. But yeah, I guess if I did, it's possible Daddy might have mentioned it to Argent. He talks to him quite frequently. You want me to find out?"

"No, please don't say anything."

After a long silence, she said, "So you're not giving up on this."

"No, I'm not."

"And now you won't tell me your plans, will you?"

"I—it's not that I don't trust you Kristin, but—"

"I promise I'll never mention anything to my father about you again. Okay?"

What could he say? "Sure."

She laughed. "You don't mean it, but I'll change your mind. I really am quite loyal." She reached out and stroked his bandaged hand again. "My one-handed lover."

He couldn't help himself. "One hand is all I need."

"Thanks for seeing me so promptly," Dylan said the next morning.

"No problem," said Dr. Silverburg. He peered across his cluttered desk. "What happened to your hand?"

"Just a little boating accident."

"Oh." He looked down at the papers in front of

him and adjusted his half-rim reading glasses. "Well, I've read it, and all I can say is that it's a classic post-mortem report."

Silverburg was chairman of County Hospital's Pathology Department. Dylan had sent the report over by messenger before the appointment, and now he was getting the benefit of Silverburg's expertise. He hoped it would be worth the $350 an hour consultation fee he was paying out of his own pocket.

"Really? In what way?"

Silverburg paused to consider his answer. He was a short, wiry man in his fifties with pronounced cheekbones and hands that seemed disproportionately large. His hospital office overflowed with papers, documents, charts, and slides. Files were stacked on the floor, spilled out from bookcases, covered the windowsill behind the credenza. He said, "I mean 'classic' in the truest sense of the word. I have seen this report thousands of times."

"I don't understand."

"It's simple. You have a copy?"

"Certainly." He pulled it out of his briefcase.

"Turn to . . . let's see, page three. You got it? Okay, now follow along with me." Silverburg started reading from the "gross" pathology—the description of the internal body organs as they looked to the naked eye, rather than the microscopic examination of tissue from those organs. He read a description of Nicole's heart, then put the paper down and continued talking. Dylan, following along on the page, saw that Silverburg was reciting, word for word, exactly what appeared in the report.

"What the hell?"

Silverburg stopped reciting. "Now, a certain amount of this is quite customary. Every pathologist is similarly trained, and we all dictate alike. Surgeons, too—operative reports about the same operation will be almost identical; everyone uses the same stock phrases describing normal structures and organs. But in every postmortem report, I mean *every* report, there will be *something* different, something to distinguish that patient from all others. The liver may be larger, or smaller, the coronary arteries will have gradations of plaque. In this case, however, *every* single organ and system is *exactly* at the mean. Without deviation. It's as if a computer wrote it."

Dylan struggled to assimilate this. "Wait a minute. What you're telling me, then, is that there is no way to tell from this report that it's an autopsy of Nicole Girard?"

Silverburg chuckled. "Hell, I can't tell you that this is an autopsy of *anyone*. No one is this normal. No one."

"But—wait a minute. What about the pulmonary distress? The report says her lungs showed objective finding of that, and her heart—"

"Mr. Ice. Everyone who dies has pulmonary distress. Everyone who dies—their heart stops. These are patently normal findings for death. But they don't tell us *how* the patient died. Or why." He paused for a few seconds, his eyebrows twitching like caterpillars. Then he said, "Frankly, Mr. Ice, I can't tell you for sure that an autopsy *was* done on this patient." He tapped the report on his desk. "Normally, I'd just pick up the phone and call the attending pathologist, but I've never heard of this man. He's not a member of the University Hospital pathology department, and I notice that the signature of the department head is missing."

"That's right. Dr. Argent, the patient's attending

physician, brought this guy in from out of town, supposedly an expert in AIDS pathology. Argent arranged everything, and I haven't even been able to find out where he's from."

"That's highly unusual. Highly unusual."

"Yes, I know. That's one of the reasons I'm here." He took a long breath, his head swimming with the implications. "If you had to find out how this patient died, at this time, how would you do it?"

"I think you know how it's done, Mr. Ice. We do another autopsy."

"Can you do that? I mean, a whole new autopsy? Aren't some of the parts . . . missing?"

Silverburg shrugged. "You're quite right. The major organs are examined, weighed, measured, and either preserved or disposed outside the body. She wasn't embalmed afterward, was she?"

"Not to my knowledge."

"Good. Well, then, since I assume you would be looking for some medications that might have caused a respiratory or cardiac arrest, we would take tissue samples for toxicological analysis."

Dylan was rapidly gaining serious respect for this doctor. "How did you know that I suspected medications might have caused her death?"

"C'mon, now. Why else would you be going to all this trouble? She's not a crime victim, is she?"

"That's the point. I don't know."

Silverburg seemed unsurprised. "Well, in any event, I must warn you that if she died from a drug toxicity—intentional or unintentional—trying to find the cause is worse than looking for the prover-bial needle. In order to test for a drug, we have to suspect it first. And to suspect it, we have to detect it. You see the problem."

"But there are some routine things you always test for, right? And you also would have the medication record from her hospital chart."

"Yes, that's true. I'm not saying it's impossible, just very difficult. Now, on the other hand, if she died from trauma of some sort—well, that's considerably easier to detect, even with the passage of time."

"I understand. At this stage, there's nothing we would want to rule out."

"Well, this can be done. You represent the patient's parents, right?"

"Uh, yes."

"Then they can consent to a disinterment and second autopsy."

"Don't we need an exhumation order?"

Silverburg smiled. "I'm no lawyer, and I don't want to tell you your business, but my understanding is that as long as there is family consent, you don't need to go to court. Unless the Missouri code has recently changed."

"Uh, frankly, I didn't know that. This isn't an area I usually practice in. I'm sure you're right."

"A lawyer who admits he doesn't know everything! What a treat!"

Dylan grinned back. "I'm afraid I have to say it often." He thought for a moment, then continued, "I'll have to discuss this with my clients. In the meantime, can you give me a report?"

"A report? A report on what?"

"Just summarizing what you've told me today."

"Of course. If you like. Any pathologist could tell you the same."

"Yes," said Dylan. "That's exactly the point, isn't it?"

CHAPTER TWENTY-FOUR

There was, Dylan thought, no easy way to ask the question. He pulled his chair closer to the Girards' kitchen table, hoping he had laid sufficient groundwork. He had methodically reviewed the entire history of Nicole's treatment and her death. He said earnestly, and pompously, "What I'm about to ask may be a shock, but I wouldn't ask unless I was utterly convinced of its necessity."

Henry's face was blank and impassive; Amanda appeared nervous, even fearful. She wore a flowery yellow print dress that clashed with her complexion, and she fingered the arm of her wheelchair nervously.

"We need to find out what really killed Nicole," Dylan continued, taking the plunge. "Because I don't think she died from AIDS."

Amanda gave a little start. Henry said slowly, "That's a pretty big statement, son."

"Yes, it is."

Henry rubbed his eyes with the palm of his hand. "I guess I can understand why you say it. Because of the autopsy and what that NIH feller told you, right?"

"That's right. I mean, there's more to it, but that's it, essentially."

"Well now, just how do you propose to find out what really happened?"

Amanda said, "Don't you see where he's leading, Henry?"

They both stared at her.

"I know exactly what you're getting at, Mr. Ice. You want to dig her up, don't you?" Her voice was shrill, and her hands were twisting the chain of the silver crucifix hanging from her neck. "Dig her up so they can do more tests on her, isn't that right?"

"Another autopsy," Dylan said softly.

"Hasn't she had enough tests? Haven't enough people been poking around my poor baby?"

"Amanda—" Henry said.

"I don't want her dug up, you hear me? She's finally got some peace. She's with the Lord, and it don't matter to the Lord how she died!"

"Mrs. Girard—" Dylan said feebly.

"Give us a few minutes," said Henry. He nodded toward the living room.

"Of course," said Dylan.

He went into the living room and tried not to listen to the fierce whispering from the kitchen as he thumbed through back issues of *People*. Eventually Henry Girard wheeled Amanda into the living room. She wore a resigned expression.

"We talked it over," said Henry. "And we don't like the idea, that's for sure. But I told Amanda that if we didn't do this, we would always wonder."

"Yes, that's true."

"Anyway, we'll do it, but only if it can be done right away. We don't want to have to think about this one day longer than we have to."

"I was hoping you would say that. Let me get my briefcase. I've got the papers all ready for your signature."

Ten minutes later, Dylan left the house, his hand aching but his spirits high.

It occurred to Dylan that he had spent more time in cemeteries during the last month that he had in his whole previous life. He hoped it wasn't an omen.

Although it still was early, the July heat was already intense, shimmering waves of hot air rising from the graves of the Gates of Harmony cemetery. Dylan took off his suit jacket and loosened his tie as he watched the small tractor with the big shovel dig into the new grass on Nicole Girard's grave. The overturned earth was dark and loamy, proof that the grass had recently been watered.

Standing next to Dylan was the aptly named Michael Dolor, the cemetery director. He was short, with graying brown hair and a pencil-thin mustache, wearing a suit so black it seemed to drain the pigment from his skin.

Neither Henry nor Amanda Girard, understandably, wanted to be present for this, and Dr. Silverburg awaited the body at his pathology lab.

Trying to make some conversation, Dylan asked, "Do you have to do this often?" He nodded at the digging equipment.

Dolor sniffed, "Oh, yes. We disinter fairly frequently. People like to upgrade their plots—their families do, I mean—and we have to move them around. Sometimes the family wants their relatives transferred to other cemeteries. We don't often get them back, though. You are returning the remains to us, aren't you?" He licked his lips anxiously. "Or does the family want to sell the plot?"

Dylan tried to keep the distaste out of his expression. "You'll get the body back tomorrow, after the autopsy."

"Good," said Dolor. "Then we don't have to remove the vault." He scurried over to the grave site to tell the shovel operator. The burial vault, Dylan knew, was constructed of steel-reinforced concrete, designed to prevent the ground from caving in around the casket as it deteriorated, or as heavy equipment passed overhead.

Dolor returned to Dylan, rubbing his hands. "This really saves time. I'm short of help today, and I've got to get my crew started on three interments for this afternoon."

"Business must be good."

"Pretty good. Speaking of business, do we bill your office for this, or the family?"

"My office," said Dylan, although he would have to pay the bill himself. Between Janis's "tuition" at the rehab center, and the money he was spending on this case, his savings were rapidly disappearing.

The shovel operator dug down about three feet, revealing the top of the burial vault; then he stopped while another employee jumped down, opened the vault, and attached hooks to the vault cover. The cover was lifted off and laid on the ground.

Dolor said with unctuous satisfaction, "See that vault? It's a Wilbert Cameo Rose, especially designed for women. Just a hint of soft pink rose on a field of white. Got a personalized nameplate, too."

"Very nice," said Dylan dryly, turning away just

in time to see a familiar limousine drive up the narrow pavement toward the grave.

The limo drove as far as it could, parking on the shoulder just behind the hearse that Dylan had rented to take Nicole's body to the hospital. The limo's rear door opened and two men got out, then walked quickly toward them. The man in the lead was John Tyler, director of Fletcher's Evangelical Foundation; following him was Henry Girard.

Maybe, thought Dylan, Henry just wants to be here for the disinterment. But even as he thought that, he knew he was fooling himself.

Tyler strode up to them, nodded at Dylan, and said to Dolor, "Morning, Michael."

"Morning, John," said Dolor. "What brings you here?"

Tyler ignored Dylan; his eyes were evaluating the progress of the disinterment. The casket was already swinging freely, about one foot above the open vault. Tyler said, "Put it back."

Without hesitation, Dolor turned and ordered his men to lower the casket back into the vault.

"Now wait a minute," said Dylan. He turned to Girard, who walked up slightly out of breath. "What's going on, Henry?"

Girard looked down at his feet and took a deep breath. "Sorry, Dylan, but Amanda and me, we've changed our minds. We don't want that autopsy after all."

Dylan looked at Girard, then at Tyler, then back at Girard, his heart sinking. "Now why," he said finally, "am I not surprised?"

■　　■　　■

"All right, Dylan," Hudson said, his face grave. "I've given you some slack. A lot of slack, in fact. Now suppose you tell me what the fuck you think you're doing."

Dylan sat in his customary chair in Hudson's office. It was only a couple of hours since he had been at the cemetery, but they had been long hours. He had tried to talk Henry Girard out of revoking his consent for the disinterment, but—as Dylan had surmised—Henry had already talked with Fletcher. Fletcher sat at the right hand of God, and when Fletcher advised against the autopsy, that was it.

The grave had been left open while Dolor's men went on to other business, and Dylan had tried to call Fletcher from a phone in the administration building. Fletcher either wasn't available or wouldn't take his call, and in the end Dylan had to admit defeat. When he dragged back to the office, he was summoned to Hudson's office.

"I don't know how to answer that, Paul. To what exactly are you referring?"

"You know damn well what I mean. What were you doing with this autopsy business? Who the hell told you to start playing Perry Mason again?"

"The client," Dylan said softly.

"That's bullshit." Hudson not only sounded angry, he looked it—unusual, for him. He prided himself, Dylan knew, on his ability to stay in control. "Henry Girard would never have dreamed of getting a second autopsy if you hadn't suggested it."

"Maybe. But the truth is, once I did suggest it, he agreed. Anyway, why not? After all that's happened, I'd think you'd be anxious to—"

"Because Vernon Fletcher doesn't want us to,

that's why!" Hudson roared. "Do I have to spell it out?"

"You've discussed this with Fletcher?"

"Of course. How the hell do you think I know about it? He called me this morning, extremely upset, asking me what I was doing, allowing you to run around half-cocked like some amateur detective."

Dylan could sense that, although Hudson was sincere, he wasn't entirely displeased with having received a phone call from Fletcher—a phone call that, in the past, would undoubtedly have gone to Kaster.

"You mean," said Dylan slowly, "that you're going to let one client dictate how the case of another client is handled?"

Hudson laughed. "You're still not thinking straight, Dylan. If Fletcher gives the word, we dump this little estate case in a minute." He grimaced. "But that's not necessary. The client agrees with Reverend Fletcher. No more investigation. You aren't Pamela Holtz, and you're not representing Charlene McConnell. You'll do exactly as I say, or I'll take you off the case."

"If that's how you feel, why don't you take me off the case now," said Dylan hotly.

Hudson glowered at him. "You know, Dylan, I thought you were smart. I really did. You had a great future with this firm. You can still have it."

Dylan felt a pang of anxiety. "Are you saying—"

"I'm not making any decisions right now. But I'm very unhappy with the way you're handling this, Dylan. I've got to tell you that."

So Barry was right all along, thought Dylan. As soon as he lost favor with Fletcher, everything changed.

"Is that all?" Dylan asked.

"Yes." Hudson, waved his hand dismissively. "That's all."

After the meeting with Hudson, Dylan found it hard to work. Barry was in court, and he didn't feel comfortable telling anyone else the extent of his reprimand. In a law firm, the scent of death was strong; any hint that his job was in jeopardy would result in a shunning even the Puritans could admire.

He tried to dictate some interrogatories in a contract case but didn't accomplish much. He wasn't used to dictating and was frustrated by not being able to see his progress on a computer screen. Maybe he would try typing with one hand.

His emotions bounced around his skull—anger, embarrassment, anxiety. He couldn't afford to lose his job, especially with his responsibilities toward Janis. Anyway, it wasn't just a job, but a career. It would be very tough to get another position at a law firm after being dismissed from Cameron Barr.

But he couldn't play Hudson's game, either. If he didn't find out what really happened to Nicole—well, it wasn't an option he was willing to consider.

By five thirty, he was exhausted, and Barry hadn't returned from court. He decided to leave early; the hell with billable hours. He'd make it up later in the month.

He drove home slowly. The stress of the past week, he realized, was having a cumulative effect, and he felt dull and lethargic. His hand ached.

At his town-house parking lot, Dylan drove his Buick into his reserved spot. As he opened the door, someone grabbed his arm and jerked him forcibly out of the car. He had no time to react; his body was twisted around, both arms jerked behind him, and he was half-carried, half-dragged about fifty feet to an idling black Lincoln. A rear door opened and he was thrown onto the empty rear seat.

When he raised himself up he saw Skoler getting in behind him. Another man—the same man who had been in the bow of the pace boat on the Potomac—faced him from the driver's seat, pointing a very large pistol at Dylan's forehead.

Dylan thought briefly about trying to get out the other side, but discarded the idea in the face of that pistol. Instead, he slid up against the door, as far away from Skoler as possible.

"You know, you're a real pain in the ass," said Skoler.

They're not gonna kill me, he thought. They would have done it already. "What do you want?" Dylan kept his voice as even as possible, despite his thudding heartbeat.

"What we want," Skoler said, reflectively, "is for you to stop sticking your nose up other people's asses. Apparently our last conversation was too wet for you to understand."

"Who do you work for?" countered Dylan. "Dr. Argent?"

The two men exchanged a quick glance, then the driver spoke for the first time. "You talk too much," he said. He was younger than Skoler, with long stringy blond hair and a bad complexion.

Skoler reached out and put his massive paw around Dylan's left hand, enclosing the bandaged fingers. He squeezed. The pain came instantly; Dylan bit back a scream.

"From now on, you're not gonna talk to anybody about Nicole Girard. You understand what I'm saying, nigger?"

Despite the gun, Dylan tried to jerk himself away. Skoler kept his grip, and Dylan's action only increased his agony. He had never felt such intense pain; he felt vomit surging up his throat.

Suddenly there was a loud bang! and Dylan involuntarily jerked back again, sure he had been shot. But the noise had come from outside the car; all three of them turned to look out the front, where a man in a dark suit stood next to the hood, pointing a massive two-barreled shotgun directly at the windshield. He dropped one hand from the shotgun and slapped the hood again.

Skoler let go of Dylan and swiveled around to look out the back; another suit stood behind the car, legs spread, holding a pistol in the two-handed grip cops use.

"Put down your weapon NOW!" yelled the man in front. Slowly, the driver complied.

"Ice!" continued the man with the shotgun, "Ice, get out of the car."

Dylan was happy to oblige. He practically jumped out of the car, then quickly moved away, holding his throbbing left hand.

"Now, both of you, get out of the car and get on the ground!" said the man with the shotgun.

For a moment, Dylan thought they would comply, but then the engine roared and the Lincoln jerked backward, knocking aside the man with the pistol. The car slammed into a red Toyota, crushing the fender, then, with a squeal of rubber, turned and drove down the parking aisle toward the lot exit, disappearing in a cloud of blue exhaust smoke.

Dylan was sure the man with the shotgun would

fire, but he didn't—he was hurrying over to his partner, who had ended up on the hood of a nearby car. The second man said, "I'm all right, Mike. I'll just be a little sore tomorrow."

Dylan walked over to them. "I hope you're cops."

The first man was in his thirties with a short haircut and a smooth, composed face. "Close. We're federal agents. I'm Michael Brent. My partner here is Tom Rackman."

For the first time, Dylan relaxed. In fact, his legs turned liquid and he nearly fell to the ground; Brent caught him as he sagged. "Whoa," said Brent. "We better get you home."

Dylan managed to pull himself up. "Sorry. Just a little delayed reaction. Can you tell me how you happened to be here?"

Brent exchanged glances with Rackman, who now was talking softly into a throat mike. "Let's go up to your apartment," Brent said. "Agent Markham will explain it all to you."

"Markham?" said Dylan feebly.

"Just come with us," said Rackman.

"Sure," said Dylan. "Why not?"

Dylan's apartment door was unlocked. Two more agents—dark suits, athletic, short haircuts—sat at the dining room table. In the living room, talking on Dylan's phone, was a tall, heavy-set man about fifty with a receding hairline and sturdy features. As they entered the room, he hung up the phone, turned to Dylan, and extended his hand. "T. J. Markham, Mr. Ice." His bearing and stance said ex-military.

"Can I see some ID, please?" Dylan asked.

Markham looked only momentarily surprised. Then he nodded, pulled a badge wallet from his inside suit jacket, and flipped it open in front of Dylan's face. Dylan had a momentary glimpse of a gold shield and a picture ID before Markham returned the wallet to his jacket.

Dylan shook hands, then sat down on the couch. "All right, Mr. Markham. You want to tell me what you're doing in my apartment, what this is all about, and do you have a warrant?"

Markham nodded at Brent and Rackman, who went into the dining room. Markham sat down across from Dylan. "Mr. Ice, you're a very popular guy, you know that?"

"You always answer a question with another question?"

Markham grinned. "Actually, yes. That's my job." He laughed, a barking sound. "Sorry. You certainly deserve some answers. Okay, I'll start at the top. We're federal agents working with the inspector general of the Department of Health and Human Services. HHS, as I'm sure you know, includes NIH. We're looking into certain irregularities in a clinical trial that is being conducted by the Midwest Immunological Research Institute. Dr. Rosati informed us that you could help in this investigation, and so we decided to contact you."

Something Markham said didn't make sense, and Dylan couldn't think why. He shoved the thought aside. "By breaking into my apartment?"

Markham smiled, a touch of steel behind the eyes. "That's not how it happened, Mr. Ice."

"Suppose you tell me how it happened." Dylan felt himself getting angrier. He knew he was being

Daniel Steven

ungrateful—these men had just saved him from
Skoler—but the cavalier way they had made themselves at home grated on him.

"Agent Timson and I called your office and were
told you were on your way home. We saw your car
enter the parking lot and got worried when you
didn't come right up. I sent some men down to check.
Then, when Rackman told me you were attacked, I
decided we better enter your apartment to make sure
there wasn't someone else waiting for you."

That sounded phony, but Dylan was in no mood
to argue the point. "The guy who attacked me. His
name is William Skoler."

"We know," said Markham.

"Do you know who hired him?"

"Dr. Argent, we think, although we can't prove
it. Based on the information you gave Dr. Rosati,
and other information we have independently, we
believe that Dr. Argent may be submitting false data
on his clinical trials in order to obtain continued
funding from the federal government. That's a
felony, and we think that Argent may be trying to
cover it up."

"Well." Dylan sighed. "Finally. I'm glad I'm not
the only one who thinks Argent is crooked. Okay.
What's next? Call the local police? There's a detective who's investigating Skoler. Now that you can
back me up—"

"I'm afraid not," said Markham.

"What?"

Markham shook his head. "No local cops, Mr.
Ice. We don't want to arrest Skoler right now; he's
our only link to Argent. Unfortunately, we don't
have enough evidence to arrest Argent; he's very
clever. That's where you come in."

"Me? What can I do?"

"Well, you've apparently made Argent nervous enough to send Skoler and his pal after you. And you tried to get another autopsy on the Girard woman. Why was that?"

Markham leaned forward for the answer, and Dylan had another sudden stab of anxiety. His subconscious was sounding an alarm, but he couldn't interpret the signal. Dylan said slowly, "My clients weren't satisfied with the original autopsy, that's all. They wanted to know for sure that she died of AIDS."

"I see," said Markham thoughtfully. "That might explain a lot."

"What would?"

"Uh, the autopsy."

"Exactly. So why don't you get one? Go to the U.S. Attorney and get an exhumation order."

"Good idea," said Markham. "We'll have to consider that." He continued quickly, "What about this McConnell woman? What do you know about her?"

Dylan repeated what he had told Detective Peterson in connection with his sighting of Skoler outside McConnell's house.

"You know that she's disappeared?"

"McConnell? No, but I'm not surprised. I knew she was leaving town, and she was afraid of Argent. She thought he was behind Holtz's death."

"Yeah. We know all that. Now, you're sure there's nothing else you can add?"

Dylan shook his head. "No, but I'll tell you if I do. You got a card?"

"Uh, just a minute." Markham patted his inside pocket, then said, "I'm fresh out." He pulled open a small notepad and scribbled the name of a local hotel. "This is where I'm staying locally. I'll be here for a few days. If you want, I'll leave a man here to watch your door. I doubt Skoler will return, but—"

Dylan took the piece of paper.

"Thanks, I'll be all right."

After they left, Dylan closed and double-locked the door, then went into the bathroom and slowly undid the bandage on his hand. There was still blood oozing from around the sutures on the stumps of his fingers, but it didn't look like there was any real damage. At least he could avoid a trip to the ER.

He opened the medicine cabinet and popped open his bottle of codeine, taking two. That ought to knock him out for the night. He wrapped a clean ace bandage around the taped-together fingers, as he had been shown, and went into the kitchen.

He found a can of vegetable beef soup and put its contents into a pan to heat. Through a buzz of fatigue and stress reaction, he tried to sort things out. Things that didn't make any sense, beginning with Markham.

First point, he said to himself as he stirred the soup. Markham had shown him genuine identification, but his hand had held the wallet in a way that allowed Dylan to see only the picture ID, not the badge. The picture ID had been from the Department of the Treasury. Dylan was no expert, but he was pretty sure that Treasury agents didn't handle HHS cases. Treasury had jurisdiction over IRS investigations, customs, and the Secret Service. It was conceivable that the IRS could be investigating Argent, but then why hadn't Markham said so?

And then there was the fact that he had no business cards. What cop didn't have business cards? They handed them out all the time to witnesses.

Second point. There were too many agents. Five agents that he had seen, all investigating a possible violation of a clinical trial funding? There had been fewer cops investigating the O. J. Simpson case.

Third point. If the feds suspected Argent of negligence or worse in the death of Nicole Girard, why wouldn't they just get the body exhumed? Why all this dancing around him, asking what he knew?

Unless—the thought came to Dylan suddenly—unless they were afraid of what they might find in the autopsy. No, that wasn't right. Afraid of making *public* what they might find. Maybe that was it.

He sat down at the kitchen table to eat the soup, but found he had no appetite.

So what should he do about all this? Should he be content to just sit back and be everyone's pet, the good boy who does what he is told?

He felt dizzy. Maybe the codeine was starting to kick in. Well, whatever he needed to do, it would have to wait. He staggered to the bedroom and stripped off his pants and shirt. He was about to get into bed when he stopped, then went into the walk-in closet.

Inside the closet, Dylan reached into the pocket of the old raincoat hanging at the far end and pulled out his new pistol—a 9 mm Glock Model 17 with ten-shot magazine. He felt a guilty pride of ownership.

The gun reminded him of Kristin, who had helped him shop for it after the attack by LaShawn Johnson. She had helped him function-test the magazine, even helped him learn to shoot the damn thing.

He made sure the safety was on, then placed the

pistol in the night stand drawer and crawled into bed. He was asleep almost instantly.

Craig Hagen didn't like what he was hearing, and made that clear.

"Look, Craig," said Markham. "I'm doing the best I can. I can't just start throwing my weight around, not unless you want the whole world to know what's going on."

"Obviously not," said Hagen, his voice sounding more nasal than usual over the long-distance phone connection. "But we've got a time problem here. I need to know very soon whether this is a fruitful line of investigation."

Markham settled back on his bed, staring out the hotel window at the St. Louis skyline. "I think I can answer that. There's no question in my mind that this guy Argent is screwing around with you. He's a weasel if I ever saw one."

"And the patient who died? Nicole Girard? What about her?"

"Argent tells a good story, but I think he's lying. That's all I can say for sure at this time. And you were right about that lawyer, he's the perfect bird dog. We've got a tail on him."

"You're not relying on him, I hope?"

"Of course not." Markham's lips compressed in annoyance. "And please don't tell me how to run an investigation."

"Yeah, yeah," said Hagen. "All right. Just do your best."

Dylan came awake all at once, panting. What?

He looked around the dark bedroom in bewilderment, his heart slowly regaining its normal beat. The digital clock read 2:23. What had awakened him?

He had been dreaming. Of the cemetery.

They had left Nicole's grave open, he said to himself, wonderingly. Of course.

He got up and went to the bathroom, where he splashed water on his face and checked the dressing on his hand.

His head still felt light as he dressed unsteadily in black jeans, black sweatshirt, and black running shoes. Rummaging in the bottom of his closet, he found an old gym bag and threw into it a halogen flashlight and a pair of leather gloves.

He opened the front door cautiously, wondering if Markham had left someone to watch the apartment. For what it was worth, he didn't see anyone.

Thirty minutes later, he was back at the Gates of Harmony Cemetery. He feared there might be a night watchman, but he saw no lights in the administration building as he pulled into the parking lot, headlights off.

From the trunk of his Buick, Dylan removed a screwdriver from the tool kit and put it in the gym bag with the other articles. Then, crouching low because it seemed like the thing to do, he scurried across the parking lot, the gym bag banging against his butt.

Although there was almost a full moon, the sky was overcast and he had to use the flashlight to avoid tripping over headstones and other obstacles. He tried not to let his imagination work overtime with the concept of being in a cemetery in the middle of the night. Inevitably, however, scenes from all the horror movies he had ever seen began percolating inside his head.

It was harder than he expected to locate Nicole's grave; everything looked different in the dark, and it was starting to rain. Not a thunderstorm, thankfully; that would have been too uncanny. Just a warm, soft summer rain that soon had his clothes soaked. He stumbled between headstones, occasionally switching on the flashlight to read the inscriptions.

He was beginning to doubt his sanity when he nearly fell into the grave.

After Tyler ordered a stop to the disinterment that morning, Dolor had sent his heavy equipment crew off to dig graves for the afternoon funerals; the men had simply replaced the heavy vault lid and covered the grave with a big stretch of the fake grass they always used at funerals.

Dylan had feared that the workers might have come back at the end of the day to fill in the grave, but now he had stepped on the artificial turf and it sagged with his weight almost to the top of the vault. With some difficulty, Dylan managed to scramble out of the grave and pull one edge of the turf off its mooring stake, exposing the top of the vault to his flashlight beam.

Placing the flashlight on the ground, he set about lifting the heavy vault cover. It took all his strength; finally he was able to push it up and lean it against the side of the grave trench.

The casket was now exposed. He expected to see a flash of lightning, hear a roll of thunder—or at least some organ music. None of that happened, but it did seem to rain harder. Dylan found himself giggling with relief. It's the codeine, he thought. Stiffen up. Then he giggled again at his choice of words.

The hell with it. Now or never. His heart accelerated, and he felt a coldness down his spine. The rain, he thought. Dripping down the back of my sweatshirt.

He slid down into the narrow space between the vault and the casket and examined the edges of the casket until he figured out the locking mechanism—a bolt and cap assembly. Although the vault was big enough to allow him to pull out the two bolts that freed the lid, he had difficulty doing it one-handed— he had to hold the flashlight with his injured left hand—and the rain didn't make things any easier.

When the coffin lid was finally free and ready to raise, he paused, looking around. Above him, the moon broke through the cloud cover, sending diffuse silvery light over the graves. He smelled the wet grass and earth, heard the sound of the rain against the coffin.

So far he hadn't broken any laws. The grave had already been open when he arrived. But once he lifted the lid and looked at the corpse he was guilty of a felony. An offense that would get him disbarred from the practice of law. The fact that no one knew about it—yet—didn't make any difference. *He* would know.

He sighed. There never was any doubt in his mind he would do it. He wanted to *know*. What really held him back now was fear of what he might see. Fear of what he might not see.

What he might not see. That really was the key. The chance of him recognizing some cause of death other than what purportedly killed Nicole was minimal, unless she had died of something obvious like a blow to the head or a gunshot. But if there was an autopsy incision, that would tell him a lot. At least he could eliminate the possibility that Argent had faked the whole thing because he knew that a *real* autopsy would incriminate him.

Okay, enough stalling.

Dylan reached out and, very slowly, lifted the lid of the coffin until he could prop it open. The rain was falling in, but there was nothing he could do about that. Slowly, he shone the flashlight into the dark cavity in front of him.

Unexpectedly, the coffin had an inner lining covering the body. His right hand shook badly as he reached down to grab the zipper tab at the top. He slowly pulled the zipper down—it moved easily—revealing dark hair and the partially decomposed face of a woman.

A woman who was definitely *not* Nicole Girard.

CHAPTER TWENTY-FIVE

Dylan carefully shut the office door behind him and took a seat across from Barry, who looked up from his computer screen with a puzzled expression. "Dylan? You all right?"

"I've been better." Dylan lowered his voice and leaned forward. "Last night I went to the Gates of Harmony Cemetery. I opened Nicole Girard's coffin. Inside—"

"You what?" Barry rose out of his seat. "Jesus Christ, Dylan, you realize that's a felony?"

"I know it is. But that's not the point—"

"The hell it isn't! Wait a minute." Barry went to his file cabinet and removed a folder. "You got any money on you?"

"Money? What for? Don't you want to hear what I have to say?"

"How much?"

Seeing that Barry wasn't going to be diverted, Dylan shrugged and said, "About seventy-five bucks, I guess."

"Give me fifty, then sign and date this." He took a document from the folder, then slid it across the desk toward Dylan. It was a retainer agreement, and Dylan understood.

"I don't want there to be any question that what you're telling me now is privileged," said Barry, as Dylan signed and passed the cash across. "Otherwise, I've got a duty to report this, if not to the cops, then to the bar disciplinary committee." Barry looked so grave it was almost comical.

"Good thinking."

"Here's a receipt for the cash." Barry pulled a legal pad toward him and prepared to take notes. "Now, tell me what happened."

Dylan told him, starting from the time he left the office the previous afternoon. He related the attack by Skoler, his rescue by the federal agents, what they told him about Argent, and how he decided to go to the cemetery.

"You just woke up and decided to go disturb a grave? Is that what you're saying?"

"Yes. But I didn't 'disturb' it. The grave was already open. Just the vault and coffin were closed."

Barry rolled his eyes. "Go on."

"It's pretty simple. I went to the cemetery, pulled back the temporary covering over the grave, and opened the coffin."

"And saw what?"

"I saw the body of a woman. And . . . it wasn't Nicole Girard."

"You're sure about that?"

"Of course I'm sure! It wasn't her!"

"Take it easy, Dylan. I'm your lawyer, remember? Now, how old was this body? I mean, about what age was the woman when she died?"

"I'd guess she was in her mid-thirties. Hard to tell for sure."

"Of course. The body wasn't embalmed, was it?"

"No."

"So it was already decomposing, right?"

"Yes," said Dylan, getting more annoyed.

"And you don't have a lot of experience looking at decomposed bodies, do you?"

"Barry," Dylan said evenly. "I'm not an imbecile. I understand that dead bodies don't look the same as live ones. But there's no question she wasn't Nicole Girard."

"Then who the fuck was it?"

"I don't know! I didn't recognize her. All I know is, it wasn't Nicole."

"I see." Barry leaned back in his chair and stretched. "Okay, let's go with this. What do you think it means, that it's not Nicole?"

"Dammit, Barry—"

"C'mon, tell me what you think."

Dylan got up and paced around the office. "I think it's obvious that Argent is responsible for Nicole's death. That explains why he was so reluctant to give up the medical records and autopsy, and why the autopsy is so generic."

Barry nodded. "Okay, I follow that. But then who's the woman in the grave?"

"I don't know. I guess he had to provide a body to the mortician."

"Are you saying he *killed* this other woman to cover up Nicole's death?"

"Why not? He probably killed Pamela Holtz, and assuming Skoler works for him, he's tried to kill me." But then he shook his head. "No, it doesn't feel right. Maybe she was just someone else who died, and he substituted her. God, I don't know."

"Yes. But if Argent faked Nicole's autopsy—

which he apparently did—then why bother switching bodies? I mean, what's the point?"

"Maybe he was afraid that Holtz would get an exhumation order. If he killed Nicole, or she died as a result of his negligence, he couldn't risk that happening."

"Dylan. If Holtz got an exhumation order and found *this* body, the shit would hit the fan anyway. The question remains, why switch one dead body for another dead body?"

Dylan sat down heavily. "Obviously, I don't have any answers."

"I agree. So what are you going to do?"

"I don't have much choice. I've got to tell the police."

"The police!" barked Barry. "What will you tell them? That you illegally opened a coffin and think you found the wrong body? Don't be absurd."

"Detective Peterson knows about Skoler," said Dylan stubbornly. "I could tell him the whole story—"

"No, you can't. As your lawyer, I forbid it."

Dylan smiled. "All right, but I certainly can tell this guy Markham. He's investigating Argent, for God's sake."

"I thought you didn't trust him."

"I don't, but I can't hide this."

"Dylan, I've got the same problem with him as I do with the police. You're admitting to a felony."

"So what the hell do you—" he was interrupted by the sound of Barry's phone.

Barry answered, said a few words, grimaced. He hung up and said, "Our master calls." He stood and straightened his tie. "I don't have any answers, Dylan, but I sure as hell don't think you should do anything without thinking it through."

"I don't know."

"Unfortunately, I'm leaving for K.C. this evening, along with our fearless leader. That's what this meeting now is about. We're resuming the depositions in the International Grain case. Can you hold off doing anything until I get back on the weekend?"

"Three days!"

"C'mon, Dylan." Barry picked up a bulging accordion file and headed toward the door. "Just think about it. Call me tonight—I'll be at the airport Hilton."

"All right," Dylan said, reluctantly.

Barry grabbed his shoulder and squeezed. Dylan followed him out, then returned to his own office.

At his desk again, he found he couldn't concentrate, so he wandered the halls for a while, dropping into the offices of other associates and chatting, answering the inevitable questions about his hand. He even spent some time with Rhonda, complimenting her on her new chartreuse nail polish. She looked at him oddly, but smiled.

He needed her now that he had to dictate so much. So far she had been resentful of the added burden; he could ask Hudson for another secretary, but now was probably not the time to do it. He would have to live with Rhonda for a while, and if that meant noticing her shade of nail polish, so be it.

At lunchtime, Dylan decided to get out of the office. None of the other associates were available, so he went by himself to an inexpensive restaurant in the shopping mall across the street.

He barely sat down in the fake leather booth when someone else slipped in across from him.

"Hey," he said, annoyed, "this is—" then he recognized Markham.

"Mr. Ice," said Markham. "You're a busy man."

"I try to be." Dylan felt somewhat intimidated by Markham's bulk and sheer presence. The guy had an enormous chest. "What do you want, or are you just following me?"

"Mr. Ice," Markham repeated. "I think you're holding out on us. Is there something you're not telling me about Dr. Argent and Nicole Girard? Because if there is, we'll find out. And I want you to be on the right side of this thing."

"What thing?"

Markham smiled broadly, light glinting off a gold filling in the back of his mouth. "Let's not play games." He lowered his voice. "You visited Nicole Girard's grave last night, and looked into her coffin. Why?"

Dylan pushed himself back in his seat. "You *have* been following me!"

"No shit."

"You gentlemen ready to order?" asked the waitress, walking up with her hand cocked over an order pad.

"Give us a minute," said Markham gruffly. When she left, he said, "Well?"

The waitress's interruption gave Dylan time to think. Clearly, Markham wasn't upset about Dylan's little crime of grave disturbance. Dylan said, "You seem to be paying an awful lot of attention to one lousy fraud case. There are defense contractors who probably rip off more in one hour than Argent has in his whole life. How many agents do you have on this case, anyway?"

Markham sucked in his breath. "Don't be cute, Ice."

"I'm not being cute, but I do know Treasury agents don't investigate for the Inspector General of HHS—the FBI does. I checked."

"Checked?" Markham chuckled. "Who the hell with? Take my word for it, Dylan, I'm the appropriate person to investigate this. And if you don't start cooperating, you can explain it to the U.S. Attorney's office."

Dylan looked away and considered it. Somebody with authority needed to get to the bottom of Nicole's death, and it might as well be Markham. Barry was wrong about this. He sighed and said, "Okay. I meant to tell you anyway."

"Yeah? What?"

"It wasn't Nicole's body in the coffin."

Markham gave a low whistle and looked around, as if worried someone had overheard. "You sure about that? I mean, we looked in the coffin, too, and—"

"You did?"

"Of course we did. Unfortunately, the agent didn't have a recent photograph of Ms. Girard."

"Well, trust me, it wasn't her. Argent switched the bodies."

Markham nodded. "Of course. That accounts for the autopsy report!"

They had that, too, thought Dylan. Why do they need me? He said, "So what are you gonna do? Exhume the body and arrest Argent?"

"It's not that simple. We don't want to tip him off before we're ready. He could destroy documents and other evidence."

"Well, what, then?"

Markham frowned, his forehead creasing unpleasantly. "That's none of your business, Ice."

"Does that mean you're not gonna do anything?"

When Markham didn't reply, Dylan said, "Anyway, Argent's switching of bodies is a criminal offense. It probably means he murdered her. It's a matter for the local police, not the fraud unit of HHS. Not you."

"We don't want the local police involved at this time. And do *you* really want the cops to know you opened a coffin without permission? After your client specifically denied you permission to get an autopsy?" He shook his head. "Not something you'd want the bar to know about, is it?"

Dylan felt himself redden. "Bullshit. If you did that, I'd tell them about this conversation."

Markham's response was a broad smile. "Good for you, kid." Then his smile disappeared. "But don't push your luck. If you go to the police now, you'll be spoiling a major investigation. You're putting yourself right in the middle of something bigger than you, and you're shitting on your friends."

"Oh? And who are my friends?"

"We are. The government," Markham stood up and turned to leave.

"Whose government?" said Dylan as Markham strode out of the restaurant.

Afterward, he didn't feel like eating.

As Dylan settled back into his office after lunch, Rhonda buzzed him. "Kristin Fletcher on line three," she said, curtly.

Dylan picked up the phone. Just what he needed to take his mind off his problems. "Hi, Kristin."

"Hi, Dylan." Her voice was strained. "I just talked to my father, and he told me about your little adventure at the cemetery."

For a second Dylan was shocked; then he realized she meant the abortive attempt to get Nicole's body removed for the autopsy. That seemed days ago, not a mere twenty-four hours.

"Yes," he said carefully. "I'm sorry your father got involved."

"Dylan, honey," she purred, "I warned you about him, didn't I? Don't cross him."

"I didn't think I had."

"Well, no permanent damage to the relationship, anyway. I took care of that. So what happened after Henry Girard showed up?"

Dylan had an unsettling feeling in his stomach. Was the question coming from Kristin or from her father? "Nothing much. I tried to change his mind, but I'm afraid your father's opinion carries more weight."

She laughed. "Of course. So what are you going to do now?"

He didn't want to lie to her, so he said, "I'm not sure, Kristin. I'll have to think about it."

"But what are your options?" she persisted.

"I don't know."

"I see. Well, what are you doing tonight? Let's have a late dinner."

Five minutes ago, he would have been thrilled with the idea. Now he said, "I'm sorry, I can't. Hudson wants me to work late."

He had never turned her down before. There was a moment of silence on the line, and then she said, "Maybe tomorrow, then?"

"Sure," he said, hanging up before he changed his mind.

At six forty-five, Dylan packed his briefcase and headed for the elevator, hoping that none of the partners noticed him leaving so early. He just didn't feel like working.

The building's underground parking lot was well lighted. Only the partners had reserved spots, so Dylan's Buick was parked about as far from the elevator as possible. His hand ached like hell, and he decided that he'd take a long, soaking bath when he got home.

Later, Dylan would assume it was his preoccupation with his hand that kept him from having any premonition about what was about to happen. He would have thought that his subconscious would notice something strange about the Buick, some noise, *anything*.

He unlocked the door, threw his briefcase in, then got behind the wheel. As he reached for his shoulder belt, a massive arm came out of nowhere and wrenched him violently backward. His head was in a hammer lock, his throat constricted painfully. He tried to wrench himself free, but the arm was too strong, and he couldn't get enough air.

As he began to black out, a voice hissed in his ear, "Ain't nobody around to help you this time, nigger."

The voice was unmistakable.

Skoler.

CHAPTER TWENTY-SIX

The wide black terry-cloth gagging in Dylan's mouth sucked up his saliva, making it impossible to swallow, and the heat inside the car's trunk was suffocating. His wrists were tied behind his back as he lay in a fetal position, smelling his own sweat.

Worst of all was the gut-squeezing fear of what would happen next—and the helplessness. He wondered whether he could stand this a minute longer without losing his mind.

Suddenly the car swooped up and down in a characteristic motion: speed bumps? A parking lot? The car slowed, and for a moment his hopes were raised; then, inevitably, he thought of all the gangster and crime movies where the victim was taken out of the trunk and shot, or thrown over a bridge—or worse.

He cursed his own stupidity. Why had he assumed that Skoler wouldn't try again?

The car made a series of rapid turns, then slowed and stopped. The car doors slammed as Skoler and another person got out; he distinctly heard their shoes on some hard material, probably concrete.

The trunk lid lifted and he was dazzled by the sudden light. At least he knew they weren't outside; there was the gasoline fume smell of another parking garage. The movement of his limbs caused agony as they lifted him out and roughly shoved him into a large wooden box reeking of garbage. There was barely enough room for him to sit upright, knees against his chest. He felt the crate being lifted onto something: a dolly, it sounded like, and the dolly being rolled along the floor.

Dylan tried not to think of what was going to happen, concentrating instead on determining, from his sense of hearing alone, where they were going. He felt the dolly roll onto a smoother surface, probably carpet. Then the sound of a chime announcing the arrival of an elevator; a brief lurch and they went up.

The crate was trundled out of the elevator, and he could hear muffled voices as the dolly went down a linoleum-floored hall. There were some sharp turns, some lurches, and then the crate was lifted off the dolly onto the floor. He felt a draft of air on his head, looked up and saw a typical ceiling of acoustical tile, then Skoler's face blocking out the light.

Skoler reached in and hauled him out of the crate with surprising ease.

"Careful!" someone said. "Not so rough!"

Skoler tried to set Dylan on his feet, but his legs were numb and he collapsed onto the floor. Preston removed the gag from Dylan's mouth. Looking up, Dylan saw a familiar form standing next to Skoler.

"Dr. Argent, I presume," said Dylan, trying manfully to overcome his fear and sound insouciant.

Argent didn't smile. "I apologize for the rough

treatment, Dylan. I told Skoler to bring you here, but I didn't specify how." He leaned down and helped Dylan to his feet. "C'mon, we've got a lot to discuss."

"You want to *t-talk*?" Dylan stuttered, knowing how grateful he sounded, but unable to keep it out of his voice.

"Yes, of course," said Argent.

A wave of anger flooded Dylan. He couldn't control his outburst. "You fucking *asshole*, you scared the fucking shit out of me!" Dylan tried to take a swing at him, but his legs gave out again and he fell to the floor.

Argent and Skoler grabbed him by the arms and lifted him onto a long vinyl sofa. Dylan sank down on the cushions and rubbed his cramped legs, taking deep breaths to calm himself. He looked around. They were in some part of Argent's laboratory: counters with sinks and lab tables were scattered around the room, some with centrifuges and incubators. There was a strong smell of antiseptic.

Argent ordered Skoler and the other man—whom he called Preston—to leave the room. Skoler scowled at Dylan on his way out.

As Argent poured a Styrofoam cup of coffee, Dylan said, "If you wanted to talk to me, you could have used the phone."

"That's true," said Argent. "How do you like your coffee?"

"Uh, black."

Argent brought him the coffee and Dylan immediately swallowed the hot liquid. His hands shook from the realization that he was not about to be killed. At least not yet, anyway.

Argent took a lab stool from a nearby counter,

pushed it near the couch, and sat down. He said, "But I wanted to show you some things, and talk with you personally. And I didn't want the federal agents to know you were coming here."

"Oh. So you know they're following me?"

"Obviously. They've got an observation post set up across the street from your office parking garage, as well as outside your apartment. No one saw Skoler bundle you into his car, so as far as the feds know, you're still at your office."

"I see. And all this was just so we could have a little chat?"

"Yes. I want to explain why you should stop making a damn nuisance of yourself."

"How have I done that?"

"C'mon, Dylan. You should have left the Girard case alone, instead of requesting medical records, talking with Dr. Rosati, trying to get a new postmortem. And telling agent Markham everything you know."

"So why haven't you just killed me, like Pamela Holtz? Not that I'm objecting," he added hastily.

Argent shook his head. "I'm not a murderer, Dylan. I had nothing to do with Holtz's death, although I admit I wasn't sorry it happened."

"You didn't hire those White Lords?"

"No," said Argent, looking Dylan directly in the eye.

"Then who did?"

"If I told you, you wouldn't believe me."

"I'm not sure I believe you, anyway." Dylan actually was very glad to hear Argent deny it. It meant his chance of living had just increased. "Skoler tried to kill me in Washington." Dylan held up his left hand.

"That wasn't on my orders," Argent said patiently. "Originally, he was supposed to prevent you from talking to Dr. Rosati. But he screwed up, and I'm afraid he's not the most balanced individual, so he took it out on you. I apologize, but he's all I have to work with at the moment."

"That's comforting. So now what?"

"As I said, I intend to explain why it's in your own best interest to back off and not report anything to Markham or the police. Of course, I don't expect you to do that without good reason." He stood up. "Feeling better? Ready for a little information?"

"I'm okay," Dylan said tersely.

Argent smiled. "Good. First you need to know the real reason I resisted your attempts to get Nicole Girard's medical chart and autopsy."

"I've seen what's in Nicole's coffin."

"What?" Argent said, standing up in surprise.

Dylan was pleased to see that he had penetrated Argent's composure. "That's right. I looked inside her coffin last night. Who is the woman, by the way?" He couldn't resist adding, "And did she die of natural causes?"

Argent shook his head. "You amaze me, Dylan, you really do." He took a deep breath and continued, "The body in Nicole's coffin *did* die naturally of ovarian cancer. She was a homeless woman. And, yes, that's the reason I resisted giving you the medical records and autopsy, but it doesn't *explain* anything, does it?"

"No. I suppose you are culpable in some way for Nicole's death, and don't want that discovered."

"You're wrong," said Argent with a smile, composure recovered. "Come with me."

Dylan didn't see much choice but to go along,

although he had a feeling he would be better off not knowing Argent's dirty little secrets.

Argent led Dylan through a rabbit warren of laboratory rooms. Dylan realized this whole section of the top floor was part of the new construction he had seen when visiting MIRI in the spring. Several of the laboratories were guarded by uniformed security cops. Once again, Dylan wondered how Argent could afford the expense of such a large security force. And why.

Eventually they reached some double doors. Argent entered a code into a security panel to the right of the doors, not bothering to hide the digits from Dylan. A lock clicked loudly. Argent opened the doors, and they walked into a small anteroom leading to a large single door made of steel, with padded door panels. There was a security station with a computer monitor and video screen to the right of the door. A tough-looking security cop sat in the chair in front of the video monitor. He rose as they entered.

"Sit down, Lewis," said Argent. Then, to Dylan, he said, "Take a look." He nodded at the television monitor.

Dylan stepped forward. The picture was rather grainy, and it took a moment for his eyes to adjust to the scene. He saw a standard hospital bed, a small sofa beneath a curtained window, a couple of chairs. In one of the chairs, a woman sat with her legs curled under her, reading a book. Dylan leaned forward for a better look.

It was Nicole Girard.

The air released from Dylan's lungs, and he literally jumped with surprise. He thought of eight things at once, all the little pieces and facts of the mystery coming together in one gestalt.

He felt Argent's heavy hand on his shoulder. "Quite a shock, isn't it?"

Dylan suddenly realized that Argent couldn't let him go, now that he had seen this. But why show it to him at all? He realized he should try to escape, right now, while Argent thought he was still in shock from the revelation.

Instead, cursing his cowardice, he allowed himself to be guided back through the doors to the original office.

When Dylan resumed his place on the couch, Argent picked up his coffee. "You okay now?"

"I'm fine," Dylan said. And then, before he could stop himself, "You bastard." *Good,* he thought. *Get angry.*

Argent ignored the epithet. "Dylan, Nicole Girard has a very special quality. Her body produces antibodies that destroy HIV better than any antiviral drug we have. In fact, PHT therapy using her blood serum is so effective, I can detect no viral load whatsoever in persons who receive it. This is comparable to some of the results achieved by triple-drug therapy, but without any of the side effects or the compliance burden. No twenty pills a day, no risk of actually *increasing* the virus's resistance. Unfortunately, we can only get enough serum to help one or two recipients, and, like all PHT, the recipient must continue to receive the therapy, on at least a monthly basis, or we risk a rebound effect. Anyway, when I found this out, I asked Nicole to continue as a donor beyond the term of the original clinical trial. She declined."

"So naturally you drugged her and held her against her will. Any self-respecting scientist would have done the same."

Argent's eyes glinted dangerously. "There's no need for sarcasm, Dylan. I didn't do it lightly or easily; if there was another way, I would have taken it. She wanted to come in every week, instead of remaining an inpatient. I couldn't risk that."

"Why not?"

"Dylan, she's one in a billion. What if she got run over by a bus? Or fell down some stairs? Or was a crime victim?" He shook his head sorrowfully. "I couldn't risk it. Or, more accurately, I might have—except for one additional point."

"What's that?"

Argent rose, his eyes shining. He stepped closer to Dylan and said, excitedly, almost like a child, "I have identified the factor that makes her antibodies so different—and so effective." Dylan suddenly noticed that there were dark shadows under his eyes, deep furrows in his forehead. The man is exhausted, he thought. And probably wasn't too rational to begin with.

Dylan said carefully, "So, you think you can develop a cure?"

"A cure?" Argent chuckled. "Yes, for those receiving it, my enhanced PHT treatment is a cure, or close enough. Unfortunately, Nicole doesn't have enough blood for the whole world. No, not a cure—but something more realistic, and almost as good. A vaccine!"

Dylan could see Argent was picturing himself accepting the Nobel Prize for medicine. He knew he shouldn't be arguing with him—it could hardly do him any good—but he said anyway, "So you think this justifies kidnapping. A federal crime, by the way."

He expected Argent to blow up, but instead he

stepped over to Dylan and said softly and very seriously, "Which is worth more—the many or the few? If you could save a million lives by killing one person, would you do it? Or would you let millions die for a principle?"

Dylan was startled by his sudden intensity. "It's a false issue, because it doesn't happen that way in real life. Only in freshman philosophy courses."

"But it's happening *now*, right *here*, Dylan. Assume what I say is true. Assume I can prevent AIDS, but not without Nicole. Does she have the right to refuse that obligation? Have you ever seen a person die of AIDS? Have you?"

"No, but—"

"Do you know how many people in the world will die from AIDS in the next five years? *Millions*, Dylan. *Millions*."

Argent's sincerity was obvious, and Dylan, forcing himself to examine the issue, could see Argent's point. If it truly was that black and white . . . but it wasn't. He shook his head. "It's all hypothetical. You could have gotten Nicole's cooperation, voluntarily. And even if she wouldn't cooperate, she can't be that rare. There must be others like her."

"Perhaps there are, but we don't have years to look for them."

Another connection was made in Dylan's mind. "So this is why Markham hasn't moved more aggressively against you! He's not investigating your misuse of funds, he's after the PHT treatment!"

"Misuse of funds? Is that what he told you?"

"Yes."

"That's bull. He's here because Nicole was to be sent to NIH for further research. Dr. Rosati knew she was a unique PHT donor—all the data from this clinical trial was funneled through him. That's why we faked her death, so that Rosati wouldn't get her. Unfortunately, your trip to Washington tipped him off that Nicole's death was suspicious. And that brought our mutual friend Markham here."

"It still doesn't make sense," insisted Dylan. "Why doesn't Markham just subpoena your records? Get a search warrant?"

"He doesn't know Nicole is alive, just that her death is suspicious." He waved his hand dismissively. "It's Inspector General bullshit. Rosati's pissed off, and he complained to the IG."

"Except that Markham isn't from the IG's department. He's Treasury."

"Treasury?" said Argent, puzzled.

"Yeah, Treasury."

"You're sure about that?"

"Yeah, I checked."

Argent thought about it for a moment, then shrugged. "Well, it doesn't make any difference. They've got no evidence of wrongdoing, anyway. As long as you keep your mouth shut."

"I will," said Dylan quickly. "You've convinced me."

Argent laughed. "Don't ever go into politics, Dylan." Then his expression changed. "You *will* keep your mouth shut, though. I'm very sure of that."

"Look, I said I would—"

"Because if you don't, you'll inconvenience me, I admit. But you won't be helping Nicole, and you'll be hurting your own health."

"Is that a threat?"

"Not at all. Let's say you tell the police, or Markham, that Nicole is alive. And let's say you are believed, which is a big *if*. They'll need a search warrant, and they'll have to come in past my security stations. You may have noticed, I have a lot of security. Anyway, that will give me plenty of time to react, and it's something I've planned for. By the time the cops get to this part of the laboratory, Nicole will be gone." He grinned nastily. "And, since Nicole has already been declared dead, if they don't find her body—or evidence that she still is alive—they will feel pretty stupid. And so will you."

"I see. But how does that affect my health?"

Argent didn't answer; instead he picked up a nearby phone, dialed, and talked briefly in a voice too low to understand. Then he turned back to Dylan. "A picture is worth a thousand words."

Skoler and Preston entered the room, and Argent said, "We're going to Treatment Seven."

Skoler pushed Dylan ahead of him as they all followed Argent to a nearby room. A woman Argent introduced as his wife, Linda, stood next to a treatment table, fiddling with an intravenous line that snaked into the arm of a patient. Linda turned and nodded at Dylan. "Hi. We've been waiting for you. Please come in."

Puzzled, Dylan stepped farther into the room, around the end of the treatment table. The patient came into view; she was blond, in her twenties— with a sudden shock, Dylan recognized her. She smiled at him, the light sparkling off her clean white teeth. "Hello, lover," she said, reaching up with her left hand to remove the blond wig and shake out her bright red hair.

Kristin.

It was as if his brain had been struck by lightning. Dylan looked at the bottle of intravenous solution dripping into Kristin's arm. He pointed at it and said hoarsely, "Is that—"

"It sure is," said Argent smugly. "Doesn't she look great?"

Dylan stared first at Argent, then at Kristin, little doors opening and closing inside his head as conclusions exploded. He stuck out his hand, pointing at Kristin. "You—me—us—" he managed.

Kristin returned his gaze without chagrin or remorse. "About five years ago, I led a pretty wild life. I don't even know who I caught it from." She shrugged. "I really do like you, Dylan, but this was necessary, for a lot of reasons. Anyway, nobody stopped you from wearing a condom."

Argent nodded at Dylan, looking satisfied. "Did you really think it was a coincidence that you met Kristin in the hospital? And didn't you find it odd that the esteemed Reverend Fletcher suddenly started pouring his hard won-treasure, fleeced from his national flock of the religiously duped, into an AIDS research center?" Argent sighed. "It all seemed to be working out nicely. We wanted to make sure that Nicole's case was handled by an inexperienced lawyer, someone who wouldn't be sharp enough to notice the discrepancies. Unfortunately, you were a little more persistent than we expected."

"Gaa," said Dylan, unable to articulate.

Argent continued, "It bears repeating that you have several good reasons to cooperate with us now. First, it's the right thing to do. Second, you can't help Nicole. Third, as long as you do cooperate, you'll receive PHT, just as Kristin does."

Dylan heard what Argent said, but he wasn't really listening. He concentrated on the idea that

Kristin had AIDS, and they had screwed without condoms, not once but many times.

Through a tunnel, he heard Argent say, "By the way, an AIDS antibody test would still be negative. It takes three to six months after infection before it shows positive."

Sweet Jesus, Dylan thought. *I must be infected. Oh my God, oh my God.*

All Dylan's fear and rage released in an explosive, guttural scream, and he surged forward to grab Kristin and smash her fucking head.

He almost reached her before Skoler's hairy arm jerked him off his feet and slammed him against the wall.

CHAPTER TWENTY-SEVEN

Dylan struggled against waking up. Waking up meant facing reality, and that was to be avoided. He looked at the bedside clock, disoriented. It was six thirty A.M.; he had to get ready for work. He sat up, rubbed his eyes, and memory returned.

I've got AIDS. It was like a kick to the groin.

Dylan went into the bathroom, remembering all that had happened at MIRI. After he tried to attack Kristin—at least she had looked momentarily afraid—Skoler had painfully restrained him while Argent made it very clear what would happen if Dylan didn't cooperate.

He had been too preoccupied with the prospect of having AIDS to listen carefully—or to care.

He sank down on the toilet seat, putting his head in his heads. He stayed that way for minutes, until finally he felt he could go on. Then he forced himself to stand up. *Don't think. Just move.*

After shaving carefully, he took a shower. *Don't think,* he kept telling himself. *Don't think, just move. Breathe in, breathe out.*

After his shower, he put on his bathrobe and went to the kitchen to make coffee.

Seated at the table was T. J. Markham.

"Morning, Mr. Ice," Markham said.

Dylan stared at him, then said resignedly, "What next?"

"Sorry," said Markham, obviously not. "I let myself in."

"What do you want?"

"Have a seat. Let's talk." He motioned toward the coffeemaker on the counter. "I took the liberty of making some coffee."

"Sure. Why not? My house is your house." Dylan poured a cup of coffee and sat down. "So now what?"

"Where did you go yesterday?"

Now's my chance, Dylan thought. Tell him.

It was a mighty temptation. He could drop the burden, tell all about Nicole and Argent's grandiose schemes. It was the right thing to do, and he had always done the right thing.

But was it?

Argent assumed that he would choose his self-interest over all else. That the prospect of having AIDS without Nicole's PHT therapy would guarantee his silence.

"Well?" repeated Markham.

Maybe if he trusted Markham, he could have taken the plunge. Instead he said, "I was at my law office."

"Not according to your colleagues. You were seen leaving the office between six and seven P.M. Your car, however, remained in the parking garage."

"I got a ride home."

Markham reached across the table and grabbed Dylan's right wrist. "We don't have a lot of time, Dylan, and you're playing games. I don't know why but I don't really care, either. Tell me where you were last night. Tell me what you know about Girard and Argent." His grip tightened, his face very grim.

I've got AIDS, thought Dylan, *and this asshole thinks he can scare me.* He laughed.

Markham blinked and let go.

"You tell me what you're really investigating, and I might help you. If not, then get out of my apartment. Otherwise—" Dylan stood and went to the wall phone, "I'm calling the cops."

Markham stood, glaring at him, obviously wondering if he was bluffing. "This isn't a game, Dylan. I like you, but if you don't start cooperating, you'll find yourself in federal custody. Do I make myself clear? You've got my number."

Then he left, leaving behind a trace of pungent aftershave.

Spots. Tiny red spots in black tissue paper. That's all she could see, all that mattered. Dots.

And memories. Photographs, jagged images, cold edges, flashes of heat. Nightmare headless monsters. Sad-faced children. Shiny needles plunging— "Time to wake up," a voice said cheerily, the words flashing inside her head, strobing, each letter composed of millions of tiny red dots, blinking on and off.

She opened her eyes and the world flooded in.

"Good morning," said Argent. "How are we feeling today?"

She shook the sleep from her mind, coming awake slowly. "I'm having nightmares."

Argent clucked his tongue. "I'm sorry, but that's

a side effect to the medication. I'll adjust the dose."
He nodded at Linda, who stood on the other side of
the bed; she placed a rubber tourniquet around
Nicole's upper arm and probed for a vein.

Nicole watched the familiar procedure tiredly.
When the blood was drawn, Argent said brightly,
"Anything you need? More tapes? Books?"

"Your head on a platter."

"Sorry." He grinned.

"How long do you intend to keep me here?"

Argent sighed. "I really wish you wouldn't talk
that way."

"I'm supposed to like being kidnapped."

"We've explained why this is necessary," Linda
said.

"Necessary for *you*. Not for me. What happens
when you're done with me? You've already told
everyone I'm dead. You'll have to kill me for real,
won't you? You can't let me suddenly rise from the
grave."

Argent said, "None of this would have been necessary if you weren't so selfish. If you had agreed to
stay in the hospital and participate in this important
experiment."

"Fuck you!"

Argent smiled indulgently. "Anyway, we do feel
bad about this, and if there was any other way,
believe me, I would take it. But the potential of my
work is so great . . . someday you'll thank me. You'll
be hailed as a great heroine, and you'll go along with
it, because you'll be too ashamed to say you tried to
sabotage my efforts. We'll explain that we faked
your death in order to keep the project a secret, and
you'll agree."

"Don't hold your breath," said Nicole. But then,

because he seemed in an unusually expansive mood, she continued, "Why *me*? What makes me so special, anyway?"

Argent paused, taking a blood pressure cuff from a shelf on the wall. He poised, about to put the stethoscope earpieces in his ears. "A genetic accident, probably. A one-in-a-billion mutation." Argent put the cuff on Nicole's left arm and pumped it up. After he finished taking her pressure, he said abruptly, "You're in good shape. We'll see you tomorrow."

After they left, Nicole swung her legs over the side of the bed and went to the window. It was barred, of course, but it was the closest she could get to being outside. For a while, she stared at the line of trees in the distance. Then she went to the bathroom.

Afterward, she lay down on the couch, her hands behind her head, staring at the ceiling. She knew that this room was on the top floor of the research center, hidden in a restricted area of the laboratory. The door was solid steel, and there was always a guard outside it. The only people she saw were Mark and Linda Argent—and three interchangeable guards who brought her meals.

Nicole had cable television, a VCR, books, a stereo, exercise equipment, everything to make her life bearable. Or so they thought.

Every day was exactly the same as the next. She wondered about Charlene, about Pamela Holtz, even her parents. It was eerie imagining them at her funeral, mourning her. Did they ever think of her now? She even wondered about Dylan Ice, the lawyer who had seemed genuinely interested in her fate. If only he had pushed a little harder, if he had been more suspicious about her conduct at the guardianship hearing. . . .

She was making herself crazy.

Nicole stared at the ceiling, slowly realizing the significance of what she saw there. Square acoustic ceiling tiles, set between thin metal rods that, she knew, hung from the real ceiling—the roof, since this was the top floor. She had often hung plants from the ceiling rods in her office building.

She lay there, thinking furiously. Assuming she could get up there—and that was a big assumption—could she crawl into the space above the hallway, into the next room, or get onto the roof?

The thought of freedom was breathtaking.

Wait. The tiles probably couldn't support her weight. But she could move from rod to rod. Yes, it might work. It would work! She could do it tonight!

She forced herself to calm down, think it through. There was the problem of the video camera, mounted high in the far corner, its little red light always blinking. She had almost gotten used to it. There was no place to be alone except the bathroom—even Argent wasn't low enough to put a camera in there.

Or was he? Her heart jumped again as she considered the possibility of a hidden camera.

If so, she'd kill him. Somehow, someday, she'd find a way. She swore it.

Well, there was no way for her to be sure. She'd just have to take a chance. Anyway, she'd first have to figure out how to get *up* to the bathroom ceiling. Standing on the toilet or sink wouldn't work; she didn't have enough arm strength to pull herself up. She'd almost have to be on a level with the roof beams.

It would be easy to drag some furniture in there, but Argent's goons would see it on the video monitor. No, there had to be some other way.

The nightstand—that was the answer. Days ago, she had talked Argent into letting her put the small nightstand into the bathroom to hold her toilet articles. It could work.

She spent the rest of the day visualizing how.

Nicole woke with a start at three fifteen A.M. She had meant to stay awake, but must have dozed off. Luckily, she wasn't too late.

Slowly, she rolled out of bed and walked into the bathroom. If there was anyone at the video monitor, they would know she went to the bathroom, since the suite was always illuminated by a small low-watt fixture on the wall. She figured she had about twenty minutes before they got worried or suspicious.

She closed the bathroom door, switched on the light, grabbed a towel and jammed it into the space between the flush pipe and the wall. Then she picked up the nightstand—not easy to do, her muscles were like putty—and jammed two of its legs on top of the towel. The other two legs rested on another towel spread across the toilet seat.

It was an unsteady arrangement, barely useable, but it was the best she could do. Nicole looked around the tiny room. *Now or never.*

She took off her nightgown and tied it around her neck. Clad only in bra and panties, she stepped first on the toilet seat, then, unsteadily, one knee at a time, onto the top of the nightstand.

Teetering dangerously, she still was able to reach

over her head and push up slowly on the ceiling tile. It lifted easily, and she shoved it off to the side, revealing a dark space and the true concrete roof about a foot above. She pushed up the adjacent tiles, so that the thin metal on which the tiles rested was revealed.

This is going to be much harder than I thought, she said to herself. It might not even be possible. She shook off the thought—she *had* to do this. Grabbing the metal bar above her head, she tested it to see if it would take her weight. The nightstand swayed dangerously, and she had to stifle a scream.

She managed to steady everything and try again. The bar felt solid; there was no give.

Now was the time. Taking a deep breath, she put both hands on the bar—almost level with her head—and lifted herself up. Involuntarily, she pushed off with her legs, knocking the nightstand out of balance. It toppled to the side with a sickening crash, leaving Nicole dangling from the ceiling bar. "Oh, shit," she whispered.

Now feeling desperate, she tried to pull herself up and over the bar, but didn't have the arm strength. She did manage to swing one leg up and over, and that helped, but the bar was so narrow that it cut painfully into the bare flesh of her thigh.

Panting heavily, she slowly tried to lift and roll herself onto the top of the beam, and almost accomplished it when she heard the cracking sound.

The metal beam on which she hung was never meant to carry much weight, and the vertical rod that attached it to the concrete ceiling above was slowly ripping out of its mooring. Nicole had time only for a brief burst of panic before the entire assembly pulled out of the roof, flopping downward like a gate.

Nicole dropped; she lost her grip on the rod and fell toward the toilet.

There was time for a brief impression of flat impact, of shocking pain and the metallic taste of blood, before she mercifully lost consciousness.

CHAPTER TWENTY-EIGHT

Every President of the United States knew the job's biggest defect was the total lack of privacy. Unless personally experienced, it was impossible to understand the 360 degrees of scrutiny, the magnitude of the invasion into private space.

Other people with private bodyguards could send their bodyguards away, could go off by themselves, take a stroll on a deserted beach without anyone watching.

They could go to the bathroom without exciting comment.

But not the President.

Thomas Banfield left the afternoon Cabinet meeting four times to use his private bathroom, where he experienced explosive liquid stools. Each time, he thought the crisis was over, but the cramps and abdominal pain returned in minutes.

He could see the concern on the faces of his cabinet officers. Craig Hagen came over to whisper in his ear, "Maybe you should just cut this short. Forget the press conference."

Banfield shook his head. It was too important, this opportunity to announce his new jobs initiative on the eve of the nominating convention. Osborne's relentless campaigning and the rumors about Banfield's health were affecting the polls, and Osborne had gained five points in the last week. Today was an opportunity to take the offensive.

Now, as Banfield sat at the head of the table, about to call in the press, he began to regret not taking Hagen's advice. The cramps and pain were back, and he felt nauseous. *Suck it up*, he told himself. *Mind over matter.* He tried to watch calmly as the cameras set up and the Washington press corps surged into the room, surrounding the Cabinet table.

Banfield introduced his Labor Secretary, trying to control his expression as she explained the terms of the proposed bill. Then, inevitably, it was time for questions, and the correspondents turned his way.

He was supremely conscious of the cameras on him; a sound bite from this would surely be on the evening news. Banfield tried to concentrate on the questions, but it was very difficult; his bowels were ready to explode and he felt stomach acid battering at his throat.

"Mr. President?" said the correspondent. "Could you repeat that, please?"

Banfield realized they were all looking at him strangely. Hagen was at his side, taking his arm, trying to lift him from his seat.

It was all too much. Trying to move seemed to trigger everything. He managed to turn his head as the vomit came surging up his throat, spewing onto the carpet, directly onto the seal of the republic beautifully rendered in blue and gold thread. He felt his bowels give way, too, and then his head seemed to float above the crowd until it began to sink, ever so slowly, below the level of the table.

■ ■ ■

When Banfield awoke, he was in his own bed and had no memory of how he got there. He still felt a trifle nauseous, and very weak, but otherwise okay. His wife was there, staring at him stonily, along with Roger Schreiber, his personal physician, and Craig Hagen.

"How are you feeling, chief?" Hagen asked, but before Banfield could answer, the bedroom door opened and Peter Rosati hurried in.

"Jesus Christ, Craig! You called Rosati!" Banfield said. "Why not just take out an ad?"

Hagen stepped forward and patted Banfield's hand in an almost fatherly way. "It's all right, sir. We snuck him in. No one knows he's here."

"He's stable," Schreiber said to Rosati. "Febrile, but pulse and respiration okay. Pressure one forty over ninety-five. Liver is enlarged and tender, and he's a bit yellow."

Rosati nodded and opened his bag, taking out his stethoscope. "Let me examine him alone for a few minutes."

Banfield didn't say anything until Rosati had finished his poking and prodding. Then he asked, "Guess your PHT didn't work, Peter. So what is it? A bad case of the flu?" He tried to grin.

"I don't know," said Rosati. "Not without stool and blood cultures. It could be something as simple as the flu, or it could be another opportunistic infection, *Cryptosporidium*, although we usually don't see that with your CD4 count. More likely, it's cytomegalovirus; that would account for your jaundice. We need to get you to the hospital and run some tests, X rays, ultrasound, endoscopy."

Banfield shook his head. "Not now."

"You don't have a choice, Mr. President. The whole world knows you're sick."

Banfield propped himself up on his elbows. "Get Hagen and Schreiber back here."

After Rosati repeated his recommendations to Hagen and Schreiber, there was a long silence. Finally Hagen said, "Mr. President, we don't have to give up. Obviously, we won't send you to NIH. We can admit you to Walter Reed or Bethesda Naval. Schreiber can do it, and handle all the tests. They're the same tests you'd give to a non-AIDS patient anyway, aren't they?" He looked at Rosati.

"Mostly," Rosati said.

"Okay, so we tell the press you've got a bad case of gastroenteritis, and you're being admitted for diagnosis and supportive therapy. No big deal."

Banfield knew they were right. Anyway, there was no alternative. He thought of all that he wanted to do in his second term, all the mistakes he wanted to correct, all the hard lessons he had learned from his first four years. He thought of how awful it would be seeing Osborne in the Oval Office. Craig was right; he couldn't cop out.

He thought of living until he was old.

Finally, he said, "What if it *is* an opportunistic infection? What then?"

"Depending on what it is, we have drugs to treat it. The problem is your CD4 count. If it keeps dropping . . . well, Mr. President, you'll *have* to start the antivirals."

His options were narrowing. The circle was getting smaller. Banfield suddenly felt very tired and collapsed against the pillow. "All right, Craig. Let's go to Bethesda Naval. It's closer to Dr. Rosati's office than Walter Reed."

As they all filed out, Marianne came into the bedroom. *His* bedroom; they hadn't slept together for years. She pulled a chair over to the bed and looked at him. And, for the first time in a very long while, he saw something close to affection in her eyes. At least there was no anger.

To the world, Marianne Banfield was a refined and accomplished First Lady, a former school administrator who had willingly subordinated her career to that of her husband. At forty-nine, she was still very attractive, with high cheekbones framed by golden hair and a perfect mouth.

They had met while he was rising in city politics, serving as a city councilman; she was a school board member who had opposed his cost-cutting efforts until they had fallen in love and he co-opted her.

It was when he met Jason Conner that their marriage deteriorated to what it was now: political convenience. They never had children, and Marianne's interest in sexual relations was minimal. She enjoyed the role of political wife—had, indeed, accomplished a great deal in education policy—and he needed her by his side.

In one way, of course, it was fortunate they were estranged, or she might have AIDS, too. He had told her about Conner's letter, had confessed his infidelity. Her reaction had been cold indifference. She never mentioned it again.

Marianne put out her hand and, almost fearfully, stroked his cheek. "I'm sorry."

"Sorry? For what?" He was genuinely puzzled.

"Sorry that all this happened. Just . . . sorry."

He felt tears wetting his eyes, an unfamiliar sensation.

"Thank you," he said softly. "Thank you."

Senator Theodore Osborne pushed the rewind button and grinned. He had just watched, for the fifth time, the wonderful spectacle of the President of the United States throwing up and passing out in front of the assembled Cabinet and White House press corps. "I couldn't have ordered a better event to kick off my campaign."

"We oughta make that a commercial!" said Barcus, and they all laughed. All except Turk Finnegan, who once again felt an unexpected pang of sympathy for his old boss. He was, in fact beginning to feel more guilt from being a Judas than pleasure from revenge. He tried to remember the hurt he had felt at his abrupt dismissal. That helped a little.

The gang of four were back in Osborne's senatorial office—Finnegan had been hustled in wearing a wig and eyeglasses—gleefully discussing the afternoon's incredible events.

McPeak said, "It's time to move, Senator. If we wait, they'll put some sort of spin on this that will make us look bad if we try to dispute it."

Osborne turned to Finnegan. "How will they handle this, Turk?"

Finnegan took a sip of coffee from his Wedgewood china cup. He cleared his throat and said, "It's tough to say, without knowing whether this is AIDS-related or not."

"Assume it is," McPeak said.

"Okay, then you put him in Walter Reed or Bethesda, where you can limit access and where the personnel are all under military orders. You treat him, hope for the best, and tell the public he's got the flu."

"But what if it's serious?" McPeak asked. "What if this is a real AIDS crisis?"

Osborne said, "If it is, what we do doesn't matter, he's finished, and not just politically. Unfortunately, we can't assume that." He picked up a gold-plated letter opener in the shape of a sword—a gift from a military contractor in his district—and tapped it lightly on his cheek. "No, I think it's time to crank up the pressure."

"What are you thinking?" asked McPeak.

"A letter," said Osborne.

"A letter? Are you kidding?" said Barcus.

Osborne smiled. "A letter to the President."

CHAPTER TWENTY-NINE

After her abortive escape attempt, Argent put Nicole back in bed restraints until a video camera was installed in a corner of the bathroom ceiling.

That left Nicole only one alternative.

Days ago, during the routine daily drawing of blood, Linda Argent had dropped the butterfly needle she usually pocketed for disposal, and Nicole surreptitiously retrieved it from the floor.

Now, moving quickly, she dragged a chair into the bathroom, grabbed a towel, stood on the chair and threw the towel over the camera lens. Then she jammed the chair against the closed door.

Nicole pulled the needle out of her pocket and looked at it. It was only about a half inch in length, not long enough to reach her heart. Her jugular vein? No, her wrist would be easier. She stuck a washcloth between her teeth. Then, methodically and forcefully, she began stabbing the needle into her left wrist, trying to pierce a vein with every jab.

Soon her wrist and hand were covered with blood. The pain wasn't bad, but felt dizzy. Got to keep going, she told herself, still jabbing as the bathroom door crashed inward.

■   ■   ■

For two days Dylan didn't go to the office. He called Rhonda and told her he was sick, which certainly was the truth. He didn't bother asking for his phone messages. Barry, still in Kansas City, called several times, but Dylan gave him the same story.

He hardly slept; all he could think of was all the horrible ways of dying from AIDS, the wasting diseases, the cancers, the weakness. AIDS dementia.

Many HIV-positive people developed AIDS in less than five years after infection; what if he was one of those—what they called a rapid progressor?

Even if he took the medications and staved off AIDS, being HIV-positive meant he would never be able to marry, to have children. What woman would want to be with him, even if they did practice safe sex?

Now, on Friday morning, unable to get out of bed, Dylan realized he needed to talk with someone.

He also realized that his only close friend was Barry, who would insist on calling the police once he learned Dylan's story. Barry would never look at him the same way, either, after learning he had AIDS. No one would. He knew how *he* looked at people with AIDS. That would all be directed at him now.

Dylan didn't bother fighting the waves of depression. He kept thinking of how he had been duped by Argent and Kristin, how all along she had reported everything to her father, or to Argent.

He thought of how they had made love, so uninhibited, so . . . forceful. And all the time she knew. All the time.

And it was humiliating to realize how easily they had bought his silence. He could stay healthy, he could be normal, be like everyone else. Just let Nicole remain a victim.

It wouldn't be forever, he consoled himself. Not if Argent really had a cure. In the meantime, he could be assured that life would go on, and no one need ever know he had AIDS. How many people could resist that?

His father, maybe. A man who had burned his draft card and gone to jail for a year might be willing to suffer even this for principle.

Apparently he wasn't the same man as his father.

Maybe he could tell Janis?

No. He quickly discarded that. She was just turning her life around. This was a burden she didn't need.

Okay, you're slipping, he thought. Do something, anything to show you still can control your own fate.

All right, then. Back to basics. Analyze the situation. The first thing he had to do was find out his chances of actually having AIDS. He vaguely recalled that heterosexual transmission of the AIDS virus was not as easy as homosexual transmission.

He forced himself out of bed, stretched deliberately, then padded in bare feet to the computer in the den. He logged on to the Internet and started searching Web sites. After an hour, he turned off the computer, satisfied.

The data were clear. HIV existed in vaginal secretions and menstrual blood and could be transmitted to male sexual partners, particularly if there was a sore or cut on the penis, but surprisingly few men were infected that way. As near as he could determine, if he had had intercourse with Kristin only a few times, his chance of getting HIV would be pretty small. Unfortunately, they had had sex numerous times—at least a few dozen.

They also had had oral sex; and because the mouth is lined with mucous membrane, contact with Kristin's infectious vaginal secretions could have allowed HIV to enter his body through tiny cuts in his mouth such as those caused by tooth brushing or flossing.

Argent hadn't misled him about the AIDS test. The standard HIV ELISA antibody test took at least three months after infection before showing positive. Still, it was worth getting, both to serve as a baseline and because it was almost three months since he met Kristin. And if the test was positive now, it would settle the issue.

All right, that would be a first step. In the meantime, he would try to act and think normally. *Right.*

The first step to acting normally, Dylan decided, was eating breakfast. He went into the kitchen and found some eggs that didn't look too old, and some turkey bacon. In a few minutes he had cooked a bacon omelette and sat down with a fresh cup of coffee. He also flicked on the kitchen TV and tuned it to CNN *Headline News.*

Dylan sat through the weather and sports and was almost finished with breakfast when the top of the news rolled around again. The first story was about the President entering Bethesda Naval Hospital, apparently suffering from a bad case of intestinal flu. There was a humorous commentary by the correspondent, who related how even Presidents sometimes couldn't be too close to a bathroom, recalling President Bush's infamous bout of flu at a Japanese state dinner.

There was file footage of the President entering the hospital for his last checkup, and something in the picture caught Dylan's eye, making him sit up and look hard at the screen. In the background of the shot there were a couple of men in suits with ear-pieces and a faraway look in their eyes. Secret Service agents.

The picture was only on the screen for a few seconds, but Dylan was reasonably sure of what he saw.

One of the Secret Service agents was T.J. Markham.

Oh my God, Dylan thought.

Markham. The White House!

Now he understood why Markham's ID was from the Treasury Department—the Secret Service was part of Treasury.

Dylan scurried to his front door and retrieved the newspaper, spreading it out on the living room floor. He found the article on the President entering the hospital, but it didn't have much more detail than the CNN story.

Then something else caught his eye. It was a full-page ad on page three, titled "AN OPEN LETTER TO THE PRESIDENT OF THE UNITED STATES." He read:

Mr. President,

Recently, your opponent has released his medical records, including the results of his testing for sexually transmitted disease. We, the undersigned bipartisan members of Congress, business and civic leaders, and private citizens applaud this as a positive step toward our goal of informing the American electorate about all factors relevant to a voting decision. Although it is unfortunate that the moral and physical health of this country have deteriorated to the point that such information is necessary, we cannot ignore the realities of our times.

Senator Osborne's release of such information may be the first step in making such information routinely available in future presidential elections. Because the law does not require such disclosure, it must be given voluntarily. Your recent refusal to do so may set an unfortunate precedent.

We therefore implore you, Mr. President, in the name of democracy, to firmly set the standard for future candidates. We ask that you take a simple blood test at a public clinic or laboratory and publish the results immediately.

The letter was signed by a Who's Who of conservatives, but with a few names in the President's party.

So there it was. Now, finally, Dylan understood why Markham and the Secret Service were so interested in Nicole's case, and why they hadn't come down harder on Argent.

"The President has AIDS," Dylan whispered. *The President.*

How did he get it? And when? If the President were a homosexual—God, the implications were enormous.

This changes everything, Dylan thought. *Even Argent might not know this.* And *that* knowledge gave him a sudden feeling of release, a feeling of—power.

All his life, Dylan had done everything asked or expected of him. He had given up his own adolescence to raise Janis. He had worked hard and been responsible, because it was the right thing to do. His dues were paid.

Argent set him up. He had let Kristin and Fletcher and Argent make a fool of him. *I've played the game on their terms.*

Dylan carefully cut the article out of the paper, folded it, and put it in his wallet.

No more, he thought.

CHAPTER THIRTY

Like most cops, Detective Sergeant Chester Peterson lived on coffee, and he was at his customary place near the pot when his partner yelled, "Chuck! Call on line five. That lawyer who lost his fingers!"

Peterson returned to his desk, picked up the phone, and punched the line. "Mr. Ice?"

"Yeah, it's me. I've located Skoler. He's in a car across the street from my apartment, in a black Ford Taurus, tag number KLD 043. It looks like he's still following me."

Peterson scribbled down the tag number and looked at his watch. He had to be in court in an hour; on the other hand, he really wanted to pick up this creep Skoler. It would be a good collar. "Okay. I'll take care of it myself. I should be there in about fifteen minutes—call this number again if they leave—and thanks."

Dylan watched as the unmarked county police car stopped next to the unmarked Secret Service car, and Peterson and his partner jumped out, guns drawn.

He didn't wait to see what happened next;

instead he hurried down to his car and drove past the little police drama. The Secret Service agents had assumed the position against the hood of their car while Peterson patted down their pockets.

Peterson soon would find their guns and shields, but by then it would be too late for them to follow him. Dylan was free of his tail.

It was a twenty-minute drive to a seedy area of north St. Louis. He parked on the street, hoping his car would survive, and entered the AIDS clinic. He had purposely dressed down, wearing a dirty pair of jeans and an old T-shirt, and he fit in with the ten or fifteen people in the waiting room. He tried not to notice that some of them looked pretty sick.

Dylan checked in with the receptionist, a plump African-American in her thirties; she smiled warmly at him.

In less time than he expected, he was called into a small cubicle, where he was introduced to a slim Pakistani woman holding a clipboard full of multi-part forms and pamphlets. She introduced herself as an AIDS counselor, gave him some pamphlets, and told him the mechanics of the test.

"We are assigning you a number," she said in her sing-song accent, "so the results of the testing will be completely anonymous."

"How long will it take to get the results?"

"We are asking you to return in one week, you see, to give you the results."

"You mean I can't get the results over the phone?"

"Yes, you can," she said disapprovingly, "but this is not wise. It is better you come here, so if the results are positive, we can help you deal with this."

"I appreciate that, but I'll be out of town."

She shrugged. "In that case, you are calling this phone number." She picked up a business card from a box on the counter, then peeled a numbered sticker off a form on the clipboard, and placed the sticker on the rear of the card. "You give this identification number to the clerk." She gave the card and the form to Dylan.

She guided him into another cubicle, where he handed the form to a young Korean woman wearing a lab coat. She drew a tube of blood, and minutes later, Dylan was back outside on the sidewalk. As simple as that, he thought. He tucked the business card in his wallet.

Now compartmentalize, he thought. Don't think about it anymore. He returned to his car and headed for his next destination.

"You have a phone call, Mr. Sasscer," said the pretty blond secretary, as Barry followed Hudson and the opposing attorney out of the conference room. Barry frowned; there weren't a lot of people that knew he was taking depositions at this Kansas City law firm. She escorted him to a nearby file room with a wall phone.

"Hello?"

"Hi, Barry. It's Dylan."

"Dylan! Are you all right?"

"I'm fine, but I need your help and don't have time to explain. You're still representing the Kreeger brothers, right? The guys I met at your birthday party?"

"Of course. Unless you know something I don't. Why?"

Dylan sounded relieved. "Good. I need a very

big favor, Barry, and I'm gonna ask you to just do it, without questions." His tone was strained but assured.

"Go ahead. Hit me."

When Dylan finished explaining, Barry said, "I can try, that's all I can say. It may not be possible, they may have other commitments. But you have to tell me—"

"I can't. Not yet. And I'm dead serious about this. Please, just try. If they can do it, call me on my cell phone."

Again, that strange timbre in his voice. It was against his better judgment, but Barry said, "All right. This once. I'll—"

"Thank you. I'll wait for your call."

"Shit," said Barry.

"You lost Ice?" Hagen asked incredulously. "How the hell did that happen?"

"Simple," said Markham, inhaling deeply from his cigarette. He breathed the smoke into the receiver. "He called the cops. Told them that Argent's pet thug—some lowlife named Skoler—was following him. So the cops tried to bust my men. They identified themselves, of course, but by then it was too late, he was gone."

Hagen looked down the hall of the hospital, where the day nurse was checking in with the Secret Service agent before entering the President's room. "He must know what Argent is up to. Maybe Argent bought him off. You should have leaned on him harder."

"I will, when I find him."

"Why can't you just move in on Argent? Go in

there and find out what's going on so we can end this thing. This all may be a wild goose chase, but we need to know if there's any help there."

"On what basis? What the hell am I supposed to arrest him for?"

"Ice told you he switched bodies."

"That's a local criminal matter. How do I justify the Secret Service's involvement?"

"Well, then, go in covertly."

"Too much security. It's not worth the risk."

"T.J., at some point risk ceases to matter. If we don't get some help for Tom—" Hagen shook his head, even though Markham couldn't see it. He wasn't ready to give up yet. The President would survive this crisis, somehow. "We're fucked either way, at this point," Hagen continued, "so give it a day. If Ice doesn't show up, take Argent down, and worry about the consequences later."

"All right," Markham said slowly. "If that's what you want."

Markham hung up the phone and began pacing around the room, considering his next move, when the phone rang again.

"Agent Markham?"

"Ice!"

"Yeah. Sorry about the mix-up with your agents."

"Where are you, and what the hell are you doing?"

"I've got the information you want."

Markham sat down on the bed, pulling the phone closer to him. "Hold on." He quickly walked to the door between the suites and pointed at Brent, lounging in a chair. Markham pointed at the phone next to Brent's bed; Brent nodded.

Returning to his phone, Markham said, "Sorry, I had to put out my cigarette. Go ahead."

Dylan chuckled. "Right. Okay, here it is. Nicole Girard is alive and well, and living on the top floor of the institute. Argent faked her death."

"Holy shit." whispered Markham.

"Nicole has antibodies that will knock HIV out more effectively than any other treatment. Better than any of the antiviral drugs. And he's used this knowledge—and her blood—to develop a cure. Or at least, he thinks it's a cure."

For once, Markham had no words.

"Are you there?"

"Yeah. Go on."

"Argent is getting nervous about you guys. He's going to move Nicole—and his whole operation—out of the country."

"What?"

"That's right. So I suggest you get there, if you want to stop him."

"Jesus! When?"

"Sometime after five."

Markham's training reasserted itself. Never take information without considering source and motivation. "So how did you learn all this?"

There was no answer; it took a few seconds for the dial tone to sound in his earpiece.

CHAPTER THIRTY-ONE

In the future, Dylan decided, the hospital would have to install metal detectors at its entrances. As it was, he walked through the main doors of MIRI with the Glock pistol in his valise. He looked at his watch. If Markham was as efficient as he suspected, there wasn't much time.

After leaving the AIDS clinic, he had changed in his car to a blue sport jacket, gray slacks, and green patterned tie. Now he walked past the reception desk to the public restroom for another quick change. Ducking into a stall, Dylan removed the sport jacket. From the valise he removed a freshly pressed lab coat, a cell phone, and a stethoscope. He put on the lab coat, draping the stethoscope around his neck in the manner of physicians. The cell phone went into the coat's side pocket. Finally, he checked the pistol's safety and stuffed it into the waistband of his slacks.

He would have to leave the valise and sport jacket in the stall; physicians didn't carry hand luggage.

Dylan exited the stall and checked himself in the mirror, twirling around to make sure the gun didn't create an obvious bulge. The only defect in the outfit was the lack of a hospital name tag or pocket stitching, but there was nothing he could do about that. Anyway, most people assumed you were who you appeared to be. On first impression, he definitely looked like a physician, and that was all he needed.

As he exited to the corridor, Dylan saw Markham and his men striding toward the reception desk. He quickly turned away and walked down the hall to a public phone cubicle, picked up the receiver, and pretended to dial while watching the action at the reception desk.

As he expected, Markham and Company paused long enough to flash their badges at the receptionist, then jumped onto the elevator, leaving behind one agent to guard their rear. Dylan couldn't help smiling. In a few minutes, Dr. Argent and his security team would have their hands full.

Dylan hung up the phone and walked casually to the staircase at the end of the corridor.

Just another day in paradise, thought Nicole as she tried to cut Salisbury steak with a spoon. After her suicide attempt, Argent had taken every potentially dangerous object away from her, including forks and knives. She managed to sever a piece of the tough meat with the edge of the spoon but didn't bother to eat it. God, she was sick of hospital food.

Then she reminded herself they were always watching, and if she didn't eat, they'd feed her intravenously. The video camera in the ceiling seemed to mock her. She gave it the finger, then reluctantly brought the meat to her mouth, chewing mechanically. It tasted like cardboard.

She managed a few more bites, ate some of the waxy lima beans, then pushed the tray away and sank back onto her pillow.

Nicole could barely lift her arms. Her left wrist was secured in a way that made it impossible to remove the bandage one-handed, and she was so fucking tranquilized that she doubted she could lift it off anyway.

That's the point, Nicole, she thought. That's the point.

She looked at the digital clock. As usual, they were giving her dinner at five P.M. That meant she had a whole evening to face. Maybe she should get up and try to watch television from the couch. Yeah. That would be something.

Her legs swung out over the bed, and she stepped onto the cold linoleum floor in her bare feet. She wore only a pair of panties and the hospital gown, but she was long past caring about modesty. The security guards watching her on video—Larry, Curly, and Moe, she called them—had seen every part of her by now, many times, in every kind of personal activity.

She walked back and forth in front of the couch, trying to get the feel of her legs, then realized she had to relieve herself. Afterward, in the bathroom, she stared at herself in the mirror. *Death warmed over,* she thought. She laughed, enjoying the thought, realizing that she didn't mind. She felt no desire at all to be attractive. To be anything, in fact. What she wanted, more than anything else, was oblivion.

I guess I've truly given up. I don't even feel like killing myself anymore. Too much effort. She shuffled back to the couch. It took all her energy to lie down, and she didn't bother with the remote control for the television. The ceiling tiles were interesting enough.

Suddenly there was the sound of the heavy metal door sliding open. She didn't look; she knew it must be one of the stooges coming to retrieve her dinner tray. But she heard what sounded like two pairs of feet on the linoleum and an uncharacteristic huffing noise, like someone panting.

"Nicole?" said a voice. She sat up and looked.

In the doorway was an absolutely startling scene. A familiar-looking doctor held a pistol to the head of the guard she had named Moe, who looked suitably impressed. "Nicole! You know who I am? Are you all right?" the doctor asked.

"Dylan Ice!" she said in wonderment. "What are you doing here?"

"No time for that," Dylan said quickly. He pushed Moe forward, ordering him to lie down on the floor. She noticed that Dylan's left hand was bandaged, but he reached into the left pocket of his lab coat and, with his thumb and index finger, pulled out a roll of surgical tape. He handed it to her, and she automatically took it. "Quickly. Tear off some long strips."

She stared at him stupidly. "C'mon!" he yelled at her. "Don't you want to get out of here?"

Nicole didn't think she had any capacity for hope, but his words energized her. She shook her body like a terrier and forcefully ripped off hunks of tape, handing them to Dylan. He used the first piece to gag Moe, the others to tie his wrists and feet together. Then he stood up, looked at her, and grinned.

"Hello," he said.

"I can't believe this is happening," she said. "Are you really here?"

He actually bowed. "Dylan Ice, Hero First-Class." Then his expression tightened. "You have any clothes?"

"A few. Jeans and shirt." She moved to the closet.

"Put 'em on, quickly."

She changed right there, while Dylan paced nervously at the door, looking past the security station.

"They took my shoes," she said.

"All right, you'll have to go barefoot. Nothing we can do. Let's get out of here."

She followed him out of the room, and she had her first look at the world outside her prison. It was a small anteroom, filled mostly with the guard desk. "Wait a minute." Before Dylan could answer, she picked up a heavy paperweight from the desk and flung it at the video monitor. The screen shattered on impact, sending shards of glass everywhere.

"Christ! What did you do that for?"

"I'll explain later," she said with satisfaction. Then she looked at the floor, covered with shards of glass. "Uh, maybe you better carry me over this part."

Dylan scooped her up and carried her forward a few feet, then set her down. "You hardly weigh a thing."

"Dr. Argent's patented weight-loss plan."

There was a second security door, already open. They walked out into a large laboratory area, empty of people. "Okay," said Dylan. "Here's the plan. We cross this room, then there's a hallway leading into the main corridor. On the right side of the hallway there's a door to the stairwell. We—"

"Put the gun down, asshole," said a voice from the far end of the room. Nicole caught a glimpse of a very large man with a shiny head, coming through the doorway.

"Skoler, you bastard!" Dylan roared, raising the gun in his right hand and firing twice, explosions of sound that were almost physical. Nicole leaped backward, through the open security door, and felt a sharp pain in her right foot as she stepped on a piece of glass.

Dylan ran toward the other end of the room, and Nicole saw Skoler momentarily raise his head above a lab table, an expression of utter surprise on his face. When he didn't see Dylan, he crawled between two lab tables, pausing to fire his pistol once, wildly. She heard the bullet ricochet off a pipe in the ceiling, sounding just like in the movies.

Dylan jumped onto a counter and fired downward, and it all ended in an instant. There was a cry of pain and the sound of something metal hitting the floor. Dylan jumped off and motioned her forward.

"Jesus Christ, Dylan!" was all she could manage.

Dylan grinned at her. "That was easier than I thought." He added conspiratorially, "That's the first time I ever shot anybody."

She walked past the counter and saw Skoler on the floor, groaning and holding his left shoulder. Blood was oozing through his fingers. Dylan ignored him. "C'mon," he said, taking her hand. Then he noticed her foot. "Shit, you're bleeding!"

"It's all right. I stepped on the glass after all. It doesn't hurt much."

"Yeah, but that's very valuable blood. You shouldn't be giving away freebies. Let me see."

She lifted up her foot and he examined it while she supported herself by leaning on his shoulder.

"It's not bad," he said, "and anyway, we don't have time to bandage it. Someone will have heard those shots."

It was amazing, she thought, that they both could be so casual about all this, like they were playing parts in a movie. She was tranquilized, she knew, but how could he be so calm? Perhaps this was a common reaction to danger; she didn't know.

"So let's go," Nicole said.

They moved into the hallway, Nicole leaving a trail of blood on the floor. Now there were other people around, frightened people who saw Dylan's gun and disappeared. They made it to the large corridor, and Dylan walked swiftly toward the door with the large Exit sign. They were about halfway there when a voice said, "Ice! Freeze right there!"

Dylan stopped and swung around toward the voice, but thankfully didn't raise his pistol. She was sure the voice would shoot if he did. "Hello, Markham," said Dylan. "I thought you'd still be interrogating Dr. Argent."

At the far end of the corridor, about twenty feet away, were two men in business suits, one standing, one kneeling, holding pistols in a cop's characteristic two-handed grip. Another man came up behind them in a white coat—Argent. "You disappoint me, Dylan," said Argent. "I thought we had a deal."

"And I thought Markham would slow you down."

"You were wrong," said Argent.

"Enough!" said Markham. "Put the gun down, Dylan. I don't want to shoot you."

When Dylan hesitated, Markham said, "Take a look—"

The door to the stairwell opened slowly, and

Nicole saw two more men in suits, crouching, guns pointed at Dylan.

Dylan said, "You make a deal with Argent, T.J.? He'll double-cross you."

"Just put down the gun, Dylan. Don't worry about Ms. Girard—we'll take good care of her."

"Yeah, I'm sure you will. She's a very valuable person. At least her blood is." He turned to face Nicole. "Sorry," he said simply. "But I did try." Very slowly, he leaned down and placed the pistol on the floor. As he straightened up, the two men in the stairwell rushed Dylan and grabbed his arms. Markham and Argent also came forward.

And because everyone concentrated on Dylan, no one stopped Nicole as she took two quick steps forward and scooped up the pistol.

"Shit!" someone said, followed quickly by a chorus of "Don't fire!" and "Don't shoot her!" from Markham and Argent.

"C'mon, Nicole," Argent said earnestly, stepping forward. "Put it down. You'll have to shoot some people just to get out of this corridor, and then I won't be able to stop people from shooting *you*. And you can't let that happen. Whatever you think of me doesn't matter. You've got something the world needs. Please."

Nicole looked at Dylan. He shrugged. "I screwed up, Nicole. Sorry. But now it's over."

"Over?" She thought of what her life had been like for the last few months. It looked like the faces of her captors might change, but life would be the same. A prisoner. A blood cow. Something to experiment on.

"I'm not going to shoot anyone," she said, putting the pistol to her temple. "Anyone else, that is."

"Jesus H. Christ," one of the men said.

"I seem to be more valuable to other people than to myself," continued Nicole. "But, you know, I really don't give a shit anymore. Either I walk out of here, or I'm dead. Nothing else." She looked at Argent and Markham. "You decide. You got thirty seconds. Dylan, count it off."

Dylan's eyes seemed to fill his face, but his expression was approving. "You got it. One. Two. Three. Four. Five—"

Markham and Argent whispered furiously; Nicole caught the word *bluffing* a couple of times, and she turned her whole head to smile at them, sweetly. She began to look forward to the end. God, the pistol felt wonderful—a smooth, cold friend. If only she had had one before—"Twenty-five, Twenty-six, Twenty-seven—"

"All right!" said Markham. "You win. Go ahead, leave."

Nicole didn't put the gun down, although it was getting heavy. She nodded at Dylan. "Him, too."

"All right," said Markham. He barked an order, and the two agents let go of Dylan.

This struck Nicole as a little too easy. They had to be planning something. And how far could she and Dylan get, anyway? Even if they made it to his car, they would be followed. Maybe she should take advantage of this opportunity—

Something of what she was thinking must have showed in her face—or maybe Dylan was unusually empathetic—because he whispered, "Don't! Trust me, we'll make it!"

It was tough to turn her head while keeping the gun poised at her temple, but she managed to look at him. "Okay."

He took her left hand. "Just walk behind me. .Don't drop the gun." He pushed the agents aside to clear a space. "That pistol has a hair trigger," he announced generally.

"Be careful!" said Argent, scooting forward.

Dylan led her into the stairwell, and then started *up* the stairs.

"What are you—" she started to say, but he shushed her.

The stairs led through a pair of double metal doors to a landing just below the roof. As soon as they were through the doors, Dylan turned and slammed the doors shut, then looked around for something to block the exit. He grabbed a large concrete planter and rolled it on its edges until it was flush against the doors. Nicole doubted it would hold for long.

Dylan looked at his watch, as if time was important. Then he said, "We're not too late. Oh, and you can give me the gun now."

With relief, she did. "By the way, I flipped on the safety before I dropped it on the floor."

"You mean—" she started to say, but Dylan wasn't listening; he pulled a cell phone from his pocket, extended the little antenna, and frantically punched a number. After a long moment she heard him utter one word: "Now!"

Behind them, she heard a thumping and scraping as the concrete planter slowly pushed outward from the door. Dylan grabbed her hand and pulled her up a ramp to the next level of roof, which opened onto the helicopter pad. The rough concrete hurt her bare feet, but she ignored the pain.

"What are we gonna—" Nicole started to say, but her words were drowned by rapidly increasing engine noise. She looked up to see a small blue helicopter approaching from the west. It stopped about fifty feet above the helipad, hovering. The words *Kreeger Aviation* were written in script letters across the door. Dylan windmilled his arms and the helicopter slowly settled down on the pad.

Dylan pulled her across the helipad and through the rotor wash toward the open door of the helicopter, practically throwing her inside. He jumped in behind her, yelling "Go! Go!"

The pilot looked around and said, "What's the rush?" but pushed on the throttle and the engine sound increased dramatically. Then he pulled back on the controls and the helicopter lifted off.

As they rose, Nicole looked down to see Argent, Markham, and the other men running onto the helipad, looking upward, their hair and clothes flying in the down draft. Argent raised his fist and shook it.

For the first time in months, Nicole Girard leaned back and laughed, deeply and truly.

CHAPTER THIRTY-TWO

The helicopter flew low over the civil aviation runway at Lambert and landed gently in front of the Kreeger Aviation hangar. The rotors wound down with a whine, and Dylan helped Nicole unbuckle her safety belts while the pilot, Tom Kreeger, busily turned switches, running down his shutdown checklist. Then the door was opened from the outside.

"Hello, Brian," Dylan said to Tom's twin brother, as Brian helped them out of the helicopter and out of range of the still moving rotors.

Brian looked at Nicole's bare and bloody feet. "What happened to you?"

"It's a long story," said Dylan, as Tom popped open his door and joined them. Standing next to each other, Tom and Brian were indistinguishable except for the clothes they wore: each had the same square-jawed face, short-cropped blond hair, and expressions of permanent impatience.

They started walking toward the small trailer that served as the brothers' office.

"Looks like you were being chased," said Tom. "You're not in trouble with the cops, are you?"

"Like I said, it's a long story. And I don't want

to get you involved. As it is, you'll be questioned by the Secret Service, asking you—"

"The Secret Service?" said Tom and Brian together. "What the hell for?"

"I could tell you, but as the saying goes, then I'd have to kill you." Dylan grinned. "Do you really want to know?"

The brothers looked each other. "Uh, since you put it that way, no," said Brian. "We're in enough trouble with the FAA."

Dylan nodded. The brothers ignored Federal Aviation Administration regulations whenever it suited them. Although their private charter service was very successful, they paid a small fortune in fines to the FAA—and legal fees to Cameron Barr. "Air pirates," Barry called them, but smiled when he said it. The brothers never endangered their passengers, they just couldn't understand niceties like filing flight plans and obtaining commuter route approvals.

They all entered the trailer. Inside were two steel desks and an enormous blackboard covered with flight schedules.

"We've got to get moving," said Dylan. "Is my rental car here?"

"Yeah," said Brian. "They just dropped it off." He picked up a key ring from one of the desks.

"Great," said Dylan, taking the keys. He turned to Nicole. "We've got to get out of here—right away. Are you okay?"

"Yeah. But we need to talk. I want to know—"

Dylan put up his hand. "Hold it for two minutes." He said to the Kreegers, "Thanks, guys." He pulled out his wallet and handed Brian a credit card. Brian pushed it back at him. "Forget it. It was a favor for Barry. Anyway, if the feds are after you, I can't take your money."

Dylan grinned and shook their hands. "They'll ask you where we went, so you can be honest and tell them you don't know."

"Got it," said Tom. "Good luck."

The brothers stayed in the trailer while Dylan and Nicole hurried out to the parking lot behind the hanger. Dylan located a red Jeep Cherokee and tried the key. It worked.

"Shit," said Dylan, as they got in. "Why did it have to be red?"

"A Jeep?" Nicole said.

"We might need four-wheel drive," he said enigmatically, pulling out of the parking lot and heading for the airport exit.

Nicole reached out and touched his right arm. "Dylan, I don't want to sound ungrateful, because you saved my life—truly—but I'm not going to do any more blind following. I've gotten free of Argent, and now I have to—"

"Do what?" interrupted Dylan. "Go tell the police you're Nicole Girard, a woman who died a month ago? You've got no identification. If they don't tell you to get lost, they'll hold you in custody while they check the story. And you can't go home—there will be federal agents all over the place."

She considered that. "You're right. I'll go see Pamela Holtz, first. She'll know what to do."

"Nicole. Let me tell you everything that has happened. When I'm finished, you can decide. Okay?"

"Okay."

So he told her. It wasn't easy remembering all the details while also concentrating on driving, but

Dylan thought he did a pretty good job. Except for one item: he couldn't bring himself to tell Nicole about his relationship with Kristin. If he told her that, she would suspect he had AIDS, and he didn't want her to think that. Not yet, anyway.

She didn't say much during his explanation, asking only an occasional question. When he finished, she said in a firm voice, "So Argent killed Pamela and Charlene. Is that right?"

"He denies involvement in Pamela's death, for what that's worth. Charlene is just . . . missing."

"But the last time you saw her, she was being followed by the man you shot—Skoler."

"Yes." Dylan sighed. "I'm afraid so." He turned the Jeep onto the entrance ramp for Interstate 40.

Nicole stared out the window for a long time, watching the scenery roll by on the interstate. Finally she said, "You're right, Dylan. I've got to hide. Because there is no way I'll be anybody's lab animal again. Never." Her voice was low but determined. "If my blood is so important, I'm willing to help. But it will be on my terms."

"I understand. The question is, how are you going to hide, where are you going to go? The Secret Service will be watching all the airports, bus and train stations. Your description will be everywhere. You've got no passport or identification. You don't even have shoes. Do you want to ask your parents for help?"

"Hell, no!"

"Uh-huh. Well, I'm willing to take you wherever you want to go. On the other hand—"

"On the other hand, you've already got this all figured out, so quit playing games. I realize you're not trying to push me, but let's cut the bullshit."

"Okay." Dylan grinned.

Nicole shifted position so she could look directly at Dylan. "And why are you doing all this, anyway? Aren't you risking a lot for someone you barely know?"

Dylan changed lanes to pass a big truck, flicking his signal, then returned to the right lane, checking his side and rearview mirrors conscientiously. "I guess I am. I can't answer your question."

"That makes me nervous."

"You're too suspicious. Argent says you're paranoid."

"Shit!" She laughed.

"Trust me," he said archly.

She managed another laugh. "Sure, why not? I'm being chased by God knows who, I have nothing except the clothes on my back, and no shoes. Why not trust a renegade from a big law firm?"

"That's the spirit!"

"Would it be presumptuous to ask where we're going?"

"I'm heading toward a place where we can stay until we figure out what to do."

"Where, already?"

"My father's place. It's in the Ozarks, near the White River. The nearest paved road is ten miles away, and he's got some dogs that are better than any alarm system."

"The Ozarks? How far away is that?"

"About two hundred fifty miles. On the way, we'll stop and get you some clothes and shoes and, hopefully, we'll avoid the cops and Argent's thugs and state troopers and Secret Service and FBI and CIA and Interpol and space aliens and whatever else they choose to send after us." Dylan realized he felt wonderful, marvelously free and alive. He looked across at Nicole and grinned.

She looked puzzled at first, then, slowly, smiled back.

The President of the United States sat up in bed and burped. It was a long, low, extremely satisfying burp—an omen of good health.

Banfield felt better. The nausea was all gone, his stomach felt reasonably normal, and his fever was down. He had survived another opportunistic infection and his mind felt clarified. Rosati and Schreiber had just been in to see him and pronounced him over this crisis. Unfortunately, he would have to remain in the hospital for another week or so.

Hagen came into the suite. "Tom. You're feeling better?"

"Yes, I am, Craig. Yes, I am. Bring me up to date."

Hagen sat in one of the cushioned chairs at the end of the bed. "There's been some interesting news from T.J. in St. Louis. We were right about Dr. Argent—he was hiding something. Apparently he faked the death of the blood donor—the Girard woman—because her blood carries a remarkably effective strain of antibody. He used her blood to develop a powerful PHT treatment."

Banfield straightened up. "What! Is it a cure?"

"No, but close enough, at least for the near term."

"That's tremendous!" Banfield allowed himself a burst of hope. *At the last minute, a reprieve.*

But Hagen shook his head sorrowfully. "There's a problem. Remember that lawyer who tipped Rosati to the situation? With the name of 'Ice'?"

"Yes, yes."

"Well, for some reason, he decided to rescue the Girard woman from the evil clutches of Dr. Argent. Without *our* help, that is. Both of them have disappeared."

Banfield didn't say anything.

"Don't worry, we'll find them," said Hagen hurriedly. "Markham's throwing a net over the whole Midwest. We've got the FBI and border patrol involved. And once we find the woman, then Dr. Argent—who is anxious to help, now that Girard has escaped—says you can be given a PHT treatment almost immediately. Dr. Rosati has looked at his data and agrees."

Banfield felt like he was on a roller coaster. "And the woman? You think she'll be cooperative after all this?"

"She may not be."

"But we'll use her anyway?"

Hagen looked surprised. "Of course."

"Of course," said the President. "Hand me that water, will you?"

Banfield reached for the cup from Hagen and took a long sip from the straw. Calm down, he told himself. He couldn't let himself get too excited, it might not work out. He forced himself to think dispassionately. "What about Osborne?"

"His letter has caused a lot of problems. Even some members of your own party are now asking that you get tested for AIDS. Just to clear the air, they say."

"That's natural," said Banfield. "They've got to cover their asses. I'd do the same in their place."

Hagen looked at him sharply. This charitable understanding was unlike Banfield.

"What are you planning to do about it?" said Banfield.

"There's not much we can do. We put a tail on Finnegan, like you ordered, and he sees Osborne almost every day. The bastard. Oh, and I know how he found out."

"Yes?" said Banfield.

"It's my fault, Tom. I should have destroyed Conner's letter. I meant to, but instead I left it in the document safe. Turk must have seen it when he was packing to leave."

Banfield groaned. "When we get back to the White House, give the letter to me. I want to burn it personally. Did he make a copy?"

Hagen shrugged. "No way to tell. Probably not, or Osborne would be doing more than just making insinuations. He would have used it by now."

They looked at each other gloomily. Finally Hagen said, "From the data provided by Argent, Rosati assures me that Argent's PHT treatment is so effective that we can get away with saying you're HIV-negative. So, until we find the woman, we stall. Blow smoke. Unless you have a better idea?"

Banfield shook his head. There was an idea germinating in his mind, a wildly strange and intoxicating idea. He wasn't ready to give in to it, not yet, not unless things really didn't work out. "Maybe I'll think of one, Craig. Maybe I will."

CHAPTER THIRTY-THREE

Nicole woke from troubled dreams of needles and guns to find herself in a very strange place. Instead of the too-familiar hospital room, she was in a moving car, her head wedged into the gap between passenger seat and door. She sat up quickly, the shoulder belt jerking at her.

For a moment she thought she still was dreaming. Then she recognized Dylan and memory returned.

"Have a good nap?"

Nicole swallowed; her mouth tasted dry and foul. "I don't remember falling asleep."

"You sort of passed out. Probably all the tranquilizers. It'll be a while before they're out of your system."

"Yeah." Nicole looked out the window; they were driving on a two-lane paved road, somewhere out in the country. The light from the moon was surprisingly bright, and she could see pastures and scattered stands of trees. "Where are we?"

Dylan looked at her. "Almost there. We just passed through a very small town called Norfork, which is about thirteen miles from the metropolis of

Mountain Home. That's the last civilization we'll see for a while."

Nicole nodded and stretched. They had bought a pair of shoes for her at a drug store in Missouri—cheap running shoes—and they seemed to be too tight. She reached down and loosened the laces.

"I bought a Coke at the gas station. You want a sip?" He passed it to her, and she took it automatically. The Coke felt great swishing around her mouth, and she drank deeply before handing it back to Dylan. Keeping his eyes on the twisting road, Dylan took the can and finished it in two big gulps.

Interesting, thought Nicole. Although HIV couldn't be caught by such casual contact, most people would refuse to drink from her cup or glass. Dylan hadn't even hesitated.

Dylan continued, "Since we're almost there, I better tell you about my father. So you won't be surprised."

She rubbed her eyes. "What about him?"

"Howard is one of the last true hippies, so his slant on life may seem a little strange to you. He is still wrapped up in causes no one else really cares about. And sometimes he has acid flashbacks—he'll start talking to inanimate objects or pulling things out of the air."

"Oh," Nicole said. "I see. Well, after what I've been through, we'll get along fine."

"Shit!" said Dylan, jerking the steering wheel to the right. The Jeep swerved violently, fishtailing as Dylan turned onto a narrow gravel road. The car skidded to a stop; then Dylan slowly drove down the road, gravel crunching loudly under the tires. "Sorry," he grinned. "I nearly missed the turn."

Nicole's heart rate eventually slowed down, and

Dylan continued as if nothing had happened, driving considerably faster than Nicole would have liked. After a gradual rise and several sharp turns, the road came to an abrupt end. The car's headlights picked out a stone-strewn dirt track—barely more than two tire tracks—leading off to the left.

Dylan reached down to the center console and flipped a lever, putting the Jeep into four-wheel drive, then gunned the engine. The Jeep jumped up the track, rumbling up and over rocks, stones, and dead tree branches. Nicole had to grab the grip above the door to minimize her bouncing, and it was impossible to talk without biting her tongue.

They traveled this way for at least another mile, a truly frightening experience in the dark. Nicole couldn't see anything beyond the scope of the headlights, which danced around crazily. Dylan, however, drove with assurance.

Suddenly he slowed the car, and Nicole saw a chain-link gate and fence crossing the track. Dylan stopped close to the gate; it was partly open, a padlock hanging loosely from the latch. A large rusty metal sign was wired to the front of the gate:

PRIVATE PROPERTY. NO TRESPASSING.
NO WARNINGS. VIOLATORS WILL BE SHOT.

"I thought you said he was a hippie," said Nicole, pointing at the sign.

"A hippie," Dylan said. "Not a Democrat." He got out of the car, opened the gate fully, then hopped back in and drove through.

"What if it was locked?" Nicole asked.

"Howard always forgets to lock it. And if it

was, I would have climbed over the fence, gone up the hill, and gotten the key."

"Oh." Nicole briefly wondered if she wasn't better off with the Secret Service.

They drove almost straight uphill for about three hundred yards, then pulled into a large clearing surrounded by old-growth trees. At the far end of the clearing, nestled in the side of a large hill, light poured out of an absurd structure. It looked like something made with spare parts: the center was a log cabin, and on either side were mismatched additions, one made out of siding, the other out of stone and bricks. The roof was in darkness, but what she could see appeared to be partly shingle, part tile, part metal. Dylan drove closer.

"What the hell is that?" Nicole said.

"Howard's house. It's built over an old mine shaft." Dylan braked and parked the Jeep next to an ancient Ford pickup. "He calls it the Shire. You know, from Tolkien, *Lord of the Rings*."

"It's amazing." Nicole opened the door, jumped out, and started walking toward the structure.

"No! Wait a minute!" yelled Dylan, and she stopped, then turned to face a new sound coming from the other direction.

Two very large dogs jumped out of the shadows and ran toward her, mouths wide open, large canine teeth flecked with saliva. They didn't bark, and somehow that made them scarier. The dogs circled her, growling hideously; then the larger one gathered himself into a crouch and leaped.

Nicole barely had time to cringe before she was knocked off her feet. She rolled in the dirt, screaming, a heavy body on top of her. But then she realized she wasn't being bitten. And that the body was—Dylan's.

He pushed her down and stood up to face the dogs. They jumped on him, rolling him into the dirt.

"Oh my God!" yelled Nicole. "Help! Someone help!"

A tall, thin man appeared out of the shadows, carrying a long stick. No, not a stick, a shotgun. He pointed it at Dylan, then relaxed and let the barrel drop.

"Do something!" shrieked Nicole, but he just looked at her vacantly. He was in his late fifties, face creased and sunburned, thinning blond hair tied in a long ponytail.

"S'all right," he said.

"Yeah, it's okay, Nicole," Dylan said from the ground, and suddenly she realized he was *laughing*. The dogs hadn't attacked him; they were licking and nuzzling him, and he stroked them in return.

"Shit!" yelled Nicole. "Goddamn it, they scared the fucking *shit* out of me!"

Howard Ice cocked a finger at Nicole and asked Dylan, "Who's the chick?"

Dylan, still trying to smother laughter, rose to his feet and brushed himself off. "Nicole Girard, meet my father, Howard Ice."

Nicole had no choice but to step forward and shake Howard's hand.

"And these two," Howard said, pointing at the dogs, "are Bilbo and Frodo. They're *very* sorry for scaring the shit out of you."

The two enormous dogs seemed to understand his words, dropping their heads and whining softly. Nicole thought they were a mixed breed, with the strongest element being Siberian husky, or something like it. They had intelligent faces, with wide-spaced eyes and brown and white coats.

"Go on, Frodo," said Howard, stepping forward and prodding the bigger dog with his toe. "Tell the lady you're sorry."

Frodo slowly walked toward Nicole, tail swishing softly, head down. He stopped in front of her, lay on the ground, and crawled forward. "Go on," prompted Howard again, and the dog extended his paw toward her.

He looked so piteous, and the scene was so absurd, that Nicole couldn't stay angry. She squatted, took the paw, shook it gently, and patted his head.

"Okay," said Howard. "Hup!"

Frodo jumped up with a joyous bark and began prancing around like a puppy.

"That's incredible," said Nicole.

"Howard understands animals. Better than people."

"I hope you didn't come here to insult me," said Howard. "You in trouble?"

Dylan sighed. "You could say that. It's a long story. How about some coffee?"

Howard Ice's home was truly weird. It combined elements of the original coal mine entrance structure—over a century old—with parts of several buildings erected by succeeding owners. Howard had modified it all to his taste, adding log walls, a primitive kitchen, and lots of rough-hewn, mismatched furniture.

They sat at a log table, drinking coffee cooked on a wood stove. Dylan finished telling Howard the whole story, with Nicole adding appropriate commentary, and now they sat in silence as Howard got up to adjust one of the gas lanterns.

"I thought you were gonna let the county fix the power line," said Dylan as Howard returned to his seat.

"Changed my mind," said Howard. "Too much trouble."

"Jesus, Howard. You promised."

Howard shrugged. "I'm not a total Luddite. I've got a gas generator that will run a TV, radio, and a cell phone. When I want to, I can get in contact with the outside world. I just don't want to." From his breast pocket he took out a small plastic bag and some rolling papers. "Got some real good home-grown here, Dylan." He pulled a couple of papers out of the pack, licked them together, and expertly filled the joint with marijuana from the baggie.

"Howard."

"Yeah, yeah," said Howard. "I thought maybe you'd changed." He looked at Nicole. "As a son, he's been a real disappointment. How about you? It's good stuff, grow it myself."

"Thanks," said Nicole, "but I've got enough drugs in my system right now."

"Okay," said Howard, lighting the joint and drawing deeply. "Ah. So what are your plans?"

Dylan said, "I've got some ideas, but maybe it should wait until tomorrow."

"Well, if you want to get out of the country, I can help," said Howard. He rubbed his hands together. "Just like the old days. You'll need new passports. I've still got some good contacts—"

"Who said we were leaving the country?"

Howard smiled beatifically. "You got the feds

after you. What else?" To Nicole, "You want to stay in hiding for the next few years?"

"I don't know." Inevitably, Nicole was breathing in some of the marijuana smoke, and combined with everything else in her system, and all that had happened, she felt like her head was too heavy for her shoulders. "I need to lie down," she managed to say.

She saw their concerned expressions and was vaguely conscious of being escorted to a room that looked as if it had once been a toolshed. There was a pair of bunks built into the wall; Dylan helped her into a sleeping bag on the bottom bunk. She could barely find the words to thank him before she fell asleep.

"Originally it was a coal mine, designed to provide fuel for the steamboats coming upriver from the Mississippi. But the vein in this hill gave out almost immediately. Some friends of mine bought the property—it's about ten acres, altogether—in the seventies, and I bought it from them after Dylan's mother died."

It was the following morning, and, after a surprisingly delicious breakfast of buckwheat pancakes and fresh raspberries, Howard was giving Nicole the grand tour. They had passed through a series of doors and were now in the atrium of the mine.

Frodo and Bilbo tagged along, occasionally nuzzling Howard's hand or the back of his knee. Light filtered in from a dirty skylight that slanted diagonally toward the house, but ahead of them the tunnel narrowed and tapered off into darkness. A crude workbench was built into the earth on the right, holding a rack of cheap flashlights and an old-fashioned kerosene lantern.

Howard lit the lantern with some safety matches. Then, holding the lantern high, he escorted Nicole over a pair of narrow-gauge railroad tracks to the edge of the darkness. They forged on into the dark tunnel, passing wooden supports every few feet, walking downhill. The air had a moist, earthy smell, and the old rusty railroad tracks were slippery with moisture.

Suddenly the tunnel dipped down several feet and twisted to the right, and Howard stopped. Waving the lantern ahead of him, he said, "This is as far as we go. From here, the tunnel branches into two forks, and the floor is covered with about a foot of water. Seepage from an underground stream that feeds the White."

"How far under the hill are we?"

"Vertically, only a couple of hundred feet, but the tunnels extend horizontally almost half a mile."

They walked back through the main tunnel, Howard pointing out various interesting features left behind by the mining company and subsequent owners. A couple of times he stopped and attempted to grab something in the air. Each time he turned to her and said knowingly, "Streamers." Remembering what Dylan had told her, she just nodded.

When they came back into the main room, Dylan wasn't there.

"He's probably on top of the hill," said Howard with a grin. "His Thoughtful Spot. Just go around the north side of the hill, you'll see a trail."

Nicole recognized the Pooh allusion and smiled back at him, realizing how much she already liked the older man. He was truly a gentle soul, even if he was a bit whacked. She thanked him and walked outside.

The sun was so bright it hurt her eyes, and there was a fresh breeze blowing from the west. In the daylight, she could see the beauty of the land. Howard's place was higher than the surrounding country, and her view to the east showed a mixture of hardwood trees and fields of tall grass. She walked into the clearing and headed around the side of the hill; she easily found the dirt path leading upward. The air was thick with the scent of honeysuckle.

It was an easy climb to the top, and she caught her breath as she saw the view to the west. The White River glistened in the sun a hundred yards away, the water a deep emerald, its banks lined with dogwood trees.

"Beautiful, isn't it?" Dylan approached from her left, along the crest.

"Really. Now I see why Howard lives here."

Dylan nodded. "He loves the solitude. There are a lot of fishing lodges and resorts around here, but river traffic is pretty spread out. No major roads next to the river, so there's no vehicular noise." He pointed westward. "Across the river, there, is the Ozark National Forest. It's an incredible ecosystem, hundreds of species of mammals, birds, over sixty species of fish, and hundreds of types of plants. Just sitting here, I've seen deer, mink, turkeys, songbirds, even eagles."

Nicole grinned at his obvious enthusiasm. "I can see you like it. How long did you live here?"

"Well, I never did, not really. Just my school vacations. My mother died when I was almost eighteen, and Howard didn't move here full-time until I was in college." His face took on a wistful expression. "I've often wondered whether, if my mother had been here . . ." his voice trailed off, and he said quickly, "There's a different feel to every season, some new phenomenon of nature to see."

They sat down together on a patch of wild grass and watched the river for a while, Dylan continuing to tell her about the river. "The White is very cold. Mountain fed. That's why it's so good for trout. When the hot summer air hits the water every evening, it creates a wall of mist that's almost surreal. You should see the sun setting through it. Then, in the winter, the same mist rises and freezes on the tree branches, forming incredible prisms of ice crystals."

"Sounds beautiful. I'd love to do some sketches from here."

"Good idea, but we can't stay here that long. We've bought ourselves a couple of days, maybe a week or two at best, but they'll find us."

"I know," she said, even though she wasn't ready to think about it. Yesterday she had been a prisoner in a claustrophobic hospital room, thinking that death was the only viable alternative. Now she was smelling the wind and the plants and feeling the sun on her face. "It's just tough for me to adjust so quickly."

He nodded. "Here's what I suggest. I'll contact a friend of mine in my law firm—Barry Sasscer—he's the guy who helped us get the helicopter. I won't tell him where we are, but I'll ask him to act as our intermediary, to pass my messages to the Secret Service."

She could see that he was going slowly, trying not to push her into what he thought was best, but that he had it all worked out. "Go on."

"Through Barry, I'll offer a deal. You'll turn yourself over to them, but only on your terms."

"*My* terms?" she said, smiling.

He smiled back. "Hey, it's just an idea. Tell me if you have a better one."

"No, I'm sorry. Please, go ahead, really."

He picked up a flat rock and flung it out into the valley. "Look, the government is the lesser of two evils. You'll go to NIH and allow them to use your blood for research purposes or whatever, provided they keep Argent away and compensate you for your time and cooperation."

"How much?" Nicole asked, amused.

"Twenty million. Ten in advance, wired to an overseas account set up by Barry."

"Jesus!"

"Hey, it's the President's life, for God's sake. They'll pay it. And when they're done with their research—no longer than six months—they have to provide you with a new identity. If you're as special as Argent says, you'll need that to have a normal life. And the money, of course."

Nicole croaked, "Once they have me—"

"Oh, you'll have protection. Complete documentation of all that's happened, to be kept by me and certain other individuals."

"Does your friend—Barry—know about the President?"

Dylan shook his head. "No, and I won't tell him. That knowledge is too dangerous. But he doesn't have to know that to play messenger."

Nicole lay back in the sweet grass and stared at the blue bowl of the sky. "And if I don't want to do this? What then?"

He didn't hesitate. "We get you out of the country. I was thinking we could try floating down the White to the Mississippi. Get to New Orleans, then onto a ship. Or maybe slip into Mexico."

"I don't know, Dylan. I just don't know."

"We can always take the second course. But if you want to take the first option, we need to get started right away. I'll have to go into town to contact Barry—Howard's cell phone can be overheard by anyone with a police scanner."

"I need time to think about this," she said.

"Of course." Dylan rubbed the bandage on his left hand in what had become an unconscious gesture. It reminded her that he had lost those fingers helping *her*. And now he was trying to get them both out of this mess, and she was "thinking about it."

She sat up again and put her hand on his sun-warmed shoulder. "Dylan, I appreciate all this. Maybe I haven't said it enough, but I really do. I almost can't believe that you've done all this for someone you barely know, and you get nothing out of it but pain and trouble. It's got to be the finest thing that anyone has ever done for me, really."

He seemed genuinely uncomfortable, almost guilty with embarrassment. "My pleasure," he mumbled.

Nicole smiled. "Call your friend. It's worth a try."

CHAPTER THIRTY-FOUR

The cafeteria was in the basement of the big white frame building housing the Second Start program, and smelled strongly of macaroni and cheese. There were six long Formica tables, all empty except for the one nearest the door, where Barry sat nursing a cup of coffee.

"I don't understand," said Janis. "You mean you really don't know where Dylan is?"

Barry nodded. "He called me from a pay phone. He's afraid they're tapping my line at the firm. I don't think so, but he's right to be paranoid. Anyway, if I don't know where he is, I can't tell. I'm trying to help him out of this mess, Janis. In the meantime, he asked that I see you and tell you that he's all right. And that you shouldn't worry about him." The last part he invented, but it seemed warranted.

"Not worry! What the hell am I supposed to do? I can't believe he would do this. He's normally so . . ."

"Steady?" finished Barry. "I know. It's not like him, that's true."

"And this is all because of that girl he likes?"

Barry couldn't help smiling. She had arrived directly at the point. "I don't think that's all of it, but certainly it's a big part." He had already painstakingly explained everything he knew about the Nicole Girard case, at least up to the time Dylan went to the hospital to rescue her. At that point things became cloudy. The Kreeger brothers told him Dylan had a woman with him, but Dylan never introduced her or called her by name. Now Barry knew it was Nicole, but why had they run? And why hadn't the feds arrested Argent for kidnapping? Dylan wouldn't tell him.

Barry had asked these questions of the federal agents who interrogated him about his role in getting the helicopter for Dylan. They had refused to answer, if they knew.

Paul Hudson also was leaning hard on Barry, demanding to know where Dylan was.

"Do you think he left the country?" asked Janis, her face pinching with anxiety. Barry belatedly realized that for Janis, this was serious on a deeper level: Dylan was her only real family. He was her father and mother and brother all in one. "Will he lose his job?"

Barry idly picked up a plastic salt shaker and twirled it around his finger. "I don't know, Janis, truly I don't. Yes, it's possible he could lose his job if he doesn't show up soon. But I don't think so."

"Shit!" Janis put her head in her hands. "I miss him. If I only knew where he was—" she looked up suddenly, comprehension coming into her eyes.

"What?" said Barry. "What are you thinking?"

"Nothing," she said, her expression converting to a look of wounded innocence.

Barry dropped his voice. "Janis, if you know where he is, you gotta tell me."

"I have no idea. No idea at all."

Dylan hadn't planned to spend more than a day or two at the Shire, but as the time stretched longer, he began to wish it wouldn't end. He and Nicole should have been neurotic with worry; instead they both adopted Howard's attitude toward life: Don't worry, be happy.

They were active. Dylan acquainted Nicole with all his old activities: hiking, climbing, canoeing, and fishing. Although too weak to do much at first, she delighted in being outdoors, and they spent hours together on the river, catching trout, sunning themselves on rocks, picnicking, talking. Nicole blossomed in the warm summer air, color returning to her face. Her hair became glossy, her features less drawn.

As Dylan sat on a rock in the river, his feet dangling in the current, watching Nicole fly-cast fifty yards downstream, he finally forced himself to think about what he had so carefully avoided telling her: his probable HIV infection.

He didn't want her to think he was helping her for personal gain. And if he told her now, she would assume the worst.

Perhaps it wouldn't have mattered if he didn't actually have some hope they might have a real relationship. He could admit that to himself now. The incipient attraction had been there all along, from their very first meeting in the hospital. Spending this time with her had confirmed it.

That night they made a campfire on the hilltop, roasting marshmallows—Howard had an astonishing supply of munchies—and watching the night sky. They talked about the prospective deal with the feds. Nicole was still ambivalent.

"I wonder if I can stand one more doctor poking and prodding at my body, drawing blood. And the smell of antiseptic. God, how I hate it."

"I know," Dylan said. "The problem is the alternative."

"Yes," she said, and he left it alone.

Then they talked about themselves, about their childhoods, and Dylan asked, hesitatingly, about her marriage.

"That's how you got AIDS, right? I mean, that's what your parents think, anyway."

She pulled a marshmallow off a stick and took a bite. Then she said, "Yeah. I got it from him."

"How long were you married?"

"Not long. I was very young—only eighteen. He was in his late twenties, a local rock musician with gigs in St. Louis. I think I married him more to get out of St. Charles and away from my parents than anything else. It wasn't long before I discovered his late-night rehearsals involved more than just music. Even unsuccessful musicians have groupies, and he was doing drugs, too. I left him, got a part-time job, and went to college. I didn't know he infected me with HIV until I got a routine physical. To be fair, he didn't know he had HIV, either."

"What happened to him?"

She shrugged. "He was a rapid progressor. Dead within five years."

"Oh."

"I know that sounds very cold, and maybe it is, but I couldn't even bear to see him."

"So you didn't love him?"

Dylan saw her squinting through the smoke at him. "I thought I did, before he infected me. I hated him for that. Why all this interest in my marriage?"

"I was just curious. I mean, it's interesting that you once had a regular relationship with a man."

There was a long pause, and he was afraid he had gone too far. But then she laughed. "Sure I did. And I could again, if I wanted to."

"You could? But . . . what about Charlene?"

She looked somber. "You sure ask a lot of personal questions."

"I'm sorry."

She laughed again. "That's all right. At this point, after all that's happened—like that guardianship hearing—I'm pretty much desensitized to embarrassment. Look out!"

His marshmallow was aflame. He quickly pulled it out of the fire and stomped on it.

"I think it's dead," Nicole said sagely.

"Guess I got distracted."

As he took a new marshmallow out of the bag, Nicole said, "Dylan, if you're trying to find out my sexual orientation, just ask."

He reddened. "Uh, yes. I guess so." He picked up Howard's wineskin and took a drink.

"Okay." She sighed. "I thought about this a lot when I was in the hospital, and I've decided I don't believe in sexual classifications—homosexual, heterosexual, bisexual, whatever. They're just cultural categories. I think sexuality is a continuum: people are just more at one end than another. You know, lots of cultures, both historically and today, don't view it as odd that people have both homo- and heterosexual experience, neither to the exclusion of the other. It's all sex, you know. Just mucous membranes rubbing against each other."

Dylan nearly choked on his mouthful of wine.

Nicole laughed and paused to take a drink of wine. "I certainly was heterosexual until after my divorce. When I found out I had AIDS—this was in the eighties—I thought it was the end of sex for me. And then I met Charlene. We grew very close, and she wanted a sexual relationship. I was always curious about lesbianism anyway, and I never had any moral hang-ups. Anyway . . . I tried it. And liked it. Luckily, female-to-female transmission of HIV is very rare, and anyway we practiced safe sex."

"Oh," said Dylan, embarrassed, thinking this was more than he really needed to know. "What about your, uh 'marriage' to Charlene?"

"That was Charlene's idea, really more of a political statement than anything else."

"Well," Dylan said laconically, "that's very interesting."

She laughed again. "Shit, Dylan, I hope you're a better poker player."

"What do you mean?"

"I mean, you wouldn't happen to have a personal interest in this issue, would you?"

He wanted to tell her how he felt, but then he remembered: *I've got AIDS, too. How convenient that I'm pushing her to deal with the feds. It really is the best thing for her, but it may seem different with the knowledge that I have an interest in the outcome.* "Let's just say I'm interested in your background."

■   ■   ■

"Twenty million dollars?" asked Banfield. He sat on the couch near his bed, dressed in an old blue silk robe with the presidential seal.

"Twenty million," Hagen confirmed.

"Everyone wants to be rich. What a fucking country." He stood and walked to the window, putting his arm on the sill. The sleeve of his robe flopped down to the elbow, revealing his bare arm, wan and skinny. "What do you think, Craig? Is this worth it?"

Hagen looked up from his notes, surprised. "Worth it? Of course. We get the woman, Rosati gives you the treatment, which has no side effects, we fake an AIDS test, and the campaign goes on without any more worries about . . . relapses."

"What about this six-month part? If she only stays with us six months, it won't get me through my second term."

"Well, she'll have to see reason on that."

Banfield turned to face him. "I see. Where do we get the twenty million?"

"Ten million. Once she's with us, we won't bother paying the other half." Hagen couldn't understand why Banfield didn't see the logic of all this. Usually he was so quick. Well, maybe it was the medication.

"Okay, where do we get the ten million?"

"Either from your reelection fund, or from one of the contingency funds in the White House budget. I'll figure it out and wire the money this afternoon." Hagen stepped forward and put his hand on the President's arm. "This is our answer."

The warmth of Hagen's hand felt good. They

stayed that way for a while, each savoring the contact. For a moment, Banfield allowed himself to think of how it might have been. Then he recalled himself to the hard reality of a hospital room. "All right," he said. "Do it."

"I will. Meanwhile, Markham's still looking for them, and Dr. Argent is under surveillance. If he finds them first, we'll be on his ass."

There was a knock at the door, and the First Lady entered. Hagen hastily dropped his hand.

"Hello, Marianne," said Banfield.

She stepped forward and pecked him on the cheek, then stood back to look at him while Hagen scuttled over to the couch.

"You're looking better," she said.

"Feel that way, too. I'm checking out of the hospital tomorrow."

"Good. Because I didn't want to leave until then."

"Leave?"

"Yes. I thought I'd go back home for a while. See some old friends."

Hagen looked at Banfield, expecting an explosion. Once he was out of the hospital, he would have to get back into campaign mode, and that meant the First Lady at his side. She was an excellent campaigner.

Banfield just shrugged. "Okay, honey. See you next week."

When she left, Banfield said dolefully, "You know, Craig, I still love that woman."

"Uh, yeah, Tom. I know." Then, to counter the mood, Hagen continued, "Something funny happened this morning—Turk Finnegan asked for an appointment. He wants to see you. Alone."

"Turk?" said Banfield. "That's strange."

"Not if you think about it for a second."

Banfield nodded. "Of course. He's Osborne's messenger. He wants to deliver surrender terms, and get his revenge at the same time."

"That's how I read it. I'll tell him to get fucked."

"No!" said Banfield. "Don't do that. I'll see him."

"What? Why? So he can humiliate you?"

"Maybe I deserve it," said Banfield.

That infuriated Hagen so much he had to leave.

Later that day, Hagen cornered Rosati in the hallway. "He's acting very strangely, Peter. I'd almost say depressed."

"You find that surprising? The man has AIDS."

"But *this* man is the President. He doesn't get depressed, he makes some *other* poor bastard get depressed."

Rosati shrugged. "I've noticed his mood, too. Hopefully, it's just the normal emotional adjustment."

"Hopefully? What do you mean, 'hopefully?'"

"There's always another possibility when someone has CD4 counts as low as his."

"Go on."

Rosati looked around the hallway, as if the Secret Service agents might be eavesdropping. "ADC. AIDS dementia complex. It's a—"

"I know what the fuck it is," Hagen said fiercely. "It's what Argent said Girard had." He sat down heavily on one of the plastic chairs that lined the hallway. "Are you gonna do the diagnostic tests? A spinal tap?"

Rosati shook his head. "No. Not for depression alone. But at the first sign of anything else, I'll have to schedule them."

"What other signs?"

"Delusional thinking. Irrationality. Excessive irritability. Suicidal thoughts." He nodded. "Definitely then I'll have to do the testing."

"No, you won't," said Hagen crisply.

"What?"

"No testing for ADC," he repeated. "Not unless *I* personally authorize it."

Rosati looked into Hagen's eyes. After a moment, he said, "All right."

Argent noticed that Fletcher seemed nervous. Nervous and impatient. Argent adopted a soothing tone as they walked through the amazingly large, perfectly tended garden on Fletcher's estate. "We'll find them. It's just a matter of time."

"Yeah, but how much time?" said Fletcher. "How long can Kristin go without her treatment?"

"She's in no immediate danger. Her CD4 count is still good."

"For how long?" Fletcher persisted.

"There will be a rebound effect," Argent admitted, "if she doesn't get an infusion soon."

Fletcher kicked at a plastic watering can, left behind by one of the gardeners. It went sailing over a hedge. "That's unacceptable."

"Look," Argent said, getting angry. "I was *this* close to finishing my vaccine. No one wants to find her more than I do. I've got Skoler's men searching for her, and you've got your security people looking, too. There's nothing more we can do."

"Have you figured out why the feds want Nicole?" Fletcher asked.

Argent shrugged. "Rosati knows her value, and

he probably has some important patients he wants to treat with my methods." He added musingly, "He's working on a vaccine, too—"

"I've got a helicopter standing by twenty-four hours a day," interrupted Fletcher. "If my people locate her, I'll let you know right away, so you can prepare a treatment for Kristin. Here." He pulled a small object from his pocket—a beeper.

"What's this?" said Argent, amused.

"It's a special beeper, connected to my phone system. I'll beep you the minute we locate her."

"Sure, sure." Argent pocketed the device.

CHAPTER THIRTY-FIVE

Dylan parked the Jeep in front of the Shire and rushed into the house.

He saw Nicole sorting some of Howard's dishes into similar piles; Howard plucked idly at his guitar, lying on the floor with both feet on the sofa.

"It's done!" Dylan said. "The feds have accepted the terms. Barry says they didn't even negotiate."

"Far out," said Howard. "What about the bread?"

"It's been wired," said Dylan. "Ten million dollars to a Swiss account." He looked at Nicole. "You are now officially rich." He pulled a slip of paper from his pocket. "Here's the account number."

Nicole took it, looked at it briefly, and stuck it in her jeans pocket. "Just out of curiosity, why couldn't you or Barry get the money? You know the number, too."

Dylan shook his head. "It can only be accessed in person, by you. Barry sent them your photograph."

"I see," said Nicole, thoughtfully. "But that means I have to get to Switzerland."

"Far out," repeated Howard. "Ten million American dollars."

"Do I detect some mercenary instinct, Howard?" Dylan asked.

Howard pulled the E string of the guitar, loudly. "Nah. Just commenting."

"What's next?" said Nicole.

"Barry's waiting for the signed agreement. He'll make copies, then distribute them to several trusted people. Tomorrow we'll drive back to St. Louis and turn you over to Markham. I didn't want them coming here and getting Howard involved."

"So this is it," said Nicole. She didn't sound happy.

Dylan sat down on the couch. "You can still change your mind."

She sighed and sat down next to him. "No," she said. "No, I don't like it, but it's probably the best way."

Howard stood up. "How about I make my special dinner?"

Dylan groaned. "Brown rice and carrots? What's the alternative?"

Nicole stood up. "I can cook the trout I caught this morning."

"Good idea."

Janis hated bus rides, but there was no other way. She had slipped out of the barracks at dawn, trudging the half mile to the nearest bus stop. After two transfers, she arrived at the Trailways station in the county, where she bought a ticket to Mountain Home. The ticket consumed almost all her money; she barely had enough left to buy something to eat on the way.

In Mountain Home, she caught a local bus to

Norfork, where there were still some people that remembered her. She hitched a ride with the owner of a fishing store driving south to Calico Rock. He even took her partway up the gravel road to the mine.

She walked the last few miles to the Shire, entering the house just around dinnertime.

Dylan coaxed Bilbo off the kitchen table—Howard let the dogs sleep wherever they chose—and started to set the table with Howard's varied assortment of cracked china and metal plates. Nicole was broiling the trout, struggling with the old wood stove. He was just moving to help her when the front door opened.

The dogs didn't warn us, was Dylan's immediate thought. Then he saw why.

"Dylan!" Janis squealed. "I knew it!" She ran to him and hugged him before he could recover from his surprise.

He pushed her out to arm's length. "What the hell are you doing here?"

"I figured it out. Where else could you hide? Pretty smart, huh?"

"Groovy!" said Howard, coming into the room. She rushed to him and they hugged affectionately. Then she noticed Nicole at the stove.

"Hiya," Janis said.

Nicole said, "Hello, Janis."

Janis looked back at Dylan. "Don't be mad, Dylan. I'll leave in a day or two. I just need a little vacation from that program."

"Oh, my God," said Dylan, putting his head in his hands.

"What's the matter?" said Janis, getting angry. "What's the big deal if I spend a few days here?"

Nicole came over to the table and sat down next to Dylan. "It's not her fault, Dylan. She doesn't understand." To Janis, Nicole said, "You were followed."

"No way. I had to change busses three times," Janis said hotly, as if that settled the matter.

Dylan groaned again. "Okay. We've got to leave right away." He stood. "If we can get to the main road before—"

The sound of barking interrupted him. "Shit!" said Dylan. "Howard, where's your shotgun?" Dylan looked at him, but Howard wasn't listening. At least, not to Dylan. His head was cocked to one side, his eyes on a portion of the wall above Janis's head.

"He's flashing," said Janis.

There was only one other exit from the house—out the east wing, past the mine entrance. "Stay here," Dylan commanded, and scooted to the front door. There was a familiar Jeep Wrangler parked just outside the door; Frodo and Bilbo were leaping and barking around it. "Shit!" said Dylan again, with even more feeling. He stepped outside and looked down the car track toward the road: It was empty.

"That's something, anyway," he muttered, and called Bilbo and Frodo to his side.

Kristin stepped down from the Jeep and smiled at him. "Nice dogs." She was dressed in a tank top and tight jeans; a large purse hung over her shoulder, banging against her thigh.

"You followed Janis," Dylan said flatly.

"Of course. Can we talk?" Without waiting for

an answer, she pushed her way past him, into the Shire. Dylan followed with the dogs.

Janis and Nicole watched her enter, puzzled. "Who's she?" Janis said.

"Hello, Janis. Hello, Nicole," said Kristin. She actually reached out and shook hands with Nicole. "I'm Kristin Fletcher."

Then Kristin looked around the room. She nodded at Howard, still sitting in the corner, concentrating on invisible colors and shapes. "That must be your father, Mr. Natural."

"What do you want?" Dylan asked, wondering if it was possible she had come alone.

"I think that's obvious," Kristin said. "My T-cells are falling like shit through a pigeon. I need Nicole."

Nicole laughed. "So you were one of the beneficiaries of my blood? Why would I want to help you now?"

Kristin shrugged. "I see that Dylan didn't explain everything. Well, that's understandable. I guess he wants you for himself."

"What are you talking about?" Nicole said, reddening.

"Kristin—" said Dylan, hoping he could cut her off, but she said quickly, "Didn't you know that Dylan and I were lovers? He didn't mention that little item?"

"Kristin, you bitch!" Dylan lunged forward, but she neatly sidestepped, and in one smooth movement, pulled a pistol from the purse and pointed it at him.

She continued as if nothing had happened, "I've got AIDS, Nicole. Your blood was keeping me healthy. And Dylan was fucking me. Unprotected, all summer. You figure it out."

Nicole looked at Kristin, mouth open, then at Dylan. Her expression was so full of surprise, pain, and dismay that Dylan wanted to scream. Instead, he stood numbly.

"Dylan!" Janis cried. "Is that true? You've got AIDS?"

"No!" he said, looking at Nicole. "It's not true! It's just that—" his words were interrupted by the rapidly escalating sound of an aircraft engine. A helicopter. It sounded like it was coming down right on the Shire.

"My father," Kristin said, and Dylan felt himself sag with despair.

"Fuck!" yelled Kristin suddenly, as Nicole ducked through the doorway leading to the east wing.

Kristin lunged after her just as Howard came to life. He lurched upward, stumbling deliberately into Kristin's path.

"Get out of my way!" she shouted, trying to push him aside.

"My fucking house," said Howard, shoving her backward. Dylan came forward and tried to grab her, but she sidestepped away, yelling something unintelligible. When Howard just smiled, Kristin raised the pistol and quickly, easily, fired two shots into his body. The force of the bullets shoved him back against the doorjamb, where he collapsed to the floor.

As Janis screamed silently in the rising crescendo of the helicopter engine, Kristin, keeping her gun leveled at Dylan, stepped over Howard's body.

Because of the helicopter noise, Kristin couldn't hear the growl of the dogs, and probably didn't even see them coming until it was too late. She turned to the right just in time to catch Frodo's slavering jaws on her neck.

Bilbo hit her low, knocking her off her feet, and the two dogs rolled her into the corner. The pistol fired once, the ricochet whining off the floor, and then there was nothing to see except fountains of arterial blood as the dogs, in a blood frenzy, ripped her open with fang and claw.

"Where the hell have you been?" said Markham's voice, sounding slightly tinny through the speaker of the car phone. "I've been trying to get you for almost an hour."

"I was in a restaurant," said Hagen into his car phone. "I forgot to take my phone with me. What is it?"

"We got them."

"Where?" Hagen tried unsuccessfully to keep the excitement out of his voice.

"Northern Arkansas, near the White River. I'm in a National Guard chopper just south of the Missouri border, following a helicopter that picked up Argent in a big hurry. And guess who owns that chopper?"

"Who?"

"The Midwest Evangelical Foundation."

"Fletcher! What's he got to do with this?"

"I don't know, but from the radio traffic we've intercepted, it's clear they're after Girard, and they're headed for some place near Mountain Home."

"You're tracking them on radar, aren't you?"

"Yeah, but I had to involve the Air Force."

"Don't worry about that, I'll clean it up later. What else are you doing?"

"I've contacted the nearest FBI field office, in Fayetteville, and told them to get some people on the road. As soon as we know exactly where Fletcher's helicopter lands, I'll send them in."

"Okay. I'm going back to the hospital to tell Point Guard. Call me there as soon as you hear something or get there, whichever comes first."

"Will he authorize whatever is necessary?"

"Of course," said Hagen, feeling much less confident than he sounded. "Just don't let her get away again. You got it?"

"I got it," said Markham, hanging up.

"I think we've got the whole story now, boss." Mitch McPeak hung up the phone and leaned back in his seat on the campaign plane. Outside the window, the air at thirty-five thousand feet was full of dark, black clouds. "That was our investigator. They've tracked down Conner's landlady, an old bird named McGee, living in some dump in Jacksonville."

Osborne sat across from him, idly playing with an unlit cigar. "And they interviewed her?"

"Yeah. The day after Conner was shot at the White House, some people she thought were cops showed up at the apartment. She can't remember what they looked like, but I'll bet it was Markham and his boys. Anyway, these 'cops' tear the place apart, searching for something."

"And?"

"And that's it. A year later, she sold the building and retired to Florida. But the point is, it's corroboration. Assuming the letter is genuine, it's exactly what you'd expect Banfield's people to do."

Osborne nodded. "Yes, it is. But it isn't proof."

"C'mon, Senator, we've got to do something! This is a dynamite stick! We gotta throw it!"

Osborne seemed unaffected. "This is nice, but it's not enough. We need evidence. Until then, all we can do is spread rumors."

"All right." McPeak sighed. He picked up the phone again.

CHAPTER THIRTY-SIX

Dylan and Janis reached their father at the same time. Howard breathed in gasps as Janis cradled his head; Dylan ripped open the bloody T-shirt, exposing two ragged bullet entries, one in the shoulder, the other about five inches away in his chest. Dylan ignored the shoulder wound, concentrating on the bright arterial blood welling out of the other entry. He felt in vain for a throat pulse. Howard's pupils were dilating, his skin turning white.

"We gotta get him to a hospital!" Janis said.

"He's not gonna make it, Janis." Dylan felt remarkably calm, realizing he had no time for grief. Janis had now seen both her parents die violently, and she was only sixteen.

They had to get away before Argent came in.

The chop-chop-chop of the helicopter wound down, and almost immediately several men rushed through the front door.

"Jesus Christ! What happened here?" someone said, followed by the sounds of loud growls and paws hitting the floor. Janis hugged Dylan as the gunshots exploded, and when he managed to look around he saw both Frodo and Bilbo lying on the floor, and a man he didn't recognize holding a pistol and bleeding from a dog bite on his lower arm. Two other men—part of Fletcher's private security force—covered Dylan and Janis with their guns.

Dylan saw Argent peek into the room to make sure the shooting was over, then stride forward, followed by Fletcher.

It took a moment before they grasped the identity of the mess in the corner that once had been Kristin Fletcher.

Markham fingered his microphone button as the OH-58 Kiowa helicopter followed the river south. "Bravo Two, report your position."

"Bravo Two," said a voice in his headset. "We're on State Route Five."

"Did you copy the Air Force transmission about the landing zone?" Markham said to the FBI agents. "You know where it is?"

"Roger, Bravo One. We've got it on our map, it's about twenty miles southwest of here."

"Get there as fast as you can, Bravo Two. I'll stay airborne in case the target takes off again."

"Roger, Bravo One."

Switching frequencies, Markham called Hagen.

Dylan and Janis were shoved into Howard's bedroom by a very tough-looking man holding an enormous automatic weapon. Janis began to cry, and Dylan tried to comfort her as best he could.

He was beginning to consider the possibilities of escape when they were dragged back into the crowded living room to face a semicircle of people:

five security men and Argent. Both Howard's and Kristin's bodies were gone; Frodo and Bilbo, however, were stacked in the corner like firewood, trails of blood still on the floor. Fletcher sat on the couch, in Howard's usual place, his eyes as big and red as saucers, staring fixedly into space.

Argent still wore his lab coat. He poked Dylan in the chest with a finger. "Where is she?"

"I don't know."

Argent slapped him, hard. The impact bloodied his mouth and made his head swim.

Dylan swallowed the blood and said, "You asshole, I don't know!"

Argent hit him again, harder, knocking him backward. Dylan struggled forward, aching to smash Argent's face, but one of the guards wrenched him back. Janis screamed, "Stop it! He really doesn't know!"

Argent turned to face her, and she continued quickly, "She ran out through there, before my father was shot." She pointed at the door leading to the mine shaft.

Argent nodded and said, "Good." He turned to the man with the automatic weapon, dressed in a black jumpsuit. "Hear that, Matson? She's got to be around here somewhere. She can't have gotten far on foot. Tell your men to spread out and start searching. Just remember, don't harm her! No matter what."

Matson nodded but looked at Fletcher. Argent followed his gaze and said, "He's in no shape to give orders. Just listen to me, I'll tell you what he would have wanted. Now—"

"Shut up, Argent," rumbled Fletcher suddenly. He slowly got to his feet, his face a study in anger and grief one moment and then—no expression.

Fletcher said to Matson flatly, "Here are your orders. You will search for the woman Nicole Girard. You will find her. But you will not bring her back."

Argent did a double take, then stared in disbelief. "What? What are you saying? Don't you understand how valuable she is? How important to the vaccine?"

"Of course I do, you asshole," said Fletcher. To Dylan, Fletcher's swearing was almost as startling as what he was saying. "That's precisely why I want her killed. I never wanted you to cure AIDS—just my daughter. You've heard my sermons. Did you really think I didn't believe what I was saying, that I was that insincere?"

"Insincere?" sputtered Argent. "You killed Pamela Holtz! Is that the act of a religious person? And if you really believe AIDS is a punishment from God, why did you want to save your daughter?"

"Yes, I've been a sinner," Fletcher said, sadly. "Kristin was my weakness. But I don't have that reason anymore."

Argent went pale. For a moment he stuttered, until finally he managed, "You can't kill Nicole. It would be a sin against all mankind—"

"God allows self-defense," said Fletcher. "And that's what this is. The defense of all that is really right, really good, all that the Bible teaches. Don't preach to *me* about killing!" he thundered.

"What about these two?" asked Matson, pointing at Dylan and Janis.

Fletcher's head swiveled to look at them, and Dylan saw no trace of sympathy in his eyes. Fletcher said, "Dylan. Do you remember that time in Tahoe? When you and Kristin were in the sauna?"

"That was you," Dylan said, understanding.

"Yes," said Fletcher venomously. "Yes, that was me. I've had to put up with a lot of things—and a lot of people I detested, even niggers like you, because I loved my daughter—" he almost choked up again, "but of all the things, that galled me the most. Well, to everything there is a season, and for every crime there is a punishment." He looked at Matson. "Tell your men to get going, before she gets too far. But you stay here, with Rogers." He indicated the guard holding Dylan. Matson nodded, then gave a quick volley of orders to the other three guards, who trotted through the door to the mine shaft.

As soon as they were gone, Argent reached out and grabbed the pistol on the belt of the man holding Dylan. Then he stepped back, raising the gun toward Fletcher.

Matson immediately squatted and kicked out with his feet, catching Argent a vicious kick in the ankle. With a scream of agony, Argent collapsed. The pistol fired, and everyone ducked for cover.

Dylan grabbed Janis's arm and hauled her off her feet and backward through the doorway toward the mine. For a second he thought of going that way, into the mine, but instead took Janis the other way, to the exit. They were outside the house, running toward the woods as three more shots exploded behind them.

The edge of the woods seemed to get no closer, but finally they made it. Dylan turned around and saw two of Fletcher's goons coming out of the house, and another two he hadn't seen before coming around the side from the helicopter. "C'mon!" he said to Janis, pulling her hand.

■   ■   ■

Nicole was very wet and very cold. For almost twenty minutes she had stood in the foot-high water in the mine tunnel. The water was oily and foul smelling, and condensation dripped from the porous tunnel roof. If only there was a place to sit . . . She hugged herself and rubbed her arms.

She had grabbed a flashlight when she passed through the mine entrance, and occasionally, just to ease the sense of claustrophobia—and to make sure no snakes were creeping up on her—she flicked on the flashlight. The batteries were weak, so she couldn't do it often.

I shouldn't have hidden here, Nicole thought. Her original idea was to stay in the tunnels until whoever was in the helicopter had left. But soon after that she heard gunshots, and the suspense of not knowing what happened was enough to drive her crazy. She almost convinced herself to go back to the house when she heard unfamiliar male voices echoing down the tunnel.

One of the voices suddenly cursed violently, and Nicole wondered if he had met a snake. But the sounds were getting closer. She flicked on the flashlight and headed farther down the tunnel, trying not to make splashes in the water. An intersection appeared, with the tunnel splitting in two. She took the right fork, went about fifty yards, and then, in the dim light of the dying flashlight, saw that the tunnel abruptly ended in a wall of exposed rock. Jagged holes in the rock were marked with the impressions of pickaxes.

A sudden skittering noise to her right made her wheel around, her flashlight following the sound, and she saw an enormous rat blinking at her from an opening about a foot above the water level.

Shuddering, Nicole stepped back, and the rat turned and disappeared.

Behind her, the voices were getting louder, and she realized she couldn't go back. Nicole forced herself to move closer to the right side of the tunnel and examine the opening. It was a large crack, over a foot high, extending deeply into the solid rock for some distance beyond the reach of her feeble flashlight beam. She didn't see the rat, and she flicked off the flashlight. In a moment, the sound of little paws on rock mingled with the dripping of the water. He was still in there, somewhere.

Suddenly a strong beam of light flashed into the tunnel, barely missing her as she pressed up against the side. "I'll check this branch," said a voice.

There was no time to think about it; Nicole stooped and squeezed her body into the crack in the rock face, wriggling along the ledge, feeling sharp rocks dig into her breasts and belly. She stopped when she thought she couldn't be seen from the tunnel.

Now light from the tunnel leaked into the crack as the man played his flashlight along the wall. At the same time she heard a sniffing sound on her other side and felt the brush of something on her right hand—the hand holding the flashlight.

Somehow she managed not to scream.

Dylan and Janis sprinted through the woods, heading toward the river and the boat docks. The underbrush was thick, and they crashed through thorn bushes, stumbling over tree roots. By the sound of it, however, their pursuers were having the same problems. If they could just make it to the river, Dylan thought, they could row across. Except that his old racing scull held only one person, and Janis would be a liability in Howard's canoe.

Suddenly they burst into a small clearing. There was another stretch of woods ahead, then the river. A familiar oak tree rose majestically in front of them. Dylan stopped and looked at Janis; she was panting hoarsely. He pointed at the tree trunk. "Janis, look. Remember the climbing tree?"

She nodded, not having enough breath to speak. He continued, "If I boost you up to the first branch, do you think you can climb to the top and stay there?"

"No!" she gasped. "I'm not leaving you!"

He shook her shoulders. "You have to, Groovy."

Numbly, she nodded. He could hear crashing in the underbrush nearby. "Quick!"

They ran to the base of the tree and he half boosted, half threw her up to the first branch. She quickly disappeared into the thick foliage.

Dylan turned around and saw the first of the two men burst into the clearing. The man saw him, yelled, and fired a quick shot that missed. Dylan dodged behind the tree, then ran like hell for the far side of the clearing, weaving and bobbing. Had they seen him boost Janis into the tree?

He flopped down at the edge of the woods and looked back to make sure the men didn't see Janis. Both men were running full speed across the clearing, neither one looking at the tree. Just to make sure, Dylan stood long enough for them to see him clearly, then ran toward the river.

He came out the other side of the stand of woods and ran down the slope to the small boat dock. His old racing shell was beached under the tarp, oars lying next to it. Howard's canoe was in the wooden storage shed. He thought of sabotaging the canoe, but there wasn't enough time.

He picked up the shell and oars and launched it just as the first shot whistled around his ears. As he turned to face them, he saw the men aim several more shots, but he was a moving target and they were pretty far away, firing short-barreled pistols. As he headed out into the river, they realized this, too, and ran down the little beach to launch the canoe.

Normally, he would have no trouble outdistancing the canoe, but the water in the Bull Shoals Dam must have just been released, because there was a very strong current. His little shell wasn't meant for rough water, and he had to work hard to push through to the center of the river.

The two men in the canoe, surprisingly, knew how to paddle. They weren't catching up, but their combined work kept them from falling farther behind. It also kept them too busy to shoot.

He was now more than halfway across, and he turned downstream, placing the shell with the current. The little hull almost skimmed along, and now he outdistanced the canoe. As the men realized this, they stopped paddling and started shooting. Luckily, hitting a moving target at over a hundred yards, from a bobbing canoe, was beyond their skill.

His shoulder muscles ached with fatigue, and his breathing was ragged, but Dylan rowed until the canoe was out of sight, hoping he had drawn them far enough away from Janis. Finally he eased up and drifted, exhausted but relieved.

At that moment Fletcher's helicopter popped

over the line of trees on the eastern shore, the engine sound growing louder as it accelerated toward him.

"It's up," said Kelly, the National Guard pilot, pointing at his radar display. A little green blip on the circular grid flashed on and off.

"Okay," said Markham. "Head for it. I want him in sight."

The nose of the helicopter tilted down and began moving forward.

Fletcher grabbed Matson's arm and yelled, "There he is! See him? There, on the river!"

They were in the plush rear of the big corporate helicopter, looking through the side window; Fletcher picked up the intercom mike and said to the pilot, "Bring us down over the river, I want to get a shot at him!"

The pilot looked back at them and said, "Sir, there's not much room to maneuver here—"

"Do it!" Fletcher ordered.

Matson said skeptically, "Reverend, this copter isn't armed. How do you expect—"

"Open the fucking door!" Fletcher moved to it and swung back the lever; the door slid back into the fuselage, triggering an alarm in the cockpit. "What the hell?" yelled the pilot.

Matson shrugged, took his weapon off his shoulder, and moved to the opening, where he grabbed a side strap to hold on. They were hovering above Dylan's boat, but they were still too high for a good shot.

Fletcher lunged forward to the cockpit, and

Matson saw him talking earnestly with the pilot. The helicopter descended.

Bullets spattered around Dylan, and he looked up to see Matson leaning out of the open door of the helicopter, holding on with one hand and shooting with the other. Fighting a wave of fear and panic, Dylan forced himself to increase his stroke and turn for the western shore. There was a brief respite while Matson reloaded; then two bullets hit the shell, one breaking his oarlock.

Dylan dove over the side.

The water was very cold, but he swam underwater for as far as possible before popping up. He was still about a hundred yards from the riverbank. Then they saw him, and the helicopter's shadow descended. He gasped and dived.

"Christ, they're shooting at someone!" said Markham, using the binoculars. Fletcher's helicopter had just come into view, and he could see the muzzle flashes on the side; as they neared, he saw a figure holding an Uzi or a Mac 10—some kind of short-barreled automatic weapon—in the open door. He swung the lenses down to see the shooter's target. There was an empty rowing shell . . . then, about fifty yards away, he saw a head bobbing in the water.

Markham swore and said to Kelly, "Put me on the air traffic frequency." The pilot flipped a dial, and Markham said into his mike, "NC1303, cease firing and ground your aircraft immediately. This is a United States Army aircraft. Repeat, you are required to immediately cease firing and set down in the nearest suitable clearing. Do you copy?"

"There's an Army helicopter over there, they want us to stop shooting," shouted Fletcher's pilot over the engine noise coming through the open door. "What should I do?"

Fletcher yelled back, "Ignore them until we kill this bastard."

"But, Reverend—"

"They won't shoot at us, you idiot! We might have Girard on board!" He went forward to the cockpit, where he pulled the copilot out of his seat and sent him back to help Matson. Then he took the copilot's seat, put on the headset, and said, "Now do exactly what I say."

Dylan stumbled out of the water, almost too cold and exhausted to care that he was now a much larger target. Running up the rocky beach, he tripped on a tree root and fell onto his chest, scraping his knees.

The fall probably saved his life, because the helicopter overshot him and had to turn to get Matson's door facing him again. Dylan got up and started running. There was a long ravine ahead, the remains of a dried-up or diverted tributary; he ran to the edge and staggered in, disappearing from view.

"They're ignoring us," Markham said needlessly. He couldn't believe Fletcher, or whoever it was, would have the balls to do this. They were deliberately firing at Dylan Ice, ignoring the fact that there were witnesses in an armed helicopter.

Markham keyed his mike. "NC1303, we are armed. Repeat, we are an armed U.S. Army aircraft. You are ordered to cease firing and land immediately."

No reply.

Markham said, "NC1303, this is your last chance. Ground your helicopter or you will be fired upon." It was an empty threat; he didn't dare shoot them down until he knew whether Fletcher, or Argent, or whoever it was, had Girard on board.

Still no reply, but the helicopter suddenly broke left and accelerated away. "And good riddance," said Markham. They could follow in a minute, but first he wanted to check Ice. He said to Kelly, "Bring it over that ravine. I want to see if they got him."

They flew to the ravine and hovered just above treetop level while Markham looked down. He couldn't see Ice.

Fuck!" yelled Kelly suddenly. Markham looked up to see the other helicopter coming back, right at them. Kelly twisted his controls desperately to dodge the other copter's rotors, and succeeded, but they lost so much altitude that their undercarriage struck the top of a tree, jarring the whole helicopter and instantly sending Markham's heart into his throat.

For a moment it looked like they would plunge into the forest; then Kelly regained control and they cleared the trees.

When they gained altitude and circled back, they could see Fletcher's helicopter making another pass at Ice.

■   ■   ■

The metal taste of fear was in his mouth as Dylan scurried down the ravine, bullets spraying around him. Suddenly he saw a massive tree trunk that had fallen into the ravine, a long shadow underneath it.

He dove head first, praying there was enough space. There was, but only barely; he took off a layer of skin as he rolled underneath, getting a faceful of moss and slime. Then the bullets tore into the bark above him.

"Well, shit," Markham said, as they saw Matson expend another clip of ammunition on the ravine.

"Aren't you going to let me fire on them, sir?" Kelly said. "They're murdering that man!"

"I can see that."

"We've go to do something!"

"No, we don't." There was no way he was going to risk firing on the helicopter. Unless—unless he could take out the shooter without risking anyone else on the chopper. It was a crazy idea, but it might work. Markham thought it over for a few seconds, then said, "Get us about fifty yards away from the shooter."

Kelly immediately pushed on the collective and they zoomed forward. Markham got up, popped the Kiowa's door, and pulled out his Walther autoloader. Just like being back in 'Nam, he thought. He yelled at Kelly, "Get me close enough and I'll take out the son of a bitch."

Kelly nodded, then brought the Kiowa next to the civilian helicopter, but with Markham on the other side.

"Ready?" shouted Kelly, and Markham gave him a thumbs-up. Immediately, Kelly spun the

Kiowa in place, bringing Markham around to face the open door of the other craft.

The man in the door was concentrating on blowing away a tree trunk below, and didn't even look up until the first of the Walther .45 ACP slugs crashed into the doorframe.

It wasn't easy aiming a pistol from a hovering helicopter, but Markham was a superb shot; the second and third bullets caught Matson in the neck and chest, and he fell backward, finger still on the trigger of his Uzi, spraying bullets into the helicopter's ceiling.

"Holy shit!" yelled Markham. "Get us out of here!"

Kelly veered away just in time, as hydraulic liquid and fuel began spraying from the rear of the civilian helicopter's engine pod. Almost instantly the whole engine burst into flame.

Fletcher's helicopter seemed to come apart in slow motion, fire spouting everywhere, pinwheeling across the sky before falling into the forest.

CHAPTER THIRTY-SEVEN

Banfield knew it was bad news as soon as he saw Hagen's expression. He swiveled in his chair and looked out the window across the White House lawn. "Sit down, Craig."

Hagen sprawled into a chair. "You're not gonna believe this, but she got away. At least, we can't find her."

Banfield swiveled back to face him. "Markham was right there! What the hell happened?"

Hagen nodded. "Markham was there, but it's a crazy story. You know that this local evangelist, Reverend Fletcher, was bankrolling Argent's operation?"

"Yes, yes."

"Well, the reason for that unholy alliance was that his daughter had AIDS. Argent was using Nicole Girard's blood to give the daughter PHT. That's why Fletcher and Argent were together, along with part of Fletcher's private army. But by the time Markham's men arrived, everything was over. Ice's father was shot dead, Kristin Fletcher was killed by some guard dogs, Nicole Girard had disappeared, and Fletcher was in his helicopter chasing Ice.

Markham shot the helicopter out of the sky, which makes Fletcher dead. A fucking bloodbath."

"Sweet Jesus," said Banfield.

"I said you wouldn't believe it."

Banfield put his head in his hands.

"For what it's worth," Hagen continued, "both Ice and his sister survived. And Argent is fine, except for a concussion, apparently received during an intramural squabble with Fletcher."

Banfield lifted his head. "What about spin control?"

Hagen shrugged. "Luckily, the place is so isolated the local cops never knew it happened. Not a problem."

"But I still don't understand how Girard got away."

Hagen shook his head. "Argent says she ran out of the house just before Fletcher's helicopter arrived. I assume she got into the woods and made it to a road. We've done infrared scans of the woods, and all the usual checking of exit routes. There's a description of her at every bus and train station, airport, and rental car company in the area."

"I see. And what about the lawyer—Ice?"

"If he knows where she is, he isn't saying. There's no way he could know, though, unless they prearranged a place. Anyway, we've got him under surveillance. If she contacts him, we'll know about it."

"So the deal is off? We gave her ten million bucks already."

Hagen spread out his hands. "It's gone, Tom. Ice had it wired to a Swiss bank. We could try to get it back, but it would mean contacting the Swiss government—"

"No. Forget it."

Hagen looked at the floor. "I did my best."

"I know you did, Craig." Banfield was surprised how disappointed he felt. He had really believed this would work, and now he had to face reality.

It seemed like his whole life was closing down around him. He was still very weak and slightly sick, and Dr. Rosati had made it clear his CD4 count was so low he could get another infection at any time. He had to start the drug therapy—it was now or never. It would be tough to hide, and even tougher keeping pace with Osborne.

He could resign the presidency now, or withdraw from the race, or do nothing and lose the election. All three courses would result in Theodore Osborne becoming the next President of the United States.

Hagen interrupted his thoughts. "Just to make your day, Turk is here for his appointment."

"Good. Send him in."

It almost felt like coming home, thought Finnegan, as he stepped into the Oval Office. He shook Banfield's hand, expecting the same reaction he had received from Hagen: a cold, menacing stare. Instead, the President greeted him warmly and motioned him to his customary seat next to the desk. Was it possible he didn't know?

"So," Banfield said, as he took his seat behind the *Renown* desk. "What can I do for you, Turk?" He looked much older, thought Turk. Thin and gray.

me to apologize, Mr. President."

logize? For what?"

nk you know, sir."

Banfield picked up a pencil, swiveled his chair, and looked out across the lawn. "Yes, I do, Turk," he said, swiveling back. "I thought you might be here to gloat. Or to deliver your new boss's terms."

Finnegan sat up straighter in the chair. "I don't work for him. And I'm not here on his behalf."

"I see. Osborne doesn't know you're here?" The tone was skeptical.

"No."

"Ah, right. You're here to apologize."

Finnegan plunged in. "I was very angry at being displaced by Hagen. Looking back, I realize what was going on. You were getting sick, and weren't willing to take me into your confidence. And you were right. I *couldn't* be trusted. I proved that when I saw Conner's letter and took that information to Osborne."

Banfield stared at him, respect in his eyes. "That's right, Turk. But if it helps any, it was against my better judgment. I wanted to bring you inside, but I let myself be talked out of it."

Finnegan nodded. "I understand. Anyway, the deeper I got in with Osborne, the worse I felt. It got to the point where I couldn't sleep at night."

"I believe you, Turk."

"Anyway, I finally resolved that I couldn't do it anymore. That's when I called for this appointment. There's nothing I can do to make it up to you now, but it's very important to me that I tell you, face-to-face, how sorry I am." He exhaled a long breath. "That's all I wanted to say, Mr. President." He stood up.

"Sit down, Turk," said Banfield. "You said you took the *information* to Osborne. You didn't make a copy of the letter?"

"No, I didn't."

"Why hasn't Osborne gone public with this? Instead of nibbling around the edges?"

"He's afraid to, Mr. President. Without the letter, he's got no proof—just my word. And I won't help him now."

"Does he know that?" Banfield asked sharply.

"Uh, no. I haven't told him yet. But I will," he added hastily.

"Not so fast." Banfield stood up and slowly walked around the office, pausing to look at the Lincoln portrait. When he returned to his desk he asked, "Are you willing to make amends?"

"Amends? What kind of amends?"

"I'd like you to do something for me."

"Of course." Finnegan's face flushed with pleasure.

But when Banfield told him what he wanted, Finnegan's expression faded. "I don't understand, Tom. How in the world will this help you?"

Banfield leaned forward and said in a very low voice, "Turk, you know me. There's a reason I'm doing this, but I can't tell you now. I promise you, however, that when it's over you'll understand."

Finnegan looked into Banfield's eyes and said, "All right. If that's what you really want."

"It is, Turk, it is. And something else. Craig doesn't know about this, and I want it to stay that way."

Finnegan grinned. "A pleasure, Mr. President."

Two days later, Turk Finnegan stood in front of Osborne's desk and placed a manila envelope on the dark wood surface.

"That's it?" said Osborne.

"That's it," said Finnegan.

Osborne was almost giddy with triumph as he unfolded the letter. It was the original, not a photocopy, he marveled. In a crisp, neat handwriting, he read:

Mr. President,

It seems very strange to address you that way. Congratulations on your victory.

I have tried to contact you many times, but you haven't returned my calls nor answered my other letters. I'm not angry, though, I understand why you wouldn't want to talk to me. I don't think what we did was wrong, it just happened. I enjoyed it very much, and I think you did, too.

But something has happened that you *have* to know about. And I'm telling you this in a letter only because I can't tell you in person, as I should.

Mr. President—Thomas—I have AIDS.

I didn't know I had it when we were together four years ago, during your campaign. That's the truth. And it's even possible I got it after we were together. Anyway, about three months ago, I got a very bad cold that wouldn't go away. That's when I got tested.

You may not be infected; for all I know, you may already have tested negative. I hope so. But if you haven't been tested, you should be right away. Even if you haven't had any symptoms.

I know this must be a terrible shock, and I'm truly very, very sorry if you got it because of me.

Please call me at my apartment in Ohio, 612-555-2525.

The letter was signed, "Sincerely yours, Jason Conner."

Osborne carefully folded the letter along its original crease lines and put it on his desk, placing a crystal pyramid paperweight on top. He looked at Turk Finnegan, who stood at the window, gazing across the Capitol grounds.

"How in the world did you get this, Turk?"

Finnegan shrugged. "I still have some friends in the White House."

"Friends!" scoffed Osborne. "Those aren't friends, they're blood brothers! There's got to be more to the story."

"That's all I can tell you, Senator," Turk said stiffly.

Osborne nodded. Normally, he would have pushed harder, but he was too happy to be bothered. Anyway, what difference did it make? The letter was genuine, he was sure of that.

Osborne buzzed his secretary. "Find Mitch and tell him I want to see him right away."

Ten minutes later, after McPeak had also read the letter and recovered his breath, he said excitedly, "This is it, Senator. The smoking gun. *Now* do we go public?"

"Yes. Yes, now we do. Set up a news conference for this afternoon, in time for the evening news deadlines. Tell all the networks they'll be getting a big story. The biggest story of the year. Hell, maybe the decade."

McPeak grinned. "You got it, boss."
Turk Finnegan allowed himself a smile.

"Any questions?" Osborne asked unnecessarily as he looked at the mass of wiggling reporters in the Senate Press Room. Now that he had finished his prepared remarks, he reminded himself to keep his expression grave.

A wave of hands shot up, shouting his name. He chose the *Post* reporter in the front row—a known administration sympathizer.

"Senator, you say you have proof of these allegations," said the man. "Why haven't you shown it?"

"Oh, we will if necessary," said Osborne. "I wouldn't be standing before you if I had any doubt whatsoever about these very serious charges. But the proof I will offer is, by its very nature, raw and embarrassing, and I'd like to avoid making this situation more sensational than it already is. The President not only has a fatal disease, but he has lied to the American people about his health. I challenge him to take an AIDS test. I challenge him to release the medical records of his recent stay at Bethesda Naval Hospital. And, most of all, I challenge him to do the right thing for his country." That's a hell of a sound bite, he thought.

"Senator! Are you suggesting that the President resign?" This question came from a network correspondent.

"No, I am not," Osborne said quickly. "That's not my place. I do think, however, that a man with a potentially fatal disease should not be running for a second term. Regardless of the moral issue." He pointed at the White House correspondent of the *Wall Street Journal*.

"Senator," said the reporter, "will you show us this alleged evidence?"

He knew they would come back to that. "Certainly, Bill. If necessary. If the President chooses to deny that he has AIDS, you'll be the first to see it."

For a moment, that stilled them, as everyone realized the threat implicit in Osborne's words. Mitch McPeak took the opportunity to step forward and say, "No further questions. That's all for now."

Osborne hustled off the stage, escorted by his own security team, feeling very close to being the next President of the United States.

Thomas Banfield flicked the off switch on the remote control, and Osborne's image disappeared into black. A good news conference, thought Banfield. He expected that major portions of it would make network news.

"That bastard," Hagen said softly. The other presidential aides watching the news conference in the Oval Office sat in stunned silence. "What kind of proof could he have?"

"It doesn't really matter, does it?" Banfield said, conscious of the stares from the other members of his staff—none of whom had been privy to his secret. They would never look at him the same way, he thought. And there would always be people reluctant to shake the President's hand. "The point is, he says he has the evidence." He let that sink in, then said, "I'd like to be alone for a while."

Jerry Nachman, his appointments secretary, spoke up dazedly. "You've got the Algerian ambassador waiting for you in the Blue Room."

"He'll just have to wait," said Banfield. "Please."

They all filed out, still stunned. Hagen looked like he was going to stay, so Banfield had to say, "You, too, Craig."

Hagen, defeated, nodded and left.

Banfield quickly moved to both doors, locking them. He returned to his desk, where he pulled toward him a clean, crisp sheet of White House stationery. With the gold-filled fountain pen Marianne had given him, he carefully drafted the note, the simple two paragraphs that would forever end Theodore Osborne's chances to be President.

When he finished, he read it again, then carefully folded it in half and placed it prominently on the center of his desk. He pulled another sheet of paper to him and composed a second short note, this one addressed "Marianne."

It was time. He felt remarkably calm and clear headed, and realized that he had ached for this sort of peace for longer than he could remember.

Banfield leaned to his left, pulled open the bottom drawer of the desk, and removed the nickel-plated single-action Colt revolver, a present from his father. He twirled the cylinder, observing that it was fully loaded, and hefted the pistol in his hand. It felt good.

Standing up, he looked around. Not in the Oval Office; that wouldn't be fair to the country, or to his successors. He moved across the room and opened the door to the President's private bathroom. He stepped inside the shower stall, closed the stall door, and looked at his watch. It was exactly 5:30 P.M.

Without further thought, the President of the United States cocked the pistol, placed it in his mouth, and fired.

CHAPTER THIRTY-EIGHT

Senator Theodore Osborne sat alone in his office, a ruined man.

Not just ruined, he thought despondently. *Hated.*

On the desk in front of him lay the Conner letter, the letter that should have been his ticket to the White House. So much paper, now.

After the first shock of the President's suicide and Hagen's release of the suicide note, public feeling had coalesced strangely. Instead of contempt for a weakling, they saw Banfield as a sympathetic figure, forced to ultimate defeat by the machinations of a ruthless, power-hungry politician.

Of course Banfield's suicide note was full of lies; Banfield had never offered to withdraw from the race in return for keeping the letter a secret. If he had done so, Osborne would have accepted. But who would believe him now? Osborne was the man who had hounded the President to death, the man who wouldn't be satisfied until he ruined the President personally as well as politically.

The slyest trick of all, of course, was that Arthur Sinclair, the Vice President, had become President, and his calmness and grace during the succession had transformed him from a political joke to a major player. He had taken Banfield's place on the ticket, and even if Osborne hadn't lost his popularity, Sinclair would be tough to beat. And Finnegan had a prominent place at Banfield's funeral.

Osborne had tried fighting back by releasing the Conner letter, and a few of the right-wing papers published the thing. The major media wouldn't touch it.

He picked up the letter and carefully, methodically, ripped it into pieces.

The convention was next week, and he knew he would have to release all his delegates, or they would bolt anyway. Sighing, he buzzed his secretary.

"Yeah, Senator?" she said, and Osborne noticed that even his loyal staff seemed affected by the general viewpoint. "Get me Mitch, please."

"He said he was busy this afternoon, Senator."

"Oh. Well, tell him I want to see him when he comes in."

"Right," she said, hanging up.

It was not even slightly ironic to Osborne that Banfield, in death, had succeeded in finally defeating him.

When square-riggers still plied the Caribbean, their last sight of land before entering the Atlantic Ocean on the journey home was the North Sound of the British Virgin Islands, otherwise known as the Bitter End.

It was a fitting name for the remote peninsula of the island of Virgin Gorda, although now the yacht club that took its name was a huge complex of waterborne tourism. Dylan didn't care about the rest of the yacht club; his attention was centered on the slim pier and fat boathouse that composed the brand-new British Virgin Islands Crew Club.

As he leaned over the railing of the club building to admire the neat row of sculls on the beach and tied at the pier, the late-afternoon sun glinting off the white tops of the shells, he realized just how much he loved this place, how at home he felt in the islands.

In BVI, no one thought twice about his skin color, or his racial heritage. Most of the natives were of mixed race.

Just a month earlier, while still at the firm—trying to make up for his absence and pacify Hudson—he had seen the advertisement in a rowing magazine for a coach to help start the BVI Olympic rowing team. And just like that, he made the decision.

"Dylan," said a man's voice behind him. He turned to see Patrick, the deeply tanned native who served as his assistant coach. "You better get going if you want to meet the plane."

"Right," said Dylan.

"I'll get things ready at the club. I reserved a villa."

"Perfect." The Beachside Villas were scattered along a narrow beach—not luxurious, but with a great view.

Dylan went down to the main dock and boarded the forty-five-foot cruiser for the thirty-minute trip across the North Sound to Beef Island Airport, Tortola. He stood near the bow, his white shirt and shorts splashed with sea foam.

He arrived at the airport a few minutes late, but so was the flight from Puerto Rico. When the two-engine propeller plane landed in a buzz of reversed engines and flaps, he found himself grinning. He watched the airport crew swing a ladder up to the door of the plane, and the passengers disembark. Almost all were tourists.

Nicole was the last person out. She scanned the tarmac, saw him, and waved.

He waited while she passed through the perfunctory customs without much concern; by now her fake passport was well proven, filled with genuine visa stamps.

He hadn't been sure she was even alive until two weeks ago, when he received her letter, routed through Barry. He had immediately written back, and they had talked on the phone several times.

It still seemed miraculous to him that she had been able to accomplish so much. After spending a day in the old mine shaft, first hiding from Fletcher's men, then the Secret Service agents, she had managed to hitchhike and walk from Arkansas to Mexico. From Tijuana she called Barry, who wired her some money. That was the last they had heard from her.

Now he knew she had gone to Geneva and claimed the President's money. If the new administration ever tried to retrieve the funds, they were too late. More likely it was charged to some contingency fund and forgotten.

Finally Nicole emerged from customs. They hugged warmly, and she kissed him on the cheek. "You look great, Dylan." She held him at arm's length. "Brown and happy. Like a native."

"I feel that way." She looked good, too, her hair cut short in a European style, face clear and glowing with health. She wore dark green slacks and a lightweight silk blouse that fit well.

She pointed at his hand. "Looks like it's all healed."

"Yeah." He held it up to show her, no longer embarrassed by the stumps. "C'mon, let's get your luggage before they lose it."

They chatted amiably all the way back on the ferry, leaning on the rail. She told him she was almost through with her work at the Swiss AIDS research center, where she had volunteered for PHT research. "They think they can duplicate Argent's work," she said. "Anyway, it looks hopeful."

This brought them into sensitive territory. He changed the subject by saying, "You know, Argent and his wife disappeared soon after you did. They took most of the institute's endowment with them, too. So now he's a fugitive, and if they catch him, *he'll* be the one under restraints."

She laughed, that melodic sound he had noticed the first time they met in the hospital. Then her expression changed. "How's your sister doing?"

"Great! She completed the drug program— successfully—and is living with Barry while she finishes high school. Then, if her grades are good enough, she might try college. It'll have to be a state college, of course, but what the hell. Oh, and the cops finally caught the gang members who were chasing her—busted them for armed robbery."

"That's wonderful, Dylan." She put her hand on his. "I'm happy for you. And you don't miss practicing law?"

He shrugged. "Truthfully, no. Well, I miss the intellectual challenge, but the rest of it—no. I didn't even realize how unhappy it made me until I stopped. I may go back to law eventually. Not in a

big firm, though. Maybe I'll try criminal defense."
He smiled. "My father would have liked that."

Nicole squeezed his hand. "That's another thing
I'm sorry about. Shit, there's so much you've lost
because of me, but most of all your father."

"Yes. And you lost Charlene."

She grimaced. "I haven't given up hope yet."

"No, of course not." The police still carried her
as a missing person, but Dylan had a feeling the
secret of her fate died with Reverend Fletcher.

They stared at the water for a while. "Do you
ever think about President Banfield?"

She nodded. "Yeah. But I don't feel any responsibility. What about you?"

"Truthfully, I do, sometimes. But I can't think of
anything I would have done differently."

"No, me either."

There seemed nothing else to say, so they just
enjoyed the view as the boat entered the North
Sound.

After a refreshing swim in the fresh-water pool,
they had a seafood dinner, talking about nothing
serious. Nicole retired to her villa, and Dylan to his
small room in the Clubhouse.

The next day Dylan checked out a small sailboat and
they sailed around the North Sound, stopping at
Pusser's Bar. Sitting on the deck, taking in the gorgeous scenery, they each drank a powerful rum drink
called the Painkiller.

"It's a good name," said Nicole, as she finished
hers with a small hiccup.

Dylan chuckled. "I agree." The drink lowered
his inhibitions enough to broach the subject he had

been avoiding. He could think of no tactful way to put it, so he said, "Why are you here, Nicole?"

She raised her eyebrows. "That's a strange question. You want me to leave?"

"No, of course not. It's just that . . . there are some things we've never discussed."

"I know. I was waiting for you to bring it up."

Great, thought Dylan. Well, here goes. "You remember when Kristin Fletcher barged into Howard's house, what she said about my having AIDS? About getting it from her?"

"Yes, I remember," she said softly.

"And that I denied it?"

"Of course."

"Well, at the time, I hadn't tested positive, but that's because it takes between three and six months after exposure before an antibody test turns positive—"

"Dylan, I always knew you thought you were infected."

"How?" Dylan said, startled.

"After fifteen years of being HIV-positive, I can tell. I remember the way you drank my soda in the car."

"But you can't get AIDS—"

"Dylan, there's always some hesitation, at least the first time."

"Damn. And all that time I was agonizing over how to tell you."

"Dylan, I never thought that you were helping me for that reason. I'm a better judge of character than that, I hope. You're not Kristin."

"No, but I did have a relationship with her." He sighed. "That's the single most stupid act of my life. In fact, it may cost me my life."

"Maybe."

Dylan lowered his voice to a whisper. "I'm still testing negative, but it's only been four months, and the doctors say you can't be absolutely sure for six months. It's like Russian roulette until then. Every other week I get tested, it's agony all over again."

She nodded sagely. "At this point, I'd say the chances are good you've dodged the bullet. But even if you do test positive, it's not the end of the world."

"Yeah, I know all about the new treatments, but they're not a cure. And damn expensive, too."

"Dylan, you're too gloomy. If not for HIV, would you be here now?" She gestured at the scene around them. "Isn't that why you're not slaving away at that law firm? Because the threat of AIDS made the whole thing seem ridiculous?"

He was almost offended, but then conceded, "All right, you've got a point."

"Anyway, you don't have to worry about the cost of anything. You're a rich man."

"How do you figure that?"

"Well, you're worth five million dollars."

Dylan gaped at her, and she giggled. "You should see your face. I intended to tell you over a nice dinner with champagne, but I can't beat this environment. Dylan, I took half the President's money and put it in a Swiss bank account, in your name. It's not a gift, either—it's rightfully yours. Without you, I wouldn't be alive, much less rich."

"Thank you," he whispered, overwhelmed.

"And, as long I'm in a giving mood," Nicole said, "here's something else. My body's resistance to HIV is unique and special. I can't help the world, but I can help one person. Hopefully, you won't need it. But if you do—"

"Don't say it. I'm not asking—"

"Shut up," she said, suddenly forceful. "That's why I'm here. To tell you this."

Dylan could think of nothing to say.

Nicole breathed deeply of the warm air. "Maybe I'll even stay for a while."

"I'd like that! Very much. Uh, does that mean . . ." his voice trailed off as he found he lacked the courage to ask what he was thinking.

Her eyes were merry as she said, "I don't know what it means, Dylan. Really, I don't. The only thing I know for sure is how I feel about you."

"And if Charlene reappears?"

"I'm finished with that phase of my life, Dylan. Regardless of what else happens, it's time for me to move on. What do you think?"

"Well," said Dylan slowly. "It's definitely worth a try." He took her hand, feeling the warmth spread up his arm to his chest.